cou[...] [...]nself defending [...] poor and [...], the chronic petty criminal, the innocent and the guilty. He discovers that he not only likes it but that he is also very good at it, that the challenging stagelike atmosphere of the criminal court appeals to him and that, finally, he is needed, desperately needed, by a segment of society which can neither cope with a complex legal system nor afford a lawyer of Ben's caliber.

We live through this crucial month in Ben's young life and are party to the startling contrasts which he sees daily as he moves between the two worlds.

We meet the people who impinge on his life and who, ultimately, help him decide which world he will live in: the beautiful, rich divorceé Sally Rochester, whose desire for Ben is boundless and prideless; Pat Forrester, a partner in Conyers and Dean, whose life and career are crumbling in full view of the entire firm; and Marvin Gold, the Deputy Defender, who uses his brilliant legal talents to defend people who are bent on destroying his family's home in a riot.

RITTENHOUSE SQUARE is a deeply moving novel of one man's encounter with himself. It is highly instructive in the vagaries of the law, both financial and criminal. And it is, finally, a perceptive portrait of the paradox which is today's modern city.

rittenhouse square

rittenhouse square

a novel

by

Arthur R. G. Solmssen

Little, Brown and Company   *Boston · Toronto*

Published simultaneously in Canada
by Little, Brown & Company (Canada) Limited

PRINTED IN THE UNITED STATES OF AMERICA

The stage really exists: Philadelphia has courts and a district attorney's office and a defender association and the sort of law firms, banks and clubs you would expect to find in a large American city. On the other hand, all of the characters and their stories are entirely fictitious; they were invented by the author who has, when it suited his purpose, taken some liberties with real occasions. For example, the Orchestra does not give its regular concerts in the summertime; but this is a novel and not a history.

rittenhouse square

On the way back to my room I sat down on a bench in Rittenhouse Square and tried to decide what to do with my life. It was only six o'clock so I still had a few minutes before I would have to dress for Kellerman's wedding dinner.

The Square was just about empty now: most of the newspaper readers had drifted on to their cocktails, the nursemaids had taken the little rich children home to the apartment houses, and it was too early for the night crowd. Pigeons hopped and fluttered undisturbed around the fish pond. On the wall of the pond a lonely little colored boy sat studying a comic book.

I stretched my legs, relishing the way my muscles ached after the first squash game in six weeks. The hot and cold shower had been good too, and the Scotch, but the talk with Ordway Smith ...

All right, back to the issue: My month on the outside was over. On Monday I would have to return to my desk at Conyers & Dean — unless I could decide to take my chances in this other world. The thing with Sally Rochester was over — unless I could make up my mind to stop screwing around. I suppose that everybody comes to a fork in the road once in a while, but here I was having to rechoose my job and my whole life in one weekend.

Marvin Gold would call before Monday, and Sally would be at Kellerman's wedding tomorrow. It was fish or cut bait, on two levels.

As I watched the little black boy solemnly chewing his gum and turning the pages of his comic book, I tried to sort out all of the things that had happened to me in the last four weeks. Looking up at the towers of the Rittenhouse Connaught I thought especially about Forrester and wondered for the hundredth time if what happened to him could happen to me, or whether Ordway Smith's analysis, detached and cool like Ordway himself, was the right one after all.

I felt sleepy now. Can you just sit down and decide something, or does the answer have to come bubbling up from your subconscious? Or should you talk to somebody? It must be nice to have a father or somebody you could go to and ask for advice about things like this. Or an uncle, or some old professor that you have known for years, somebody who would bring you into his study — a quiet room with books all around the walls and a fire burning in the grate — and he would ask you to sit down in a leather armchair like Boyle has in his office, and then he would light his pipe and say something like, "All right, tell me all about it. Begin at the beginning."

book one

$15,000,000

SCHUYLKILL STEEL CORPORATION

Thirty-Five Year 4¾% Debentures, due September 1, 2000

Interest payable March 1 and September 1

Price 101.20% and Accrued Interest

Copies of the Prospectus are obtainable from the undersigned.

FIRST HUDSON CORPORATION

McTAVISH BROS. & STRAUSS   LONSDALE, JNO. R. BRECKENRIDGE & CO.
Incorporated

WILLIAM C. LUFTSCHREIBER & CO.
Incorporated

        JOHN J. O'RILEY & CO.

NASSAU SECURITIES CORPORATION

D. W. BENJAMIN'S SONS & ROSENHEIM, INC.

A. B. CORCORAN & CO.

        PELL AND PELL
Incorporated

MITTERSILL, TAFT, VON GABLENZ & PEABODY

chapter 1

Begin at the beginning? Everything connects back to something else, so how can you tell where all this began? I might as well start that morning Forrester didn't show up at the closing for the Schuylkill Steel Debentures.

We were gathered in the William Penn Trust Company's second biggest conference room, which is supposed to convey the impression of cool Colonial dignity but on this occasion seemed hot and too full of people. The brokers from First Hudson were beginning to fidget, and Frederick Lacey, the lawyer for the bank, was leafing around in my carefully arranged document stacks, trying to find something wrong.

The closing had been scheduled for eleven o'clock, but at eleven-thirty two essential ingredients were still missing: the No Stop Order telegram from the Securities and Exchange Commission, and my boss, Patrick Forrester. Although he had allowed me to handle this job pretty much on my own, the partner in charge does have to appear at the settlement, if only to shake hands with the clients and to sign the opinion which says that Conyers & Dean find everything to be okay and that "said Debentures are valid and binding obligations of the Company in accordance with their terms and the terms of the Indenture."

So far, this deal had rolled along without incident.

In March the Directors of Schuylkill Steel decided to borrow some money for an addition to their rolling mill, and we sat down to negotiate with First Hudson Corporation. In April we prepared the papers, and by the middle of May we had cleared a fat registration statement through the SEC. First Hudson had already sold the bonds to their customers. If nothing went wrong at the closing, our client Schuylkill Steel would get a check for $15,178,124.40 and, after a decent interval — say twenty-four hours — my employers Conyers & Dean would present their bill of $28,750 plus out-of-pocket expenses. Nothing had better go wrong.

I decided to call my office. There wasn't the remotest chance that the SEC would stop this issue, but the underwriters just won't settle without that telegram. As I reached for the telephone, Frederick Lacey said:

"Ben, is this Mr. Black's signature on the Indenture?"

I put down the receiver. "No, Mr. Lacey, that's Vernon Benson's signature. Mr. Black has signed all the other papers, but Mr. Benson had to sign the Indentures because —"

"Well, how do we know he's authorized?"

"Mr. Lacey, it's in the Board Resolution, and it's on the signature certificate, that's item forty-three . . ." Lacey knew as well as I did that Vernon Benson's signature bound Schuylkill Steel, but I had to dig to the bottom of the largest pile to find the right papers for him. Lacey's duties at the closing were purely ceremonial; while we were preparing the Indenture, he had made sure that William Penn Trust Company did not assume one milligram of responsibility unless it was required by federal law; now that this 186-page book was printed and signed, he was just here to fly the flag of the Messrs. Openshaw, Prescott, Pennington & Lee, who had been counsel to the bank for forty years. All our big law firms have these fierce old warhorses who must be kept doing something because they don't want to retire; Mr. Lacey's specialty is nit-picking other people's trust indentures and finding errors in closing papers. No whippersnapper just out of school is going to slip defective documents past Frederick Lacey, Esquire.

"Hmm, Vernon Benson, yes," he said, examining the signature certificate through bristling eyebrows. "Here you have him Executive Vice-President, and on the Indenture . . ."

"Mr. Lacey, that Indenture was printed two weeks ago," said Morton Black, the Treasurer of Schuylkill Steel. "Vernon was just promoted —"

"What difference does it make?" asked Elliott Day, one of First Hudson's New York lawyers. "Just ink-in the word 'Executive.' "

"It doesn't make any difference, Mr. Day," said Lacey. "It's just that here in Philadelphia we like to have things right — if possible."

I dialed the telephone. "Oh Mr. Butler!" My secretary began to chatter: "I was just on the way over. It was here all the time, they had the telegram and they just put it in your mailbox and those girls *know* I wouldn't come up to get the second mail until eleven-thirty —"

"Okay, well just bring it over now, please. Any sign of Mr. Forrester?"

"Mr. Forrester? Isn't he over there with you?"

I had the call transferred, but Forrester's phone didn't answer and they couldn't find his secretary.

"Can't we get some of these preliminary things out of the way now?" asked Elliott Day, looking at his watch. "I have a meeting in New York at three . . ."

"Oh, aren't you going to join us for lunch, Mr. Day?" said Angus MacDonald, the bank's Trust Officer.

"Say, Ben, should we open a special account for this money?" Morton Black wanted to know. "Or should we just make a transfer to the general account? Can't we put in an order for some Treasury Bills right now?"

"Ben, I was explaining to Mr. Black that if he buys a

9

certificate of deposit with what he won't need for the first six months . . ."

I wished that Forrester would come. A big closing is really a two-man job: one tends to the paper work and the other talks to the people. I haven't learned how to do both at the same time.

Suddenly the tall oak doors swung open and Ellsworth Boyle rushed in. Boyle is not the most senior partner in Conyers & Dean, but for practical purposes he runs the firm. He is a director of Schuylkill Steel, and although jobs like this one are turned over to special working groups, everybody knows that the company is his client.

He circled the table, shaking hands. "Morning, morning, morning." Red-faced and out of breath, he sat down at the head of the table. "Well, Pat Forrester has some trouble at home, wife suddenly ill, shame, nothing serious though, I'm glad to say. Called me up. Understand you have the whole thing wrapped up, Ben. Fred here giving you a hard time as usual?" He began to shove papers around. "Something about an opinion, you want me to sign an opinion?"

CONYERS & DEAN he scrawled at the foot of each opinion letter as I turned the pages for him. He never stopped talking. "Hell of a note, thought I was going to get away without doing *any* work on this deal . . . That's the secret of successful law practice: get other people to do the work . . . Sure it's okay for me to sign this, Ben? . . . Mr. Day, how's Henry Spratt, we were in law school together, did you know that? Henry was smart, he went to New York where you can make some money . . . This issue's all sold out, I hear, all sold out before the agreement was signed, that's what I call investment banking. Yes sir, big profits for big risks, that's what they always tell me. If I could start over again, I'd be an investment banker, right, Mr. Poole? The lawyers do all the work, the bankers make

10

a few telephone calls, borrow some money for twenty-four hours, make a few deliveries, twelve dollars per bond times fifteen thousand bonds, let's see — well, it's a nice piece of change . . . Okay, Ben, anything else?"

I whisked the opinions out from under him, and right on cue Angus MacDonald's secretary entered and handed me a yellow envelope. I ripped it open, glanced at it, and passed it to Elliott Day. "May I close?"

Day read the telegram and nodded. "You may close, sir."

"Could I have a look at that, Ben?" asked Frederick Lacey.

"Oh, I beg your pardon, Mr. Lacey."

"My God, boy, don't forget the *Trustee!*" shouted Ellsworth Boyle. "Suppose the SEC says that we're not allowed to use the William Penn as Trustee?" Ignoring the laughter, Lacey read the telegram and handed it back to me. "That appears to be in order," he said with dignity.

I glanced at Ellsworth Boyle. "Fire away," he said, and I began to hand out and explain the documents while the others ticked them off their copies of my Closing Memorandum.

Twenty minutes later we were finished, the checks were delivered, and I nodded to the uniformed bank messengers who were leaning patiently against the walls. They picked up the heavy sealed suitcases and filed out of the room. The New York lawyers shook hands and departed too; everybody else took the elevator up to the officers' dining room.

In the washroom I found myself next to Ellsworth Boyle.

"Nice clean settlement, Ben," he said. "Come in to see me before the office meeting tonight, will you?"

That would be the Ridgeway merger, putting three companies together and selling stock to the public at the

11

same time. A small but complicated deal, and I might have a couple of people working for me. I knew that I should be happy about it, but I wasn't; I was tired. I wanted to ask what was wrong with Sheila Forrester, but Boyle was already striding out into the sea of white tablecloths.

chapter 2

By five-fifteen all the lawyers at Conyers & Dean — except those who were out of town or sick — had gathered in the "big" library, which occupies most of the thirtieth and thirty-first floors of the Franklin Tower.

The younger partners often grumble about the rent paid for that enormous room — modern law libraries are filled with steel book stacks and work cubicles like those on the twenty-ninth floor — but the older men are used to the place, and everybody likes to show it to visitors and new clients. The north wall is pierced by three tall Georgian windows looking across to City Hall; the other walls are filled from floor two stories to the ceiling with books. A narrow balcony circles the room twelve feet above the floor, and from its railing hang two dozen gilt-framed portraits of old Philadelphia lawyers, including Judge Conyers and Mr. Dean. A heavy crystal chandelier is suspended on a chain from the dark distant ceiling, and little reading lamps illuminate the long refectory tables.

The other big firms don't have "full office" meetings any more: they don't have room, and all decisions are made by committees of partners anyway. We still have full meetings; the older men are used to them. On the last Monday of every month (except July and August) Mr. Woolstonecraft pushes the tables back against the walls and arranges about fifty chairs in a sort of U around the senior partners' table. Mr. Woolstonecraft came to us as an asset of the Hyde Estate, having been Clarence Pickford Hyde's butler since 1923.

I sat on a table between Patterson Fox and Randy Kellerman, with my back against the books. Nobody tells you where to sit, but everybody always settles down in pretty much the same formation: the seniors — Alfred Dennison, Taylor Chew, Boyle, a couple of others — are behind their table, facing the semicircle. The other partners sit along the right arm of the U, with the older men toward the front. The associates sit on the left, and since they outnumber the partners two to one, that side of the room is crowded, with the youngest men spilling over on tabletops and radiator covers. Occasionally a partner who comes in late will sit down on the left, just to show that we're casual and you can sit where you like, but I've never seen an associate on the right.

You can laugh about these customs and smile at the airs some of the men give themselves and complain about the pay and the incredibly long hours, but as I watched the room filling up I had the same old feeling. These are the best and I'm glad to be with them. When lawyers in Chicago and Los Angeles and London think of Philadelphia, they think of Conyers & Dean. "Prestigious" is what *Time* called us last year in a story about the Hammond Soap case. A silly word, but it made me feel good.

Patrick Forrester sat quietly in his chair, looking down at the carpet and listening to Ordway Smith. They were both in their usual places, on the right and well in front; the two most powerful junior partners, the rising stars in our particular sky.

Ordway Smith is one of these men who has everything. He is young and handsome and rich and happily married to a beautiful girl from a famous family. He may not be a brilliant lawyer, but he is so frank and

14

charming in his admiration for his intellectual superiors that they cheerfully do his paper work for him. In fact, like most successful lawyers, Ordway never seems to be doing *any* work. You will rarely find him trying a case or writing a brief or looking up a point of law. He spends his time seeing people or attending meetings or talking on the telephone. Philadelphia, Rittenhouse, Racquet, Merion Cricket, Radnor Hunt, Gulph Mills — you name the club, Ordway belongs to it. He is a director of the Fairmount Chemical Company which was founded by his great-grandfather; he sits on the boards of the Greater Philadelphia Movement, the Committee of Seventy, the Art Museum, the Orchestra, and one of the fancy girls' schools. No Sunday society section is complete without a picture of Ordway in a white tie sipping champagne with the French Consul or welcoming Joan Sutherland to the Academy of Music. Ordway knows his job, and he does it well.

Patrick Forrester is also about thirty-six, but his success is grounded on a brilliant mind and unlimited capacity for work. He has no money: his father taught English at one of the suburban high schools. He runs our securities group. We work night and day on stock issues, bond issues, corporate acquisitions, proxy fights — that sort of thing. We never go to court. We prepare instruments so complicated that only bankers and securities analysts and other lawyers try to read them. Our job is to see that every hole is covered and that our clients get their money. Forrester works and works and works, in his shirt sleeves, smoking one cigarette after another, with files stacked on the floor around him and printers proofs spread across the tables and the telephone ringing and secretaries and lawyers and messengers running in and out.

I found him in this atmosphere that day he rescued me from slavery to Leslie Patch.

When I first came to Conyers & Dean, fresh from the

University of Pennsylvania Law School, they put me into a bullpen behind the library stacks on the twenty-ninth floor, together with Randy Kellerman (just out of Virginia) and Sam Atwater (just out of Harvard). The walls were painted green; a single dirty window faced into an air shaft so we had to keep the lights on all the time. There was barely enough room for our three shabby desks, which were always strewn with the yellow lined notepaper we used to draft our research papers. Dusty law books were piled on the floor and the windowsill.

I know that most lawyers have to start out in places like that, but still I didn't like it. Sam Atwater was given to deep expressive sighs; the problems he had to solve always seemed unsolvable. Randy Kellerman, who is engaged to probably the richest and plainest girl in town, spent most of his time on the telephone. In the morning he called around to see who wanted to have lunch; in the afternoon he conferred with Roseann about their plans for the evening. These were just minor annoyances. My real problem was Leslie Patch, an older man, the partner in charge of real estate.

Our job was to look up points of law for people who were actually working on cases and dealing with the clients. Since we were not assigned to any particular partners, anybody could send for us and give us work. We quickly learned that different people do this in different ways. Some of them will tell you the whole story and take you along to meetings so that you can meet the clients and let you participate in the job; others will just throw abstract problems at you, order a memorandum covering every conceivable legal issue, and then tuck it into the file without another word — unless they don't like it.

Leslie Patch is the most extreme of this second type, and for some reason he developed a special interest in me. He began to pile mountains of work on me, and much of it was clearly unnecessary research into the remotest points

16

of law — points that would never come up. He seemed to enjoy assigning work. The worst of it was that he did it in such an offhand manner. The others had warned me never to walk past his office, but even in the elevator or the toilet, just the sight of me would inspire an idea for research. "Say Ben, will you stop in to see me later? I've thought of an interesting question about the insurance clause in our Form 27 Lease." Some of his ideas were good, but often I would present him with a memorandum representing a week of work only to discover that he had abandoned the idea or forgotten about it.

Gradually I realized that he was looking for companionship. Apparently he thought we had something in common because we both had worked our way through college and law school. He was an insecure and lonely person: self-absorbed, humorless, argumentative. The other partners avoided him, and he found it increasingly hard to catch younger men to help him. The more work I did for him, the more he gave me. I found myself sliding into the real estate department. He began to invite me to have dinner with him: "Just two old bachelors wedded to the jealous mistress, eh, Ben?" Over drinks and dinner he would tell me about his life, his struggles to climb from the freight yards of the Pennsylvania Railroad, where his father worked, to a partnership in Conyers & Dean, and of all the big deals that would have fallen apart but for his expert guidance and encyclopedic knowledge of real property law. After the third martini he would begin to hint that snobbery and jealousy were holding him back in the firm. He was not a likeable person, and his pathetic solicitation of friendship made me squirm.

One morning last summer Patrick Forrester sent for me. I went upstairs right away, but it wasn't easy to get into Forrester's room. He was on the telephone, and Patterson Fox Junior was waiting for him to sign a stack of opinions. Philip Rieger, another partner, was leaning in the door, and Forrester's secretary scurried back and forth with letters and files. I sat down to wait.

Forrester was bending over the proofs of a registration statement which lay in the glare of his desk lamp. He was explaining changes to his printer, moving the gold pencil slowly down the margin annotations. His lined dark face was closed in concentration. Although it was only ten o'clock in the morning, he looked tired.

When he finished with the printer he signed Fox's opinions, talking all the time to Rieger about a client's investment letter problems. After both of them went away, he asked his secretary to come in for dictation and then turned to me.

"Are you busy, Ben?"

That's always the first question. They know we are in there almost every night but they always ask anyway. The correct answer is something like "I'm busy but I'd be glad to help you just the same."

I said: "Mr. Forrester, I'm so damned busy, I don't know how I'll ever finish the things that are on my desk." He looked startled, so I went on quickly, "I'd like to work with you because I've heard that your jobs are exciting, but if you want me you'll have to cut me loose."

Forrester swiveled back and lit a cigarette. Then he asked me what I was doing and I told him.

"Hmm," said Forrester, and then his telephone rang. For ten minutes he argued with a vice-president of First Hudson Corporation about a footnote in a prospectus. While he was talking the other line rang, and his secretary picked it up. He finished with the first call and looked questioningly at her.

"Mr. Benson, Schuylkill Steel."

"All right. One second."

"Mr. Forrester can speak to Mr. Benson in just a moment."

18

Forrester turned to me again. "Look, Ben, I guess I'll have to get in touch with you later."

"Certainly, Mr. Forrester. Any time."

I assumed that would end the matter, but an hour later I had a call from Ellsworth Boyle himself. "Ahh — Ben, Pat Forrester seems to be in sort of a bind on one of his SEC registrations, really got too many deals cooking now, so I've arranged with Leslie that you can put off some of his things for the time being. Go on up and see how you can help Pat this week, will you?"

That was the beginning. Overnight everything changed for me. Our client Baxter Instruments was trying to buy all the stock of an electronics firm in Cambridge. Some Baxter stock was to be offered in exchange for theirs. We had six weeks to complete a job that usually requires three months. That very night I flew to Boston with Forrester, and he left me up there for three days to check out their records. Of course I had no idea what I was doing but I can follow instructions and Forrester knows how to give them. We worked steadily on the Baxter deal until it was closed and then started right in on an issue of convertible debentures for a small new company. I had to do most of the work because Forrester was called into a proxy fight involving one of Boyle's companies. As soon as that was straightened out, we flew over to London for three weeks, again on Baxter's behalf, to work out a loan agreement for their English subsidiary.

I sat at Forrester's side in every meeting and drafted papers for him and listened and watched, and I guess he liked me because I never went back to that room behind the library. They found me a tiny private office, then I got my own secretary, and at Christmas I discovered a two-thousand-dollar bonus in my pay envelope. When I meet Leslie Patch in the corridor he looks right through me.

Forrester is hard to describe because he keeps his

19

identity on the inside. His armor is silence: he knows how to sit still and listen with the third ear, so that he hears not only the words people are putting out but the thoughts they are thinking. He can sit in a room full of arguing lawyers and accountants and high-pressure executives, quietly drawing intricate geometric diagrams on a tablet; when they finally stop he tells them what is going to happen. This is a remarkable gift, and he pays a high price for it. Everything is on the inside, the machine is always running at full speed, but there is no place for the steam to escape. At first I thought he was one of these serene people who are quiet on the inside too, but as I came to know him better I began to notice how his hands shake when he lights a cigarette; how much whiskey he drinks, with no apparent effect; and how the drawings he prepares during conferences are becoming more and more elaborate, convoluted and puzzling.

Well, on this particular day I went back to the office after lunch and spent the afternoon putting together a permanent file for the Schuylkill Steel Debentures. These files are taken to the bindery, where they are transformed into corpulent black volumes with gold-lettered spines; then they join the ranks of similar trophies on the bookshelves of Forrester's office.

I was pretty sure that he would call me, and he did.

"Ben, I'm sorry I left you in the lurch this morning, but I just had to get Sheila to the dentist. She had an abscess in her tooth and it was killing her, so I just called Ellsworth Boyle . . ."

"That's all right, Pat. We had everything ready ahead of time, but I'm sorry to hear about Sheila. Is she all right now?"

"Oh yes, he fixed her up in an hour and I took her home and put her to bed. Did everything go all right? Any trouble with Lacey?"

20

"No, just minor stuff, Pat. Everything was fine, we got the money, they invested it in Treasury Bills, and everybody seems to be happy."

"Good boy," said Forrester, and hung up.

At quarter to five I had come upstairs and reported to Ellsworth Boyle's oak-paneled suite, but Miss Leaming said he was still attending the meeting at Hammond Soap Company, so I went into the library and read some advance sheets.

The big room was full of men now, talking and smoking and glancing at their watches.

"Let's get this show on the road, for Christ's sake," muttered Randy Kellerman. "We'll never make the six-oh-five as it is ..."

"All right, fellows," said old Mr. Dennison, as if he had heard, and banged his pencil against the edge of the table. Ordway Smith settled back into his chair. The talking stopped. "Ellsworth seems to be late, but I guess we'd better begin. Let's see now, I don't believe I have anything to announce. Do I? No. Well, Taylor, how are things in the mortuary department?" Taylor Chew announced again that absolutely all wills drawn in this office must be reviewed by someone in the estates department and will you all please see to it that Miss O'Connor has a copy of every will that you've written? Because we're always getting questions from banks or other people and then sometimes it takes a day or two to track down the instrument in question, and it makes a rotten impression on the various trust departments in town ...

"Anybody else have anything? Leslie?"

"Well, as a matter of fact," Leslie Patch took a deep breath, "I wonder if anybody can give me a thought on this rather interesting question that's just come up." He launched into a long story involving a tract of land on the Main Line, two mortgages, two lawsuits, and four million

21

dollars. As usual, he was less interested in legal advice than in announcing that he had brought in a big deal.

"Show and Tell," whispered Randy.

"Well, that's quite a mess you have there, Leslie," said Mr. Dennison. "Does anybody . . . Oh, here's Ellsworth."

Boyle came clambering in over people's legs, squeezing between hastily moved chairs, and settled down beside Dennison. "Sorry to be late, Alfred, damn Soap Company meetings always overtime . . . go ahead, go ahead . . ."

"No, no, nothing important, just shooting the breeze —" Leslie Patch pursed his lips — "Go ahead, Ellsworth, you've got a whole list of things there . . ."

"Well, okay," Ellsworth Boyle pulled his chair forward, adjusted his glasses, and looked at the list Miss Leaming had typed for him. "First of all, securities group closed the Schuylkill Steel Debentures this morning, fifteen million bucks, Mr. Butler at the helm and everything shipshape, so I guess we can pay the rent this month." He looked up. "By the way, Ben, I didn't get a chance to talk to you before, but you'll be our man at the Defender next month. Give you a little change of pace, and some trial experience."

Before I could digest that, Leslie Patch sat up straight and said: "Why, that's ridiculous! You're going to send a trained securities lawyer over there to defend all those niggers, those dope addicts and burglars . . ."

There were groans: "Oh come on, Leslie!"

"No, I think he's right," said Ordway Smith. "The Defender has a full-time staff; they get paid by the United Fund and the City; why do we have to give up men we've trained —"

"It's just for one month —"

"It'll be good for him —"

"One at a time, fellows," shouted Boyle. "Did you want to say something, Alfred?"

"Yes," said Mr. Dennison quietly, and everyone shut

22

up. "Back in the thirties, some other men and I set up this Defender Association to represent people who are accused of crimes but can't pay their own lawyers. It's grown into quite a big outfit now, because as you know the Supreme Court has said that every defendant *must* have a lawyer. If he can't afford one, you've got to give him one free. The United Fund and the City support this outfit jointly, but all the big firms have been sending young men for a month at a time to add to the staff. We've been sending one man every year, because we feel it's our duty as lawyers, and also because it's good training for the men."

Mr. Dennison stopped a moment, and then he added: "Of course I don't have anything to do with selecting the men to go, but I thought you'd like to know the background."

For three seconds there was silence. Then Leslie Patch said: "Alfred, we don't have anything against the program as such. But if you've got a man who can do a fifteen million dollar bond issue — Well, if Pat doesn't need him any more, we've got an awful jam in the real estate department right now —"

"Let me answer that," said Ellsworth Boyle. "We had originally scheduled Sam Atwater to go over there next month. Now he can't go, I understand. What's the story on that, Harry?"

Harry Rex, one of the partners in the litigation group, took his pipe out of his mouth and said: "The story is that Sam's been working on the Hammond Soap case, the antitrust case, with Ames Mahoney, and now the thing has come to trial in Chicago, and the trial might go on for maybe three or four months out there. Sam has catalogued all the files, it would be impossible to take him away —"

"Okay, well there's your reason," said Boyle. "Ben Butler just finished a big job, and he's done nothing but research and financing since he got out of law school, and we think he ought to get into court."

"Why?" somebody asked. Some partner up front; none of the associates had said a word through all this.

"You really want to know why?" Everybody looked at Patrick Forrester. Had Boyle cleared this with him? "I'll tell you why. If a man doesn't get into court when he's young, he'll *never* get there. And all his life he'll wonder whether a man who's never faced a judge, who's never talked to a jury — all his life he'll wonder if he's really a lawyer at all."

The room was silent.

"Well," said Ellsworth Boyle, "I think we've kicked this thing around enough. Ben, you clear up your desk this week, and on Monday morning you go see Walter Simon, the Chief Defender —"

Ordway Smith leaned forward. "Have you asked him if he *wants* to go?"

"Yes, I do!" I shouted, and the room exploded with laughter.

chapter 3

"All right now, Mr. Randolph, let's see if we have this straight: You were just standing there on the corner?"

"Yes, *sir*."

"Corner of Tenth and Fitzwater?"

"Yes, *sir*."

"And what were you doing?"

"Wasn't doing nothing."

"And the police car stopped and they arrested you?"

"Yes, *sir*. They did that."

"Why did they do that?"

"Why did they? I don't know that."

"You weren't doing anything at all?"

"No, *sir*."

"What time of day was this?"

"What time of *day*?"

"That's right. What time of day."

"I don't know what time of day it was. Not very late."

"Well, was it dark?"

"Yes, *sir*."

"It was dark?"

"Yes, *sir*. It sure was dark."

I sighed. This was taking too long. It was almost two o'clock, I had interviewed a dozen men, and two more were waiting outside the booth. I was tired and hungry, and Mr. Wallace Randolph stank.

"All right, then they arrested you. Did they say anything? Did the policemen say anything?"

Long, agonized concentration. "I don't know, I don't think they say anything."

"They just dragged you off without a word?"

"They say where I get the box."

"What box?"

"This here box I had."

"You had a box with you? What kind of a box?"

"Just a regular . . . box. Packing box? Like, you know, a regular box?"

"Was anything in it?"

"I don't know what was in it. They say they was resisters in it."

"Resisters? What are they?"

"These little radio resisters. They play music, you know, you can carry them around?"

"You mean transistor radios? You had a box of transistor radios?

"Yes, sir."

"How many radios were in the box?"

"I don't know how many. Fifty, they say."

"Fifty transistor radios?"

"That's what they say."

I still had not reached the space marked "Hearing" on my interview form.

"All right, Mr. Randolph. They took you to the police station, right?"

"Yes, sir."

"And then next morning you had a hearing with the judge?"

"Yes, sir."

"Now listen carefully, Mr. Randolph: I want to know *who said* what at your hearing before the magistrate."

"Who said what?"

"That's right."

"I said I didn't take them. I said I didn't know nothing about them radios."

"Mr. Randolph, were you the first one to testify — to say anything?"

His face scrunched up in terrible concentration.

"Were the policemen there? The ones who arrested you?"

"Yes, sir. One of them, he was there."

"Anybody else?"

"That detective. He was there."

"A detective? What did he say?"

"He tell the judge about how they broke into the warehouse and take things."

"What warehouse?"

"That warehouse right there on the corner."

"What corner, Mr. Randolph?"

"That's what I just *tole* you! Tenth and Fitzwater."

"A detective said that a warehouse right there at Tenth and Fitzwater had been broken into. What else did he say?"

"I don't remember what else he say."

"Did he say what was missing from the warehouse?"

"Yeah, he say some resisters missing."

"One box of resisters — I mean *transistors* —?"

"Yeah."

"What else did he say? Did he say what time it happened?"

"No, he didn't say that."

"All right now, did the policeman say anything — the one who arrested you?"

Again, excruciating mental effort. Nothing came out.

"Did the policeman tell how he arrested you?"

"Yes, sir. That's what he told them."

"What did he say you were doing?"

"What was I doing?"

"What did *he* say *you* were doing?"

27

A long pause. Then: "He say I was in the alley. But I wasn't."

"What did he say you were doing in the alley?"

"*He* say, I was running down the alley."

"Carrying this box?"

"Yes, sir."

"And where was the alley in relation to the warehouse?"

"Was what?"

"Was the alley behind the warehouse?"

"Yes, sir."

I sighed again and wrote down my client's version of the magistrate's hearing. My report would probably be the only preview our trial attorney would have of the Commonwealth's case against Randolph.

"All right now, Mr. Randolph, did you say anything at the hearing?"

"I say I didn't break into no warehouse."

"What about the fifty radios? Did you tell the magistrate where you got them?"

"Yes sir, I told him."

"All right now, tell *me*."

"Well, see, I was standing there on the corner, see, and this fella come along —"

"Just a minute, Mr. Randolph."

"Hah?"

"You want me to finish this story for you?" The dark face frowned at me. "A man came along and asked if you would just hold that box for him for a few minutes while he made a telephone call?"

"Yeah!"

"He said he would give you a dollar if you would just watch the box for him?"

"Two dollars!"

"All right, two dollars. You don't know the man's name, do you?"

"No sir, I sure don't."

"But you've seen him around?"

"That's right."

"And he left you standing there all alone, on the corner of Tenth and Fitzwater, holding a box with fifty little radios in it, and a minute later the red car drove up and the police arrested you, and that's all you know about it."

"You got it just right! That's how it sure was!" Mr. Randolph's face was all white teeth. I rubbed my eyes. My stomach was growling.

"Mr. Randolph, I've been down here one week interviewing prisoners. You know how many times I've heard that same exact story? Seven times! This is the second time I've heard it *today*."

The grin had disappeared and Mr. Randolph was looking sullenly at his cracked shoes. "Well, that the way it happen . . ."

On my first day at the prison I had watched my classmate Marvin Gold, the Deputy Defender, handle this situation. A skinny truculent white boy had just told him the man-came-along-and-asked-me-to-hold-this story. "Okay, buddy, back to your cell," Marvin had said quietly. "I don't have time to listen to this crap. Goodbye, we'll see you in court." The prisoner had tried to change his tale, but Marvin wouldn't listen, and he had to be reinterviewed by somebody else. The second time he told us the truth.

"Mr. Randolph, I'm your lawyer. I'm supposed to represent you. If *I* don't believe you, do you think the judge and jury will?"

"I don't want no jury," said Mr. Randolph quickly.

"Okay, that's up to you; we can waive the jury." Surprisingly, most of these people are more frightened of juries. "But you've still got to convince the judge, and your story doesn't make any sense."

Mr. Randolph shook his head. "That's the truth, that's the way it happen . . ."

"All right, if that's the truth I'll write it down here and the lawyer who tries your case in court will do his best for you. But it's pretty hard for us to help you if you don't trust us."

The man was old enough to be my father, and as I sent him shuffling back to his cell I wondered why he should trust me, after all. Had he ever seen me before? Would he ever see me again? I was part of the system, just as much as the police and the judges and all the other people who run the world he doesn't understand but has to live in.

The last customers were two acne-faced nineteen-year-olds who had stolen a car for a joyride and had driven it across the bridge to Camden, New Jersey, thus inadvertently committing a federal offense. They were scared to death and wanted to plead guilty, so my job was mainly to find out about their family backgrounds. Since neither had a police record, we would probably bring in their parents to beg the judge for another chance.

Finally I was finished. I signed out at the prison office, waited for the guards to unlock the series of sliding grilles and the heavy steel door, and then stepped out into the sunny summer afternoon. Across the street I boarded the bus, and half an hour later I walked into the crowded offices of the Defender Association on the tenth floor of one of the seedier downtown office buildings. I smiled at the receptionist, negotiated the narrow passage between the six typists and walked into Marvin Gold's office.

"Oh, I'm sorry," I said. Marvin was talking with a man who sat in front of his desk with his back to me.

"Just a sec, Ben," said Marvin. "Be right with you."

I backed out and closed the door, but almost immediately it opened again and a dignified-looking little man came out, followed by Marvin.

30

"Well, thank you anyway, Mr. Gold," said the little man, shaking hands.

"Okay, Max. I'm sorry I can't help you but I'm sure you'll find a lawyer who will." The little man nodded politely to me and headed for the door. Marvin waved me into his room, followed me in, and settled back into his swivel chair.

"What did you think of that gentleman?" he asked.

"Perfectly respectable-looking man."

Marvin nodded. "Downtown business type?"

"Mmm . . . No . . ." I rubbed my chin. "Sort of an upstate business type, I should say . . ."

"Notice the Shriner's pin, did you? Well, say a banker from Shamokin? Cashier of the People's National?"

"Yeah, something like that."

Marvin nodded again. "You know who that was? That was Maxwell Moriarty, one of the oldest bad-check men in the business. He just got out, and guess what he wanted? Legal advice."

"That's quite flattering, isn't it?"

Marvin grinned. "Oh yes, it's flattering. Even wanted to pay me. You'll never guess what he's interested in."

"The law of negotiable instruments?"

"Are you kidding? Max Moriarty knows more about negotiable instruments than any professor out at the Law School. No, he'd like a little memorandum on the subject of extradition treaties — with special emphasis on what countries don't have extradition treaties with the United States!"

I started to laugh.

"Well, it really isn't funny," said Marvin, who was smiling too. "I think the old bastard is about to pull a really big one this time . . . Oh well, never mind him. How'd the interviews go?"

I opened my attaché case and handed him the sheaf of notes. He took a cigar from the box in his drawer

31

and lighted it with great deliberation. Then he creaked back in his chair, put his feet on the desk and began to leaf slowly through my interviews.

Marvin is only a year older than I am, but he looks at least forty-five because he is fat — terribly fat. I don't know why; he is the only child of poor parents and maybe his mother made him eat too much. He must weigh over two-fifty and he only comes up to my shoulder and he has to wear very thick glasses, so the overall effect is far from impressive. Marvin never said much in class, and I must confess that during our first year of Law School I was not aware of him. In August, when those of us who had made the grade were ordered back to work on the Law Review, Marvin and I found ourselves in adjoining library stalls. We did our first Case Note together. When he discovered that I had a job washing dishes in the Houston Hall cafeteria and was therefore not quite what I apparently look like, he let down his guard a little. I guess I did too. We became friends. I learned that his father had come from Russia as a boy, that his parents owned a shoe store in a Negro neighborhood, and that Marvin had earned his B.A. at Temple night school while selling shoes in the daytime. He wanted to be a lawyer so badly that I cringed for my companions of the first year, those amiable tweed-coated bridge players, most of whom were following the line of least resistance into their fathers' firms. I caught the bug and began to work very hard, but next to Marvin I was a loafer. He sat in the library every night until it closed; not satisfied with the heavy daily case assignments and the Law Review work, he chased down collateral points suggested by the lectures, helped one of the professors draft a new criminal code, and wrote briefs for the Civil Liberties Union.

"Don't you ever get tired of books?" I once asked him.

I remember that he smiled a little and shook his head. "Ben, I've spent all my life in a shoe store. To

32

me these books are — Well, I could say that to me they're food and drink." Then he was embarrassed and made a joke of it.

For a boy who grew up in the slums, Marvin didn't have much firsthand experience with life. He liked to hear me talk about parties and dances and women — especially women. I should explain that at this time I had two or three things going at the same time and with my schoolwork and the dishwashing job life became a little complicated and it was helpful to be able to talk to somebody who didn't know the people involved. Over late beers at Tony & Al's or The Deck or Smokey's, Marvin would encourage me to tell him stories that just reinforced my playboy image. I am not in fact a playboy, but maybe I did enjoy performing the part for Marvin's entertainment.

Well anyway, he graduated with the highest grades in our class. Only a very naïve person would consider that sufficient qualification for a job with Conyers & Dean or any other downtown emporium, and Marvin is not naïve. He signed up with the Defender and was quickly promoted to the number two position on the staff. We always planned to have lunch together, but first I was busy and then he was busy . . .

The swivel chair creaked again as Marvin shifted his weight. He was nearly through the folder. "These are not half bad, my lean and hungry friend. Not half bad. At least, you seem to realize that the guy who tries the case in court has never seen the defendant and has to rely on the interview."

"Do I look as hungry as I feel? I never had lunch."

"Yeah, well, the joys of public service . . . Hmm, you didn't believe Mr. Wallace Randolph's story? My goodness, that's his story, let him stick to it."

"That's not how you handled that kid the other day."

"A momentary flash of ill temper, dear boy. Don't do

33

as I do, do as I say." He put down the papers and turned in his chair, causing more squeaking and clanking. "Well, I think it's time to call it a day. Want to go across the street for a drink?"

"Sure," I said, getting up. "Oh wait a minute, Marvin, what day is this?" I took out my little pocket diary. "Oh hell, I'm sorry, I'm supposed to be at a dinner party in Paoli in an hour. I'll be late as it is, but I'll see you on Monday."

"Ah, what a gay life you socialites lead," said Marvin, putting on his jacket. "So long, Ben, I'll see you next week. You're doing a good job."

chapter 4

As I parked my car in Ordway Smith's circular driveway, I realized that this wasn't the big buffet dinner I had expected. There were only three other cars. Walking past the lilac bushes to the big Colonial farmhouse, I bet myself ten dollars that they had an extra woman to take care of — somebody's cousin or sister or college roommate.

"How *nice* to see you, Ben," said Marion Smith as she opened the door. They were all in the library, talking and drinking. "I don't think you know my sister, Sally Rochester . . . This is Ben Butler, from Ordway's office . . . This is Mr. Morris, Benjamin Butler . . . Of course you know Sheila and Pat . . . and this is *Mrs*. Morris, Benjamin Butler, who works with Ordway and Pat . . . Oh, here's Ordway, he always makes me do the introducing . . ."

"Because you do it so beautifully, m'dear," said Ordway, coming in with a full ice bucket. "Nice to see you, Ben. What can I fix you?"

Mentally I paid myself the ten dollars and looked at Sally Rochester, who was very carefully not looking back while she conducted an animated conversation with Mrs. Morris. She was a younger and bigger version of Marion Smith, a tall strapping redhead with sort of a sullen look on her face, maybe a little on the heavy side, but the look had something . . .

"Say, you're not by any chance the son of Loring Butler, are you?" Mr. Morris's bloodshot eyes examined me across his martini. "There's something about your face . . ."

"Yes, sir, he was my father. Did you know him?"

"My God, I certainly did know him, we started at the bank together in thirty-five, well you must have been just a kid . . ." He stopped, but this happens to me all the time.

"I was six years old when he was killed, Mr. Morris."

Morris looked at the carpet and shook his head. "Yeah, I remember it all now. A terrible shame, plenty of single men stationed in Washington, sitting around in offices, and they put a man like Loring Butler in the infantry —"

"Well, he was in the National Guard, Mr. Morris. How are things on the second floor these days?" I had by now remembered: Mitchell Morris was the vice-president in charge of the trust department of the William Penn Trust Company.

"Oh, we're making a living, I guess . . ."

"Mitchell, will you tell Pat that story you told me at lunch yesterday?" Ordway Smith moved Morris a little to the right, and I saw Sheila Forrester sitting on the sofa, alone. She had that look they get at a certain stage: husband working all the time, children growing into more and more problems, never enough money for the life they lead — a brave but tired look. She gave me a pale smile as I sat down beside her.

"May I get you another drink?"

"No thanks, Ben. How've you been? I haven't seen you for a long time."

"I'm fine, Sheila, but I'm sorry to hear about your tooth, that must have hurt. Is it all okay now?"

"Tooth?"

"Your abscessed tooth, when Pat couldn't make the

steel company closing the other day, that's how I heard about it."

"Oh, that," she said vaguely. "Yes, that's all right. Tell me, where are you living now?"

I told her about my room on Spruce Street, but I was thinking about something else. For the second time this year, I had a wrong feedback from Forrester. One night last winter I couldn't find the library copy of a Commerce Clearing House service I needed, and I knew that there was another one in Forrester's office, so I went upstairs. The whole thirty-first floor was dark and empty, so I just marched right into Forrester's room, and by God there he was, sitting in the dark and looking out the window. It was embarrassing for both of us; he mumbled something about thinking over a problem and I got the book and vanished, and neither of us said another word about it. But I didn't like this business about the Schuylkill Steel settlement; why would he have to fake an excuse for not being there?

Sheila Forrester was telling me about teen-age baby-sitters; it seems that some of them allow the children to watch television all night and leave dirty dishes standing around.

"Tell me about Sally Rochester," I suggested.

"Oh, haven't they briefed you?" I shook my head. "Well, it's a familiar story," she said. "Seven years of marriage, two lovely children, one eighteen-year-old secretary, good-bye Mr. Rochester."

"They're divorced?"

Sheila nodded. "She just got back from Las Vegas. Well, here comes Ordway so you'd better go over and talk to her. You're next to me at dinner and Marion's looking at us."

Ordway arrived with the martini pitcher for Sheila and asked me to go help myself, so I walked over to the tray, made myself another Scotch-on-the-rocks and joined

Sally Rochester, who was now talking to Mitchell Morris.

"No, they hadn't brought in those French revues when we were there," Morris was saying.

"We were just talking about Las Vegas," Sally said to me. "Have you ever been there?"

"No, I haven't. Did you have a good time?" My God, did I say that? Nothing to eat since breakfast and two stiff drinks, but still . . . Morris turned to Pat Forrester, and Sally said: "I didn't know dark men could blush that prettily, so I see you've been told."

"I'm sorry, I'm not used to alcoholic beverages."

"I'll bet." It came out "All bet" because she had this nasal debutante drawl they seem to pick up from each other. It always reminds me of the hours I stood around at the Saturday Evening Dancing Classes, where I didn't know anybody because I went to public school. She extracted a cigarette from her purse and I lighted it for her, thinking: What-kind-of-law-do-you-practice-my-isn't-that-fascinating.

"What kind of law do you practice?" she asked, blowing out smoke and squinting at me. She had little lines beside her mouth. She wasn't used to being a single woman at parties and making conversation.

"Well, I'm practicing criminal law."

"How *fas*cinating! Oh, you're kidding me."

"No, I'm not." I told her about the Defender and my prison interviews. It was easier than trying to make the Schuylkill Steel Debentures sound interesting. She was grateful to have me talk while she listened. I looked carefully into her eyes, and it was there. You can't describe it but you can see it, and if it's there then it's just a question of how long she thinks she ought to fight it.

The three blond Smith children came down in their bathrobes to say goodnight. Then we moved in to dinner.

We sat by candlelight around an oval mahogany table. From each wall a dark ancestor brooded down upon us.

38

Ordway carved the roast and the maid passed the vegetables in silver dishes. A setting for eight does not allow the host and hostess at both ends so Mitchell Morris was at the foot, between Marion Smith and her sister. Pouring a layer of Cabernet Sauvignon on top of the martinis, he began to dominate the table. He told three stories in a row, and only the first one was funny. Ordway seemed to be encouraging him, but with determined efforts Mrs. Morris and Marion Smith broke up the general conversation. The way the heads turned left me isolated; on my right Sheila Forrester was talking to Ordway and on the other side Marion Smith was working hard on Morris. In that fix you are supposed to lean forward and involve yourself with another group but I just sat back, observed the scene, and tried to see myself in Ordway's role. Did I have the equipment? Answer: Negative. With luck I might become another Patrick Forrester. Poor Boy Makes Good in Prominent Law Firm. Motivation: Hunger. For that matter it seemed to me that Forrester looked even more tired than usual.

"Don't you think so too, Ben?"

I should have known that Marion's training would not permit her to let me sit there woolgathering, conspicuously out of it. I agreed with her as heartily as I could, the table turned, and I kept up my end for the rest of the meal. We had vanilla ice cream with strawberries, and then the ladies went upstairs. Ordway brought out his Cognac and cigars.

Mitchell Morris turned to me. In the candlelight his face was the color of the roast beef. "Ben, I hear you had a tussle with Fred Lacey the other day."

"Oh I wouldn't call it a tussle, Mr. Morris. Mr. Lacey was just guarding your interests very carefully."

"I don't know, old Fred is getting a little hard to deal with these days. In fact that whole firm is beginning to slide a little, in my humble opinion. Now you take that

39

Pemberton Estate thing, Ordway . . ." As Mitchell Morris began to develop his complaint against the Messrs. Openshaw, Prescott, Pennington & Lee, I sensed that both Ordway Smith and Pat Forrester were watching me over the rims of their brandy glasses. Morris was talking high treason against the firm that had represented his bank for a generation, and while this was exactly what two rising partners in Conyers & Dean wanted to hear, it was not necessarily for the ears of a very junior associate. I could hear the voices of Ordway and Marion as they planned this party: "I don't think we need to have Butler this time; after all, we want Morris to talk business, and this boy —"

"But I've already asked Sally and she's all alone over there. Randy Kellerman's engaged. Would you rather have Leslie Patch?"

"Christ, no!"

"Well, some single man from outside the firm?"

"No, that would be worse."

"Then it has to be Ben Butler."

The Messrs. Smith & Forrester were playing their roles to perfection: Just by the way they frowned and nodded and judiciously blew cigar smoke around, you could see that it hurt them to hear their friends at Openshaw, Prescott vilified by this unhappy client; on the other hand the Pemberton Estate was unquestionably a fantastic mess.

"And you know what happened then?" Mitchell Morris's face was shading toward purple. "Bill Pennington had the unmitigated gall to send over a bill for sixty-five thousand dollars. *Sixty-five thousand dollars!* Said he had time cards. *Time cards!* I said, 'Do you realize this has to come out of our trust department budget?' I said, 'We can't hit the estate for this, you know.' What I wanted to say but didn't was 'Who do you think got us into this jam, anyway?' Judas Priest!" He expelled his breath and swallowed most of his brandy.

"Well now, Mitchell, maybe you're being a little hard

40

on Bill Pennington and his boys." Ordway pushed his chair away from the table, leaned back, and launched into a detailed discussion of the Pemberton litigation: how it all started, the personalities of the litigants and their lawyers, who did what, who *should* have taken what position, and why — it was an amazing performance, full of inside knowledge and good humor. Ostensibly Ordway was explaining why Openshaw, Prescott, Pennington & Lee had to handle the matter the way they did; on the other hand, you could not escape the conclusion that someone with a little more insight, someone who understood the second Mrs. Pemberton as well as Ordway did . . .

"Jesus, Ordway, that's the first sensible discussion I've ever heard about this miserable mess. Do you think you could write me a memorandum —"

Ordway roared with laughter. "Not a chance, Mitchell, I'm too young to get disbarred! This is Bill Pennington's can of worms — and yours, of course."

At this point the ladies came down, the coffee was carried into the living room, and everyone began to mill around. The front door was open and I stood on the steps for a moment listening to the cicadas pulsating in the darkness. The smell of fresh hay rose from the fields.

"I think they want to play bridge," said Sally Rochester beside me.

"Oh my gosh." Now I was in trouble. "Your sister didn't tell me that. I don't play bridge. Will that ruin her party?"

Sally giggled. "You don't play bridge? Not at all? How *priceless!* No, they've got one table and Mrs. Forrester is dead. She'll take him home soon anyway. Wait here a second." She went back into the house. A few minutes later Pat appeared at the door, carrying a tray with glasses, water, and bottles of Scotch and bourbon. I opened the screen for him.

"Non-cardplayers have been ordered to the terrace," he said.

41

"Pat, I'm awfully sorry if I spoiled the game for you."

"Nonsense, I don't even want to play. We're going home in a few minutes and glad to have an excuse. I'll carry this over."

Sheila came out and handed me the ice bucket. We walked around to the terrace.

We sat there for an hour, talking quietly and drinking and tossing our cigarette butts in high arcs across the boxwoods. Sally and Sheila talked about their children. I listened to them, and watched Forrester as he smoked, his feet propped against the fieldstone terrace wall, his eyes on the line of black trees at the top of the hill. I realized that I had hardly heard him say a word all evening. Of course he had reason to be tired. While I was doing the Schuylkill Steel thing, he was keeping his eye on it, taking care of a complicated little acquisition for Baxter Instruments, and getting another company listed on the New York Stock Exchange. In April he finished a merger for Riverside Controls. Still, I didn't understand why it was necessary for him to lie to Ellsworth Boyle, and to me . . . Whatever it is, I thought, I would like to help him with it. That sounds stupid, of course. Nobody can ever help anybody. Well, Forrester helped me. I was getting desperate doing scut work for Leslie Patch, and Forrester changed my life —

"I mean ninety cents an hour, and then they can't even let the water out of the bathtub . . ." She turned to Sally again. "Do you have somebody full-time up there?"

"Well — uh, actually, I've been terribly lucky." Sally sounded apologetic. "My Aunt Helen's down in Georgia all winter, and she had this old colored woman, and her children had moved up here, you see, so she wanted to come up here too . . ."

"You *are* lucky," said Sheila in a flat voice.

"Well, but you see, I had to go away to Nevada and leave them alone all that time . . ."

42

Pat Forrester stood up suddenly and said, "Listen, friends, I'm sorry but I've got to work tomorrow —"

"Oh gosh, what time is it?" asked Sheila, as we all rose. The Forresters said goodnight and went into the house. We heard the voices in the living room, and then doors slammed and their car went crunching out the driveway.

"Well, I suppose we should go in," said Sally.

"Is that a pool down there?" I asked.

"Yes, and a tennis court behind the trees. Do you want to walk down?"

"Sure."

"Oh, and bring a bottle. You may not be accustomed to alcoholic beverages, but I've become a little addicted, I'm afraid."

The pool was in the middle of the meadow, in the bottomlands fifty yards below the house. Sally kicked her shoes off and walked out to the end of the diving board.

"Are you going for a swim?" I asked.

"No," she said. "Bring that bottle out here and pour me a drink."

I stood behind her, feeling the board sag beneath our weight, and poured the whiskey into the glass she held up.

"That's fine. Now you can go sit down over there someplace."

"Yes, ma'm." I left the bottle on the diving board and sat down at the edge of the pool. I could barely see her in the darkness. She was splashing the water with her foot.

"I hear you're a terribly good lawyer," she said after a while.

"Well, I'm glad you hear that," I said.

"It must be fun to be very good at something. Why did you decide to be a lawyer?"

"Oh, I don't know. I suppose I was pushed into it a little. My father wanted to be a lawyer, but there wasn't enough money, so he went to work in a bank, and then he

43

was killed in the war when I was a little boy, and I guess my mother just sort of made up her mind that that's what I was going to be. Anyway, she persuaded me to start law school, and I did pretty well there. I seem to have a feel for it, or something."

"And of course you love it," she said. "That was my husband's trouble, he hated his work and it just soured him all the way through."

"What did he do?"

"He still does it. Works for his father. Marine insurance; they sell insurance for ships." I could hear her pouring more whiskey into her glass.

"Wasn't he interested in something? Most people —"

"Golf," she said, sloshing her foot in the pool. "He's one of the best golfers around here. He could have been a pro. Bobby Rochester; have you heard of him?"

"No, I'm sorry, I don't play golf."

She laughed. "No bridge, no golf? You're eccentric!"

"Just a bookworm."

We carried on this conversation for a while. I told her about my poor boy's life: my mother's job as a lady stockbroker, my scholarships at college and law school, and my little room on Spruce Street.

"Well," she said. "You're a real Horatio Alger boy, aren't you?"

"Where did you ever hear of Horatio Alger?"

"What's that crack supposed to indicate? As a matter of fact, I'm not nearly as dumb as I look."

"I didn't say you looked —"

"At least I didn't discuss baby-sitters with you, did I? By the way, what's the matter with your friend Forrester?"

I said I didn't think there was anything the matter with him.

"Oh come on, now! He sat there glooming to himself all night, hardly said a word to anybody — Ordway claims he's so brilliant . . ."

44

"He is," I said. "He's got one of the finest legal minds in town, and on top of that, he's a leader. I mean people like to work for him. We have this securities group, you see, and he's the head of it —"

"Well, be that as it may, I think he's got problems. And his wife's a bore. Do you happen to have a cigarette?"

I went back out on the diving board, gave her a cigarette and lighted it. Without moving it from her lips, she poured Scotch into our glasses. I sat down beside her on the board.

"Slowly but surely he moves," she said through the cigarette.

"You're pretty jumpy, aren't you?" As a matter of fact, one thing I have learned is that you *never* move first. You let them do it, and they nearly always do.

She removed the cigarette and took a long drink. "You must forgive me, it's been a long time since I've sat in the dark with a young man. I don't know the right lines any more."

"You're doing pretty well. Are you drinking that straight?"

"You the kind of person who puts swimming pool water into Scotch? Yes I drink it straight, that's the only way I can get to sleep at night —"

"Sally? Are you down there?"

"We're down here at the pool, Marion. Is the party over?"

"Well, the Morrisses just left, yes." Marion's white dress appeared at the other end of the pool. "God, that man's a terrible player. I'm afraid I finally showed it a little and Ordway's furious with me." She sat down. There was a flash of white as she took off her shoes and dipped her legs into the water. "Oh boy, that feels good! Yes, I think we can swim tomorrow. Bring them over after lunch."

45

"I thought I'd ask my friend here if by any chance he plays tennis," said Sally.

"Oh sure, Ben, do come out. That would be fun."

I said I'd like to.

A cigarette glowed in the darkness and Ordway materialized. Hands in his pockets, he strolled around the pool, stooping to pick up the whiskey bottle from the diving board. We all moved toward the house.

Under the hall lights Marion looked sharply at her sister. "Sal, dearie, I think maybe you'd better stay over. The bed's all made up in the —"

"Why? My God, you think I'm *drunk?*"

"No no, of course not, but it's late and you have had a few —"

"Don't be crazy, Marion. That was before, I'm perfectly all right now, no trouble for weeks, and anyway I've got to take Robbie to the dentist at nine o'clock." She pulled her coat from the closet and I helped her put it on.

"Why don't you let me take you home?" I asked as we walked out to the cars. Ordway was still carrying the bottle, which was nearly empty.

"That's a good idea, Ben," said Marion enthusiastically, as if it had just occurred to her. "Then you pick her up tomorrow and bring her over with the children."

"Oh cut it out, Marion, he's got other things to do. Let's not make a big production out of this!"

"Well, thanks ever so much —" I began, turning to Marion, but Ordway touched my arm. "Hold it," he murmured.

Sally said good-bye to us, climbed into her station wagon and slammed the door. Then she turned the key, but nothing happened.

"All right, Ordway!"

"What's wrong Sal? Won't she start?"

"Ordway, goddamn you, you hook up this car again —"

"Sally!" gasped Marion.

We all looked at each other for a second. Sally's eyes were blazing. Then she jumped out of her car, walked over to mine, got in, and slammed the door.

"Well —" I began again.

"Good night, Ben," said Marion quickly. "I'm mortified that she's behaving this way, but she's been through an awful lot and it really is better if she doesn't drive —"

"Ben understands, m'dear," said Ordway, gently moving me toward my car. "Good night, old man, you've been a tremendous help, we'll look forward to some good tennis tomorrow. Good night, sister Sal." He closed my door and I drove off.

"Where to, Madam?"

"Oh, shut up!"

"Well, you have to tell me where you live!"

She gave me an address in Bryn Mawr, one of those Stockbroker Tudor mansions on the steep hill.

We drove along in silence for a minute or so, and then she said "I'm sorry I made a scene in front of you, Ben. They're only trying to look out for me. Our parents were killed in an accident when I was still in school and Marion has sort of brought me up, but even so, I've *had* the Kid-Sister-with-a-Problem Bit. I did get smashed a lot last winter, but I'm over it now, I just take enough to let me sleep but they insist on treating me like some kind of a *case* or something . . ."

When she got all that out of her system she calmed down and told me about her children and her attempts to make a life for herself, to get out of the house, "but I'm like all the rest of these girls, I don't know how to *do* anything, so all anybody wants me for is to get my picture in the paper with a string of pearls and three other Dumb Doras planning something for the Devon Horse Show, or something." She had studied archaeology at Vassar, and

47

she thought that she might become a volunteer guide at the University Museum . . .

As we drove between the gateposts and up the long driveway, I said something about what an impressive establishment she had.

"Oh, it's impressive all right, but you should see the heating bills. It belonged to Bobby's grandmother; I wish we could sell it, but they claim they can't get anything for it, so we have to wait for the College to buy it — or so Ordway thinks. I'd much rather have a smaller modern house somewhere, but they tell me it's wiser to insist on staying here for the time being — oh God, I'm so *sick* of the negotiating and bargaining — I'm sorry, Ben, you're really getting an earful of woe tonight."

I stopped under the stone arch protecting the front door; she was out of the car before I could get around to the other side.

"Well, that's another thing I'm going to have to learn again — husbands don't open the door for you." She burrowed in her purse for the key, and then looked up again. "Thanks very much for taking me home. And you really don't have to come out tomorrow, you know."

"I'll be here at two o'clock."

She unlocked the big wooden door and opened it. Turning around, she said: "Guess what?"

"What?"

"I can read your mind, and you're probably right. Good night, see you tomorrow." She closed the door.

chapter 5

"Name and number, Officer."

Assistant District Attorney Willis F. Donahue's voice betrayed the fact that he had been trying cases in Room 453 for a long, long time. In his rumpled suit, he blended well with the room itself — an enormous dreary hall of marble and wood and dirty green paint, dim despite the windows on three sides and the lights high up in the murky ceiling. In back of us, behind the wooden railing, the seats were filled with policemen, impassive-looking women, and bums who had found an entertaining place to spend the morning.

The Judge was a polite little man from somewhere upstate, sitting in the city by order of the Chief Justice because our dockets are overloaded. He kept himself occupied by writing on a yellow pad; apparently he was noting every word of testimony, even though the court stenographer was doing it too.

On the counsel table in front of me I had carefully spread out our meager file in the matter of *Commonwealth v. Perez:* A & B; AA & B; CCDW. A copy of the bill of indictment, the prison interview, the investigator's report. Our client, a slim olive-skinned Puerto Rican boy with slicked-down blue-black hair was accused of attacking a friend (male) with a knife, cutting the same friend with the same knife, and carrying a concealed deadly weapon (the knife). Mr. Perez, whom I had met when he was brought from the cell room, sat behind me, calmly cleaning his fingernails with a paper clip. The smell of the prison was on him, but I was used to it now.

The policeman on the stand identified himself as Patrolman C. W. McGrath, Number Twenty-seven twenty-two.

Leaning heavily against the rail and scowling at the bill of indictment in his hand, Donahue asked:

"Officer, on the ah — twelfth of March of this year, at about eleven P.M. were you in the vicinity of — ah — Thirteenth and Spring Garden?"

"Yes, sir."

"Please tell his Honor what you observed." This, like almost all of these trials, was a "waiver." With consent of the court, the D.A. and defense counsel (me), Mr. Perez had waived his constitutional right to a jury trial because he thought he could do better with a judge alone.

Reading from his notebook in a flat monotone, Officer McGrath stated that while proceeding north on Broad Street in car number 473, together with Officer Beazley, he had received a radio report dispatching him to a taproom at such and such a number North Thirteenth Street, fight in progress. I could have objected because while a witness can refresh his recollection, he can't just read his testimony from a notebook, but I had already learned the first rule of trial practice: Never object if you're not being hurt.

"All right then, Officer, you drove to this taproom, right?"

"Yes, sir."

"And there was a fight going on?"

"Objection!" That wasn't just leading; that was putting words in his mouth.

"Sustained," said the Judge.

"All right, what was going on when you got there?"

"Well, there was all these people standing around in the street and we stopped and Beazley got out. They were holding this guy . . ."

I jumped up. "Your Honor, is he telling what he saw?"

The Judge stopped writing and looked up.

"Did you see them holding this man?"

"Your Honor, I just told him Beazley got out and he . . . I had to pull the car over out of the way . . ."

Donahue turned and called back into the room, "Is Officer Beazley here?"

"Officer Beazley, Officer Beazley," shouted the tipstaff, and somebody else took up the cry in the corridor.

"Officer Beazley's on vacation," said Officer McGrath.

"Well, wasn't he subpoenaed?" asked the Judge.

Donahue began to riffle around in his file.

"Officer Beazley was not subpoenaed," announced Officer McGrath stiffly.

Turning back toward the stand Donahue began, "Didn't you tell the Grand Jury—"

"If your Honor please!" My voice sounded a little too loud.

"All right, Mr. Donahue," said the Judge. "Counsel to side-bar, please.

Donahue and I walked around the railing and stood directly in front of the marble bench. The Judge leaned over and said, "What the hell . . ."

"I can't help it, Judge," said Donahue. "They've got this file all screwed up. One of the policemen told the Grand Jury that the crowd was holding this guy . . ."

"What'd he do, cut somebody?"

"Yes, sir, the guy was bleeding all over the place . . ."

"Well, have you got him here?"

51

Donahue didn't know. He went back to check the bill of indictment, and then the tipstaff called, "Julio Martinez! Julio Martinez!"

"I guess he's not here either, Judge," said Donahue. "I guess I'll have to ask for a continuance."

Now it was my turn. "Your Honor, this man's been locked up since March. He's got a wife and three children at home . . ."

"Has he got a job?"

"He had one, yes sir, and they say they'll take him back, it's the Mayer Knitting Mills, he was a maintenance man . . ."

"Any record?" asked the Judge, turning to Donahue, who leaned over to look at the card the police clerk was holding up.

"No record, your Honor," I said, and Donahue nodded in confirmation.

There was a silence. Then I said "Your Honor, after all the man's actually served —"

"All right," said the Judge. "That's all you have, is it, Mr. Donahue?"

"Yes sir."

"All right." He raised his voice. "The court finds the defendant not guilty on all bills. You're a lucky man, Mr. — uh — Perez. You can go home now. Next case."

Mr. Perez, who was still cleaning his fingernails, raised his head as he heard his name, and discovered that everybody was looking at him.

"Hey, wha' happened?" he whispered to me.

"You've been found not guilty. You can go home, Mr. Perez." I started to write the result on the outside of the file envelope.

"I'm not guilty?" Mr. Perez was showing emotion for the first time. The guards were starting to lead him out. "Hey, where they taking me? What's going on?"

52

"They couldn't prove their case against you. They brought the wrong policeman, and Mr. Martinez didn't show up. So they let you go."

"Oh."

"These officers are going to take you back upstairs and give you your stuff, and then you can go home."

"Oh." He still looked very puzzled. "Well — uh . . . well, *thanks*."

"Okay, Mr. Perez."

I turned back to look at the Judge.

"I think your client was the most surprised man in the room," said the Judge.

"That's for sure," said Donahue, putting his papers together. "Bring out Frank Bush."

Commonwealth v. Bush was a mess of the kind you don't even know exists until you spend some time in the criminal courts. Having read the file, I was curious what the man would look like. They brought out a fat little fellow with a shiny face, sideburns, a tiny moustache and shifty eyes. He wore a double-breasted pinstriped suit over an open sport shirt. He had been living with a woman who was the mother of two small children — apparently not his — and he was accused of making some kind of sexual advances to one of the children, a twelve-year-old girl. The indictment people had him charged with everything they could think of: Rape, Statutory Rape, Sodomy, Solicitation to Commit Sodomy, Indecent Exposure, Corrupting the Morals of a Minor, and Disorderly Conduct. The Grand Jury had indicted on all counts.

Donahue put the mother on the stand, a plump washed-out woman well over forty, wearing a hat and gloves. She cried, but she didn't know anything. Then he put on the little brother, aged ten. Uncle Frank came into the bedroom and went into Mary's bed. Did he get in the bed? No, he sorta leaned on the bed and kneeled on the floor. Did Mary do anything? She said cut it out, and then she

53

called Mama, and Mama woke up and ran in and turned on the light and started yelling.

"Cross-examine," said Donahue.

The room was quiet with outrage. I looked at the Judge, who was still writing on his yellow pad. Should I emphasize that it was dark in there? Should I ask whether Uncle Frank had been drinking? "No questions," I said, and the little boy disappeared.

Donahue put on the little girl. They ought to figure out some way to try these cases in private. Her voice was so low that the court crier had to stand beside her and shout out her answers. Donahue tried hard, but it wouldn't come. Uncle Frank had put his hands on her, as they used to phrase it in the old novels. That was all Donahue could get her to say. Finally he gave up and turned to me. "Your witness, counselor."

"No questions."

When the little girl was gone, I stood up and said: "Your Honor, I demur to the evidence in Number 463, 464, 465, 466, 467, 468 and 469."

"Counsel to side-bar."

We went up again. "I'm not going to let this man go," said the Judge.

"But your Honor," I began. "He's not guilty of what they've charged him with —"

"I know it, but I want a psychiatric examination. How long will that take?"

"Couple of days, your Honor," said Donahue.

"All right, I'll sustain the demurrers on all the bills except the disorderly conduct one — which is that? Number 469? All right, I find him guilty on Bill Number 469. Sentence deferred pending psychiatric report. I'm not letting a man like that on the street without a checkup."

We went back down, the Judge made his ruling in public, and I tried to explain it to Frank Bush. Then the guards took him back to the cell room, and I had to explain it again to the children's mother.

"You mean I can't take him home now?" she gasped. "He's been in jail for three months, how'm I supposed to feed these kids? They took away the Unemployment, and the Relief is only . . ."

"But you had him arrested, Mrs. Blake . . ."

"Well, for Christ's sake, whatd'ya expect me to do? The children were yelling . . ." She began to cry, and one of the policewomen led her away.

That was the last case on the list. "Court stands adjourned until Monday morning at ten o'clock," shouted one of the attendants, everybody rose, the Judge climbed down the stairs into the robing room.

"You're getting the hang of it, my boy," said Donahue as we packed our files into our briefcases. "Some day you're going to bump into one that's been properly prepared upstairs." Or a D.A. who's read his files before trial, I thought. I thanked him and turned to go, but there was a hand on my elbow.

"Hey Clarence Darrow, how about some lunch?"

It was Sam Atwater, my former roommate at Conyers & Dean: portly, bespectacled and smiling.

"Sambo! Why aren't you in Chicago?"

"Come on, let's eat and I'll tell you all about it." We moved out of the courtroom and down the long tiled corridor toward the elevators.

"Want to go to the Racquet Club?" asked Sam.

"No, let's just go over to Porter's."

As we descended to the street and picked our way through the Penn Square traffic, Sam explained that the judge presiding over the Hammond antitrust case had come down with the flu.

"So they dismantled the whole trial, forty lawyers and ten filing cabinets of evidence, and sent everybody home? Couldn't they find another judge?"

Sam shook his head. "Not that bad. They sent everybody home, but the judge will be okay in two weeks and they couldn't clear another one, so we locked up all the stuff at the Chicago firm and came home."

"What did the plaintiffs say?"

"Not much. They're right there in Chicago, so what do they care? No, this is just a breather for everybody, but I'm sorry I missed out on the Defender."

I followed him into Porter's Ale House, the nearest thing we have to a London pub. At lunchtime it is jammed with secretaries and young men from the offices in the neighborhood. We carried our sandwiches and beer away from the bar, moved slowly through the dark smoky room, and found an empty table back in the corner.

Sam bit into his rare roast beef and mustard on white, munched meditatively for a moment, and said: "If that judge had crapped out a week earlier, I'd be over there instead of you. How do you like it?"

"Well, it's different. So far I've just done prison interviews and a few simple waivers —"

"Yeah, that was a real charmer I watched, just now. Must make you feel great to send that pig back where he can get at that little girl again."

"You know better than that," I said. "You sound just like a layman. They had him charged with half-a-dozen things he didn't do! I'm supposed to present his side and if they can't prove what they've charged him with I've got to demur to the evidence, don't I? We've got an adversary system in this country —"

"Please! I heard it all in first year Crimes. You've learned the lesson. But most of them are guilty as hell, and you know it." He raised his stein and noisily swallowed some beer.

"Sure, most of them are guilty of something, though not necessarily what they're charged with. And once in a while — maybe once or twice a week, they tell me — you

56

get somebody that by God really seems to be innocent and of course that makes it all worthwhile — or anyway, it should."

"It should? What's that supposed to mean?" Sam looked puzzled.

I leaned back in my chair and looked at the dirty plaster ceiling and tried to explain. Seventy-five or eighty per cent of people we defend are Negroes, and most of them seem to be completely untouched by the whole procedure. "Sam, it's an endless parade of black faces, sullen, closed black faces. You get the feeling that they just simply don't give a damn what happens at the trial. It's our ball game and they're not playing and they couldn't care less if we decide they're guilty or innocent or what."

"Ben Butler meets The Negro Problem." Sam took another drink. "The fashionable word is alienation, my boy. Where have you been all these years?"

"But where's it all going to lead, Sam? Almost half the people in this city are black, did you know that? Can you run a city where half the people are living in a different world?"

Sam shrugged. "The only answer I know is a commutation ticket." He finished his beer and wiped his mouth with a paper napkin. "You're the last guy I would expect to agonize over social problems. Well anyway it sounds like an interesting tour. I hope they'll let me go next year, but I wouldn't be surprised if the Hammond case is still in litigation then. I may spend the rest of my *life* on this thing; nobody else can find the papers."

He suddenly looked so tired and discouraged that I quickly asked "What's new at the sweatshop? I feel as if I'd been gone for months."

Sam recounted the usual routine: some secretaries had been shifted; Leslie Patch was bitching loudly that he couldn't get any help in the real estate department; the guessing was that Crosby would make partner in September but Dahlquist would not — "and you've seen about Randy's wedding."

"To Roseann? That's in the fall, isn't it?"

Sam shook his head. "Slight revision. Wedding takes place on the Fourth of July."

"But that's only — Oh." Sam was grinning.

"Well what the hell," I said, "they were engaged, weren't they? Will it be a small wedding?"

"You don't know Mrs. Hyde, do you? A small wedding for Roseann? People might think there was something funny going on. No, it's going to be the whole schmier. Five hundred people and tents and an orchestra. In fact my guess is you'll be an usher. He's got to ask one of us to represent the firm, and you look better in a morning coat. You know, all this talk about a merger instead of a wedding is really true. For Kellerman of all people to pick that one — He must really be in love with her. *You're* the one who should have arranged a shotgun wedding with Roseann Hyde. Poor but intelligent, man of the people who made his own way —"

"Thanks anyway."

"So she isn't very pretty. You can't have everything, Butler."

"Do you want some coffee?"

He nodded and I fetched two cups of coffee from the counter. When I sat down again Sam's mood had changed. "Say, what's the matter with Forrester?" he asked.

"What do you mean what's the matter?"

"Well, he's in there all the time with his door shut —"

"Maybe he's trying to get some work done."

"But what's he working on? There used to be half-a-dozen people trying to get in to see him, and now he locks himself in there and never talks to anybody —"

I'd had some thoughts like this myself, but neverthe-less I resented his question. "Listen, Pat's been working

58

night and day all spring. There isn't another partner in the firm who's put in the hours —"

"All right, all right!" Sam raised his hand. 'Say no more. Patrick Forrester is the hardest worker and the finest guy and if you say one word against him his people start foaming at the mouth. It's an article of faith at C & D."

I drank my coffee. A busboy was collecting dishes from the tables and behind the bar they were removing the sandwich stuff. We were the only customers; it was almost two o'clock.

Sam studied me carefully and then decided to continue on this tack. "The other day I sat beside him on the train. He didn't have anything to read, so I offered him part of my *Bulletin*. Know what he said?"

I waited, looking down into my empty cup.

"Said he'd given up reading papers. Finds nothing of interest in the papers." Sam looked at me over the tops of his glasses. "A lawyer who finds nothing of interest in the papers? Just a little eccentric, don't you think?"

"I don't know," I said. "Sometimes I get bored with them too; same old stuff every day . . ."

"All right, have it your way. It's not eccentric, it's perfectly normal for a busy successful lawyer to stop reading the newspapers."

He stood up. "Well, I've got to get back. Mahoney keeps getting brilliant ideas for me to look up. Do you have to go down to the hoosegow this afternoon?"

"No, I'm through for the day. I'm going to the Orchestra."

"The Orchestra on Friday afternoon? How elegant!" We paid our checks and walked out into the blinding sunlight. "Got a date?"

I didn't say anything.

"Come on, Butler. Cut the crap! I'm chained to a wife, a mortgage, two babies and an endless antitrust

59

case . . . I have to live vicariously through your adventures. Who is she?"

We were almost at the corner of Broad Street, where I would have to turn south.

"Her name is Sally Rochester."

"Who dat?"

"Ordway Smith's sister-in-law."

Sam stopped, a disgusting leer on his face. "Ah yes indeed," he said. "The big redhead. Bobby Rochester, magnificent golfer, they got divorced, didn't they?" He put his hand on my shoulder. "My boy, I would say there are definite possibilities there, definite *possibilities*. Not only that, but —" His eyes narrowed. "Why you sly son of a bitch. Friday afternoon Orchestra, eh?" He shook his head. "*Very* sophisticated."

"So long, Sam. Take a cold shower when you get upstairs."

"Good-bye, you lucky bastard. I'll tell all the boys how hard you're working."

I glanced up at the clock on City Hall tower, and just then it began to bong, so I sprinted down the block to the Academy of Music. As I ran through the empty lobby, the applause died down. I squeezed past the door just as the usher was closing it and dashed down the aisle amid the red and gold and the hush and the sea of faces, and then I saw the blazing hair and the empty seat. She turned, startled, and then smiled with such relief that I felt something. I really did. Ormandy's arm went up, paused, and came down on the Overture to *Figaro*.

chapter 6

She was lying on top of me, heavy and smooth and warm, smelling of perfume and whiskey and sweat. Her hair was in my face. Outside on the highway a truck was changing gears, and its headlight beams moved from one end of the ceiling to the other.

"Are you asleep?" she murmured, putting her tongue in my ear.

"Uh-uh."

"Do it again."

"Uh-uh. I can't."

"Sure you can."

"No I can't . . . *Hey!*"

"I think you can."

"Jesus, Sally!"

"See?"

Darkness.

"Ben?"

"Mm?"

"I made this all pretty easy for you, didn't I?"

"Mm." What's the correct answer to that? No, it was really very difficult?

"Ben, I used to be a nice girl, I really did, but if you knew how much I needed that . . ."

Why do they always say these things? O-God-What-You-Must-Think-of-Me Routine. The only thing is to let them talk it out and then they feel better.

"How about another drink?" I asked.

"All right — No, lie still, I'll get it." I felt her move above me, stretching toward the bedside table. A heavy girl, but strong and clean. Field hockey. Tennis. Swimming. She splashed some whiskey into the glasses, put one of them in my hand and curled down beside me. "Oh I feel so good now." Her lips touched my neck. "You're a very accomplished young man, but I suppose you've been told that before." I felt sleepy. The Scotch burned marvelously. They really are not all alike. Each one is a new and different person. It's just that they say the same things, many of them, but they are all different, and their stories are different. She was talking again, telling me about her marriage and all the trouble. I think this is as close as you can get to another person, to lie in bed with them, and that's why I can't see anything bad about it. Most people are lonely. Even if they're married.

I wonder if Atwater is lonely. Gossips like a woman. Kellerman and Roseann Hyde. Embarrassing. Makes you look stupid. Pills. Had a thing with her, took her purse to the bathroom. Married woman. A sly son-of-a-bitch, what did he mean? Marry her. Like hell. Buy a cow. Lonely. No. How many does this make? Sixteen. No. Blonde at Sugarbush. Fur cap and snow on eyelashes. Ground her teeth. Can't ski, can't do anything, no time to learn. Bad coordination. Makes this one seventeen. Booth Tarkington. Nineteen if you count those two in London. Kinsey definition. Sexual Intercourse. For purposes of this Indenture the following defined terms shall have the meanings set forth in this Section, unless the context clearly indicates otherwise. Why does Forrester keep his door shut? Go over there and say What's the trouble, can't I help you. No. Not as many as they all think. Reputation. Trying to prove something over and over again. Why? Doubts about it. Wind up like that creep today, feeling up children. No. Everybody wonders about it. Postcoital tristesse. Too easy? If Donahue had read his files — No, the other, I'm trying to think about the —

The bedside lamp cut into my eyes. "Come *on* Ben, wake up! We fell asleep and look what time it is! You've got to take me home." Her legs felt sticky against mine. She got out of bed and began to pad around the room, picking up her clothes and putting them on. I yawned and scratched myself, watching her.

"*I* don't think you're too fat."

"Ben, will you *please* get out of that bed? I told Jessie I'd be home right after dinner, and look what time it is! She might get worried and start calling people."

"Gosh, I never did give you any dinner, did I?" I got up and put on my shirt.

"I guess we drank our dinner." She sat in front of the imitation Danish dressing table combing her hair. I put my hands on her firm smooth shoulders and looked at our reflection in the mirror.

"Pleased with what you see?" she asked.

"Sure. Aren't you?"

"I should say not!" She leaned forward and carefully applied her lipstick. "Unmade bed, pillows on the floor, whiskey bottle, cigarette butts, the smiling bachelor, the blowsy sex-mad divorcée — a charming tableau."

"You mean you didn't like it?"

"Oh God, you know how much I liked it. I'm just ashamed of being such a pig. I can imagine what you're thinking: The first date and she climbs right in. These hot divorcées!"

"That's a little corny, Sal." I leaned down to kiss her, but she stood up, pushed me away, and put the comb into her purse.

"That's what they all say, is it? Poor Ben, such a bore

to hear the same lament all the time. Zip me up, will you please?"

"Look, I think you've got the wrong idea about me —"

"I know *all* about you, Mister Butler. I'm just surprised that you turned out to be so nice. Come on, are you ready to go?" She paused at the door. "Jesus, suppose somebody sees us coming out of here?"

"How many people do you know in Gloucester, New Jersey?"

"Well, they could be driving by . . ."

"All right, let's go back to bed."

"Oh come on, you idiot." She opened the door, and walked quickly to my car.

On the way home she talked again about Bobby Rochester. She had known him vaguely all her life, but he had started to court her during her senior year at Vassar while he was a Navy lieutenant in New York. "We had fun that year," she said. "He'd been at sea, but they moved him to Ninety Church Street, where he had practically nothing to do, so he'd drive up and see me, and then on weekends I'd come down to Manhattan. He always had plenty of money, of course, and we really did the town."

That summer she graduated, he was released from the Navy, and Ordway and Marion gave them a big Philadelphia wedding. After a long trip to Europe, they settled down in the old manor Bobby had inherited from his grandmother, and he went to work in his father's business.

"Well, you know, it was the normal kind of life you would expect. We knew a lot of people and went to parties. I was on committees to raise money for things — mostly things his mother was interested in — and then I got pregnant pretty soon. His family always went to Bay Head in the summer, so we had to get a house there too, and that's where we went. Bobby knew all the people there, every weekend would be one long cocktail party, always with the same crowd, of course. Bobby played golf again, and he spent more and more time at it — sometimes I got the feeling that golf was really the only thing that interested him."

"Did you get bored with him?" I asked.

"Yeah, I suppose that's what happened. I don't know, these things work so slowly, but after a while I began to see that he was just — you know, a nothing, a vegetable. All he ever wanted to talk about was his golf game, what matches were coming up, who was playing where, who made this or that score someplace . . . I guess I should have tried to work up some interest in the thing, so I would understand what he was talking about. I guess I should have done that. But he never ever looked at a book, he never even read the papers except for the sports section . . ."

"Somebody said he married his secretary?"

"Yup. That's what he did, and everybody in town will tell you it was my fault. I didn't make him feel needed, you see. Didn't make him feel that he was important. Are you racing with that car?"

"No, I'm just looking at it," I said. "That's what I'm going to get when I'm rich and successful."

"What is it?"

"Mercedes Coupe, Two-twenty SE. I'm sorry, Sal, you were telling me about his secretary."

"Oh, she was just a little twerp from upstate someplace. Eighteen years old! I guess he made a pass at her and told her his troubles and she realized that if she played her cards right maybe she could become Mrs. Robert Marshall Rochester the Fourth, and boy, did she proceed to play her cards right." Sally snorted. "Honestly, men can be the silliest vainest things! All of a sudden Bobby stopped being a dumb boring clod and turned into the most fascinating person in the world, every word that fell from his lips was pure gold, you see, and of course his lovemaking was the most, to say the least —"

"She made him feel that way?"

Sally nodded. "He began to walk around in a perfect daze. He became very lofty with me: I obviously didn't understand his type of personality; I was frigid; maybe I ought to see a psychiatrist. All kinds of interesting thoughts that obviously hadn't originated in *his* mind. It was just ridiculous."

"You had another child by then?"

"Yes, this thing with Dagmar — that's really her name, I nearly died laughing when I first heard it — this Dagmar thing began when I was pregnant with Andy, but I didn't realize what was going on for nearly a year, and then it took another year to get everything straightened out. If that's what you call it." She giggled a little. "Dagmar Rochester. Isn't that *awful?*"

I turned between the two stone gateposts, drove up the long curving drive, and stopped the car in front of her door.

"You'd better not come in, Ben." She leaned over and quickly kissed my ear. "Thank you for a lovely evening. Much the best concert I've ever attended." Then she was out on the steps.

"Hey wait a minute," I said. "What about tomorrow?"

"Do you want to take me to the Hunt Races?" she asked, fitting her key into the lock. "Ordway is riding a new horse he just got."

"Sure," I said. "What time?"

"Oh, pick me up about eleven. Night, Ben. Thank you again." She closed the door.

66

chapter 7

SCENE: Men's Toilet, The Radnor Hunt Club

The auditor squats behind the door of his stall. From this position he can see part of the floor. Enter from left a pair of dusty black riding boots and a pair of square-toed English walking shoes.

WALKING SHOES: Listen, you sure you're all right?

RIDING BOOTS: Yeah, I'm fine. *(Sound of noisy urination)* Pretty scared about the horse, though. That could have been a mess.

SHOES: One hell of a spill, George. Horses and people flying all over the place. What happened?

BOOTS: Same fucking thing I did at the Gold Cup last month — pulled him up too soon and he thought he couldn't clear it and he swerved over and that Walker kid slammed right into me.

SHOES: Too bad, you'd've had the race.

BOOTS: Goddamn right I would.

SHOES: Well, you'll be in all the papers tomorrow, ass over teakettle. The photographers were right there.

BOOTS: Big deal! *(Sound of urinals flushing)* Who was that with our gal Sal?

SHOES: Some flunky in Ordway's law firm. Ben somebody. *(Sound of hands being washed)*

BOOTS: How much did Bobby have to give her?

SHOES: Million five, I heard.

BOOTS: That's what I heard. Ordway really put the blocks to him.

SHOES: Pretty nice for this lawyer.

BOOTS: Pretty nice is right.

SHOES: I always thought that was your private stock, cousin.

BOOTS: Uh-uh. Not for a long time. She wants brains now. A barrister is just the ticket, not some brokendown steeplechaser. It's brains that count today, m'boy. Of course he'd better find himself an extra set of balls, too. You ready?

chapter 8

DEFENDER ASSOCIATION

PRISON INTERVIEW REPORT

Name: *Fernanda Runcible*   Age: *22*

Address: *1893 Columbia Ave Phil.* Color: *C*

Birthplace: *Norfolk, Va.*   Occupation: *Maid. "Day's Work"*

Family:	Address:	Occupation:
Father *?*		
Mother *Betty Runcible*	*1893 Columbia Ave.*	*Unempl. (Relief)*
Brothers *Rupert (25-married) Roger (24-U.S.Army) Randolph (19-in NY?) Renfrew*		
Sisters *Betty (17-married) Carlotta (15-home) Pats (12-home) Jean (8-home)*		
Spouse *None*		

Police Record: (List all arrests whether or not conviction resulted)

Place:	Date of Arrest:	Charge:	Final Disposition:
Phila.	*? 1960*	*Larceny (Shoplifting)*	*Charge Dropped*
Phila	*1962*	*Larceny (Shoplifting)*	*Guilty. Sentence Suspended.*

Name and Address of Last Employer:

Miss Dorothy Todd,
1801 Rittenhouse Connaught

I hereby certify that I do not have enough money to employ my own lawyer and request that the Public Defender represent me at my trial.   *Fernanda Runcible*

69

ARREST: 10 P.M. May 4 at Defendant's home, 1893 Columbia Ave. 2 Detectives.

HEARING: 10 A.M. May 5.

Detective said Defendant took two (2) diamond rings, one (1) diamond necklace and one (1) alligator purse from apt. of Miss Dorothy Todd, Rittenhouse Connaught on preceding Saturday (May 1). Purse recovered but jewels missing. Detective said Miss Todd was away and Defendant let herself in with her own key. Miss Todd not at hearing. Defendant said she was in apt. to clean but did not take any jewels. Held for grand jury.

DEFENDANT'S STATEMENT: I did not take any jewels. Miss Todd asked me to vacuum the apt. on Saturday. I have a key. The doorman saw me come in and leave. I did take the alligator purse, but Miss Todd said I could have it. There was nothing in that purse. The police found that purse in my room. I want to plead not guilty. I want the lawyers to decide if I should ask for a jury.

INTERVIEWER'S COMMENTS: Despite record, this girl makes a good impression. Prosecutrix should be interviewed. Those jewels in purse all weekend? Prosecutrix not at hearing? Jury?

Wm. C. Merangelo
ASST. DEFENDER

I put the interview report back on the table and rubbed my eyes. It was Sunday night, and I was alone in the library at Conyers & Dean, where I had spent most of the day looking up every conceivable point of law raised by the file called *Commonwealth v. Runcible.*

On Friday afternoon at five o'clock Marvin Gold had called me into his office and handed me a thin brown folder.

"Here's your first jury trial, hotshot. Burglary, larceny, receiving stolen goods; a nice issue of fact. Monday morning at ten o'clock."

I couldn't believe my ears. "Marvin, I've only been in court a couple of days, I've only tried a couple of waiver cases, I haven't even *seen* a jury trial —"

Marvin laughed. "This can't be Ben Butler, the fourth man in our class, can it? Case editor of the Law Review, wizard of high finance . . . When did all this unbecoming modesty develop?"

"Cut it out, Marvin, it's not funny!" I opened the file and took out the yellow bills of indictment. "Burglary, larceny, receiving stolen goods. This girl could go to jail for — Look, I don't even know what the maximum sentence is! How am I supposed —"

"Sit down a minute," said Marvin.

I sat down in the other chair. Marvin creaked backwards, put his feet on his desk, and ignited a cigar.

"All right now, point one," Marvin seized his thumb. "Trying cases isn't like performing an operation. I understand that these surgeons, they hold clamps and cut the easy parts and generally keep their hands in there, and every now and then they do a little more, and one day they find themselves running the show, but it happens so gradually that they never know which was their first operation. Well, it's different in court. You're either trying the case, or you're just sitting there watching. If you're trying the case, your mind is in gear every second: what's the witness saying, what's the other side going to do, what's the jury thinking, how's the judge going to rule — you're completely absorbed. The other guy at the counsel table, he may be listening or he may be trying to look up the witness's skirt. His mind can be on the trial one second and on something completely different the next second. Is that clear?"

"I guess so, but —"

"What I'm trying to tell you is that there's no way to learn to try cases except by trying them. You could sit beside me for a year and you wouldn't learn much. All right, point two." Marvin gripped his index finger. "We've got a duty toward our clients. We've got to give them the best possible representation we can. That means we do not send in just any green kid to handle a serious criminal charge. We don't send a man unless we're sure he can do a decent job. Now, in the first place we know the kind of a firm you come from; in the second place, I personally know what your record is — don't bridle, I'm just telling you the truth — and in the third place both Walter Simon and I stuck our heads into four fifty-three last week and watched you for a few minutes. You're ready for jury trials, Ben, so don't give me a big argument."

"But Monday morning!"

"Ben, that's the way we have to operate. At Conyers & Dean you can take six months to prepare a case, but *our* clients are in jail, remember. And we try three thousand cases a year! We can't spend that much time on each one. Look, you've got all weekend to find out everything there is to know about this case and believe me, that's a hell of a lot more time than Willis Donahue is going to spend on it. You've already read our *Trial Manual.* Have you looked over *Brown's Pennsylvania Evidence,* the Handbook?"

"Yes," I said. "I've brushed up on the Hearsay Rule, and —"

"All right now, just listen: You go home and take the *Trial Manual* and Title Eighteen of *Purdon's* — that's the Penal Code — and maybe *Brown's* and of course this file. You sit down and you read this file until you know every single word in it — and this is a damn slim file, as you can see. Then you pretend you're Willis Donahue and try to figure out what witnesses he'll put on, what he'll ask them and what they'll say. Make an outline of how you

72

think he'll try the case: What does he have to show to get to the jury, and how will he do it, and what if anything can you do to break down his witnesses. Okay?"

"I guess so."

"The most important thing is to know exactly what she's charged with, and exactly what he's got to present to make out his case. When you've figured out what *he's* going to do, then decide what *you're* going to do. Are you going to put the girl on, or not? If you put her on, what will you ask her? If you put her on, then Willis can cross-examine her. How much can that hurt you? You've got to decide all that for yourself, and then make up a little trial memo covering all the steps in order and all the points of law that might come up. It's easy."

I nodded glumly, leafing through the papers.

"Why did you ask for a jury in this one, Marvin?"

"That's a good question," he said. "Usually we feel if there isn't much doubt about the facts, or if the case isn't so serious, why then most of the time we figure a judge will give our people the benefit of the doubt just as well as a jury. That kind of a trial is quick and informal. And even if the judge convicts, he may still go easy on the sentence. On the other hand, if you ask for a jury, then you get the full-dress treatment: jury in the box, witness on the stand, examinations, cross-examinations, objections, arguments, speeches — the whole bit, just like on television. *Then* if the jury convicts —"

"You're in trouble."

"You're in trouble. Why? Because now the judge is under the pressure of public opinion, represented by the jury. Here all these fine people have spent all day listening to evidence, they've argued about it in the jury room, finally they've voted to convict, and now the judge is going to give the man a suspended sentence? Let him walk out on the streets? What kind of a judge is that? We've been

73

wasting our time!" Marvin scratched his chest and looked out of the window. "So that's why we waive the jury in the run-of-the-mill cases: it's safer."

"But —"

"*But!*" He turned, pointing at the ceiling. "How about the serious case, where there is a real issue of fact. 'That man came in my store and pointed a gun in my face,' says the little old grocer. 'That man was drinking beer with me all night and he never left the table,' says the alibi witness. Somebody's lying. Who's going to decide? Ten years of a man's life may hinge on it."

"So then you ask for a jury?"

"Right, because why should a judge make that decision? It's really for the conscience of the whole community; twelve people off the street can listen to the witnesses, and they know just as much about human nature as the judge. And then of course the judges are all different: you'd never waive a jury if Stellwagon is sitting. Of course, we wouldn't send you in front of him for your first case; he's murder. You'll have Judge Small from upstate. He's a nice little guy — won't give you any trouble."

Marvin's cigar had disintegrated into a wet frazzled mess. He dropped it into the ashtray and took another out of the drawer.

"You think this Runcible case presents a real issue of fact?" I asked.

Marvin nodded. He lighted the fresh cigar and enveloped his face in blue smoke. "There's something funny about it. I don't know, I haven't really studied the file, but it doesn't ring right. This is a colored girl, a cleaning girl who's supposed to have walked out of a fancy apartment house in Rittenhouse Square with twenty thousand dollars' worth of diamonds, but the woman who owned them won't talk to our investigators."

74

"Why not?"

Marvin shrugged. "I don't know why not, but she wouldn't, and of course we couldn't force her to. But you might ask her that on the witness stand."

"Have you got a theory about this case, Marvin?"

"No, you see if *you* can develop a theory."

"Well, I guess I'd better go to work on this." I stood up. "Will you be here on Monday in case I want to ask any questions?"

"No," said Marvin, smiling. "That's another reason you're trying this case. I've got to argue an appeal in the Superior Court on Monday. But give me a call over the weekend if you have any questions."

I did exactly what Marvin told me. There wasn't much in the file except the interview report, the bill of indictment, and the investigator's report.

JUNE 1   *Warren Burns,* doorman at Rittenhouse Connaught. Was on duty Saturday morning, May 1. Knows Fernanda Runcible, saw her come in, go up in self-service elevator about 10 A.M. Saw her come out "before lunch." She carried large alligator purse on way out. Mr. Burns states that nontenants not permitted in building unless known to be employees of tenants.

Dorothy Todd. Apartment 1801, refused to permit me into apartment. No statement about Fernanda Runcible, threatened to call police. Terminated interview.

Mrs. Betty Runcible, 1893 Columbia Avenue. One room, third floor rear. Mrs. Runcible not sober. Young girl (sister of Fernanda) stated

Fernanda supports family. Mrs. Runcible says
Fernanda good girl, never been in trouble.

Edward C. Kowalski
INVESTIGATOR

What can you do with a file like that?

I leaned back in my hard chair and looked up at the
rows and rows of law books lining the high walls of the
library. I had already checked every conceivable point: the
answer wasn't in those books. Beyond the little pool of
light on my table the huge room was dark, but I could
still see the stern intelligent faces of Mr. Dean and Judge
Conyers and Justice Sharswood and Mr. John G. Johnson
and all the others pondering down at me. What would
they do with this thing? What was all that about an alligator purse? Were the diamonds supposed to be in it?
Why would the girl carry the purse out in full view if
there were diamonds in it? The story didn't make sense.

It was nine o'clock. On my way home I would have
to walk right past the Rittenhouse Connaught.

chapter 9

The doorman was standing on the curb with his hands folded behind his back, watching the oddballs who always congregate in Rittenhouse Square on summer evenings: girls with long dirty hair, boys with long dirty hair, Negroes wearing sunglasses, people who could be of either sex, people looking for a variety of connections, people looking for trouble, and people just watching.

"Is this where Miss Todd lives?"

The doorman turned and gave me a quick hard look. I passed muster.

"Yes sir, right in the elevator, please." He led me through the little black-and-white tiled lobby, leaned into the elevator to push the button for the eighteenth floor and withdrew, touching the visor of his cap. "Number eighteen-oh-one, sir. First door on your right." The gate slid shut.

There were only three apartments on the eighteenth floor. I pushed the bell at 1801, and a moment later the door was opened by a tall, bony blonde.

"Oh hi," she said. "Come on in." She looked like one of these fashion models you see in magazines, hollow-cheeked and leaning backwards with a disdainful look. Her hair was carefully made-up and sprayed with something, but she wore a long navy blue housecoat. Behind her I could see the living room: some modernistic furniture, a bottle of Pepsi-Cola with a straw in it, and a copy of *Vogue* on the floor. The television set was on.

"Miss Todd? My name is Benjamin Butler —"

"Yeah? Gee, I never can remember names. Come on in and close the door, hon." She walked over to the television set and turned it off. "Are you the one from Chicago?"

"Miss Todd, I'd like to ask you some questions about Fernanda Runcible —"

"Fernanda?" She whirled around. "Say, who the hell are you, anyway? You're not the guy —"

"I told you, my name is Ben Butler. I'm a lawyer, I represent Fernanda Runcible, and I'd like to discuss the charges you made —"

"Listen, I already told that other creep who was here, I don't have to tell anybody anything." She moved toward me, looking remarkably ugly for such a pretty girl. She was frightened. "Listen, I could have you arrested, you know that? I don't know how you got in here —"

"Miss Todd, I don't understand why you're acting this way. All I want to know is what happened, exactly what the circumstances were —" Her doorbell rang.

"All right, buster," she whispered. "You better float right outa here, or you'll be sorry. You know what I mean? I have friends who can handle people like you. You know what I mean?" I thought for a minute that she was going to jump at me, but she moved past and opened the door.

Out in the hall stood a carefully dressed middle-aged man — hat, cuff links, tie clip, pocket handkerchief, gold watch strap — who stared at us through heavy black-rimmed glasses. "Er — Miss Todd?"

"I'm sorry, sir, but I don't need any insurance today," said Dorothy Todd to me. "Thank you very much for coming up, though. I'll call you if I change my mind."

"Miss Todd?" the man asked again. He looked suspicious.

"Yes, I'm Dotty Todd. C'mon in, this — uh gentleman — was just telling me about insurance, but he's leaving." We had some awkward business as I stood back to let him in while he stood back to let me out, but somehow we reversed positions and I was outside. Dorothy Todd slammed the door.

Now I noticed that I wasn't alone in the little hallway. A woman holding a bulging bag of groceries was trying to unlock the door of Number 1803. Apparently she had come up in the elevator with the man.

"May I hold that bag for you?" I asked.

She turned.

You look at somebody in a dark strange hallway past a brown paper grocery bag, and everything stops dead, as if a movie projector has been halted. Not déjà vu, the feeling that you've been here before. This was different, entirely new, a ringing silence that made my heart stand still. What shall I say about her? She was short and had dark hair and gray eyes that examined me with what appeared to be amusement.

"Thank you very much, but I can manage." She had an accent of some kind: "manatsch." She was a good deal older, maybe thirty-five, but well preserved: rounded, smooth, and elegant. She turned away from me and braced the grocery bag against her door while she tried to get her key into the lock.

"Here, if you'll just let me hold the bag —"

"Will you *please* just let me . . . Oh, look out!" The bag slipped, fell heavily and split. Between us lay a heap of bread, eggs, butter and assorted canned goods. A grapefruit rolled toward the elevator door.

"Oh my God," I said. "I'm terribly sorry . . ."

She looked at me and shook her head slowly. "A very

helpful young man, I must say. Are all the eggs broken?"

Kneeling down, I explored the mess. "No, I think they're okay — Look. Here, let me wrap them up . . ."

"No, now just wait a minute. I will get something . . ." She unlocked the door, went in, and returned with an empty plastic wastebasket. "Here, put everything in this please, and perhaps you will be so kind as to get that grapefruit over there?"

I gathered up the groceries into the wastebasket and followed her into the apartment. It was the same size as Dorothy Todd's, but everything else was different. In the living room there were mostly books — paperback novels, heavy expensive art books, books in French, books in German, books in shelves along the wall, on the tables and on the door. There was a wide sill in front of the window; on the sill stood several carved wooden figures: a bust of a thin aristocratic old man, another of an adolescent boy, a smooth polished whale, and a seagull with wide outspread wings.

In the tiny kitchenette she began to take the groceries out of the wastebasket and put them away.

"Oh thank you so much, just put it down on the counter here . . ." It was time for me to go, but I didn't.

"Er . . . Miss . . . my name is Benjamin Butler, I'm a lawyer, I'm supposed to defend a girl named Fernanda Runcible who used to work for Miss Todd across the hall . . . I wonder if I could talk to you about it for a moment . . ." It all came out in a rush, and she looked at me with some interest.

"Fernanda, that is the colored girl?"

"That's right. Did you know her?"

"You were over there with Miss Todd to ask about Fernanda?"

"That's right, but she wouldn't talk to me."

She smiled faintly. "Well, Miss Todd is a very busy young woman. When I saw you and that other man I

80

thought," — the smile became mischievous — "I thought she was especially busy this evening."

"She's a call girl, isn't she?"

"Well, it really is not any of my business, but so many gentlemen ring my bell at strange hours . . . Tell me about Fernanda . . . You say you are a lawyer for Fernanda? Is it true she stole some jewels?"

She walked back into the living room, sat down on the big yellow sofa and took a cigarette from a silver box on the coffee table. I lighted it for her and sat down on a comfortable straight-backed chair.

I told her all I knew about the charges against Fernanda. She listened quietly, smoking and watching my face. Sometimes you can be talking about one thing while thinking about another; I was talking about Dotty Todd's diamonds and the alligator purse and the doorman, but I was thinking about this woman whose name I didn't even know. I can't describe people. What good does it do to say she had black hair and gray eyes? She just knocked me out, that's all. I really wanted to forget all about Fernanda Runcible and ask her who she was and if she was married or divorced or what, and would she go out with me? Of course she was pretty old, but that just made her more interesting.

"What was the value of these diamonds?" she asked suddenly.

"Twenty thousand dollars, supposedly."

"Would they perhaps have been insured?"

Wow! "What makes you ask that?"

"Well, I have some diamonds too, and I have them insured, so that if they are stolen, I get some money. My husband said it was necessary." Her husband? She looked up, apparently reading my mind. "My husband is dead now, but when he was alive . . . Well, you see, once I had a friend, she also had insurance, and then she could

81

not find a ring, but the insurance company would not pay her for the ring, because she could not prove that it was stolen, you see if she only lost it, they would not pay . . ."

I saw what she was driving at. "There are different kinds of insurance policies. Some cover unexplained loss, but they are more expensive than the ones against theft."

"That is what I mean." She put out her cigarette in a blue porcelain ashtray and began to walk around the room. I watched her body move under the thin summer dress and tried hard to worry about Fernanda's trial. "Suppose Miss Todd had to have some money quickly," she said, looking out of the window. "Could she say that somebody had stolen her diamonds and get the money from the insurance company?"

"Well, that's an interesting idea," I said. "But in the first place, I understand that call girls who can afford to live in a place like this make a lot of money, and in the second place you're saying that she would deliberately send her cleaning girl to jail to collect some insurance —"

She turned around. "You are quite a *young* lawyer, aren't you?"

"What's that got to do with it?"

"Nothing, I suppose. But I do know this: Our friend Miss Todd has a friend too. His name is Freddie. He is a very unpleasant young man. Sometimes I can hear him shouting at her, and that is not all he does to her. He drives a white Cadillac, he does not seem to have a job, and I would guess that he can spend her money faster than she can earn it. And now he is gone."

"Gone?"

"I have not seen him for many weeks — perhaps three weeks. When was this day the girl is supposed to have stolen the diamonds?"

"May first."

"Well, I don't remember exactly, I think he was still

around in the middle of April, but then a few weeks ago we had quite a scene here. I woke up in the middle of the night, there was shouting in the hall, I got up and opened the door and there were three men trying to get into Dorothy Todd's place. They pounded on the door and shouted, but she would not open the door. They wanted Freddie, but I'm sure that he was gone by then."

"Well, what happened?" I asked. "Did they get in? Did somebody call the police?"

"Well, she didn't, apparently, and I did not want to get involved, and after ten minutes or so, they went away."

She told me more about what she had seen of Dorothy Todd and Freddie, she didn't have any positive information, but you certainly could conclude that Freddie might have some reasons for disappearing for a while. Would they try to raise some cash with a faked insurance claim? It was an interesting idea, but there was no way in the world to prove such a story. At least, I didn't know how to do it.

I was thinking about this when she said, "I am afraid you will have to excuse me now, because I must change my clothes and do some work."

"I'm sorry," I said, standing up. "You've been extremely helpful. You've given me a whole new slant on this thing." I stopped. "What kind of work do you do?"

"Oh —" She sighed a little. "I try to make things, you know. I try to carve things. Like those." She pointed to the figures by the window.

"You made those?"

She nodded. "Do you like them?"

"My gosh yes, but they look . . . well, professional. Are you really an artist? I'm sorry, I don't even know your name."

"My name is Mrs. Wesselhof. Monica Wesselhof."

"And — ah, you're not from around here, are you?"

She looked down. "No. I'm from Austria. But I am studying here. At the Museum College of Art. Do you know where that is?"

I said yes, I did, and tried to think of something else to say. She wanted to get rid of me now, but I still didn't want to go.

"Are you going over to the College now?" It was nearly ten o'clock.

She shook her head. "I can do some work here. I must make sketches for a new carving . . . When is the colored girl's case to be heard?"

"Tomorrow morning."

"Tomorrow morning? What will happen to her?"

"I don't know. Why don't you come and find out?"

Her eyes shifted and she seemed to focus on me in a different way.

"Well," she said. "Perhaps I will. Where is the court?"

I told her. Then I left and went home.

chapter 10

At ten o'clock next morning I was sitting at the counsel table in Number 453. A couple of ancient fans hummed on their perches below the ceiling. In a deep alcove, two reporters were languidly examining the trial sheets. A group of black-coated tipstaves and court criers clustered behind the wooden railing, talking and picking their teeth. The back of the room was nearly filled with the usual collection of policemen, witnesses, potential jurors and loafers. I had already looked for Monica Wesselhof, but she wasn't there.

Willis Donahue came in with an armload of files.

"Don't worry, Ben," he said. "These aren't all your case. We've got a full list in here. You sure you want a jury trial on this Runcible thing?"

"Those are my instructions."

"I think Marvin's crazy, what a waste of time . . ." He put the files on his table and was immediately surrounded by other lawyers who wanted to talk about their own cases. One of them had a doctor waiting; couldn't he please go first? Another one had a master's hearing in the afternoon; his case would only take ten minutes, Willis, no kidding —

"Easy, boys," said Willis. "The Defender has a jury trial in here, and I promised Judge Small we'd finish it as fast as possible. I don't think we can take anything else first."

"Aw come on, Willis . . ."

"All right, take it up with the Judge yourself if you want —"

"ALL RISE PLEASE," shouted the crier. "OYEZ, OYEZ, OYEZ! AllpersonsboundbyrecognizanceorotherwisehavingtodowiththeHonorabletheJudgesoftheCourtsofOyer andTerminer . . ."

"Oh-oh," said one of the lawyers, and all of them scuttled for the doors. Even I knew that the man in a black robe who was settling himself up there was not Judge Small from Snyder County. ". . . GeneralJailDeliveryand QuarterSessionsofthePeaceinandforthecountyofPhiladelphia holdenherethisdaywillnowappearandtheyshallbeheardGod savetheCommonwealthandthisHonorableCourtBeseated please!"

"Good morning, Judge Stellwagon?" Willis Donahue hadn't counted on this either.

"POLICE OFFICERS IN UNIFORM CAN REMOVE THEIR JACKETS!" shouted the Judge. There was a bustle in the room. The Judge leaned over. "Judge Small broke down on the Turnpike. I'm sitting by order of the Administrative Judge. The Administrative Judge feels I don't have enough work in my own court. What's this, a jury trial? How long's it going to take? Nobody told me they had a jury trial in here. I haven't got time to hear a jury trial today."

"Well, if your Honor please," Willis began, "This is a very simple case. The Commonwealth has only two witnesses . . ."

I didn't know what to do. Marvin Gold would never have sent me in front of Stellwagon for my first jury trial. On the other hand, if the case wasn't tried today, Fernanda Runcible might sit in prison for another month until she reached the top of the next list.

"... will certainly go to the jury before lunchtime," Willis was saying.

"Who are you?" demanded the Judge, turning his watery eyes on me for the first time.

"Benjamin Butler, your Honor."

"Judge Stellwagon, Mr. Butler is here for the Defender," said Willis.

"I can see that," snapped the Judge. "What firm?"

"Conyers & Dean, sir."

"Well, I guess we'd better treat you right," he said, "or Ellsworth Boyle will put me on the House Committee at the League!"

That was a joke, so we laughed.

"How many witnesses have *you* got?" he asked me.

"Just the defendant, your Honor."

"All right, let's go then. Bring out the defendant. Put a jury in the box."

The door to the cell room opened, and one of the attendants led out a skinny, pretty colored girl. She wore a gray sweater, narrow slacks made of chino or something like that, and dirty white sneakers. She must have been frightened, but she hid it behind a mask of wooden sullenness. I realized that I should have gone to see her in the cell room, but I had been too preoccupied with my trial memo. I introduced myself and explained that I was going to represent her. She nodded and sat down beside me as the prospective jurors filed into the box. I reviewed her story with her, and asked if she wanted to take the witness stand.

"You the lawyah."

"If you take the stand and tell your story, and really tell the truth, it would look better than if you don't. But you don't have to. And if you get up there, the district attorney can ask you questions and try to trip you up."

She shook her head. "What's he gonna ask me? All I know is I didn't take no necklace or nothin'. Don't know nothin' about it. That's all I can tell him."

"Well look, if you really did take that stuff and you get up there, the D.A. will trip you up sure as you're sitting here, and then you're dead."

"I'm *tellin'* you, I didn't take them —"

"If your Honor please, this panel is satisfactory to the Commonwealth," said Willis Donahue. While I was talking to the girl, he had asked the jurors whether they knew him or me or Fernanda Runcible or Miss Dorothy Todd of the Rittenhouse Connaught. The jurors shook their heads. I studied this collection of housewives, secretaries, telephone operators and retired men, feeling a twinge in my stomach. This was crazy! The people at Conyers & Dean who tried civil cases — cases involving fights over money — would never dream of going into court without six months of preparation: pleadings to sharpen the issues, depositions to find out all about the other side's evidence so that no possible surprise could be sprung at the trial, and a thorough investigation into the background of each juror. On the other hand, in a criminal case with a piece of a girl's life at stake, we send in a man with no experience, only the sketchiest idea of the other side's case, and no information at all about the twelve strangers in the jury box.

Nothing could be done about it. I asked Fernanda if she knew any of the jurors. Of course she didn't, and I said politely that this jury was very much acceptable to the defense. The jurors were sworn.

With a grunt Willis Donahue stood up, ambled over to the box, and began his opening address.

This was old stuff to Willis, and he didn't overwork himself. The Commonwealth would prove that this defendant worked as a cleaning girl for a lady on Rittenhouse Square. The Commonwealth would present evidence from which the jury could conclude that the defendant discovered that her employer had some valuable jewelry, found where it was kept, had access to it, and carried it out of the apartment while her employer was away on a trip. His friend Mr. Butler, on loan from a big corporation law firm, was here on behalf of the Public Defender. The Defender represents people who can't afford to hire their own lawyers. Willis hoped that the jury would listen to the evidence carefully, and also listen carefully to the charge which his Honor Judge Stellwagon would give them at the close of the case. Willis hoped that they would study the witnesses and then decide the case on the basis of the evidence. He was going to present a case based on what we lawyers call "circumstantial evidence." In other words, he was not going to present any witness who actually saw this girl steal the jewels; but if you had to bring in an eyewitness to every crime, then nobody would get convicted, because most crimes weren't committed in front of witnesses. The Commonwealth was going to show evidence from which they could *conclude* that this girl had taken the jewels, and his Honor Judge Stellwagon would explain to them later that if the Commonwealth's evidence persuaded them beyond a reasonable doubt, then they should find the defendant guilty. Willis was sure that when they had seen the witnesses and listened to their testimony, they would agree that this defendant was guilty beyond a reasonable doubt.

Willis sat down.

I glanced at my notes for the last time, and then I walked over and faced my first jury. I tried to remember everything I had ever read and heard about this inscrutable, unpredictable twelve-headed monster. For centuries lawyers have devoted their lives to the courtship of juries, studying each new clump of strangers with the fascination of a lover, always looking for the key, the switch, the pressure point, the magic words that make twelve ordinary people decide to vote one way instead of another. Nobody ever finds the key, but nobody ever stops looking.

Twenty-four eyes focused on me as I gripped the

wooden railing of the jury box. For a moment, the monster and I stared at each other; I thought I would freeze. A drop of sweat was running down the inside of my arm.

"Ladies and gentlemen," I said, and the sound of my own voice croaking in the silent room stopped my heart. It didn't sound like my voice at all; it sounded high and frightened.

Somehow I got the next words past my teeth, and then I wasn't listening to my voice any more. I don't remember exactly what I said to them. I think I said that Fernanda Runcible would take the stand to explain that she did not take the lady's jewels, and so they would be able to judge for themselves whether she was telling the truth or not. I said that while they were listening to Mr. Donahue's witnesses they should keep in mind every minute that it was the job of the Commonwealth to convince them, the jury, beyond a reasonable doubt that Fernanda was guilty. *Beyond a reasonable doubt,* I said again. "It isn't up to us to prove she's innocent. It's up to Mr. Donahue to prove to you that she's guilty. If he doesn't do that, if you can't make up your minds, if you have a reasonable doubt about her guilt, then you've got to find her innocent." When I finished that, I said the whole thing over again, in slightly different words, hoping that the repetition would make it stick in their minds, because it was the most important thing in my favor. Then I sat down.

Willis Donahue's first witness was a Detective Shannon, who testified more or less from what he had written in his notebook. On Monday, May 4, he had received instructions from Captain C. H. Dougherty to investigate jewel theft or burglary at Rittenhouse Connaught. Visited Miss Dorothy Todd, Apartment 1801, was shown around apartment, received description of jewels. He read the description: One diamond ring, platinum setting; one ring with three

90

diamonds and one emerald, platinum setting; one necklace, thirty-five diamonds, various sizes.

"Where had the diamonds been kept?" asked Willis Donahue.

Complainant stated that diamonds had been kept in an alligator purse, because complainant had heard that jewel thieves always look in dresser drawers, so she had just put them in a purse in her closet. I could have objected to all this hearsay, but it wasn't hurting me.

"Were you shown any evidence that the apartment had been broken into?" asked Willis Donahue.

The apartment had not been broken into. The lady had been away all weekend, the place had been locked. The apartment was on the eighteenth floor, and there was a doorman on duty all the time.

"On the basis of information received, where did you go next?"

On the basis of information received, the witness and Detective Castelli had obtained search and arrest warrants, had located the defendant at her mother's room on Columbia Avenue, and had taken defendant into custody.

"What did you find in the room where this girl was?"

"We found an alligator purse."

"Is this the purse you found?"

"Yes, sir."

"If your Honor please, I move that this purse be marked Commonwealth Exhibit 1 and move for its admission . . ." The purse already had a little label tied to the handle, and one of the clerks made a notation on it.

"Was there anything in the purse?"

"No, sir. Nothing."

"Did you make a search of the apartment?"

"It was only a room, but we searched the whole house."

"Just answer my questions, please, Officer!" Illegal search is a big issue in the law today. Unless the police had search warrants for the whole building, Shannon might

have fouled up the Commonwealth's case with that remark. I didn't see how the slip would help me, though.
"Did you find anything?" asked Willis.

"No, sir."

"To your knowledge, has this jewelry been recovered?"

"No, sir."

"Cross-examine," said Willis.

I stood up. "Where was the purse, Detective Shannon?"

"The purse? It was in the room, the room where they
were living —"

"*Where* in the room?"

"Oh. Let's see, I think it was on the shelf. Yeah, it was
there on the shelf."

"In plain sight?"

"No, I wouldn't say it was in plain sight." Lesson
Number one: *Never* ask a question if you don't know what
the answer is going to be! Fernanda Runcible pulled at my
jacket. "Ask him did I show it to him?"

"Detective Shannon, when you came into the room, was
this defendant present?"

"Yes, sir."

"Did you have a conversation with her?"

"Yes, sir."

"Well, please tell the jury what was said."

"We knocked on the door and this girl opened it. There
was a woman lying in the bed, and a couple of young kids
were there. They were looking at the TV. Detective Castelli and I identified ourselves, showed our warrant, and
asked about the rings and the necklace. This girl said she
didn't know anything about them. Then I asked her if
she had this alligator purse reported missing. First she said
she didn't know anything about that either, and then we
started looking around, and then she said, 'Oh you mean
this old thing,' and she fished this purse out from behind
some junk on the shelf — some old newspapers and a box
of laundry soap they had there on the shelf."

"Did she say anything about the purse?"

"She said this Miss Todd said she could have it, so she took it."

"Did you ask her when she took it?"

"Yes I did, counselor. She said she took it on Saturday."

"That preceding Saturday? While Miss Todd was away?"

"That's correct."

"And Miss Runcible consistently denied that she took any jewels?"

"That's right."

"That's all. Thank you."

"Call Warren Burns," said Willis Donahue.

"WARREN BURNS, WARREN BURNS."

The doorman who had let me into the Rittenhouse Connaught walked toward the front of the room. He looked entirely different in street clothes. I put my head down and busied myself with my files. The man was sworn, and under Willis's questions he testified that he knew Fernanda Runcible, had seen her go up in the elevator at ten o'clock on Saturday morning and had seen her come down again before lunchtime. When she came out, she was carrying this alligator bag.

"Mr. Burns, what's the policy at the Rittenhouse Connaught about letting in visitors? Can anybody just walk in there?"

"No *sir!* Nobody can just walk in there."

"Is it your job to keep people out?"

"That's right, sir. If we don't know them, we call up on the phone."

"But you let in this defendant, this girl here?"

"Well, I know her. I means she works for Miss Todd, I seen her all the time . . ."

"And that's why you let her in?"

93

"That's right. Otherwise we don't let nobody in, that's the whole reason they got us down there . . ."

"All right, Mr. Burns. Thank you very much."

The doorman started to leave the stand, but I got to my feet and said: "Just a minute please, Mr. Burns." He stopped and looked at me for the first time. "I understood you to say that you don't let people into that building unless you know them. Is that what you just told the jury?"

He looked confused suddenly. "That's the rule, yes sir."

"I know it's the rule, Mr. Burns, but is that what you always do?"

I still wasn't sure if he recognized me. He turned to the Judge, and then to the jury, but he didn't say anything.

"Is that what you always do, Mr. Burns?"

He swallowed. "That's what we're supposed to do . . ."

"Is that what you did last night, Mr. Burns?" I could feel the jury leaning forward. "You remember letting me into the Rittenhouse Connaught last night, Mr. Burns?"

"Objection!" Willis Donahue was on his feet beside me. "Your Honor, I don't know what he's driving at, but this is beyond the direct examination, if Mr. Butler is going to be a witness here . . ."

"Oh, if your Honor please, he asked this man if they let people into the building if they didn't know them —"

"Overruled," said Judge Stellwagon. He was leaning forward too.

Warren Burns looked at me. Willis's objection had served its purpose of giving the man a moment to collect his thoughts.

"You asked for Miss Todd," he said, and swallowed. "You said you was going to see Miss Todd."

"I did? Did I say I was going to see her, or did I ask you if this was where Miss Todd lived?"

"You said . . . you said she was expecting you, and she told me, she said there's somebody coming . . ."

94

"But you'd never seen me before, had you, Mr. Burns?"

"She said she was expecting somebody, she said to let him up —"

"Mr. Burns, I'm going to keep asking this until you answer me: Had you ever seen me before you let me go up in that elevator at the Rittenhouse Connaught last night?"

"No, I never seen you before!" He was truculent now.

"Thank you, that's all." I looked at the jury, and the doorman started to leave the stand. "Oh, just one more question please, Mr. Burns." He stopped, already standing outside the witness box. "Does Miss Todd have a lot of men you don't know showing up there at night all the time —"

"THAT'S OBJECTED TO, YOUR HONOR!" Willis Donahue came up like a rocket. "That's totally irrelevant —"

"Your Honor, I'm trying to show that they let people into that building all the time, that anybody could have gone up there —"

"Objection sustained. Any other questions for this witness?"

"No, sir." The point had been made, I thought. I wondered whether Willis would try to repair the damage; apparently he decided to leave it alone.

"Call Dorothy Todd."

They had kept her out in a different room. She wore a yellow silk dress and long black gloves and a huge black straw hat, and sunglasses. She sat there with her hands folded and answered Willis Donahue's questions in a low, quiet voice — very ladylike. She had employed Fernanda for about six months. Fernanda came in twice a week and cleaned the apartment. No, she'd never missed anything before. Yes, she sometimes gave her clothes and things she didn't need any more. No, she had not told Fernanda she could have the alligator purse. As a matter of fact, she had only just bought the alligator purse at Nan Duskin's a

95

couple of months before, and she had the sales slip right here.

That was a pretty cute touch, and Willis Donahue made the most of it — showing it to me, having it marked as Commonwealth Exhibit Number 2, waving it at the jury, handing it back to the clerk with a little flourish and moving for its introduction into evidence. The purse had cost forty-seven dollars.

Well now, about this necklace and the rings: Would Miss Todd please describe them to the jury. Miss Todd did, in considerable detail. I could have objected because the detective had already described them, and anyway we weren't disputing that they existed, but I had a feeling that the jury was fascinated with all this and would resent an interruption.

"Miss Todd, would you have any idea of what these jewels may have been worth?"

Yes, it just so happened that Miss Todd had a very good idea what they were worth. On the Friday before they were taken, she had removed them from her safe-deposit box and had them appraised, because she never got a chance to wear them these days and she was thinking of selling them and maybe buying some stocks that a friend of hers had told her about, and so she had taken them to this man down on Eighth Street to have them appraised, and she had the appraisal right here.

Again I could have objected, and maybe I should have, but what good would it do me? Willis would just have adjourned the trial and sent a detective to bring the jeweler into court. I kept quiet, and Willis introduced into evidence the appraisal showing that the jewels were worth just a little over twenty thousand dollars.

"All right now, Miss Todd, will you tell us in your own words what happened this particular weekend that you went away? Where did you put the jewels?"

"Well." Miss Todd took a deep breath. The point *was*,

you see, that she had to go away for the weekend, and by the time she got finished having the diamonds appraised, the bank was closed, and what was she supposed to do with the jewels now? She had to take them back to her apartment, naturally, but she didn't have a place to lock them up there. The only thing that locked was the drawer in her dressing table and she had read this story in a magazine where they said that the first place jewel thieves look is in the drawers of the dressing table, because that is where most girls keep their jewelry, you see, so that they have it when they're getting dressed, so that's the first place they look if they break in, so that's not the place to keep anything, so where was she supposed to keep them over the weekend?

She paused. Dead silence.

Well, so she thought about it for a while and then she finally got this idea — she guessed it was a pretty dumb idea — that she would just put the rings and the necklace in her purse and toss the purse in her closet with the other purses and hope that nobody would think to look there.

"And that's what you did, Miss Todd?"

She nodded. "Yes, sir."

"And you left for the weekend when?"

"On Friday night."

"Did you know that Fernanda would come to clean on Saturday?"

"Oh yes, she has a key, she often comes when I'm not there."

"But you left all this jewelry in the apartment, knowing that the girl was coming in to clean the next day?"

"Well, she wasn't supposed to clean the closet, or go through my purse!"

"All right then, when did you return?"

"I came back on Sunday night."

"And you looked for the purse?"

"Sure, I checked to see, because I'd been thinking about it and there it was — gone. I just about fainted."

"And you called the police?"

"Right away. I called them right away, but they didn't come until next morning about ten o'clock, this detective came and talked to me."

"Did you ask any of the building employees?"

"Yes, I called down and I said 'Who was in here while I was gone?' and I talked to Warren, that's the doorman, and he said nobody was in there, Miss Todd, except of course Fernanda —"

I stood up. "Your Honor, we've already heard what the doorman saw —"

"All right," said Willis Donahue, "I think we have enough anyway. Your witness, Mr. Butler."

"Miss Todd, would you mind removing those sunglasses, please?"

"What for?" She sounded much less ladylike.

"Well, I think the jury would like to have a look at you. You're the main witness, after all."

Willis Donahue was on his feet again. "If your Honor please, I understand this witness has some trouble with her eyes, and I told her I didn't think the court would object to her sunglasses, and I'm sure the jury understands —"

"You want to keep your glasses on, young lady?" asked the Judge.

"Yes sir, if I may, please, your Honor . . ."

"All right, well, ladies and gentlemen, you can make of it whatever you want, but I don't think I can compel a witness to take off her glasses. Let's get on with it, counsel."

"Very well, your Honor. Miss Todd, let's talk about these jewels some more. Let's take the necklace, first of all. How long have you owned that?"

98

"Objection, your Honor," said Willis Donahue. "What's the relevancy of that? What difference does it make how long she's owned it?"

We got into quite a wrangle, and the Judge called us to side-bar. I said that since she had testified as to the value of the jewels, I should be allowed to establish when and how she'd obtained them, and how much was paid for them. Willis insisted that it made no difference how she got them; their appraised value was in evidence, and how she got the jewels had nothing to do with the issue: Did the defendant steal them? Judge Stellwagon scratched his face, leaned back in the swivel chair, leaned forward again, and then said: "All right, I'll sustain the objection. Let's not go wandering all over the map and confuse this jury."

We went back to our places, the Judge put his ruling on record, and I faced Dotty Todd again.

"Miss Todd, I believe that you were questioned by detectives after you reported your loss, is that right?"

"That's right."

"You told them everything you knew about this case, right? You told them about how you put the jewels in the purse, and how you went away for the weekend, and how Fernanda had been in the apartment on Saturday — you told them everything they needed to know, didn't you?"

Silence. She didn't know where I was going.

"Didn't you cooperate with the police in every way, Miss Todd?"

"Sure. Of course I did."

"And how about Mr. Donahue here? Did you ever talk to him?"

"I talked to him this morning, yes."

"Just this morning? Did you talk to other lawyers from the District Attorney's office?"

99

"If your Honor please, is all this relevant?" Willis complained in a tired voice. "Of course she discussed the case with our office. That's our job —"

"If your Honor will bear with me, one more question on this line —"

"All right, go ahead, but let's not take all day with this thing."

"Miss Todd, if you told everything you knew to the police and to the District Attorney's office, why did you refuse to discuss it with the Public Defender?"

"That's objected to, your Honor!" Willis Donahue was beginning to lose his temper for the first time. "He knows that's completely improper, your Honor, this witness was under no obligation whatever to discuss anything with defense counsel at any time. And if he doesn't know it, perhaps your Honor will tell him, and will so instruct the jury!"

"Objection sustained." Judge Stellwagon turned toward the jury. "Ladies and gentlemen, you will disregard that question and the answer. Nobody has to grant interviews to defense lawyers about a crime that's been committed, and that applies to the Public Defender too. And Mr. Butler, I want you to stick to the issue in this case. If you've forgotten, the issue is: Did the defendant carry away this young lady's jewels? Is that clear?"

"Yes sir."

"All right, proceed."

"Miss Todd, I believe you told Mr. Donahue that you took the diamonds out of the bank on Friday, to have them appraised. Is that right?"

"That's right."

"And then you were going away for the weekend, so you had to leave them in your apartment?"

"That's right."

"Well, let me ask you this, Miss Todd. Where did you go that weekend?"

100

"That's objected to your Honor," Willis said. "What does that have to do —"

"Your Honor, I think we're entitled to know why she couldn't take these extremely valuable jewels with her, keep them right with her . . ."

"All right, I'll allow the question."

"All right, Miss Todd, will you tell the jury where you went for the weekend?"

"Well, I went to Atlantic City."

"Did you go alone?"

"Objection!"

"Sustained. Disregard that question, ladies and gentlemen."

"Well, did you stay in a hotel there?"

"Objection! What difference does it make where she stayed?"

"If your Honor please, they have safes in hotels, and women normally take their jewelry with them —"

"Your Honor, if our young friend is going to testify here, maybe he ought to take the witness stand and be sworn —"

"All right, that's enough now," snapped the Judge. "Young woman, couldn't you have kept these diamonds in a safe place over the weekend. In a hotel safe or something like that?"

"I guess I could have, sir, but I didn't know what to do, so I just thought if I hid them, that would be the easiest . . ."

"All right, I think that answers the question, Mr. Butler. Can we get on with it now? Do you have anything else for this lady?"

"Just a few more questions, your Honor. Miss Todd, was this jewelry of yours insured against theft?"

"Now your Honor, *if you please!*" Willis Donahue was shouting. "He knows that's a completely improper question —"

101

"I don't think it's improper at all, your Honor, I think —"

"Counsel to side-bar!"

Again we walked around the railing, picked our way among the clerks and the stenographer, and stood with our chins level to the Judge's desk.

"All right now, I've had about enough of this," he growled. "What do you think this is, a television show? I told you I want this case finished before lunch, for Christ's sake it's simple enough, now why do we have to have all this wrangling?"

"Judge Stellwagon," said Willis, "I know he doesn't have much trial experience, but that's no excuse for dragging all these red herrings around in front of the jury."

"Well, your Honor, I resent that! I think this girl is making a fraudulent claim, I think she's insured those jewels and is claiming the insurance, and this accusation against the cleaning girl is just to support her claim — the insurance company won't pay if she doesn't testify, she knows that —"

"That's what he thinks, Judge. Ask him if he's got any evidence."

"No, sir, of course I don't, but I think I'm entitled to ask her. If she's filed a claim for the insurance, then the jury's entitled to know that, because it affects her credibility."

"Oh, my God," groaned Willis. "Where'd you ever get that idea? You show me one case that says that —"

"You show me a case that says I can't ask her if she had theft insurance." I had spent two hours looking in vain for a case on this point, so I was pretty sure he wouldn't have one.

While Willis and I stood there quarreling in whispers, the Judge sat with his elbows on his desk, his chin in his hands, regarding us balefully.

"Are you trying to impeach her credibility on the

basis of insurance fraud?" he asked me. "Is that what you're trying to do?"

"Yes, sir."

The Judge shook his head. "Uh-uh. Can't do it this way. You've got to lay the groundwork, got to bring in some independent evidence first."

"That's exactly my point, sir," said Willis.

"But your Honor, why can't I *ask* her about the insurance? Isn't that the best evidence?"

Judge Stellwagon shook his head and leaned back in his chair. He had made up his mind. "Let's finish up this case, all right, men?"

As I followed Willis back to the counsel table he turned to me and said: "Anybody'd think you're getting paid for this. Simmer down, son, it's just another larceny case."

I didn't reply to that bit of advice. The Judge instructed the jury to forget my last question, and told me to proceed. The jurors were looking at me expectantly.

I took a deep breath. "Miss Todd, have you ever been convicted of prostitution?"

Willis Donahue's shout drowned the babble of surprise from the audience. "YOUR HONOR, THIS IS OUTRAGEOUS! Are we going to have witnesses subjected to this sort of thing —"

"Objection sustained," said the Judge. "Young fellow, I'm not an impatient man, but . . ."

I stood my ground. "Your Honor, I consider that a perfectly proper question. I'm allowed to impeach the credibility of this witness."

"But not in that way," fumed Willis Donahue. "Judge Stellwagon, he's making a farce of this trial —"

"If your Honor please, I have a case on this very point, if we could come to side-bar."

The Judge turned to the jury. "Ladies and gentlemen, I'm sorry that we're having all these interruptions. It's not the way we usually try cases in this court, but you will

103

appreciate that lawyers have to learn their trade just like other people." And then he gave them a broad wink. Somebody snickered. "All right, counsel to side-bar," he said wearily.

When we were face to face again, the Judge peered down at me and asked: "Are you trying to provoke me or something?"

"No, sir, Judge Stellwagon . . ."

"Because I'm about to call up Walter Simon and tell him to send somebody else over here. How many cases have you tried anyway?"

"Not very many, sir . . . but I can't see why Mr. Donahue is making such a fuss. I'm allowed to impeach the credibility of his witness by asking her if she's ever been convicted . . ."

"— of a felony," interrupted Willis Donahue, "or of a misdemeanor in the nature of *crimen falsi*. That's not what you asked her."

"Well, your Honor, there's a case right on it, Commonwealth against Mueller, in one fifty-three Superior —"

"All right, goddamn it, let's have a look at it." He jerked his head, and his law clerk dashed forward. Judge Stellwagon told him to get volume 153 of the *Superior Court Reports,* and then he turned to the jury again.

"Ladies and gentlemen, our eminent counsel here wants to teach me some law, so we'll take a five minute recess. If any of you wish to leave the room, please notify the court officer."

There was a rise of voices as people got up to stretch their legs. The Judge got up too and began pacing back and forth behind his chair. Willis Donahue and I stood before the marble front of the bench, with our hands in our pockets. I looked at Dorothy Todd, now shifting around unhappily on the hard chair in the witness-box. She didn't look especially cool any more.

The law clerk returned with the brown volume. Judge

104

Stellwagon sat down, emitted a long sigh, and began to read. He turned the pages, skimming, and then he started to shake his head.

"No, no, no," he said. "This isn't on point at all." He looked at me. "This wasn't a larceny case —"

"Your Honor, they allowed counsel to ask a witness if she'd been convicted of prostitution —"

"But this was a raid on a whorehouse." He passed the book down to Willis Donahue. "If she'd been convicted of prostitution, that would have mattered there, but that's not what we've got here . . ."

"But it would affect this girl's credibility too," I said.

The Judge continued to shake his head. "Felony or misdemeanor in the nature of *crimen falsi*. You can ask her that, and that's all. Now for Christ's sweet sake, can we finish with this witness?"

The crier called the court back into session, and Willis Donahue mumbled: "Butler, you're either dumber than I thought, or a hell of a lot smarter."

"Well, don't lie awake nights worrying about it, Willis."

Again, the Judge told the jury to forget my last question. "You see, ladies and gentlemen, it's been so long since some of us have been to law school, that we begin to think maybe we've forgotten something, so we just want to make sure. But apparently we're not overcome by senility yet: the younger generation can be wrong too." The jury chuckled happily, and I tried to blush. "All right, Mr. Butler, you have another question for this witness."

"Thank you, your Honor. I'm through with this witness."

Willis cursed under his breath. He was in an unpleasant spot now. The jury had heard the uproar about theft insurance and prostitution, and despite the Judge's instructions, they wouldn't forget such succulent items. On the other hand, Dotty Todd had never had an opportunity to deny that she'd filed an insurance claim, or that she was a prostitute. Of course, Willis could ask her these questions himself. But I didn't think he would; he didn't know what the answers might be.

I was right.

"If your Honor please," said Willis, "we have no further questions either, and the Commonwealth rests its case."

Dorothy Todd sat there.

"Thank you, young lady," said the Judge. "You may step down now."

For a moment she looked as if she wanted to say something, but then she seemed to change her mind. With all eyes in the room upon her, she stood up and, stepping carefully in her high heels, climbed down the steps from the witness-box, walked across the well of court, and out the side door which a tipstaff held open for her. When the door closed, a collective sigh rose in the room.

I turned to the girl beside me. "All right, Miss Runcible. Go on up to that witness stand."

"Oh man, don't make me go up there!"

"Did you take those jewels?"

"No, I didn't take them."

"Then you haven't got a thing to worry about. Go on."

She sat still for a second; then her chair scraped back and she stood up. The court attendants guided her to the stand, one sort of handing her to another, until they had her up there facing the room. She was sworn, and then it was my turn to question her.

I wanted to keep it short. She said that she had been working for Dorothy Todd for six months; she was supposed to come in Tuesdays and Thursdays and Saturdays to wash the dishes — two lady jurors wrinkled their noses — to vacuum the rugs and to clean up. She had a key. Miss Todd sometimes gave her clothes she didn't want any more. Well, like a raincoat, a raincoat made to look like leopard skin, only it was a raincoat? And a pair of flannel slacks. And a sweater — a gray sweater. No, not this one here. What about the purse, I asked? Wasn't that a very expensive purse? Fernanda shook her head: You couldn't tell, she'd go out one day and buy something, then the next day she wouldn't like it, wouldn't wear it, and she'd give it away. One time she bought this pair of gold — you know that stuff? lawmay? pants, but then she wouldn't never wear them, and she gave them to Fernanda, only they didn't fit, so she gave them to her girl friend —

"Well now, exactly when did Miss Todd say you could have the alligator purse?"

"That same week, must've been Thursday, I guess . . ."

"Tell the jury exactly what Miss Todd said."

"She said, 'Fernanda, I don't want that damn purse, it's too big and it don't go with the suit, so you go ahead and take it home.' "

"This was on the Thursday before that Saturday?"

"Yes, sir."

"And what were you doing, right at that time?"

"I was cleaning up the place, putting things away, and this purse was on her dressing table, and I was just putting it in the closet."

"Well, why didn't you take the purse home on Thursday?"

"Because, I already had my own purse, that I come with. How'm I gonna go home on the bus with two purses?"

I glanced at the jury. The ladies were impassive.

"So then what happened on Saturday?"

"Saturday I come in, I went up in the elevator and let myself in, there wasn't nobody home —"

"Did that surprise you?"

"Huh?"

"Were you surprised not to find Miss Todd at home?"

107

Fernanda shook her head. "Nah, she always off some-place —"

"Just a minute, your Honor," said Willis Donahue. "I don't understand what this has got to do —"

"I'll withdraw the question. Miss Runcible, did you know Miss Todd had those diamond rings and that neck-lace in the apartment?"

"No, sir, I didn't."

"Ever hear anything about any diamond rings?"

"No sir, nothing."

"Anything about a necklace?"

"No sir."

"What was in that alligator purse when you took it?"

"Wasn't nothing in it. It was empty."

"Did you take that jewelry out of Miss Todd's apart-ment?"

"I didn't, no sir."

"Cross-examine."

Willis Donahue didn't have much room to maneuver. We had not put her character in evidence, so he couldn't ask her about her shoplifting arrests. I was afraid that he might do it anyway: then I would have to move for the withdrawal of a juror, which is our quaint way of ending a trial for prejudice. The Judge would have to grant my motion, and Fernanda would go back to jail to wait for a new trial. I held my breath; I had really been pretty dirty with Dorothy Todd, and this would be Willis's method of balancing the scales.

Willis leafed through his file. If you didn't know bet-ter, you would think that the District Attorney's office had a thick dossier on this girl. The jury watched, fascinated. Finally, Willis found the papers he wanted and settled back in his chair.

"Now, Fernanda —" he began.

That was a mistake. I stood up quickly. "If your Honor please, all the other witnesses in this case have been addressed by their last names. Is there any reason why Mr. Donahue can't call her Miss Runcible?"

"I *beg* your pardon, Miss Runcible," said Willis, with elaborate courtesy. "How old are you, by the way?"

"I'm twenty-two." That didn't help him much.

Next he wanted to know how long she had worked for Dorothy Todd. Six months was the answer. Did she have any other day's-work jobs, except these three mornings for Miss Todd. Well, she did have one but she gave that up. Slowly Willis extracted her confused employment history: ever since she had left school at sixteen, Fernanda had worked for housewives in various parts of the city and the suburbs. She usually didn't work more than two or three days a week, and she never stayed with one woman more than a few months. Her reasons for leaving were vague, to say the least. ". . . she say she didn't need me no more . . . it took me too long to get way out there . . . I didn't feel too good, felt sick all the time . . . That lady, she was complaining all the time . . ."

Willis made his point. The girl was a drifter, or she had been fired by a great many women in the past six years. Why? The jury was invited to wonder. I could have objected, because this material was not relevant, but the jurors seemed interested and I didn't want to irritate them.

Finally Judge Stellwagon got tired: "All right, Mr. Donahue, she doesn't remember why she left that job. What difference does it make?"

"If your Honor please, I'm trying to show —"

"I know what you're trying to show. Let's get on to something else."

"Yes, sir."

He picked up the purse again. Did she really expect the jury to believe that Miss Todd had given her a brand new alligator purse worth *forty-seven dollars*? ? ? What exactly had Miss Todd said? Where had she been standing? Where had Miss Todd been standing? I objected, but the judge overruled me. Fernanda didn't remember where she had been standing or Miss Todd either. Well, it was only a few weeks ago, wasn't it?

I stood up again. "Well, it was six weeks ago, your Honor."

"Your Honor, here he is testifying again!"

Whack! The Judge slammed his hand down on the desk top. "I want you men to stop this wrangling! You've got a perfectly simple larceny case here, and you're making a three-ring circus out of it. She doesn't remember, Mr. Donahue. Now have you got any more questions?"

Willis tried one more approach: If she had been given the purse, why was it hidden?

"Man, you don't keep nothin' good lying around loose in there," said Fernanda passionately. "You know what we got for a lock on the door? We got a bent nail, that's what keeps the door closed. Only way to keep something is to hide it way back on the shelf or someplace."

"That's all, your Honor," said Willis in a disgusted tone of voice.

I stood up. "The defense rests, your Honor." Then I made the usual motions for a directed verdict of not guilty which the Judge denied the moment the words were out of my mouth. I asked him to dismiss the burglary charge: There was no evidence that Fernanda had entered the building with intent to commit a felony. The Judge nodded and told the clerk to endorse "not guilty" on the burglary bill.

Then Willis turned to make his address to the jury.

This time he wasn't so casual. He went over the testimony again, and hammered at the purse issue: they were sensible people; did they believe that Miss Todd would give her cleaning girl a forty-seven-dollar alligator purse? He showed them the beautiful shiny purse and the sales slip from Nan Duskin's. Now somebody was lying here, that much was clear. Now let's look at the motivation: the defendant was charged with a crime; not much question about her motivation. The jury had heard and seen her; they could decide if she would tell a lie to avoid going to prison. But what about Miss Todd? What possible reason would she have to tell a lie against this girl and come into court here and subject herself to all kinds of questions and cross-examination — and here Willis wanted to suggest that when his young friend had acquired some more experience in court, he might hesitate to ask witnesses insulting and improper questions — what reason would Miss Todd have to come into court and tell lies and subject herself not only to cross-examination but also to possible perjury charges, if her story wasn't true?

Well, of course, our young friend has suggested a motive. He wants you to believe that there is insurance fraud here. He wants you to think that Miss Todd has made this charge against this girl so that she can collect on her insurance. Now of course, that's a lot of nonsense; Mr. Butler is trying to sell the jury a bill of goods. Why? Because Miss Todd would not have to accuse her innocent cleaning girl if she wanted to collect on her insurance. All she would have to say to the insurance company would be 'A bushy-haired stranger took them.' All she would have to say is that some burglar came into her apartment and took her jewels; she wouldn't have to file charges against an innocent girl and come into court here and have herself called all kinds of names by a young inexperienced corporation lawyer who never tried a case before! And so, said Willis, flushed and breathing a little faster, he was sure that the jury would have no trouble in deciding who was lying and who was telling the truth. He was sure that the jury would not allow themselves to be led astray by a lot of courtroom tricks apparently learned from television shows; and he was sure that when they considered the evidence they had heard, and when they had listened carefully

111

to the charge which his Honor Judge Stellwagon would give them at the close of the case, they would not have trouble at all in finding this unfortunate girl guilty of larceny as charged.

Willis Donahue sat down and wiped his forehead with his handkerchief.

Everybody looked at me.

I walked over, put my hands on the edge of the jury box. They didn't look like parts of a monster any more; they looked like fellow passengers. We had been on a long voyage together, and we knew each other.

"Ladies and gentlemen," I said. "You may remember that I spoke to you before about reasonable doubt. I told you then, I'm telling you now, and I hope that Judge Stellwagon will also tell you, that you may not find this girl guilty of stealing those jewels if you have a reasonable doubt about it. Well, haven't you got a reasonable doubt now? Mr. Donahue is perfectly right when he says that somebody must be lying. You've got two completely different stories, so one of them must be lying. But *who* is lying? Is this girl over here lying? Or is the beautiful lady who wouldn't take off her sunglasses to look at you lying?"

They seemed to be interested, so I kept talking. I discussed all the witnesses and what I could remember of their testimony. I talked very slowly, and I tried to look at each member of the jury as if I were talking only to her or to him. A couple of grandmotherly ladies in front; several shabby old men, whose collars were too big for their shrunken throats; a heavy patient-looking old colored woman; two pretty secretaries who chewed gum in unison; a huge red-faced truck driver; a balding young accountant with rimless glasses; a carefully dressed telephone supervisor with blue hair, who kept a critical eye on the two secretaries; and a colored insurance salesman who wore a lodge pin on the lapel of his shiny blue suit.

"Well now, Mr. Donahue has brought up this matter

of insurance fraud when he talked to you, so perhaps he won't mind if I say something about that too. Suppose Miss Todd, maybe not Miss Todd but somebody who is advising Miss Todd, suppose somebody suggested that if her jewels disappear, she might collect some insurance. What do you think would happen if she called up the insurance company and said 'Gosh, my jewels seem to have disappeared. On Friday I took them to be appraised, so I would have some good evidence that they're worth twenty thousand dollars, just in case I lost them over the weekend, and what do you know, I went away for the weekend, and now they're gone, so please pay me twenty thousand dollars, Mr. Insurance Company. Of course, there's no evidence that anybody broke into my apartment, but anyway my jewels are gone, and you've insured them, so please pay me.' "

I stopped for a second. "What do you think the insurance company would have said? I can guess what they would have said, and I think you can too."

I turned to look at Willis Donahue, who was pretending he was reading some document on his table. "Of course, Mr. Donahue has suggested that she could have told the insurance company that a bushy-haired stranger took her jewels. A bushy-haired stranger?"

Suddenly my mind was empty. "What was the name of that doctor out there in Ohio with the bushy-haired stranger?" I asked myself, desperately looking at the ceiling for help. "That doctor who said a bushy-haired stranger killed his wife?"

"Dr. Sheppard," said three members of the jury in unison.

"That's right! Dr. Sheppard. He didn't have much luck with placing the blame on a bushy-haired stranger, and I suggest to you that if Miss Todd had blamed her loss on a bushy-haired stranger, she wouldn't have collected a cent —"

113

"Your Honor," said Willis Donahue. "If counsel is going to conduct a colloquy with the jury —"

"*Colloquy?* What's that, some kind of a disease?" asked Judge Stellwagon. A couple of jurors tittered. "He asked a rhetorical question and the jury answered it. Let's keep moving along."

Several jurors were smiling at me now. They were obviously grateful for a chance to participate in the case, and they liked me for letting them help.

I said a few more words about the Commonwealth's burden of proof, that it was Mr. Donahue's duty to convince them beyond a reasonable doubt, and if he didn't carry that burden, if he didn't convince them beyond a reasonable doubt, if they chose not to believe his witnesses because they didn't seem to be people worthy of belief, why then they should give this girl the benefit of that doubt, find her not guilty, and let her go free.

"That's all I have to say, ladies and gentlemen. Mr. Donahue gets the last word, so I'll just remind you again that if you have a reasonable doubt about Miss Runcible's guilt — if there is a reasonable doubt in your mind — then you *must* find her innocent. Thank you for your attention."

Willis Donahue was a study in virtuous outrage now: our jury system is the bulwark of our Republic; he assumed that members of the jury were responsible citizens who would judge this case on the admissible evidence presented to them; he assumed that as responsible citizens they would recognize that a lot of false issues had been raised here to confuse them — maybe not on purpose, maybe just because of the commendable zeal of a very young lawyer performing a public duty — but nevertheless Willis assumed that the members of this jury would not allow themselves to get mixed-up or confused by a lot of false issues that had nothing to do with the question. The question was: Had this girl taken the diamond rings and the diamond necklace, or hadn't she? Now, what was the evidence?

114

Willis went over the evidence again. The jury looked impassive. The Judge yawned, pushed up his glasses and rubbed his hand over his eyes. Willis reminded the jurors of their oath, told them that the evidence allowed no other inference than that this girl was guilty as charged, said that he was not going to thank them because you do not thank people who are doing their duty as citizens, and sat down.

There was a rustle in the room, a shifting of bodies, coughing, a murmur of voices. Then there was a sharp tearing sound as Judge Stellwagon ripped some papers off his yellow pad. He moved his chair forward, placed the sheets under the reading lamp, and adjusted his glasses.

"Ladies and gentlemen of the jury," he began.

It was a short, concise and perfectly proper charge. He reviewed the testimony, cautioned them to pay no attention to irrelevancies which had nothing to do with the case, explained what a reasonable doubt is, supplied the legal definition of larceny, discussed the presumption of innocence and told them that their verdict would have to be unanimous. The whole charge didn't take ten minutes. The jurors never took their eyes from the Judge's face.

"All right?" he turned toward the counsel table and peered over his glasses. "Have I forgotten anything?"

Willis and I both said that we had no additional points for charge.

"Well, you must be tired out or something," said the Judge. "Mr. Fenstermacher, you can lock up this jury, please."

"ALL PARTIES REMAIN SEATED," yelled the tipstaves in the corners of the room, and one of the other attendants herded the jurors out through the side door.

"ALL RISE PLEASE." Judge Stellwagon got up. Black robes billowing, he hurried down the steps behind the bench and out through the little door. Behind us, the rest of the room rose too, but I just sat there beside Fernanda Runcible.

I had been swimming far beneath the surface of the sea, and now suddenly I was floating up and up and bursting out into the air. Nothing in my life had absorbed my attention like this trial; while I watched and listened and talked, I was dancing this complicated dance with the Judge and the jury and Willis Donahue and the witnesses, and the world outside wasn't there. For two hours, the dance had been the world.

Now I sat there, completely drained, and realized that the sullen girl beside me had very little to do with this dance, or game or battle or whatever it was, because I had not been doing it for her; I'd been doing it for myself.

"Well, what do you think, Miss Runcible?"

She examined her fingernails. "I guess you done your best. How long they make us wait?"

Of course I didn't know, and the guards were debating whether to take her back to the cells on the seventh floor. Willis Donahue was packing his papers into the file. He looked over at me.

"You turned out to be a real gut fighter, Ben. They teach you to play like that at C & D?"

"No, I guess I tried this one pretty much by instinct."

Willis shook his head. "Some instinct."

"What do you mean by that, Willis?"

"You've missed your calling, friend. You should be doing this full time."

"Well . . . thanks, Willis." I didn't know what I was expected to say to that.

"Holy Christ," said the sheriff's deputy. "They musta rung already."

Judge Stellwagon was climbing back from the robing room, and the tipstaves were closing all the doors. "ALL RISE PLEASE."

The jury filed back into the box. The ladies were looking at me.

"Well, that was a pretty fast decision, ladies and gentle-

116

men," said the Judge. "Have you already reached a unanimous verdict?"

The foreman was one of the gaunt old men. He stood up and gulped. "Yes, sir. I mean, we have, your Honor."

The court crier marched over quickly, faced the foreman and asked: "How do you find the defendant Fernanda Runcible on bill of indictment number seven eighty-seven, guilty or not guilty?"

"Not guilty."

Silence.

"All right, ladies and gentlemen," said Judge Stellwagon. "Your verdict will be recorded, and you are discharged. Before you go, though, you might be interested to know that this little girl was arrested for shoplifting in 1960, and the charge was dropped for some reason, and then in 1962 she was arrested again for shoplifting, and she was convicted right here in this room, and Judge Morgenstern suspended her sentence, and now you've acquitted her again. A mighty lucky little girl, wouldn't you say?"

The jurors didn't look at him as they stepped out of the box and mingled with the other people in the room.

"Man, you got me off!" said Fernanda Runcible. For the first time there was a hint of some emotion in her face.

"I guess I did."

We stood up, and deputies were leading her away because they had to sign her out of the cell room and give her clothes back.

"Well," she said. "I want to thank you."

"That's all right, Miss Runcible."

"Well, you go ahead and call me Fernanda."

"Okay Fernanda, you keep out of trouble now."

"Yeah," she said. "No more trouble, man." The deputies took her out. I turned around and saw that the Judge was still sitting up there, writing something. He jerked his head at me, and I walked around the railing to the bench.

117

The Judge stopped writing and looked at me over the tops of his spectacles.

"Pretty cute performance," he said. "I guess you think you're Clarence Darrow now, don't you?"

"No sir, I'm just lucky . . ."

"That's exactly right. You're young and lucky and the jury liked you and you hit the jackpot. But don't count on winning them with stunts, boy; you got away with murder today. You know that, don't you?"

"Your Honor, I only did the best I could —"

"Never mind." He handed the papers down to one of the clerks and got to his feet. "As far as I'm concerned you pulled a stunt, and it paid off, but boy, don't you *ever* pull any stunts in my court again. Is that clear?"

"Yes, sir."

He turned abruptly and disappeared down the steps. I walked back to the counsel table and assembled my file. The room was nearly empty. Willis Donahue had gone without another word, and the court attendants were getting ready to lock up the room for the lunch recess. I put the file in my dispatch case, and then I saw Monica Wesselhof sitting there, right in the middle of the room. She got up and came over.

"Congratulations," she said, smiling, and extended her hand.

"I didn't see you," I said stupidly, as I shook hands with her.

"Oh, I could see that you were very busy. It was quite interesting. The first trial I have seen in America."

We walked out into the gloomy corridor together.

"Do you feel happy?" she asked.

"That was my first real trial," I said. "I feel . . . well, we have an expression 'walking on air.' I'm walking on air, I feel as if I'm going to blow up."

She giggled. "Please don't blow up right here. Must you go into another trial?"

118

"Oh no," I said. "I'm through for the day. I'm going . . . will you please have lunch with me?"

There was just the tiniest flicker and pause. "Yes," she said. "I would like that."

"Just one thing, I must warn you."

"About what?"

"Well, I intend to get drunk," I said.

She put back her head and laughed. "Well then, I shall get drunk with you." She took my arm, and we ran all the way down four flights of stairs to the street.

chapter 11

I suppose I should have taken her to the Bellevue or the Barclay, but I wanted a drink right away, and Mc-Gintey's was just across Penn Square. It was late and the place was not as crowded as usual. The bartender waved us back to the last booth. She asked for a stein of German beer, and I started right in with Scotch-on-the-rocks.

Although I was curious about her — who she was and what she was doing here — I was so jazzed up that I couldn't seem to stop talking about myself. I told her about my work at Conyers & Dean, about the bond issues and the trust indentures and all the big deals I'd worked on, and I told her how they had never let me go to court and now here I was apparently really really good in court and how intoxicating I found it to be face to face with a jury.

She watched me through the smoke of her cigarettes and smiled and asked questions at the right places and laughed when I tried to be funny, while I drank and talked and talked. I don't think I've ever poured myself out like that before; it was partly the booze and partly the excitement of the trial, but mostly it was just her presence.

The waiter brought our soup and sandwiches. I slowly calmed down and tried to turn the conversation. She didn't like questions about herself, but I put together the outlines.

She had grown up in a castle in the Tyrolean mountains near Innsbruck, had been married to an older man who owned steel mills in the Ruhr, and had come to Philadelphia after her husband died.

Why Philadelphia?

She shrugged: Why not? She had read about some special sculpture courses at the Museum College, her application had been accepted, so she had come over on a student visa. She had been making wood carvings all her life, but there had never been time for any formal study. Now she had both time and money, so why not go back to school?

Somehow it didn't make sense to me. "You came all the way over here, all by yourself, to live in a strange town just to study sculpture?"

She put down her coffee cup. "Well, why not? I felt I needed some real — how do you say it — training? Some professional training, and they could give it to me here, so I came. Why shouldn't I?"

"But there must be plenty of places in Europe . . ."

"Perhaps I am tired of Europe." She blew out a cloud of cigarette smoke.

"But don't you have a family, any children or anything?"

"No children, no." She looked down at the tabletop. "My father is dead and my brother is dead and my husband is dead and we had no children. So you see —" she looked up again, "I can do what I like and go where I like, and I wanted to come here. For a while."

"Well, I'm glad you did."

I ordered brandy for both of us, and then I tried to probe some more. Her mother had died when she was born and she had been brought up by her father. She helped him run the family estates — dairy farms, timberlands, pastures in the mountains. Her brother had spent the war as an officer in the German alpine troops; after the war, unemployed and bored, he had signed up with the French and

121

had died in Indochina. After her father died too, she had run the place by herself, until she met Wesselhof, a German industrialist, at a ski resort in Switzerland; he was much older, he was kind, he wanted to take care of her — and he had plenty of money to restore her dilapidated castle. They kept a big house at Dortmund in the Ruhr where his mills were, and they traveled to Italy and Spain and Greece, but most of the time Monica lived in her mountains. Her husband's children did not like her, and after he died she decided to try America.

She told me all this in a slow quiet voice, looking down into her brandy glass as she moved it back and forth across the table.

"Well, that is my story. Not terribly interesting, is it?"

"That's not the whole story," I said.

"Oh no?" She held her chin in her hands now and looked at me across the table.

"No. Are you suggesting there weren't any men before Mr. Wesselhof?"

She raised her eyebrows and looked back into the brandy glass.

"You're quite a lawyer, with all your questions."

"I'm sorry, Monica, it's none of my business."

"You see, in my generation . . . you see, we had a war, and the war . . . well, it changed many things for us . . ."

The tired waiter in his dirty white jacket was standing beside the table. "That be all, folks?"

"Will you have another brandy with me?" I asked her.

"Yes, why not?"

Twenty minutes later we were swinging down the street together. It was the middle of the afternoon, the town seemed empty in the warm hazy sunshine, and my ears were ringing. I looked up at the office buildings and thought about all the people drafting contracts and auditing statements and talking on the telephone and worrying about things. I felt the pressure of her body against my arm as she moved in step with me.

In Rittenhouse Square, bums and retired stockbrokers were dozing in the sun, and nursemaids were watching little children chasing the pigeons around. I realized that we were walking toward Monica's apartment house. For a moment I thought of changing course; I really did not want to run into that doorman or Dorothy Todd. On the other hand I wanted to be alone with Monica so badly now that I could hardly walk. Desperately I tried to think of some reason to ask her to my place. Etchings . . . ?

"Why are you laughing?" she asked.

"Oh, just because I'm feeling good." We waited for the light and crossed the street to the Rittenhouse Connaught. The doorman was not the one I had cross-examined; he touched his cap politely, and I followed Monica into the elevator. As we rose, she frowned and said: "What shall we do if we meet that girl in the hall?"

"That's just what I was wondering."

The door opened and we stepped out. The hall was empty. Monica opened her purse and took out a key. Was I supposed to say good-bye now? Should I just follow her in when she opened the door? I followed her in and shut the door and then I backed her up against it hard and started to kiss her.

"*No!*" She twisted her face to the left. The cord in her neck stood out and I tried to kiss her under the ear.

"Oh Monica, I'm so crazy for you —"

"*No!*" Her body became hard, she wrenched herself out of my arms and pushed past me into the room.

"Oh Monica, please . . ." It wasn't really me. I was sitting over on the sofa, watching a movie — a lousy movie. I have never *ever* done this before; it is corny and humiliating, and it doesn't work, but just the same I — this lunatic transformed other I — followed and grabbed her wrist.

123

She whirled around and hit me in the face.

"Hey . . ."

"Would you like to know what I am sick of?" Her face was flushed. "I am *sick* of American men who think that every German girl, every Austrian girl, wants to lie right down on the *floor* for them . . . I am so sick of it, I just can't tell you! Now please go away and leave me alone!"

"My God, Monica, I'm sorry . . . I didn't mean . . ."

Suddenly she began to giggle. "Oh, you should see your face. You are not used to this, are you? They always do what you want them to?"

"Who?"

"The girls. I think you are a little spoiled."

I moved toward her again.

"NO!" She stepped back quickly. "All right, that is enough now. You sit down there in that chair or you leave. Which will it be?"

I sat down in the chair.

"All right," she said. "That's better. Now I think you are a very nice boy, very attractive, I'm sure you are very successful with the ladies, but I must tell you that in the first place I am much older than you are —"

"Oh no, you're not."

"Oh yes, I am. And in the second place, I am very much in love with somebody else —"

"You mean somebody here in town?"

"I don't think that's any of your business, is it? You came up here looking for information about that cleaning girl, and I was able to help, and you did a fine defense of the girl, and we had a nice lunch and some drinks, and now is the time to say good-bye. Is that not correct?"

"No," I said. "The last part is not correct. You may be involved with somebody else, but I can't help it if I'm nuts about you and I want to see you —"

"Oh, this is so ridiculous! We have had one meal to-

124

gether, a very pleasant time . . . Let me ask, how old are you, Ben?"

"What difference does that make? . . . I'm thirty . . . uh, thirty-three —"

She snorted. "Thirty-three! You are not over twenty-five."

"I most certainly *am* over twenty-five."

"All right, you can be forty for all I care, but I told you that I am interested in somebody else — well, more than just interested —"

"Well, where is this guy you're so interested in?"

Her face darkened. "That is not your concern . . ."

"He's not available, is he? I bet he's married and he's got six children and he's got you stashed away here for evenings in town . . ."

"All right, that's enough, you will have to go now please. I have had enough of this nonsense."

"I've hit it right on the nose, haven't I? You're in love with somebody who's keeping you on the string, or just plain keeping you . . ."

She walked over and opened the door to the hall. "Good-bye," she said quietly, holding the door open for me.

I sat still. "All right, I'm sorry."

She just stood there.

"I said I was sorry, Monica."

"Will you please leave now?"

Suddenly a bell rang in the hall. The elevator was stopping on the eighteenth floor. Monica looked startled and shut the door.

"Was it Dorothy Todd?" I asked.

"I don't know, but I didn't want her to see you in here. Isn't this ridiculous? How did I ever become involved —"

"Monica, please . . ." I stood up and walked toward her.

125

She moved around me and headed toward the bedroom. "All right, my friend, I cannot throw you out, but I have work to do. I will put on my smock and get to work and I will just pretend that you are not here. Good-bye." She slammed the bedroom door in my face. Of course I should have gone then, but instead I poked around the living room, looking through her art books and examining the carved figures on the shelf by the window. A few minutes later she came out of the bedroom, dressed in something brown that tied around her waist, and tennis shoes. She opened a big closet, carefully spread some newspapers on the worktable near the window, and then carried a large wooden object from the closet to the table. It looked like a block of teak which had been carved into the shape of an enormous lumpy egg. From the closet she took two different hammers and a series of chisels, which she laid out like surgical instruments on the worktable. Then she walked over to the record player, switched on the tuner, mounted a stack of records and started the machine. For the second time in four days I heard the Overture to *The Marriage of Figaro*. She returned to her table, picked up a hammer and a chisel and began to tap gently at her block of teak. Stretched out on the comfortable couch, a pillow under my head, I listened to Mozart and looked at Monica's strong bare arms.

I woke up because the music stopped. Yawning and stretching, I got to my feet, turned over the stack of records and pushed the switch. The bottom record fell into place, the tone arm moved and music filled the room again. Monica did not take her eyes from the block of wood, which was beginning to look like the head of a man. I went to the bathroom and then returned to the couch. Lying on my side, I watched Monica chipping away at the wood, scattering the shavings across the newspapers on the table, stopping now and then to step back and squint at her work, completely absorbed and apparently unconscious of my presence. I was quite sober now, and tried hard to understand what had happened to me. What was so special about this one? I really don't believe all this crap about love at first sight. People read books and see movies and then they try to make their own lives romantic by persuading themselves that men and women really do put out these magic spells — Well, it never happened to me, and lying there watching her I just couldn't figure out what she had that turned me into a slob.

The tone arm moved back for the last time and the changer turned itself off. The opera was over. Monica continued to work. There was a long silence.

Then she said: "Do you have a car?"

"Yes, I do."

"There is a museum I would like to see, in the suburbs. The Barnes Foundation. Do you know it?"

"I think that's out in Merion," I said. "I've never been there, but would you like me to take you out?" I swung my feet and came over to the table.

"Yes, that would be nice of you," she said, still tapping her chisel with the hammer. "It is a private place, I think, and I must find out when it is open, and if you call me tomorrow, I will tell you." Then she turned and looked at me. "And now I really must ask you to go, Ben. Somebody is coming to see me, and you just cannot stay here. You will not make a fuss now, will you?"

"I guess I slept it off," I said. "I owe you an apology, Monica."

She put down her tools. "Oh well, perhaps at my age it is flattering, you know." She smiled. "I must say, you have provided me with a very interesting day." I tied my necktie and put on my coat.

"Do you think there'll be more interesting days?"

"I don't know. Perhaps. But you must promise to behave yourself." She came to the door and God help me,

127

it was all I could do to keep my hands away from her.

"All right. Good-bye, Monica. I'll call you tomorrow."

"All right. Good-bye." She closed the door.

When I crossed the street and walked into Rittenhouse Square I had an overpowering urge to sit down on one of the benches and keep my eye on the door of the Connaught. I found a good spot and was just about to sit down when the other occupant of the bench, a tough-looking leathery man with tattoos on his hands, woke up and asked, "You got the time, buddy?"

I told him it was a quarter to five, and then I really woke up. I hadn't even checked in at the Defender office, I hadn't reported the Runcible case, and I had not picked up my assignments for tomorrow. With one last glance across the street, I turned and marched briskly back downtown.

As I came into Marvin Gold's office, the first thing I saw was my attaché case. It was lying on Marvin's desk.

"Well, look who's here," he said, looking up. "We were about to contact the Missing Persons Bureau."

"I got an acquittal for the Runcible girl."

"So I hear. Congratulations. You must have floated out of there in a daze, because they called up from four fifty-three and said you'd left your bag and the whole file right there on the counsel table. We had to send over for it."

"God, I'm sorry Marvin, I guess —"

"Never mind, it's okay. Sit down a minute." It was five o'clock now, and the girls were closing the office. Marvin finished signing his mail. Then he strolled down the hall to discuss a trial with one of the other assistants. When he came back he handed me a typewritten list of names.

"Hey, what's this? Prison interviews again? I thought I'd graduated to court now."

"Baloney," said Marvin. "We all take our turn at

the prison. Tomorrow's trials are already assigned — they're only running two rooms — and meanwhile the prison list is backing up. You'll be back in court on Wednesday — If you're not disbarred by then, that is."

"Disbarred? What's that supposed to mean?"

Marvin shifted his weight, turning his chair, and put his feet on the radiator. "Buddy boy, you've been the principal topic of conversation around here this afternoon. First of all, Stellwagon called up Walter Simon and complained that you'd insulted a witness in the Runcible case. Did you really call that woman a whore in open court?"

"Certainly not. I just asked her if she'd ever been convicted of prostitution. I was trying to impeach her credibility —"

"Where'd you get the idea that she's a prostitute?"

"Well, one of her neighbors told me that."

"You went out and talked to the neighbors?" Marvin looked impressed. "Well, anyhow, Stellwagon gave Simon quite a chewing-out, then Simon sent for you, and of course nobody knew where you were, and then the telephone rang again and guess who that was."

"Who?"

"Mr. Ellsworth Boyle, Conyers & Dean."

"What did he want?"

"Your fair white body, that's what he wanted. He was awfully sorry, but they suddenly developed an unexpected amount of corporate work and somebody got sick so they want you back. Perfectly happy to substitute another man, but you they want back, and on the double."

I was startled at the degree of my disappointment. Two weeks ago I had never heard of the Defender.

"Well, I guess that solved Mr. Simon's problem very neatly, didn't it?" I said.

"You don't know Walter Simon. Most of the time he's affability personified, but when he thinks the operation of his outfit is at stake — look out! He just about told your

Mr. Boyle to go screw. He said the deal was four weeks because we can't train men for this kind of work in a couple of days any more than Boyle can train men for his financing jobs in a couple of days, and we've just now got you so that you can try cases in court and only this morning you'd won a difficult jury trial and if the law firms can take their men back just as they're becoming useful to the Defender why then there isn't much point to the whole loan program, is there?"

"He talked to Boyle that way? What happened?"

"Boyle backed off. Of course I didn't hear exactly what he said, but Walter began to make mollified noises, if you know what I mean, and in conclusion it was unanimously agreed that B. Butler is the hottest thing that ever came down the pike."

"So I'm staying for the month?"

"So you're staying."

"What about Judge Stellwagon? Does Mr. Simon want to see me now?"

"He can't see you now because he's flown out to Chicago for a meeting of the National Legal Aid and Defender Association. He promised Judge Stellwagon that he'd have a talk with you when he got back, and in the meantime Marvin Gold would look into the matter." He put a cigar in his mouth and lighted it. "That's what Marvin Gold is doing right now, looking into the matter. Let's have the story."

I told him everything that happened. I told him about my reception by Dorothy Todd, my meeting with Monica, what Monica told me, and what happened at the trial. Marvin puffed on his cigar and leafed around in the file and listened. When I finished talking he leaned back and studied the ceiling for a while.

"Well, I won't say it's the *orthodox* way to handle a case, but who can quarrel with your results?"

"Marvin, I didn't plan this defense; it just sort of happened."

He nodded. "That's obvious. I'd say you were damned lucky, but also you exploited every opportunity, and lots of people don't know how to do that. As a matter of fact —" Marvin produced an enigmatic smile. "I'd say that under that polite glossy big-firm exterior we're beginning to find a tricky — should I say dangerous? trial lawyer. This work takes instinct, Ben, and you've got it."

"Well, thank you kindly."

"As for Simon, I'll tell him I don't think you've done anything wrong." He shuffled the papers back into the file and handed the bundle across the table. "Okay Ben, just write up your report and put the file on Nancy's desk. I've got to run now." He stood up and put on his jacket.

"Oh, I thought we could walk around the corner and lift a few." I was thirsty again.

"I'd like to, but believe it or not I'm supposed to address the Frankford Businessmen's Association. The subject is 'Police and the Criminal.' Commissioner Armstrong will speak for the police, and I guess I'm supposed to present the other point of view."

"Well, in that case I'll see you when I bring back my interviews tomorrow," I said, heading for the door.

"Oh, just a sec, Ben. There was a message . . ." He rummaged among the papers on his desk and found the pink slips. "A Mrs. Rochester called. Twice."

chapter 12

— Hello?

— Hey Ben? Randy Kellerman. Did I wake you up? It's only ten o'clock and I thought —

— Uh . . . No . . . It's okay Randy, I've had quite a day and I must have dozed off. How are you?

— I'm okay Ben, working like hell. I just got home. Listen, the reason I'm calling, Ordway Smith asked me to be sure to tell you to come to the office dinner. It's at the Rittenhouse Club on Friday night, black tie, they put out a memo but nobody was sure whether you'd gotten it, so Ordway told me to make sure and he wants to know how many will be there —

— Friday night? Okay, sure, tell him I'd love to come. How are things at the office?

— Boy, things are *wild*. You heard about the Hammond Soap closing, I guess, and —

— No, what Hammon Soap closing? You mean the Sinking Fund Debentures?

— Sure, the Debentures. You haven't heard this story? Christ, it's unbelievable . . .

— Well, what happened?

— All right, you know the deal, perfectly straightforward deal, twelve million dollars of Debentures, twenty year maturity, sale through underwriters, full-dress SEC registration, nice fat prospectus describing the company, outlining the terms of the Indenture —

— Sure I know all that, Randy. What was the problem?

— Well, altogether a dozen people worked over the thing for three months — our people, company people, the accountants, the underwriters, *their* lawyers, the SEC . . . Everything ought to be clear, right? Okay, finally everything is buttoned up, registration statement is effective, ten thousand prospectuses printed, twelve pounds of closing papers drawn up and signed, everybody gathers in a boardroom in New York and guess what's discovered?

— What?

— There's nothing about the antitrust suit in the prospectus!

. . . .

— Ben?

— I don't believe it.

— *You* don't believe it? I was right there in the room. They were climbing up the walls! You know what it meant, don't you?

— You couldn't close.

— Damn right we couldn't close. We'd issued a misleading prospectus, materially misleading as the day is long, and it queered the whole deal.

— Couldn't you amend? Print the business about the antitrust suit on a sticker and paste it on all the prospectuses?

— Oh, we sat around for hours trying to figure out something like that, but it wouldn't work. The underwriters would have to offer each buyer his money back, you see, because of this omission in the prospectus —

— That's what I mean. Give each buyer a chance to rescind, to get his money back, and if he doesn't want to rescind —

— That was the trouble, Ben. The Hammond Debentures were sold at four-point-oh-five net interest cost, and meanwhile the market changed, and now you could buy General Motors Debentures at that price. So the underwriters weren't sure they could hold their accounts together . . .

— You mean to say the deal aborted?

— Not exactly, but we've got to start all over again, this time at four-and-a-quarter interest cost. Of course, it'll cost the company a fortune; twenty basis points in interest, plus all the printing expenses . . .

. . . .

— Still there, Ben?

— I'm here, but I just can't believe it, Randy. We've been working on that antitrust case for what, a year?

— More than that.

— Ames Mahoney and Atwater haven't been doing another thing —

— Well, sure . . .

— Randy, how could we miss something like that?

— Collective brainstorm, I guess. Missed the woods for the trees. So obvious that nobody saw it.

— What about all the brokers and analysts who supposedly read these prospectuses?

— Don't ask me. Maybe nobody reads them after all.

— Who finally discovered it?

— Huh. You'll never guess. Your esteemed servant.

— You caught it? When?

— Right there at the closing, like I told you. I was looking at the No Litigation Certificate, and I saw somebody had put in the wrong boilerplate, "No material litigation other than in the normal course of the Company's business," instead of "No material litigation other than as set forth in the Registration Statement" — you know — so I thought I'd better grab a stenographer to retype the thing, then I thought what *did* we say about the antitrust case and

then I started leafing around in the prospectus and then —
boy . . .

— Nothing there?

— Nothing. Not one frigging word. I kept thinking
well it's here someplace, maybe in a footnote or someplace, but it wasn't.

— So then you had to tell Pat? I'm glad I wasn't there.

— It was awful. Just awful.

— How'd he take it?

. . . .

— Randy? I said 'How did he —'

— Actually, not so well, Ben.

— What happened?

— Christ, I mean everybody knows it wasn't any more
his fault than anybody else's, I mean look at all the Hammond people who read over that prospectus, but after all,
he's the partner in charge of the deal, and when something
blows up, he's the one who is supposed to cope, to impro-
vise, to tell everybody what to do, right?

— Didn't he do that?

— Hell *no,* he didn't do that! He just sort of —
Well, he sat there at this board table, writing things on a
yellow pad with a pencil and then crossing it all out . . .
Ben, I wouldn't say this to anybody else, but I think he
really lost his nerve or something. I mean he just didn't
know what to do. All the brokers and the Hammond people were saying 'Why don't we do this' and 'Can't we do
that' and running in and out and calling people on the
telephone, and all the time Forrester sat there writing on
his pad. I don't mind telling you I was getting scared.

— What finally happened?

— Well, the underwriters' lawyer was Day, from Van-
Buskirk and Spratt; you know him?

— Yeah, he was on the Schuylkill Steel job —

— Well, Day just took over the whole show. Got his

135

people calmed down and told them to work out a new price, called the SEC and told them what we were doing, put a message out on the Dow-Jones ticker — what they call the "broad tape" — You know, he sort of got everything untangled so that we could start over again this week, and then he sent everybody home.

— What about you and Pat?

— Oh, it was pretty bad. Of course, Day and the brokers were embarrassed for us, and the Hammond people were ashamed. I tried to help out as best I could, but I'd never seen anything like this happen . . .

— Did Pat say anything to you?

— Yeah. After all the others had gone, we were sitting there by ourselves, with all our useless closing papers lying scattered over the table, and he said "I'm sorry, Randy, I don't know what happened to me. Take this stuff back to Philadelphia, will you?" and then he got up and walked out.

— Didn't you go after him?

— Certainly not, why should I? He probably went out to get drunk. That's what I'd do.

— Well, is he back in the office now? Something could have happened to him —

— No, nothing happened to him, he was back in the office yesterday, with a hangover.

— Did you tell anybody else what happened?

— No, thank God I didn't have to. Apparently Forrester called Ordway Smith from New York and gave him some explanation, and I guess he talked to Boyle. Anyway, nobody asked me anything. But Ben, I think something's wrong with Forrester, I really do. Somebody said he's going to take a vacation, and that sounds like a damn good idea.

— Who's going to redo the Hammond deal then?

— Well, I heard a rumor that they were going to bring you back.

— No, it seems I'm indispensable at the Defender.

— Good for you, you're well out of it. Actually there are just a couple of changes and a new set of closing papers. I can do it by myself and Rieger can sign the opinions. No sweat.

— Well, sounds like things are hopping at C & D.

— Dropping, you mean! One more thing, Ben. You may have heard, Roseann and I are getting married a lot sooner than we'd planned —

— Yeah I got the invitation, Randy, I think that's swell.

— And I wondered if you'd be willing to ush for me. The others are all people from school and Roseann's brothers —

— Why sure, I'd be delighted, Randy. Be an honor.

— Okay I'll give you all the details in a week or so. You'll have to go to whosits and give them your measurements, and there'll be one rehearsal and the dinner, of course.

— Sounds great.

— Okay hotshot, we'll see you on Friday.

chapter 13

The rest of that week I was with Monica; or rather, I was with her in the afternoons. I did jail interviews the first day, and then they sent me back to court again. My assignment list looked like the index of a hornbook on criminal law: Aggravated Assault, Burglary, Conspiracy, Drugs, Embezzlement, Forgery, Gambling . . . Rape, Robbery, Sodomy — all the things that happen every day and night in a city of four million people. My clients were the poorest of the lot, the ones who couldn't raise fifty dollars for a bail bond or a lawyer to stand up with them, sometimes stupid, sometimes sly, and frequently both. Most of them were guilty too, but often I was able to bring out facts that might soften the sentence, or show that a man hadn't really done all of the things charged to him. I didn't get another Fernanda Runcible, but once in a while I was able to throw enough doubt on the Commonwealth's evidence to gain an acquittal. A couple of times I could demonstrate that a man was really innocent. I learned that my job was just to do the best I could in each case.

The court was usually through the list by one o'clock, and when I turned away from the counsel table I would find Monica sitting somewhere in the room. We would walk across Penn Square to McGintey's and after lunch we would get my car.

I saw more paintings and statues that week than I had seen in all my life. Monica could lose herself in a picture or a piece of sculpture the same way I submerged myself in a trial. She would stand there, one foot behind the other, her hands behind her back, and standing that way, she might look at something for ten or fifteen minutes. At first this bored me and I would march around the museum and come back and she would still be standing there, or maybe she would have moved sideways ten steps, but she would still be looking at the same object.

Gradually I learned that if you keep looking at a really good painting, you see more and more; it begins to have an effect on you. I noticed this at the first place I took her, the Barnes Foundation, a strange private museum: ugly Colonial furniture and sullen gum-chewing guards and walls of drab brown cloth, and on those walls a fantastic luminous jumble of paintings, high and low and mixed up and almost on top of each other. Everything: Titian, Picasso, El Greco, Pascin, Manet, Monet; at least a dozen Renoirs, piles of pink naked flesh; a Gauguin . . . you could dip your fingers into the crystal water of some lagoon in Tahiti and feel the sun on the brown skin of the girls . . .

"You like that picture, Ben?"

I nodded, still looking.

"Why do you like it?"

"I don't know. It makes me want to go away, I guess."

"Well, he did it, you know."

"Gauguin? I know. *The Moon and Sixpence.* He died of syphilis."

She laughed. "You are too much a lawyer, Ben."

Later, in my car, she said: "You don't really want to go away from here, do you?"

I had stopped beside the river in Fairmount Park. The homeward rush of the commuters had not begun, and the Drive behind us was empty.

"No, I don't really want to go anywhere else," I said.

"I've had to work very hard to get where I am — I mean to get a job in my firm and to do well there — and before that I knocked around enough to see that the grass isn't usually greener on the other side. It just looks that way. Wherever you go, you find people working away in their little ruts, looking up suspiciously at any stranger who comes along. I guess I'm really pretty happy in my own rut here."

"You're lucky," she said.

"How d'you mean?"

"Some people don't feel that way. Some men think their own little rut is their own little trap."

"You're talking about somebody you know?"

"Oh, yes."

"Who? This guy you're hanging around for?"

She looked at her watch. "Oh, it is late, Ben. Will you take me home now, please?"

"You're just not going to talk about him, are you?" I said, starting the motor. "You know, sometimes it helps to talk about these things."

"No, I think not. I think I would rather talk about something else."

She told me a little more about herself. Her family, landowners who had received their castle from the Emperor Maximilian in 1509, maintained dairy farms and logging operations near Innsbruck. As a young girl she had watched an old woodcarver repairing the holy figures in the castle chapel; this had ignited her interest in sculpture. Her father had encouraged it and provided a workshop, in which she gradually taught herself to carve little figurines that could be sold in the tourist shops of Innsbruck. After she married Wesselhof he took her along on business trips to Paris and London and Rome and Athens, where she had the opportunity to visit museums and exhibitions, but she had never had any formal training until she came to Philadelphia to study at the Museum College.

The whole story still did not quite hang together. She had already told me that her father and her brother and her husband were all dead. I asked who was taking care of her farms while she was away.

"Oh well, my people are doing it — I hope. I had a letter yesterday, somebody wants to build a ski slope in one of my fields and put in — what do you call it? The thing that pulls you up?"

"A chair lift?"

"Yes, a chair lift. Our poor old Tyrol is becoming very crowded. I don't know if I really want all those people around . . . Still, they offer quite a lot of money —"

I interrupted her train of thought. "Monica? You're not going to stay here much longer, are you?"

She turned to me, smiling. "*Ach,* the lawyer again! Why am I not going to stay here much longer?"

"Because you've got to look after your place, for one thing. And because you're not the kind of woman who's going to sit around all by herself in a room in a strange foreign city very long. Are you going to take your boyfriend with you?"

She sighed. "You are the most persistent fellow! You always come back to the same subject, don't you? And I told you, I cannot talk to you about it. Please don't keep pressing me."

"All right, Monica."

We drove in silence for a while. I swung around the fountain at Logan Circle and turned down Nineteenth Street.

"I'm sorry you are angry, Ben. Do you want to see me tomorrow?"

"Monica, you know I want to see you all the time."

"Good-bye, Ben. Don't look so unhappy. Tomorrow will be better."

It wasn't though; it was worse. They gave me a nasty arson case to try: a man accused of setting fire to his girl

141

friend's room. Somebody had smelled smoke on the stairs and the firemen had come very fast and so only the empty room had been wrecked. One fireman testified that twenty minutes later the whole tenement would have gone up. There had been seventy-five people in the place that night — half of them children under ten. Our man claimed he was nowhere near the place, and the investigators found an alibi witness, a truck driver who swore he was in the same truck with the defendant all that evening, and that they had been drinking beer in a taproom on the other side of town when the fire was discovered. I asked for a jury trial. The Commonwealth put on the girl friend who said that our man had threatened to set fire to her place and had in fact tried to do it once before. The owner of a hardware store testified that the defendant bought three cans of charcoal lighter fluid that same day. Three indignant, positive housewives said they saw the defendant on the stairs that afternoon. I tried everything I could think of, but I could feel that I wasn't getting anywhere. During lunch with Monica, I was silent and abstracted. A really brilliant lawyer would think of something; but what? After lunch the jury came back and convicted our man. Judge Stellwagon congratulated them on their verdict and gave my client ten to twenty years.

"That man was quite guilty, you know," said Monica in the car. By the time we got out of City Hall it was too late to go anywhere, so we were just driving around in the Park again.

"How do you know he was guilty? Were you there?"

"Oh come on now! Admit it! Why should you want to free that awful man? Just think of all the people in the building, what would have happened —"

"If I were more experienced, I would have thought of something. I might have overlooked something — Oh, I guess you're right, Monica. You can't win them all, and in this particular job you can't even win most of them, be-

142

cause most of them *are* guilty. But Christ, twenty years! And suppose he's innocent and I didn't bring it out." I drove the car into one of the parking places along the river and stopped.

She sat there and looked at me and smiled and then I just couldn't stand it any more. I said the hell with it and slid across the seat and put my arms around her and kissed her on the mouth.

"No!" She turned her face, but I held her fast. My face was in her hair, and the smell of it drove me wild.

"Oh please don't fight me Monica, I'm so crazy for you . . ." Our bodies rocked together as she squirmed and I tried to press her back. A button on her blouse popped. "Oh, for heaven's sake!" she gasped. "Please *don't,* Ben, please — Oh, my God!"

Something crashed against the roof of the car; I whirled around and was face to face with a tough-looking young Fairmount Park Guard.

"Step outa the car, Mac. Keep your hands away from your body." He carried a nightstick in his hand. His own car was stopped directly behind mine.

I opened the door and got out. Monica, her face flushed, pulled her skirt down and blew hair out of her eyes.

"Let's see your driver's license and owner's card," he said. My hands were shaking as I took them out of my wallet. He regarded them, solemnly chewing his gum.

Then he stooped to peer into the car. "You all right, lady?"

"Oh yes. Yes. Thank you." She was looking down, trying to pull her blouse together.

"You want to prefer charges?"

"What?" She looked up again.

"Do you want him to arrest me?" I said.

"You shut up," said the Park Guard.

"Oh my God, no! No, no, he was not . . . No, it is

143

quite all right, thank you." She looked at her watch. "It is time for me to go home now."

"All right, take her home, Mac. And next time *stay* at home for this kind of a party." He handed me my cards, climbed back into his own car, and backed out of the parking lot.

We looked at each other.

Suddenly Monica began to shriek with laughter. "Oh Ben, Ben, you were so funny . . . You looked like a little boy caught in the kitchen . . . Oh, oh . . ." She was shaking with laughter.

"Well, I'm glad you think it's so damn funny."

"Oh Ben, he wanted to arrest you! For attacking me! And then — and then —" She had to stop to catch her breath. "And then tomorrow, you could defend *yourself* before the judge!" She grabbed my arm and collapsed in a gale of laughter.

"Jesus, what a sense of humor!" I turned the car around and drove toward the city. Out on the Schuylkill, a couple of shells were sweeping upstream and a man in the coach's launch was yelling through his megaphone. The sun sparkled on the water.

"Don't be so serious, Ben." She was still close beside me, holding my arm. "That was all so silly, it was a joke wasn't it? Please smile now, Ben."

I tried.

"All right, that's better. Now let me tell you something: I am really too old for this sort of thing, you know — sitting around in cars and wrestling and kissing — what is the word? There is an expression —"

"Necking," I said sullenly.

"Necking, yes. I am too old to be in cars, necking." She took out her purse, extracted her compact and replaced her lipstick carefully. Then she began to comb her hair. "You know if I were free, and if I felt that way about you, Ben — Well, I would just go to bed with you. You know?"

She turned to look at me. "But I am not free, and I cannot sit around in the car wrestling and fighting with you. Do you understand that?"

I said I did.

"No, not that way. Not angry. Because otherwise I cannot see you again."

I sighed. "It won't happen again, Monica."

"Please don't be angry, Ben. This is so silly of you. You must have many many other girls, girls your own age, American girls —"

"Never mind, Monica. There isn't any logic to this kind of thing and you know it. You feel something or you don't, and you just don't."

There wasn't much to say after that. When I stopped the car in front of the Connaught she opened the door and looked at me.

"Do you want to see me tomorrow?"

"Yes, of course I do, Monica."

"I have a class in the morning, but I will meet you in that bar. One o'clock?"

"One o'clock."

She stepped out and slammed the door. I drove the car around to the garage and walked back to the Defender office with my files. Again I wanted to sit on a bench in Rittenhouse Square and watch her door, and again there wasn't time. It was almost five.

"Say, your lunches are getting longer and longer," said Marvin Gold as I walked into his office. He was perfectly right, so I had to mumble something about an important meeting . . .

"Important meeting!" Marvin chortled. "I'll bet it was important. What's the matter, does her husband come home at night? Hey, remember those important meetings with the girl in the hoagie store by the Law School? You used to come back to the library smelling like salami —"

"Listen, do you want a report on my arson case?"

"Yes, *sir*. Pardon me!" Now I had hurt his feelings, but I just wasn't in the mood for this. We went over the case, which Marvin had predicted I would lose. He thought the man was guilty too. He didn't even think the sentence was too harsh. We wrote up the report and put the file away, and then he gave me the cases for Friday. I took them back to my room and worked over them all evening, trying to blot out every thought of Monica, and almost succeeding. I dreamed about her though, and I woke up before dawn, frustrated and sweating. I drank some Scotch and took a shower and went back to sleep, and when I woke up it was after nine o'clock. I took a taxi to City Hall, consumed a doughnut and two cups of coffee, and walked into four fifty-three just as Judge Stellwagon came out of the robing room.

That was quite a morning. I was sorry that Monica wasn't there to see me. I guess it was really the cases, but somehow I seemed to be inspired. Everything Willis Donahue tried went wrong; everything I did went right. His witnesses got mixed up and said all the wrong things; my witnesses went down the line. All his indictments seemed to be drawn up wrong; they didn't fit the facts, and the Judge had to keep granting my demurrers, meaning the defendants were freed. Every time I made an objection I was right and the Judge had to sustain me; Willis's objections began to sound like wails of protest.

"That's the Commonwealth's case, your Honor."

"Well, your Honor, I demur to the indictment. There was no showing of intent at the time of entry, so that he hasn't made out a burglary, sir —"

"Demurrer sustained. Say, Mr. Donahue, I've got a suggestion."

"Yes sir?"

"Why don't you offer friend Butler here a job in the D.A.'s office."

146

"I'll speak to the District Attorney about that, Judge Stellwagon."

"Yeah, you do that. What a morning! Talk about general jail delivery! By the time the Public Defender gets through around here, we won't *need* any jails. Well, the mayor will like that." Laughter in the courtroom.

"All right, call the next case."

"That's the list, your Honor."

"That's the list? Before twelve o'clock? Will wonders never cease . . . Have a nice weekend, gentlemen."

"ALL RISE, PLEASE . . ."

By the time Monica arrived at McGintey's I had finished two drinks and was beginning on the third.

"You look a little more cheerful today," she said.

"I really think maybe I'm good at this trial work."

She laughed. "Had you any doubt about that? Of course you are very good at it. That's obvious."

"I think maybe I want to keep doing it."

"Well, why not?" She took a sip of the beer the waiter had placed in front of her.

"I don't think they'll let me, at the firm. They've trained me for other things, things involving a lot of money. In fact, whenever I finish a job I've got to present something called a 'No Litigation Certificate.' My job is really keeping people *out* of court."

Monica shrugged. "Get another job."

Another job? Even in the worst drudging days under Leslie Patch that idea had never entered my head. Through all the long years of scholarship applications and examinations and after-school jobs, a position with Conyers & Dean was the target, the goal, the dream, the key that would open the door to security and a place in the world and for once, enough money. I'll never forget my mother's expression when I showed her the letter from Boyle. I

147

thought of the big library and the rows of books and the portraits looking down, and the way people react when you tell them where you work. Another job?

That afternoon she wanted to see an exhibit of Indonesian carvings at the University Museum, so I drove her out to West Philadelphia and followed her past rows of fierce grimacing masks and funny little black women and many different animals carved from exotic woods. When we came to a yard-long shark, exquisitely carved of teak, Monica took a pad from her purse and began to sketch. I walked slowly to the other end of the long gallery and then turned around. The afternoon sun was streaming in through the high windows, cutting shafts through the dusty air. Monica stood all alone, leaning against the wall, her eyes fixed upon her pad, her pencil moving steadily. What do you do when you just can't have something you want? She was right; I wasn't used to it. I didn't know what to do. Do you just keep hammering away, or do you give up?

When she was finished she seemed to emerge from a trance. Looking around, she saw me at the other end of the hall. She smiled and waved her pad and came toward me. What can you do? Can you put your foot through a glass case containing a carved Javanese coffin?

"You are looking so angry again," she said. "I thought you were happy today?"

"I'm subject to moods. Monica, I've got to take you home a little early today. We're having an office dinner and I've got to drive out to my mother's and get my tuxedo."

"That's all right. I have seen enough now. Aren't they amazing carvings?"

I drove her back to Rittenhouse Square.

"Monica, tomorrow is Saturday, and I'm free all day —"

"Oh, Ben —" She put her hand on my arm.

"He's free on Saturdays too, is he?"

"Not always."

"Not always, but tomorrow he's free. Okay. Good-bye, Monica."

"Good-bye, Ben. Thank you for taking me to the Museum, and —" she stopped.

"What's the matter?"

She had opened the door, but was still sitting there, looking at me.

"What's wrong, Monica?"

She made up her mind. "Ben, this is really good-bye. I will be gone next week. I have enjoyed *very* much being with you. And I wish you good luck and success." She got out of the car.

"Monica!" I started to get out.

"And many girl friends! No, please don't get out, it's better this way. Good-bye, Ben. If you ever come to Innsbruck, please visit me!" She turned and ran into the Connaught.

I had met her on Sunday and lost her on Friday. It seemed hard to believe, but there was nothing I could do about it, so I put the car in gear and drove away.

chapter 14

"Well hel-*lo*, dearie, I'm so glad to . . . see . . . you."
My mother was panting a little as she came to the top of
the stairs. My mother smokes too much, but what are you
going to do? "I saw the car in the drive — I've just been
at the Orchestra with Edna . . . What's the matter, dear, are
you sick?"

"No, I'm fine, Mother."

"Can you stay for supper? Gloria's here —"

"Thanks, Ma, I've just come for my dinner jacket,
there's an office thing tonight —"

"Well, I hope it's in your closet, I think I just had
it cleaned . . ."

"Yes, it's right there, I'm just putting my shoes in a
bag."

"Ben, why don't you change here and have a drink
with me?"

I looked at my watch. "Okay, Ma. Sure, I'd like that.
I'll get ready and be down in a few minutes."

I went back into my room and got undressed and went
into my bathroom and started to shave. I guess it is ex-
travagant for a person on my salary to keep a room in town
when I could live in perfect comfort at home, free. But
I've seen what happens to people who keep on living with

their mothers because it's so convenient. And my mother isn't lonely, at least most of the time, I think. When my father was killed, she found herself with a six-year-old boy and practically no money. First she got a job as a secretary in the bank where my father had worked, and at nights she studied investments and then she passed her examination and became one of the first women brokers in town. She began selling mutual funds when they were beginning to boom, and gradually she built up a following of lady investors — mostly widows and divorced women. When my grandmother died, my mother took the insurance money and put it all into Xerox stock, which is now worth fifty or sixty times what she paid for it. She says she won't be a burden to me, anyway. But during the years I was in school and college, she must have wondered if she would make it.

I think she could live on her income now, but she still goes to her office every day. Her ladies are always writing letters or coming in to see her. "Half of them haven't any investment problems, really," she says. "They're just lonely and want somebody to talk to, and those stupid men in the banks and the law firms can't understand that, they get impatient, so these girls just come to me, because I'll listen to them." So her days are busy, and she has many friends who come in the evenings to play bridge with her.

I took a shower and put on the dinner clothes and went downstairs. My mother was sitting on the couch beside the fireplace, sipping a martini and reading the *Bulletin*. My Scotch-on-the-rocks was ready on the bookshelf beside the red leather armchair.

She smiled and put down the paper. "Well, tell me all about your exciting criminal cases."

I told her a couple of stories. "Ma, I'm good at it. I like it."

"Well, that's fine, but it won't help you much at C & D, will it?"

"No."

"Ben, you don't look very well. I think this work is a strain on you."

"Mmm. Maybe so."

My mother lighted another cigarette. "How is Mrs. Rochester?"

I raised my eyebrows.

"Edna said she saw you at the Orchestra last Friday."

"Oh. Well, you see, we don't have trials in the afternoons, usually, and —"

"Dearie, I'm sure you know what's right, but there must have been lots of Conyers & Dean wives who saw you there last week, and for a boy your age to be going to the Orchestra in the afternoon — especially while their own husbands are at the office —"

"Ma, I'm up every night till midnight, getting my cases ready."

"All right, Ben, I know, but we worked *so* hard to get you into this position and I just don't want to see you make mistakes . . . Oh, nuts!" She set her glass down with a bang. "Listen to me, I sound like some mother in a soap opera. What's happening to me? You do what you want with your life, what difference does it make. Fix me another drink, please."

I carried our glasses out into the pantry. The smell of frying chicken came from the kitchen.

"Hello, Gloria, how are you?"

"Just fine, thanks, Mr. Butler. You're not staying for dinner?"

"I can't thanks, Gloria."

"The ice is already in the bucket by the sink."

"Okay, thank you." I mixed a stiff martini and brought it back into the living room.

"Aren't you having another?" asked my mother.

"I guess not, Ma. We'll be drinking for an hour before dinner."

152

My mother touched her glass to her lips. "Um, that's much better than I make them. Well, tell me about Mrs. Rochester."

"What do you want me to tell you?"

"Well, where did you meet her?"

"She's Ordway Smith's sister-in-law; I met her there at a dinner party."

"Oh yes, of course." My mother took another drink and regarded the blank fire screen between us. I have never found it hard to read her mind. She had looked up Sally Rochester and made inquiries, and I knew what was coming. "She's a Warren, you know. Her aunt was that Miss Warren, who had that place out in Devon next to Edna's mother's place, and she raised Irish setters. Her picture was in the paper all the time. But then she died and the place was sold . . ."

It can't have been easy for my mother. She grew up in Altoona, a railroad town in central Pennsylvania. Her family has been there for four generations. They aren't rich, but everybody knows them; they are doctors and lawyers and small businessmen. She was sent to the University of Pennsylvania, where she met and fell in love with a senior at the Wharton School. My father was an orphan, the son of a West Philadelphia doctor, who was in college on a senatorial scholarship. He didn't have a cent, but he did have a job lined up at the William Penn Trust Company, which was pretty good considering this was in 1935. At Christmas vacation he took the train to Altoona and asked her father for her hand, and they were married after his graduation that June. By the time the war began, I was four years old, my father was an assistant vice-president, and we had just moved from the apartment in West Philadelphia to the half-timbered cottage in Wynnewood. My mother began to live the life she had been led to expect, the quiet but steady rise through the upper middle class on the Main Line: doctors, lawyers, bank executives; the

Paoli Local; the Cricket Club; dinner parties followed by
bridge; street lights blurred by the smoke of leaf fires;
Community Chest drives; football games at Franklin Field,
with the sea of handkerchiefs moving slowly back and forth
("Hurrah . . . for . . . the Re-head and the Blue!") — and
then one day we watched the Twenty-eighth Division parad-
ing down the Parkway. My father came home a couple of
times, from Indiantown Gap and other places. I remember
him in his uniform; he gave me his brass second lieutenant's
bars when he was promoted, and I wore them on my snow-
suit. One day he took me for a walk in the rain, and we
threw empty beer bottles in the river. I wish I could remember more about him, but we have a lot of pictures
that I look at sometimes. Two years later he was dead. We
received a lot of letters from men in his company and from
his battalion commander, and several medals.

My mother could have gone back to Altoona, but her
parents had also died, there was little money, and I guess
she didn't want to be patronized by her sisters-in-law. And
maybe she had grown accustomed to the city. At any rate,
the easy matronly life was over: she had a house and a
little boy and with no family to fall back on she had to go
to work. I was sent to the public school; mother rode the
train into town every day and followed the lives of her
former friends in the society pages.

It came out all right in the end. Mother turned herself
into a successful broker, while I sweated for good grades
and scholarships ("WAR HERO'S SON WINS LEGION PRIZE"). I
made it through college and law school at Penn, and when I
got the job with Conyers & Dean, my mother knew that she
had made it. There was just one more thing.

". . . that Rochester boy, her first husband, I gather he
must have been a complete stinker. He ran off with his
secretary and left her with two little children. Is that
right?"

154

I nodded and sipped my Scotch.

"I don't think the Warrens, that branch, have a whole lot of money left, they were very badly hurt in the Depression, but the Rochesters, that's another story. Wouldn't there have to be some settlement? I mean a man like that, he can't just desert his family without —"

"I'm sure she's well provided for, Ma. Ordway Smith represented her."

"Oh well," she said. "Then you can look it up in the office files, can't you?" She was perfectly serious.

"Honestly, Mother, sometimes I wonder about you!"

"Well don't be silly, if you're interested in her it would be perfectly natural —"

"Who said I was interested in her?"

"Dearie, you wouldn't bridle like that if you weren't, but never mind about the money. Why don't you bring her over for dinner some night? Next Friday, for instance — Gloria will be here anyway, and —"

"Mother, get the wedding bells out of your head, won't you please?" It was time to go and I stood up. "I'm perfectly happy in my single state, I've been on two dates with this girl, she's a very nice girl —"

"I didn't say a *word!*"

"— and while I know you've only got my interests at heart —"

"Oh Ben, I really do. A lot of old widows with only one son would cling to him and try to keep the other women off. I've never done that, much as I may have wanted to, because I hate these prissy mother-ridden old bachelors like — Oh well, you know lots of them, they've been turned into old ladies themselves!"

I was startled by her vehemence. We have never talked about this sort of thing before. "Gee, Mother —"

She wasn't through. "I've done just the opposite. I've sat back and watched you bowl over one poor woman

155

after another, ever since you were seventeen, and don't think I don't know why the Emersons' nursemaid went back to Sweden —"

"Mother!"

"— one sitting duck after another, and in a way I thought it was good for you, but I'm beginning to get worried about it now, Ben. I don't think you really care about them any more, they're nothing but scores to you —"

"You really are exaggerating."

"No, I'm just telling the truth, dear. One conquest after another, one cast-aside after another — it's not the way to live, the way to be happy. You've got to settle down, Ben."

"Okay, Ma, I'll give it some serious thought, but right now I've got to drive into town. I'm late." I leaned over to kiss her cheek and she held my hand for a moment.

"I'm sorry I made such a scene. But you're all I've got and I just want you to be happy. You know?"

"Sure, Ma. Don't worry, when the right one comes along, you'll be the first one to know. Okay?"

She shook her head and then she stood up to follow me into the hall. "I hope you'll recognize the right one when you meet her. It seems to me there've been so many . . . Oh well enough of that. You're having dinner with me on your birthday, aren't you?"

"Sure, Ma. Don't I always?"

"And you don't want to bring Mrs. Rochester?"

"No . . . I guess not."

"Too much of a commitment?"

"Good night, Ma. Stop worrying."

"Good night, dear. Have fun." She closed the door and I walked to my car.

chapter 15

I was late, and when I got there the party was in full swing. Several banquet tables were set up in the big penthouse dining room of the Club, and behind the bar three white-jacketed stewards were frantically mixing drinks. The partners and associates of Conyers & Dean were packed three deep along the bar or carrying their glasses through the open doors to the terrace, which looked out into tree-tops of Rittenhouse Square.

Randy Kellerman and Sam Atwater turned away from the bar and opened a slot for me.

"Well, it's our man in City Hall," shouted Sam.

Patterson Fox came up behind me and put his hand on my shoulder. "The greatest criminal lawyer since Chippy Patterson, that's what we hear."

"George, let's have a Scotch-on-the-rocks for the Great Mouthpiece," somebody called, and a drink came back over several heads.

I found myself in the middle of a noisy group: Tommy Jones and Millard and Lansing Merrit, and Fox and Randy and Atwater . . . They were all talking at once.

"What's the matter with you guys?"

"We hear you're the boy wonder of the criminal courts," said Randy.

"Is it true that they like you so much they won't let you go?" somebody asked.

"I heard you got a hundred dollar call girl acquitted," said Patterson Fox.

"Oh for God's sake —"

"Hey, Ben," said Randy Kellerman, "Mary Atwater saw you at the Art Museum with a beautiful lady. Were you investigating one of your cases?" There was a roar of laughter.

"You people are obviously jealous —"

"Well, well, how's the defender of the downtrodden?" Ellsworth Boyle came through the crowd with his hand outstretched. The others fell back a little.

"I'm fine, sir. Enjoying the experience very much."

"So I hear. Tried to get you back to help out with this Hammond Soap thing and Walter Simon nearly bit my head off. A dedicated man, Walter. Being mentioned for the vacancy on Number Four Court. Well anyway, I got the impression that they're pleased with you over there, and of course that's very gratifying. What are you drinking there? — George, let's have a Scotch-on-the-rocks and a Scotch-and-water — As a matter of fact, Randy Kellerman should be able to cope with those debentures — Evening, Alfred, I called to see if you'd like to walk up the street with me —"

"Thank you, Ellsworth," said Mr. Dennison. "I snuck out a little early so that I could have a nap. Otherwise I get so damn sleepy in the evening. Well, young Butler, isn't it? What are you doing these days?"

"Why, I'm at the Defender this month, Mr. Dennison."

"Oh yes, yes, of course, slipped my mind. Did you know that I was one of the founders?"

"Oh, were you, Mr. Dennison?"

"Yes, indeed. Yes, indeed. I remember it very distinctly. We had the first meeting in David Harding's office, that was in the old Balz Building, northwest corner of Broad and Chestnut — no, I guess it must have been the

158

north*east* corner — of course that was before they merged with, that is, David's *firm* merged with the Willingham office, David himself went on the bench, as you know —"

"Mr. Dennison, may I get you a drink?"

"Well, okay, but just a finger of brandy please, and a lot of ice and water on top of it. I'll be out there on the terrace. Such a beautiful evening."

"Mr. Butler, in the flesh! We've missed your cheery face around the office."

"Hi, Ordway, thanks very much for getting the invitation to me."

"Not at all, delighted to see you. We hear you have the District Attorney's office pretty well on the ropes."

"I don't know where all these stories have been coming from. I'm just doing the regular routine work over there —"

Ordway took my arm. "Ben, step over this way a minute, will you please. Want to talk to you about something."

Apprehensively I followed him to the other end of the terrace.

"Want to talk to you about Pat Forrester," said Ordway, lighting a cigarette and leaning his elbows on the parapet. "Pat hasn't been at all well for the last few weeks. Don't know exactly what it is, guess maybe it's a combination of things, certain strains he's been under, but in any case it's beginning to cause some problems. Maybe you've heard about that Christawful mess with the Hammond Soap debentures —"

"Yes, I heard about it, Ordway."

"Well, I'm not sure if that was the result of other troubles or whether it was just another straw on the camel's back, but in any case he's not in good shape. Been acting odd around the office, been drinking a lot, and sometimes he just hasn't been showing up at all. I gather he's been having some trouble with Sheila, too." He paused for a moment. "Ben, I'm telling you all this because I think you like Pat a lot, don't you?"

"Yes, I do, Ordway."

"Well, I do too, and we've both got to help him. When you come back to the office next month you'll be working right with him, and you'd notice all this immediately, so I don't see any reason not to give it to you straight right now. We're going to have to find out what the trouble is, and we're going to try to fix it. But anyway, I want you to keep your eye on him a little tonight. He was sitting over there all by himself knocking back an awful lot of booze. I already offered to drive him home, it's right on my way, of course, but he gave me some dumb excuse, so I don't know what he's got on his mind. You live right around here somewhere, don't you?"

"Yes, right over on Spruce Street."

"All right, well, just sort of keep an eye on him will you?"

"I sure will, Ordway. Thanks for telling me all this."

"Okay, Ben. Let's go join the others. We'll be sitting down pretty soon."

In the center of the crowd I came face to face with Randy Kellerman again:

"Hey, Ben, you going to the June Ball tomorrow night?"

"June Ball? Not that I know of."

"I heard Sally Rochester was going to ask you. Roseann and I are at the same table, with Ordway and Marion —"

I hoped I wasn't in trouble with Marion Smith. I really should have called Sally back. "I guess she got somebody else, Randy."

"Okay, but you're coming to the softball game on Sunday, aren't you?"

160

I looked blank.

"Oh Lord, didn't you get that memo either? We're playing the Openshaw firm at Mr. Boyle's place. Sunday afternoon at three. You'll be there, won't you? They've got this guy Harris who pitched on the varsity at Princeton, last year they beat us twelve nothing, and they've beaten Pepper and Ballard this year . . ."

"I'm no good, Randy."

"Sure you are, when you connect you can put it over the treetops."

"*When* I connect." These softball games are played in a desultory fashion by the biggest law firms in town whenever the more athletic associates can recruit a team. Usually the event becomes a raucous picnic, with cocktails rapidly gaining over baseball. Some of the older men like to play too, and one of them occasionally provides a spacious lawn and a swimming pool.

"All right, coach, I'll try to do my share," I said.

"Attaboy. Sunday at three."

We turned away from each other.

Down at the other end of the bar Pat Forrester was standing by himself, grimly examining his glass. He looked up at me.

"Well! The tiger of the criminal courts. How's it going, Ben?"

"Just fine thanks, Pat. I'm enjoying it very much."

"So I hear. That courtroom business really goes to your head, doesn't it? Maybe you won't want to come back to the trust indentures next month."

"I seem to be pretty good at this trial work, Pat. Do you think they might let me —"

"At C & D? What kind of trial work have we got? Antitrust cases? Two years of depositions and memos of law and counterpleadings, file cabinets full of statistics about soap flake sales in supermarkets or something, and then a six month trial? Ask your friend Atwater. You'll wish you were back in the stock and bond business." His words were beginning to slur. He put his glass to his lips and took a long drink. "And God knows we can use some help." He put the glass down, "Can we have another round down here please, George?"

"All right fellows," shouted Ellsworth Boyle, "I think we can sit down now."

Ordway Smith came down the bar. "Okay, Pat, will you and Ben sit down at the other end of that table, please? Over there with Leslie Patch, and Mr. Dennison, you're up there at the other end, sir, with Ellsworth — Harry, let's not have all the younger men down at that other table, tell some of them to come up here, will you?"

"That's our boy," said Patrick Forrester, his chin resting in his hand. "A born leader if there ever was one. Hit me again please, George."

"Mr. Smith said to close the bar, Mr. Forrester. They're serving wine —"

"George!"

"Yes, sir. Right away, Mr. Forrester."

During dinner, Forrester, on my right, sat silent and morose, while Leslie Patch regaled our end of the table with every detail of a complex proceeding before the Zoning Board. Some people don't realize that other people, even other lawyers, don't want to hear about every fact and every applicable decision and who said what to whom at every stage of every conference. I couldn't help contrasting this boring monologue with Ordway Smith's witty dissection of the Pemberton case, two weeks ago. I tried to pay attention to Leslie Patch while watching Forrester consume his Scotch and then three glasses of claret.

Not until the waiters were passing the ice cream did Leslie Patch hear the sound of his own voice.

"Well — ah, I guess that's about all there is to tell about the Nicholson matter. What have you other fellows been up to?"

Silence. Apparently the others' minds had drifted off somewhere. He tried again: "Say, Pat," he said, leaning forward to look past me, his heavy glasses flashing in the candlelight, "I'm delighted to hear you're going to take a vacation. Where are you going?"

"Haven't decided yet," said Forrester, fingering his empty wine glass.

"Is Sheila going with you?"

"No."

It was so awkward that I felt I had to say something. "I'm glad to hear you're going to get a rest, Pat. When do you leave?"

"Next week. Monday, maybe."

"That's great, Pat. How long will you be gone?"

"I don't know exactly. Several weeks." Then, as if he could read my mind. "Phil Rieger is taking over the Hammond Soap Debentures. Maybe you can help him when you get back. And Randy's familiar with the deal; you won't have any trouble."

Should I say I was sorry that issue had blown up? Fortunately Ordway Smith began to bang on a glass with his spoon, the room quieted down, and Ellsworth Boyle rose to his feet.

Well, fellows, here we were again. Getting bigger all the time, getting harder and harder to retain that elusive small-firm atmosphere; just realized that he hadn't been down on the twenty-ninth floor for six months; makes it all the more important that we get together often for occasions like this just to see each other over a friendly glass and talk; we're all especially grateful to Ordway for organizing this resplendent feast. We're not having any shoptalk

163

or any departmental reports tonight; thought it would be fun to let Mr. Dennison tell us some stories about the old days in the firm, the old days with Judge Conyers and Mr. Dean.

"Oh my God," said Patrick Forrester under his breath. I knew what he meant. If I had heard these stories before, how many times must he have heard them?

Everyone applauded happily, and Mr. Dennison, his cheeks flushed from the brandy, got to his feet and stood behind his chair, holding tight to the back of it and beaming out over the rows of faces.

"Well, here we are again," he said. "It never ceases to amaze me how big we've become. How many are there now, Ellsworth?"

Boyle had to glance over at Ordway Smith, who held up one hand outstretched and the thumb of the other hand.

"Sixty lawyers, Alfred," said Boyle.

"Are you sure?" asked Mr. Dennison. There was a ripple of laughter. "The managing partner thinks we have sixty lawyers. When I joined the office we had six — and they called us a big firm! At that time our offices were in the old West End Trust Building on South Penn Square, that's where the Girard Trust is now." The old man paused to wipe his mouth with a napkin, took a deep breath, and let himself glide into the past. He talked about his salary — "less than you fellows spend for a good lunch today" — and his colleagues who were all dead now, about his classmates at the University of Pennsylvania and his professors and the judges before whom he tried his first cases and the mortgage problems of the Rapid Transit Company and finally, as always, about his hero, the great Frederick Hamilton Dean.

We smoked and shifted in our seats and watched the night fall beyond the tall windows. Familiar as these stories were, I rather liked them. They conjured up a city I never knew: a city full of horse carriages and trolley cars and men wearing black suits and straw hats; a grimy city in which the steam locomotives came chuffing along the Chinese Wall all the way in to Broad Street Station and people drank a lot of beer and watched Connie Mack's Athletics; a city of coal smoke and bricks and fat arrogant men with moustaches and cigars; a city that was run from leather armchairs at the Union League . . .

"Now at this particular time," Mr. Dennison was saying, "Frederick Dean was becoming recognized as the most effective appellate lawyer in the city. Maybe in the entire Commonwealth — yes, I would say that was true. He was simply swamped with cases, and he found that he did not have time to do his own research —"

"— and that was our job," mumbled Patrick Forrester.

"— and that was our job," said Mr. Dennison. "Many's the night I worked past midnight with some of the others — sometimes with Judge Conyers, sometimes with young Lawrence Pool — he died on the Mexican Border, a tragic loss — and then we'd rush out copy to the printers and watch them set the type, and then we'd have to check the proofs, and then maybe we'd get time for a catnap before we had to deliver the printed briefs to the Supreme Court."

Mr. Dennison paused to drink from his water glass.

"No time to read briefs," said Forrester. Down at our end a few heads turned, but the old man was listening to other voices.

"Frequently Mr. Dean would not have time to *read* these briefs of ours," he explained, putting down his glass. "Of course, he might have seen a draft, but usually he knew the law of the case so well that he didn't always bother to study our masterpieces before he began his oral presentation to the Court. On one occasion —"

"Disastrous result," said Forrester thickly.

"Shut up, Pat!" whispered Leslie Patch behind my back.

"— this nearly led to a disastrous result," Mr. Dennison went on. "When Mr. Dean began to address the Court,

165

Judge Conyers and I could hardly believe our ears. Mr. Dean was presenting the case for the appellant, apparently having forgotten that we represented the *appellee!*"

Most of us managed to produce the expected laughter.

"Yes, it's funny now, after all these years, but I assure you that it wasn't a bit funny at the time. What should we do? I looked at Judge Conyers, who was of course far senior to me —"

"Coattails," said Patrick Forrester. At the other end of the room, Ellsworth Boyle leaned forward and glared in our direction.

"You fellows heard this story?" Mr. Dennison sensed that attention was shifting somewhere —

"No, no," said several voices.

"Go ahead, Alfred," boomed Ellsworth Boyle. "What happened then?"

"Well!" Mr. Dennison licked his lips. "Conyers finally screwed up his courage and scuttled up behind Mr. Dean and pulled at his coattails. Mr. Dean leaned down and Conyers — who was a much smaller man, as some of you will recall — Conyers whispered in his ear and came back to his seat. Whereupon Mr. Dean *slapped* our brief down on the lectern" — Mr. Dennison swung his arm to show how Mr. Dean had slapped the brief — "and said, 'And that, may it please the Court, is —' "

"All that can be said for my opponent's case." Patrick Forrester's head was in his hands, but his tired voice could be heard all over the silent room.

The color left Mr. Dennison's face. "Well, I guess I have told this one before . . ."

Ordway Smith and Ellsworth Boyle were on their feet applauding and the rest of us rose too, amid a great clatter of chairs. "A marvelous story, Alfred," I could hear Boyle shouting. "A real classic —"

I couldn't look at Forrester, who was standing shakily beside me.

166

There was movement away from the tables.

"For Christ's sake, Pat!" Leslie Patch pushed his way past me, and I could see Ordway Smith approaching from the other side. Moving fast, I extricated myself and joined the crowd streaming toward the bar.

"*Mama mia!*" said Randy Kellerman, mopping his brow. "All that excitement on a full stomach!"

"Some people around here are losing their marbles," said Patterson Fox.

"A disgusting performance," said his father. "There's never an excuse for rudeness. Come on, you've had enough to drink, I want you to drive me home."

Sam Atwater spoke into my ear. "Not a thing the matter with him. No *sir!* The man's at the top of his form."

I turned away, but the voices were everywhere: "Well, he must have heard that story twenty times, don't you think?" . . . "So what? Is that any reason to hurt the old man's feelings? It was grotesque . . ." "Two Scotch-and-water, George. Light ones, please." . . . "Ben, will we see you at the June Ball?" . . . "Hell yes, somebody said he was drunk after lunch on Wednesday, right in the office." . . . "Did he leave?" . . . "I think Ordway's gone to look for him." . . . "Did Boyle say anything to him?" . . . "Any brandy back there, George?"

The toilet was full of people, but Forrester was not among them. I ran down the steps to the second floor. Right off the passage there is this little curtained-off place where you can take a leak. As I turned the corner I saw Ordway Smith disappear through the curtain.

"Pat, are you all right?" I heard him ask.

Forrester said something, but I couldn't hear it. There was a long silence. Then Ordway said: "Pat, you know what I mean. Are you *all right?* You and I are going to run this firm, aren't we?"

"You're going to run it, hotshot."

"What about you?"

167

No reply.

"Pat?"

"Ordway, you know the answer. I'm just another good technician. You can buy all the technicians you need."

"What's wrong with you, Pat?" Ordway sounded exasperated. "Why, out at Schuylkill Steel, Vernon Benson won't make a move without you, and he'll be the president next year, and look at Angus MacDonald at the William Penn — Listen, how's your book coming?"

"It isn't," said Forrester.

"Why not? No time?"

"No time, no energy."

"Pat, you've just overworked yourself. You've been pushing too hard and you're pooped and you're showing it, that's all. Take Sheila and get in the car and go up to Nantucket or someplace for a while."

"She can't go," said Forrester. "The children are still in school."

"Well, go by yourself," said Ordway. "Just take off, get lost, do nothing for a couple of weeks. Sleep twelve hours every night. You'll come back a new man."

"Okay, Ordway," said Forrester quietly.

"Come on, let me take you home now."

"No thanks, Ordway. I'm not ready to go home yet. I'll take the train."

"But I'm going right by —"

"No thanks. Really."

The curtain stirred. "Well . . . Okay then. Take it easy, will you, Pat? We all need you." Ordway stepped out and as he turned the corner, he saw me. If he cared that I had been listening, he didn't show it. "Have you got your car handy? I think you'd better stick around and look after him."

I nodded. He clapped me on the shoulder and went upstairs.

A moment later Forrester stepped past the curtain.

168

He was pale, but he smiled when he saw me standing there. "Corporal of the Guard, night relief? I guess I'd better go back up and say something to Mr. Dennison."

I told him that Boyle had already taken Mr. Dennison home.

"All right then," he said. "Let's go outside and get some air."

Hands in our pockets, we strolled out of the Club, across Walnut Street, and into the warm leafy summer night. Rittenhouse Square was full of people: old men and women on the benches, talking or trying to read newspapers by the dim streetlights; giggling clusters of fairies; part-time exotics with sunglasses and sandals and beards. Behind the murmur of voices you could hear a ball game coming over a transistor radio, and somebody idly strumming a guitar. Heads turned to follow us; we were conspicuous in our black dinner jackets. Forrester didn't notice it. I spotted an empty bench and we sat down.

We sat there in silence for a long time. Forrester smoked a cigarette, and when he finished, flipped the glowing butt across the walkway. "We few, we happy few, we band of brothers," he declaimed. "What are all the brothers saying?"

"About what, Pat?"

"About that drunken lout who hurt the feelings of a sweet old man and made an ass of himself to boot."

"I guess they all know that you drank too much. And that you've overworked yourself."

"They all know that, do they? Dear old C & D, dear old stories, dear old brothers in their dear old tuxedos."

I had to change the subject. "Pat, I heard what you said to Ordway about a book. Are you a writer? I never knew —"

"Am I a writer? I'd like to know the answer to that one myself. Let's just say I'm a man who'd *like* to be a writer."

169

"Have you published anything?" I asked.

"Yeah, but it was a long time ago. Right after the war was over."

"You were in the war, weren't you, Pat? You must have been very young."

He nodded. "Pat Forrester, boy mule skinner. I ran away from home with a forged birth certificate and enlisted, and the next thing I knew I was in the Tenth Mountain Division. We were supposed to be ski troops, but there wasn't much skiing in Italy. We carried pack mules up and down the mountains. Oh, it was a mess."

"And that's when you started to write?"

"No, that was later," he said. "When the war ended in May of forty-five, our battalion fetched up at Bolzano, in the Italian Tyrol. By that time I had a commission, and they sent me up to an Intelligence outfit on the Austrian side of the Brenner Pass —"

The Brenner Pass? My heart stopped.

The Brenner Pass is near Innsbruck, isn't it? Of course it's a coincidence, I thought, looking up at the lighted windows of the apartment houses around the Square. There are four million people in this town; how many of them were in that neighborhood when the war ended . . .

". . . so we sat around up there with nothing to do," he was saying, "and I wrote some short stories and sent them to *Collier's* — you probably don't remember *Collier's* — and damn if they didn't print one of them, and then an agent in New York wrote to me and — well anyway, I published four stories that winter — all before I was nineteen. That's my literary career."

"Well, what happened then? Why didn't you keep it up?"

"I tried to, but it didn't work," he said. "I came home the next spring and went to Harvard on the GI Bill and took one of those accelerated courses, and then I went to law school."

"Why law school?" I asked.

Forrester laughed. "Good question. I don't know . . . In the first place I wanted to make some money. My father spent his life trying to interest high school kids in Shakespeare, we were always broke, and here was a chance to learn a profession at government expense. I did pretty well in the aptitude tests, and somehow the law seemed to be a good way to combine scholarship and money . . . I thought I could keep on writing in my spare time. Well, in the meantime I got married, we had a baby, we lived in two rooms in one of these veterans housing units — this is all way before your time, but there you are trying to study, trying to be at the top of your class, the baby's crying, your wife is out working to help make ends meet, the diapers are drying in the bathroom . . . I did submit a few stories, but they were all rejected, and then there just wasn't time any more. The competition in law school was terrific; they busted out half our first-year class, and I saw right away that the law isn't worth studying if you don't put your whole heart and soul into it — I guess you've learned that too — and I did pretty well, I got a job with C & D, and then of course I was already running in the next race, trying to make partner."

"So you stopped writing."

"Yeah." Forrester rubbed his hand over his eyes. I think he was embarrassed by his monologue, but I wanted to know more.

"But then you took it up again? You're working on something now?"

He nodded. "Trying to. Not very successfully."

"What got you started again?" I asked.

"A couple of things," said Forrester. He thought for a moment, and then he asked: "Have you read those lectures by Professor Llewellyn, *The Bramble Bush?*"

The Bramble Bush is one of those slim books they ask you to read before you start law school: What the Law

171

Is About; Law and Civilization; Beyond Bread and Butter; that sort of thing. I said yes, I'd read it.

Forrester let his head roll back against the wooden slats of the park bench. "All right, you remember he discusses what usually happens in our kind of practice: either people 'go under in the surge of the law factory to be thrown up after five years upon the beach, a dry smooth shining pebble' — I think that's how he puts it, or, he says, they salvage part of their soul for something else. Well, I realized that I wasn't salvaging a goddamned thing! I was running on a treadmill, getting out deals, drawing up reams of documents to secure other people's money, beating on you younger guys to do the same thing —" He sat up straight again and looked at me. "What's the point of it all? When they take me out and bury me, you know what I'll leave behind? A bookcase full of beautifully bound registration statements!"

"So you started writing again?"

"I tried to, but it just isn't working."

"You don't have enough time, do you?"

He nodded. "In the first place, I just can't find time to do the writing. You know how we operate: I'm on trips, or I have to stay at the office until ten o'clock or I have to be at the printer's, and when I do get home for dinner I have a couple of drinks and then later I'm too tired — well anyway, you just can't accomplish anything unless you produce a certain number of pages every day. And I'm just not doing it. But the other problem is that I never get a chance to think about what I'm trying to do. You create certain characters and a situation, and then you have to sit back and let them perform for you —" He stopped himself abruptly. "You must think I've lost my mind."

"No, I see what you mean, Pat. But isn't this getting away from what Llewellyn was driving at in *The Bramble Bush?* He didn't mean that a busy lawyer should write novels at night; I thought he meant that you should use

172

the law itself to salvage something, to use the law itself as a creative outlet —" Forrester was shaking his head, but I went on. "Yes, that *is* what he meant, Pat, you look at it again, and he's right. My God, just think what you could do if you applied your legal experience to produce something that would last . . . you know, they're talking about drawing up a new federal securities code, putting together all the statutes —"

Abruptly Forrester stood up. "You're a nice boy, Ben. I've got to go now. Catch my train."

I stood up too. His manner annoyed me. I meant what I was saying, I was trying to help him, so why should he slam the door in my face? As usual, my feelings showed.

"I'm sorry," said Forrester. "I know you're trying to be helpful, but it's more complicated than you think. I appreciate it just the same, though."

"Pat, I wish you'd let me drive you home. My car's just down the street —"

"No thanks, I'm okay now, really."

"Will you be in the office on Monday? I could come over after I finished in court —"

"No, I'm going away for a little while." Another thought struck him. "Ben, I'd like to tell you something. In this business, in these law firms, we take a lot for granted. If the younger men foul up or make mistakes, we chew them out or we get rid of them, but if they just do a good job all the time we think that's what they're paid for and we don't say anything. But —" Pause. He turned to think.

What brought all this on? Looking down at the pavement, he continued. "I just want you to know how much I've valued your — well, your reliability. You not only do first class work, but you do it on time and without supervision and that's what counts. And the others realize it too."

"It's very nice of you to tell me, Pat. I certainly appreciate —"

"Just one more thing." He seized my elbow, an uncharacteristic personal gesture. "Conyers & Dean is not the world. You think it is now, but it isn't. Don't limit your horizons too much, you're still very young. If you like trying criminal cases, why not do that for a while? You're not married, you're free as a bird. Do what you want to do, Ben. Enjoy your life and don't worry about the future."

He was saying good-bye.

"How long will you be gone, Pat?"

He frowned. "Don't know exactly, not long." He looked at his watch. "I've got to catch my train now. Good night, Ben, and thank you again. I'm sorry I ruined the party for you."

"Oh you didn't, Pat. Good night."

He punched my arm and walked off, toward the northeast corner of the Square, in the direction of Suburban Station. The Connaught was the other way, on Nineteenth Street. I walked a few steps in that direction until I reached the shed where the Park Guards have a little office. My heart was pounding. I stepped behind the hedge surrounding the shed, leaned against the painted boards, and waited. Of course, he might walk around the outside of the Square, where I wouldn't see him. Or he might just ride home on the train, and what would that prove, one way or another? Or the whole crazy idea might just be a sign that something was the matter with *me* . . .

I saw the white shirtfront before he was halfway back across the Square. He wasn't trying to hide or use the outside paths or anything; he marched straight across the Square, past the beatniks at the fish pond and past my hedge. At Nineteenth Street he waited for the light, then he crossed and disappeared through the revolving doors of the Rittenhouse Connaught.

174

chapter 16

It was almost noon when I woke up. That was all right, because I had really dosed myself: all that was left of my Red Label, two Doridens to knock me out, and three aspirins to kill the hangover. I lay there groggy and sweating, but I didn't have a headache. Carefully I stood up and opened the window, letting in the warm wind from the street and the noise of the traffic.

What in God's name will I do with myself, I thought, trying to keep my mind away from that part that hurt. I went into the bathroom and began to shave, and it was just the way you can't keep your tongue away from a sore tooth. It hurt. My hand was shaking. He went up there in his dinner jacket; did he keep a complete change of clothes . . . ? Well, why not? I threw my pajamas at the chair and stepped into the shower. Best thing is to find some work to do. As I turned on the cold water I remembered Marvin Gold. He was spending the weekend at the office, reorganizing the file system. Couldn't do it during the week, he said: too many telephone calls, too much commotion. He was the only one who knew which files could be thrown out and he was going to hole up all day Saturday and Sunday . . . All right.

I had breakfast at a Horn & Hardart, read the *Inquirer,* and walked up to Market Street.

The glass door at the Defender office was locked. Marvin opened it for me. He wore a Miami Beach sport shirt, pale blue slacks and sneakers.

"Well," he said. "What keeps the playboy of the western suburbs in town on a sunny Saturday afternoon?"

I said I didn't have a date and wanted to help him, so he led me into the file room. He had pulled out most of the drawers; bulging red folders were stacked on top of the cabinets, on every chair, on the floor, and even on the windowsills. It took Marvin ten minutes to explain his plan, and then we got to work.

I soon wished that I had put on sport clothes too. My hands became black from the dirty files, and then I smeared my shirt and my pants. Dust from the old papers made us sneeze. We worked all afternoon, but we didn't make much progress; Marvin had a good story about every other file: "Hey, listen to this, Ben. This was the craziest case you ever saw —" a man who took dirty movies of his wife and daughter; a little old lady who managed to carry twelve overcoats out of Wanamaker's; a bank teller who pointed out a stickup man in open court, only the man he pointed out was Judge Stellwagon's brother-in-law . . .

At seven o'clock I gave up. "Marvin, I've got to have a drink. This dust is getting into my throat now."

We sat up at the bar in McGintey's and dined on Scotch, snapper soup, Holland beer, hot roast beef sandwiches, and coffee. Then we strolled back to the office.

As we crossed Penn Square we had to sprint to avoid a police truck that came through the red light, its bell clanging. A moment later two patrol cars followed. We watched them screeching around City Hall, headed north on Broad Street.

"What's up?" asked the newsboy on the corner.

"Search me," said the traffic cop. "Here comes another one."

Outside the office door we heard the phone ringing.

176

"Who the hell —" said Marvin, unlocking the door. "Say, maybe they're calling the Defender *before* the cops get there, for a change." We laughed. Marvin reached for the telephone and I turned on the light.

"Defender Association . . . Oh, hello Pop . . . *What?*" His face was transformed His eyes had been merry; now they were hooded. He looked like another person.

"All right, yes, I'll be right up . . . Yes, I'm coming right now this minute . . . *No!* You can't do that, Pop! No, you can't do that, that's against the law . . . No, I'm telling you what the law is, are you a lawyer now? I am *telling* you! Listen, I'll be right up, don't do anything. Nothing! You do nothing, understand, Pop? . . . Pop, I'm going to hang up now. Just don't get in a fight — stay out of trouble! Please!"

Marvin put down the receiver, glanced hurriedly around the littered office and walked toward the door.

"Ben, I'm sorry, something's come up, I've got to go home."

"What is the trouble?"

"Oh just some trouble up there, where we live. Listen, will you turn out the lights? I'll have to come back to-morrow —"

"What the hell is going on, Marvin? You look sick." I followed him into the hall and closed the door.

He was ringing for the automatic elevator, banging uselessly on the button. "It — it isn't anything to do with you, Ben." He stopped. "There seems to be some trouble up there on Columbia Avenue."

"Columbia Avenue? Isn't that in the Negro area? Isn't that what they call the Jungle?"

"That's where we live. In the Jungle. We sell shoes to the natives." He still didn't sound right. I followed him into the little elevator and we sank slowly to the lobby.

"You mean the natives are restless?"

All I got for that was a mirthless, icy smile.

Out on the sidewalk, Marvin raised his arm, and a yellow taxi clattered over to us. "So long, Ben. I'm sorry —"

I grabbed his elbow. "Marvin, will you for Christ's sake tell me what's going on?" I could hear sirens wailing in the distance. Marvin put his hand on the cab's door handle, but he didn't open the door.

"There's a big riot going on up there." He spoke in a flat, quiet voice. "The Negroes are running wild and smashing the stores. They haven't come into our block yet, but my parents are scared." He looked down at the curb. "I've been expecting this for a long time."

"Listen, I'm coming with you."

"Ben, you'd better stay out of this, this hasn't anything to do with you —"

"Shut up and get in the cab." I opened the door and pushed him in. Marvin gave the address. We drove around City Hall and north on Broad Street. The traffic was heavy, even for Saturday night, and then, amid a chorus of horns, everything stopped.

"Must be something wrong up there," announced the driver.

There were blinking red lights and sirens behind us. An ambulance eased carefully over the curb, crossed the sidewalk and disappeared into an eastbound side street.

"Driver, follow that ambulance!" said Marvin suddenly.

"Oh no," said the driver. "There's cops all over the place —"

I took out a ten dollar bill and put it on the front seat. The driver looked at the bill, looked into his rearview mirror, and swung the cab over the curb.

Marvin leaned forward and gave directions. We made two turns, crossed Broad at the next intersection and then turned north on Eighteenth Street.

Now we were in the endless dreary ocean of the city,

narrow cobbled streets, block after block after block of identical shabby brick houses, identical stoops, little stores, parked cars, and more and more milling people — black people, sitting on the stoops, leaning against the buildings and the cars, hanging out of the windows, or just standing around in groups. It was Saturday night in the summer. Suddenly everybody seemed to be running — running north. Up ahead were bright lights and even more people. Now the traffic was stopped in this street too.

"Go through that alley," Marvin said. The driver turned, and we bumped along a line of overflowing garbage cans, past grimy board fences enclosing the back yards. We turned the corner again.

Marvin pointed: "Look!"

There was a little drugstore on the opposite side. A group of Negroes — women and teen-agers — were milling around; some of them were climbing right into the window. Then I saw that the plate glass was smashed and lay scattered on the sidewalk. A woman was standing in the window, throwing handfuls of little boxes into the street.

"There must be something going on up here," said the driver as we passed, still going north.

Then he said: "Most of these stores are owned by Jews."

"Just drive the cab, please," I said.

"Listen, friend —"

"The man's quite right," said Marvin. "Most of these stores *are* owned by Jews."

Nobody said anything. At the next intersection a red police car was blocking the street. Two officers were standing beside it, looking at their broken windshield. We stopped and one of them came over.

"Can't go past here, chief," he said to the driver. "All hell's breaking loose up there."

"I've got to get to Columbia Avenue," said Marvin.

179

"Not tonight, chief. Not without a tank. We just come down from there and look what they done to our car. They're tossing bricks off the rooftops."

The cabbie turned around. "This is as far as I'm gonna go," he said. "I got a wife and children . . ."

We climbed out and Marvin paid. The driver slammed the taxi into reverse, turned around, and roared off the way we had come.

"You guys can't go up there on foot," said the policeman. We could hear the radio in his car squawking: "Twenty-second and Norris, assist officer! Twenty-second and Norris, assist officer!"

"For Christ's sake, here comes a bus," said the second policeman. Sure enough, a brand-new glass-fronted PTC bus slowly worked its way around the corner and stopped behind the patrol car. We all walked over. The uniformed driver was a Negro. His bus was empty. With a hiss, the pneumatic door opened. "Hey, let me through, will ya?" shouted the driver. He looked young and trim and efficient. "I gotta get this thing up to Ridge Avenue —"

The policemen looked at each other.

"You better take him through," said Marvin.

"Go call in, George," said the first policeman to the second. Marvin and I climbed into the bus and put our quarters into the box.

"What's going on up there?" I asked the driver.

He shook his head. "Damn if I know. They say the cops beat up a colored woman at Twenty-second and Montgomery and now she's dead, and the people up there started fighting with the cops and now everybody is running around and breaking into stores."

We sat there for a few minutes and listened to the diesel idling. Then the policeman came back to the door.

"Okay, they told us to let you through, but we've got to stay here to block the street. You men going to ride with him?"

180

We nodded.

"Well, I guess it's better than walking, but keep your heads down. Good luck."

The driver closed the door and put the bus in gear. For about six blocks everything was quiet: no traffic and few people.

We turned a corner, and suddenly we were in a blaze of light. People jammed the street and both sidewalks. The bus came to a stop. On the right side there was a crash; I turned to see a swarm of women climbing into the A & P through the broken windows. Police cars were parked on both sides of the street, but all of the officers were clustered under a flashing neon Bar & Grill sign, holding back the men who were trying to get into the taproom. As we watched, the crowd began to push the police back against the wall of the building; a nightstick flashed, the white police helmets bobbed, and then a black man was down on the sidewalk. The people in front of the A & P began to throw bottles across the street. Something hit the window of the taproom and the glass crashed into the street. The crowd began to scream. The safety glass in one of the bus windows burst into a hundred segments.

"Better get down!" yelled the driver, and a moment later a shower of bricks and bottles hit the bus. Marvin and I squatted between the seats, but the safety glass held together pretty well.

Somebody hammered on the door. The driver opened it, and two helmeted policemen climbed in.

"Get this thing outa here!" shouted the first one, while the second, a sergeant, slumped into a seat. The bus lurched and began to move forward. Something dented the roof with a deafening crash, and then we were in the next block, where everything was dark and silent again.

The sergeant was lying on the seat and the other man was bending over him.

"Did they knife you, **Fred?**"

181

"They grabbed my badge and twisted the pin — ouch! Jesus, take it easy!" The front of his shirt was sopping with blood now.

"You'd better get this man to a hospital," I said.

The policeman turned. "Driver, take us to Temple Hospital."

"That's the wrong way," said the driver. "They need this bus up on Ridge Avenue —"

The policeman moved forward, his hand reaching for his nightstick. "Listen, boy," he said through clenched teeth. "This bus is going to Temple Hospital or your brains are going to be all over that dashboard!"

"You'd better take them," I said to the driver. "The sergeant is really hurt."

Poker-faced, the driver glanced into his mirror. "Makes no difference to me, man; I don't run the company." He swung the bus to the right, toward Broad Street.

Marvin stood up. "Ben, we've got to get off here. It's only a couple of blocks now."

"You want to be walking around here alone?" asked the driver as he stopped the bus.

"We'll be all right," said Marvin. "Thanks for your help." We got out, the door hissed, and the bus drove away.

We walked as fast as we could. This street was completely empty. Now and again, ancient Negro women glared at us through open windows. We turned a corner.

"My God!" said Marvin. "They're up at the end of our street." I could see a clump of people, and then there was the familiar sound of breaking glass, and a cheer. "Come on," said Marvin. "This way."

We ran down the street in the other direction, passing a laundromat, a restaurant, a drugstore and an appliance shop. All of them were closed. I could hear Marvin gasping. At Gold's Budget Shoes the blinds were drawn behind the locked door. Marvin couldn't seem to get his key into the lock.

"Hey Pop!" he shouted. "Hey Pop, it's me!"

The door swung open, and we faced a tiny bald man with a twelve-gauge shotgun and a terrified look in his eyes.

"Marvin! You got here!"

"Marvin!" There was a shriek from the back of the store. A little woman dashed forward and threw her arms around Marvin, who looked uncomfortable. "Oh, Marvin, they're going crazy," she sobbed. "They're smashing all the stores . . ."

Marvin tried to extricate himself from her grasp. "Okay, Mom, don't worry, it'll be okay . . ." The father was carefully bolting the door with one hand while he awkwardly held the shotgun with the other. The place was dark and smelled of leather. Shoe boxes were stacked from floor to ceiling along both walls.

"This is my friend Ben Butler," said Marvin. "We were doing some work together, and this is my mother and father . . ."

"It's a pleasure, I'm sure," said Mr. Gold, gingerly shifting the gun so that he could shake hands.

"It's nice to meet you, sir," I said. "Ah — is that thing loaded?"

"Coitainly it's loaded!" snapped Mr. Gold. "What you think I got it for? I'm an American citizen, I got a right to defend my property —"

"Give me that gun, Pop," said Marvin, freeing himself from his mother. "You and Mom go on upstairs. We'll handle this."

"They ain't going to smash *my* store," shouted Mr. Gold, waving the shotgun around. "I worked all my life . . . I'm an American citizen . . . I got my rights to defend my home . . ."

"Give me that gun, Pop."

"Morris, give him the gun," wailed Mrs. Gold. She began to cry. I stood back against the shoe boxes, ignored. The little man glared at his wife and son.

Marvin moved toward him, speaking softly.

"Pop, this isn't like·Russia. This is different. They're mean and they're drunk and they're smashing stores, but they're not hurting the merchants. Even the police aren't shooting at them —"

"That's what I mean. The cops, they're just standing around with their hands in their pockets while they smash our stores —"

"They're doing the best they can, Pop, but if you shoot somebody, there's no telling what might happen."

"It's all politics," shouted Mr. Gold. "They want their votes. They can smash the stores but we can't stop them, just so the damn politicians will get their votes —"

Marvin grasped the barrel of the shotgun and gently pulled it from his father's hands. "Come on, Pop, take Mom upstairs, it's going to be all right." Marvin didn't know what to do with the shotgun either, so I took it from him, extracted the shells, and slid it between two rows of shoe boxes.

Somehow Marvin got his father and mother up the stairs. When he came back he said: "Ben, they were born in Russia, you see, and when they were children something like this happened . . . in Odessa —"

There was a shout in the street, and then the sound of breaking glass. Upstairs Mrs. Gold screamed, "It's Hirshmann's, next door."

I edged close to the window and peeked around the wall of shoe boxes. The sidewalk was packed with jostling shouting Negroes. The show window next door was outside my line of vision, but I could see a group of men carefully passing a washing machine out. As the other people cheered, they balanced it on a child's delivery wagon and trundled it down the street.

Then the crowd began to whistle and clap. I leaned forward and saw two men straining to move a huge new

184

refrigerator out of the window. They tipped it forward slowly, straining under its weight. Suddenly it slipped, toppled to the left and fell to the sidewalk with a rending crash.

A car horn began to blow and a white Thunderbird convertible stopped at the curb. A tall young Negro wearing an immaculate gray silk suit stood up in the car and held an electric bullhorn to his lips.

"YOU PEOPLE COME OUT OF THAT STORE!" His voice boomed over the whole neighborhood. "PLEASE DO NOT CARRY ON THIS WAY, MY FRIENDS —"

The crowd turned on him, hooting and shrieking. A beer bottle struck the hood of the Thunderbird, bounced off, and splintered on the pavement.

A thin girl in a white blouse and tight white trousers climbed up on the smashed refrigerator and began to scream.

"You can go to hell, Mister N-Double-A-C-P! We are black, black, black and we don't give a shit for *nobody!* You can take me down to jail and hang me up —" The crowd was screaming so hard that I couldn't hear the rest of it, but I was already trying to unlock the door.

"Ben, what are you doing?" Marvin grabbed my arm. I twisted away from him and opened the door. A hundred faces turned.

"Let's get that shoe store, that jew store!" yelled the girl, pointing right at me.

"Get off that ice box, Fernanda," I said, trying hard to sound quiet and authoritative. My heart was beating in my throat.

She leaned over to get a closer look; I could see that she was very drunk. "Hey!" she shouted. "It's my law-yah! It's the P.D." Her white teeth flashed. She was beautiful in a scary way; a savage in the jungle. "What you doin' here, lawyah?"

I held out my hand. "Come on off of there, Fernanda."
The mob was standing back and watching all this, suddenly
quiet and perplexed.

"Come on down, Fernanda."

She took my hand and jumped gracefully to the sidewalk.

"Hey man, you want to get your head stove in?" she
said. The others began to shout a lot of very dirty words
at us.

"GO ON HOME YOU PEOPLE, YOU ARE BREAK-
ING THE LAW. THIS IS NOT THE WAY WE WILL
GAIN OUR FREEDOM," said the electric voice from the
Thunderbird. Their attention diverted, the people began
to turn toward the car again.

"Why don't you send them home, Fernanda?" I held
on to her hard scaly little hand. "They're all going to get
arrested."

"No they not, daddy," she said, twisting away from me
in a little dance. "That's not your store. What are you
doing up here?"

A bottle or something flew past my head and the Golds'
window fell around us in a shower of glass. The crowd
moved closer. I couldn't see the Thunderbird any more.

Fernanda stopped jumping around and stared at me.
"Hey man, you got cut? You better let me see that —"

"Fernanda, I want you to get these people out of
here!" My voice sounded a little shrill in my ears.

"You really want me to, huh?"

"Please, Fernanda!"

She looked undecided for a moment. Then she walked
up to the smashed window, peered inside and turned,
screaming:

"Nothin' in there but a pile of shitty old shoes! Let's
go get that dress store!" Without looking at me, she
marched right through the crowd and across the street
and stood all alone in front of Schine's Paris Fashions.

Would the others follow her? We never found out, because a ragged little boy called out: "Hey man, the hoagie store's on fire!"

He was right. A few doors to the east, thick brown smoke was welling out of a little restaurant. The mob turned and ran toward the fire, and for a few seconds Fernanda and I looked at each other across the empty street. Then more people appeared from all directions: little wizened old women in bedroom slippers, sweating men in undershirts, murderous-looking teen-agers — a tide of brown faces moved in the eerie bright lights of the display windows. The air smelled of burning grease.

There was a loud *Whomp!* Dark red flames appeared behind the broken windows of the restaurant. The crowd cheered and whistled.

I turned to find Marvin standing beside me. "Some glass hit you," he said. "There's blood on your cheek." He started to dab at my face with a handkerchief. The firelight was reflected in his glasses. "You must be nuts," he said. "They might have trampled all over you."

Now we heard sirens again, and blinking red lights appeared over the heads of the crowd. A big fire engine eased its way down the street; the people fell back sullenly to the sidewalk. Two firemen dragged their hose to the yellow hydrant and began to attach it.

"Let the son of a bitch burn!" somebody yelled, and then bricks and bottles began to clatter against the fire engine. I looked up: on the rooftops across the street, a gang of boys were throwing things as fast as they could pick them up. At the hydrant, a fireman dropped his wrench and collapsed into the gutter. His helper ran back to the engine, where the others scrunched down beside the big wheels like armored infantry in the lee of a tank.

More sirens. There were headlights on the sidewalk now, and a red police jeep bounced through the mob. Two big trucks turned the corner and stopped. A score of

187

troopers in white helmets jumped over the tailgates and waded into the crowd, beating men and women to the ground with nightsticks. A policeman stepped over the wounded fireman and turned on the hydrant, and the men beside the fire engine began to point a stream of water into the burning building.

Suddenly the screaming and the roar of motors was drowned in an ear-splitting clatter. Everyone looked up to see a police helicopter hovering over the street, its searchlights seeking the men on the rooftops.

Marvin and I crouched in the doorway, ignored. "My God, I can't believe it," I whispered. "It's like a war movie."

Marvin said nothing.

In a couple of minutes it was over. The helicopter disappeared, the flames turned into hissing smoke, and the street was filled with helmeted police who straggled back to their trucks, boots thumping on the pavement, leather equipment creaking, their sweat-soaked shirts torn at the neck or sleeve . . . They looked like a football team leaving the field after a game. A hulking potbellied bareheaded sergeant, mopping his face: "Wouldn't even let us shoot those baboons off the roof —"

They had prisoners. A dozen sullen men in handcuffs were pushed into a police van, and then a couple of wild-looking girls in purple skintight stretch pants. One of the girls kicked and howled and threw herself to the sidewalk, twisting and biting and rolling her eyes. It took four cursing red-faced troopers to wrestle her into the van, and when they slammed the door, one of them held up his hand, which was streaming dark arterial blood. I wondered what I would do if they had Fernanda, but they didn't have her. Two men carried the unconscious fireman past us in a stretcher.

"What's going to happen to this town?" asked Marvin quietly.

"Well, look who's here," said a voice behind us. "It's the Public Defender drumming up business!" We turned to face a tall heavy man in a rumpled business suit and a white police helmet.

"Inspector Shay, this is my friend Ben Butler, a volunteer defender," said Marvin.

"Pleased to meet you, counselor. Your Ma and Dad all right, Marvin?"

"They're pretty scared, but they're all right now. Do you think I should move them out tonight?"

The Inspector shook his head. "Naw, these people here have spent themselves. I'll leave one car in the street, just to make sure."

"What happened?" I asked. "How did this all start?"

"Oh hell, it was nothing!" He took off his helmet and rubbed his hand across his eyes. "They say a man and woman were fighting in a car — blocking an intersection — so two officers — colored officers, I think — tried to break it up. Next thing you know, the streets are full of niggers attacking policemen, they say we beat up this woman and she's dead —" He put on his helmet again. "Listen, something like this was bound to happen. These people are so jazzed up about this integration business, and half of 'em are out of work, and now these Muslims are operating on them . . ." He waved his arm down the street. "They're sick of everything and they're mean and they want to smash things. Your folks and these other people are just sort of natural targets . . ."

"That's our historical role," said Marvin, under his breath.

"How's that?"

"Nothing, Inspector. You think this will go on all night?"

"Hell yes, this will be a night to remember. We closed all the bars and State Stores, but there's enough booze around to keep it going a while. And listen, we're

189

not allowed to shoot or use tear gas or nothing. That's straight from the top. So all we can do is run from one riot to another and try to keep them from burning the town down. We can't even stop the looting."

"But you think it's okay to leave my parents here?"

"Yeah, there won't be any more trouble, and I'll leave a car right in front . . . Why, aren't you going to stay here now?"

"Where are these prisoners going?" asked Marvin.

"Straight to the Hall. Judge Stellwagon is sitting as committing magistrate in central police court. We're going to run them right through while we have the arresting officers, we don't have enough room in the station houses to hold this many people —"

"Well, then I guess I'd better ride down with you. They'll need the Defender."

Inspector Shay and I stared at him.

"Put him to bed, counselor. He's flipped his wig."

"You're not serious, are you, Marvin?"

"You think I'm in the mood for jokes tonight?" He turned and walked into the store.

After a moment, Inspector Shay said: "That's quite a character. I guess he's trying to prove something."

"Yes." For some reason we were both embarrassed.

"Look, I have to take this bunch in now," he said. "My car's two blocks down the street. I'll tell the driver to wait for you. It's the red Lincoln with the light on the roof. Nice to meet you, counselor." He marched up the empty street.

A few minutes later Marvin came out of the store. He was dressed in a suit now.

"Aren't your parents frightened?" I asked.

"Sure they're frightened, but they won't leave." He was adjusting his necktie as we walked. "I tried to send them out to my sister's in Wynnefield, but they won't go. They just won't leave the street."

190

The next block seemed to be completely deserted. I couldn't understand what had happened to all the people who must live there. Most of the stores were dark, and everywhere the burglar alarms were ringing, unheeded. Broken glass crunched beneath our feet.

Inspector Shay's big red Lincoln came backing down the street toward us. It stopped, and the driver opened the back door. Then we were gliding silently down Broad Street toward the distant tower of City Hall.

"Marvin?"

He turned.

"Marvin, if those stores were all owned by old Philadelphia Quakers, those people would still have smashed them tonight."

He looked out of the window again. "They're not owned by Quakers, though."

"Listen, Marvin —"

"It's not hard to see how they feel." He took off his glasses and rubbed his hand over his eyes. "They are miserable, just miserable. They live in filthy stinking holes, a whole family to a room, half of them can't get a job, no place to go, no hope for anything better, and why? Because they're black. It's sort of a permanent nightmare, and it's imposed on them by white men." He put his glasses back on. "And who are the only white men they see? Who collects their rent and sells them food and lends them money? Who makes their living off them?"

I couldn't think of anything to say.

"But what are we supposed to do?" He turned to look at me. "You met my father. They brought him here when he was fourteen years old, not a word of English, not a nickel to his name, and he had to go to work. What was he supposed to do, ask for a job at some bank downtown?"

"Maybe they could move to some other section —"

"You saw my father. He's a man who sells cheap shoes to Negroes. And who would buy their store? Who knows

191

when this will happen again? We're in a revolution, and all they have is tied up in that crummy little store right in the middle of the battlefield — Well, here we are." He leaned forward. "Can you drive us right into the courtyard, Officer?"

The central police court was in turmoil. The immense dark room was jammed from wall to wall with reporters, court attendants, bondsmen, lawyers, helmeted riot police and a lot of people who had no business there. In one corner, a dozen troopers were leaning over a railing, dictating arrest reports to a couple of harassed typists. In the well of the court, two assistant district attorneys were trying to handle the charges as they were brought up, and behind them the sweating black-coated tipstaves were struggling to move the right prisoners to the bar when their cases were called.

Marvin pushed his way through the press of bodies and I followed right behind him.

Judge Stellwagon, looking down from the Bench, seemed almost glad to see us.

"Mr. Gold, are you here for the Public Defender?"

"Yes sir, and Mr. Butler will assist me."

"All right," said Stellwagon. "Will you talk to this man, please?"

Like the district attorneys, Marvin and I took turns. While he stood at the bar and handled one case, I would force my way back among the crush of prisoners and policemen to find out what the next case was about, and then I would move up to the bar with that group while Marvin elbowed himself back to the next one.

Stellwagon was sitting as committing magistrate, which meant he could discharge prisoners, find them guilty of summary offenses like disorderly conduct, or hold them for indictment by the Grand Jury. Our job was mainly to make sure that nobody was locked up by mistake.

192

"Hold him for the Grand Jury, five hundred dollars' bail." "Your Honor, he can't make bail in that amount, couldn't you fix it at two hundred? The man's employed —" "No, not with that record, call the next case." "If your Honor please, this man threw a brick at a police car, corner of Ridge and Jefferson . . ." "Which is the officer?" "Name and number, Officer . . ." "Look, we know you were doing the best you could, Sergeant, but did you actually see *this man* throw the brick?" . . . "All right, all right, he's discharged, get him out of here. Next case!"

Everything smelled of sweat and whiskey. ". . . struck a police officer with a tire iron . . ." "This man here, Officer?" "Naw, not that one, *that* one!" "What's your name, boy?" . . . "A thousand dollars' bail. That's what I said, Mr. Butler. No. Call the next case" . . . "You're sure this is the same guy?" "Counselor, I've had these same handcuffs on him since that very minute." . . . "Five hundred dollars' bail, all right, bring up those two monkeys over there . . . What? Who? I will not talk to *any* lawyer on the telephone, tell him to get his ass down here . . . I can't hear you, Mr. Gold. I WANT SOME QUIET IN THIS ROOM!"

The night wore on. More police details pushed their prisoners into the back of the room, while the Sheriff's deputies took the jail cases back into the corridor through the side doors. It was almost like a production line. "Get somebody to send out for coffee," shouted one of the district attorneys, and my stomach growled.

"Your Honor, isn't this more of a case of disorderly conduct? After all, the officer said he was just . . ." "All right, all right, adjudged guilty disorderly conduct, fined ten dollars plus costs or ten days . . . What? Oh, good morning, Fred. Have you come to spell me?" Judge Morgenstern replaced Judge Stellwagon on the Bench, and a moment later somebody touched my arm. It was Walter Simon, the Chief Defender.

"Okay Ben," he said. "You and Marvin go on home and get some sleep. I've brought in two of the other boys, and we're relieving you. Thanks for jumping into the breach."

Marvin and I stood under one of the looming arches of City Hall and looked down Broad Street. It was almost four in the morning; the banks and office buildings stood silent and empty in the pale gray light. I felt a little dizzy.

"How about some breakfast?" I asked.

Marvin nodded. A beard was beginning to fuzz the lower half of his face. We walked through the revolving doors of Horn & Hardart's, and as I squinted in the blazing light the first face I saw was Sally Rochester's.

Twenty people in evening clothes were sitting around some tables they had pushed together. Apparently this was a second breakfast after the June Ball, which had been held across the street in the Bellevue-Stratford. Sally was sitting with Randy Kellerman and Roseann Hyde and a balding pudgy guy in tails. They were all laughing and talking and smoking cigarettes, but some of them looked up as Marvin and I passed on our way to the counter. I didn't know whether I should stop and introduce Marvin, or what. I didn't feel like it. I waved in what I hoped was a cheerful manner, and then we sat up at the counter and ordered our coffee and scrambled eggs.

"Looks like you missed a good party," said Marvin.

I nodded, drinking my coffee and staring vacantly at the white tile wall in front of me. The girl brought the eggs and we began to eat.

"Had a hard night on the town, Mr. Butler?" asked Randy Kellerman, standing behind me resplendent in a dinner jacket with plaid tie and matching trousers.

"What are you supposed to be, the King's Own Scottish Borderers?"

194

"My, aren't we snotty tonight! I have a message from Sally."

"This is Marvin Gold," I said. "My boss at the Defender. Randy Kellerman."

"Nice to see you," said Randy, through his nose.

"How do you do," said Marvin.

"I'm instructed to inquire whether Mr. Butler would care to join us for a swim, out at the Smiths'."

"What, now?"

"Certainly, now. Best time of day for a swim. Ordway and Marion were at the dance, they left a while ago, but they said everybody should come on out —"

"Who's the bald guy?"

"What bald guy?"

"The *bald* guy, for Christ's sake, the one with Sally."

"Oh, his name is . . . I forget what the hell his name is, he runs one of Ordway's charities, they brought him along for Sally . . ."

"Well then, what's she want with me?"

"Delicacy forbids —"

"Oh shit," I said. "Excuse me a minute, Marvin." I swung off the stool, and walked across the room.

Sally tipped her head back and blew out a cloud of smoke. She wore a black strapless gown and a diamond necklace.

"My God, Ben, you've got a big cut under your eye," she said. "Have you been in a fight or something? You know Roseann, of course, and this is Preston Lamont, Ben Butler."

He got up and we shook hands.

"Listen, Sal, I'd love to have a swim but I'm pretty well shot." I tried to explain what I had been doing all night, but it didn't make much sense.

"How *fahs*cinating!" said Roseann Hyde, her big blue eyes bulging even more than usual.

Marvin came by, heading for the door. "I've got to

195

be getting home, Ben. You go ahead, I'll see you Monday."

"No, wait a minute . . . Sally, I've been up all night —"

"So have we. Come have a swim, it'll do you good."

"Wait a minute —" I followed Marvin out through the revolving doors, and once again we were standing on the Broad Street sidewalk. I really didn't know what to say to him now.

"Listen, Marvin, you won't get a taxi to go up there, I've got a couch in my apartment . . ."

"The subways are still running, I guess," he said. We just stood there. Suddenly he put out his hand. "Good-bye Ben. And thank you."

"So long, Marvin." We shook hands, and then he turned and walked up the street toward the subway entrance.

chapter 17

"He does *so!*"

"No!"

"I'm telling you, he does!"

"*No!*"

I groaned and tried to open my eyes. Sunlight was streaming into the garret. I really didn't know where I was. The two little boys wore identical costumes: blue polo shirts, white shorts, sandals. Then I recognized Robbie and Andy Rochester.

"Morning, fellas." I turned heavily on my side and the bed creaked. "What's the argument about?"

"He won't believe you got more hair on your arms than our father, but he doesn't even remember," said Robbie, who was almost six.

"I do so, I do so," yelled the little one.

"Well, I can't help you with that one," I said. "What time is it?"

"How are we supposed to know?" asked Robbie. "You're the grown-up."

"Look at our watch," suggested Andy.

"Good idea." I raised my wrist and tried to focus. It was twelve-thirty. I sat up in bed.

"Hey, you're *naked*," shouted Andy.

"Haven't you got pajamas?" asked Robbie.

"Why would I have pajamas at your house, silly."

"This isn't our house," yelled Andy in triumph. "This is our *garage!*"

So it was. I was sleeping in the empty chauffeur's apartment and my car was parked cosily underneath.

High heels came clacking up the stairs.

"Mo-*ther*, you can't come in!" Andy tried to close the door against her. "He hasn't got pajamas —"

"Well, I've brought his clothes to put on," she said, pushing the door open. She looked terrific: long brown legs, tight white shorts, a printed sleeveless blouse. She carried my shirt, my socks and my underwear, freshly washed and neatly folded. "Here's your laundry, sir. And here's some shaving stuff and a toothbrush. Boys, run down and tell Jessie that Mr. Butler's up and we'll eat in fifteen minutes."

They pounded down the stairs and Sally sat on the bed. "Hi," she said.

"Hi," I said and pulled her down on me. "Why only fifteen minutes?" She closed her eyes and her lips were cool and tasted of toothpaste, but after a moment she moved away from me and sat up again.

"No. Now listen." She pushed her hair back. "We've got to be terribly careful, Ben. If Bobby finds out I'm letting men sleep here — or rather if his mother finds out — they can give me trouble about the boys. Please help me be careful, will you?" She put her hand on my chest. "Because I have the most terrible hots for you, I guess that's pretty obvious."

It was, but after the maddening week with Monica, Sally and her cheerful appetite were intoxicating medicine.

After I had said good-bye to Marvin Gold in front of the Horn & Hardart, I had turned to find her beside me. She put her arm in mine and said: "My date's had enough. Will you drive me out for a swim?"

The night was gone anyway, and I was numb.

"What about the others?" I asked.

"The hell with them," she said. "They've been talking about swimming for an hour, but I'm the only one who means it."

We got my Chevy and put the top down and drove through the still Sunday morning streets. The sky was turning pale blue. On the Expressway I pressed the accelerator to the floor, and Sally's hair flew behind her like a torch.

At King of Prussia we left the Expressway, wound through the empty cloverleaf maze, and started south on 202. Then we bent off into a narrow macadam road and rushed under a long green tunnel of leaves, past meadows still shrouded in mist, until we came to Ordway Smith's whitewashed stone gateposts. The gravel clattered against my fenders as we crawled toward the house.

"They're asleep," said Sally. "Stop here, we'll walk across the field."

When I turned off the ignition we could hear the birds singing. The grass was wet and the pool was steaming in the chilly air. I was cold. The floor of the bath house creaked beneath our feet. Sally said there would be bathing suits, but in the men's compartment the pegs were bare.

"Damn," she said through the partition. "Nothing in here either, except a towel. Well, you do what you like; I'm going skinny."

The sweat had dried in my shirt. I took off my clothes and hesitated, shivering in the doorway. Sally stood on the lip of the pool, wrapped in a small yellow towel. She dropped it, launched herself, and cracked on the water in a flat racing dive. I was right behind her. The water was warmer than the air. For a moment I swam along the bottom. The cut in my cheek began to sting.

When I broke the surface Sally was coming back the other way, her head lying in the water and her arms

199

flashing in a fast chopping crawl. We swam three lengths, passing each other in the middle, and then she stopped, holding on to the wall beneath the diving board. Her hair, plastered down across her forehead, looked darker, almost the color of whiskey. I noticed for the first time that she had a few freckles on her nose. Behind her strong brown shoulders, the waves we had made slurped into the gunnel drain . . .

"No," she whispered. "Listen . . ." Her skin felt slick and cold as I pressed her against the wall of the pool. "Listen, please Ben, it's broad daylight . . . let's not start anything here . . . *please*, Ben?" She ducked her head under my arm, submerged, bumped smoothly along my body, and reappeared beside the ladder. The water streamed down her flanks as she scrambled out of the pool. She snatched up the towel and disappeared into the bath house.

When she heard me on the wooden step, the damp towel came flying into my arms. "Hurry up," she said from the darkness. "I want to be out of here before the farmer comes to look after the horses."

I scrubbed myself and put on my smelly clothes.

"Let me have that towel back," she said as I came out. "I'll try to wrap my hair. Are you cold?"

"No, I feel wonderful."

"So do I. Come on, let's get out of here before somebody shows up."

As we turned out of the driveway, she slid across the seat and took my arm. "I thought you'd lost interest in me."

"Sally, I know I should have called you, but . . . I had a bad week, a lot of things going on . . ." It sounded lame.

"That's all right," she said. "But I'd like to have gone to that ball with you. It's really just a children's party. Well, anyway."

She turned on the radio. "His eye is on the sparrow," sang the lady, "and I know He watches me." I wondered

200

how things were on Columbia Avenue. Sally put her head on my shoulder and closed her eyes.

Twenty minutes later I turned into her steep driveway and she sat up.

"Take it easy now, let's not wake anybody. Turn right here at the circle . . . Okay, through the arch and across the courtyard — Oh, damn those dogs!" Two Irish setters came bounding around the corner. Sally jumped out of the car and put her arms around them. They stood still, swinging their tails happily, and then they disappeared again. Sally walked toward the long garage on the other side of the courtyard, stooped down before the second of the five doors, and brought it sliding up. I drove in, switched the motor off and stepped out. Her station wagon was the only other car in the huge old-fashioned garage.

We stood there and looked at each other.

"What time is it?" she asked, pulling the towel from her head and fluffing her hair.

"Six-thirty."

"Well, thank God Jessie's a sound sleeper."

"Who?"

"Jessie, my cook. She's over the kitchen, she might have heard the dogs . . . Oh, the hell with it." She stroked the hair out of her eyes, and then she turned. "Come on, this way."

There was a door at the end of the garage, and behind it a narrow stairway. I followed her up. The skirt of her ball gown rustled against the curving plaster walls. We emerged in a dark musty room. I saw a tall wooden dresser and a white iron bed with a mattress and some blankets.

"Chauffeur's apartment," she said, sounding breathless.

"You have a chauffeur?" I asked stupidly.

She shook her head. I could barely see her face in the gloom. "Bobby's grandmother —" she began, but then

201

she was in my arms and her tongue was in my mouth and we were both struggling to get her dress off.

I finished shaving, put on the fresh soapsmelling linen and my wrinkled suit and climbed down the little stairs. The hot sun shone through the big chestnut trees, leaving dappled patterns on the cobblestones. I walked across the courtyard and around the outside of the enormous house, past banks of flowers lining the velvet lawn.

Robbie saw me first. "Hey, here he comes. Can we eat now?" They were sitting on the terrace, in the shade of a tall copper beech. There was a place for me at the glass table.

We had grapefruit and fried ham and scrambled eggs and rolls with butter and jam. If Jessie the cook had doubts about anything, she didn't show them as I thanked her for washing my things. When we had finished eating, I read the funnies to the boys, but underneath the funnies were fat eight-column headlines and pictures from North Philadelphia. The boys ran off somewhere. Sally and I finished our coffee and smoked cigarettes and looked at the photographs from another world. By the time I had read every word of every story, the shadows on the lawn stretched all the way down to the highway.

Sally had told them that I had run out of gas last night, so we loaded the boys and the setters into her station wagon and rode up to the village, where we bought a can of gasoline.

Driving around on Sunday afternoon with a girl, two children, and two dogs was a new experience for me. So was feeling a little boy's hand on my shoulder.

The boys wanted to help me pour the gasoline into my tank, and while trying to keep from spilling it all over their clothes I suddenly remembered my promise to play in the softball game against Openshaw, Prescott, Pennington & Lee.

chapter 18

We drove over in two cars so that I could go straight home after the game. Robbie came with me and Sally took Andy in her station wagon.

Ellsworth Boyle has a beautiful place in the Gladwyne hills, an ivy-covered Colonial farmhouse, a complex of barns and stables, and a formal garden leading to the swimming pool. We followed the dusty lane around all of this to the mowed field below the pool, where we found a line of two dozen cars and a boisterous crowd. A lot of children were running around munching hot dogs, while their parents were serving themselves from the bars set up on the tailgates of the station wagons. Underneath the big oak stood a keg of beer with an ice coil. The picnic had obviously been long and liquid, but the game was still in progress. We parked our cars at the end of the line and walked back. Sally's boys hung behind until they recognized Ordway Smith's children, their cousins, who were poking around in a large tub of ice and Coca-Cola bottles. Conyers & Dean was at bat and most of my colleagues, dressed with strenuous informality, were milling around behind home plate, drinking.

Our approach was greeted with shouts of derision. "It's the second half of the eighth, C & D is trailing twelve to nine, and look who shows up!" Sam Atwater wore a

Mexican sombrero, a gray sweatshirt stenciled PROPERTY OF HARVARD ATHLETIC ASSOCIATION and bathing trunks.

Randy Kellerman in madras shorts and a rich caramel suntan, presented two paper cups and a bottle of bourbon. "What happened to you last night? I thought we were all going swimming and next thing you two had disappeared . . . Here, Sally, you want some ice in that?"

"Better late than never, Ben," said Ellsworth Boyle, his face flushed and glistening under a red Phillies cap. "Glad you could make it."

"I'm sorry, Mr. Boyle, I just plain forgot. Do you know Sally Rochester?"

" 'Course, my dear, glad to see you, have they offered you — okay yes, give me another, Randy. Look fellows, there's no reason we can't still take this game. I'm dropping out and Butler here will take my place and let's try to put on a little burst, shall we? I mean what the hell . . ."

Sally walked over to join Marion Smith on her blanket. The other girl with them turned and I saw that it was Sheila Forrester, looking more pale and tense than usual behind her sunglasses. There was also a sad-eyed boy in an Episcopal Academy sweater. Ordway Smith was coming toward me, carrying a Thermos bottle.

"Ordway, is Pat Forrester here?"

He shook his head. "He's off on his vacation, thank God. I went over to see Sheila yesterday, just to have a talk with her, you know, and we thought her boy Henry might enjoy the game —" Ordway came closer to me. "Ben, I noticed you and Sal came over in separate cars. Does that mean you're going directly back to town? . . . Well do me a favor and drop Sheila off in Wynnewood, will you? Her boy is coming with us to visit Jack, and we've got to go out to dinner at seven —" I said I would be glad to take Sheila home, and then Ellsworth Boyle shouted that I was up.

My appearance at the plate elicited a volley of insults and whistles from the Openshaw team and their supporters.

"They're getting desperate," called my classmate Tom Moynihan from second base.

"Careful," announced the shortstop, who was William Rogers Pennington, their managing partner. "This one might be sober, he just got here."

"Don't let them rattle you, Ben." I looked at the little umpire, and was startled to recognize Angus MacDonald, from the William Penn Trust Company. I had never seen him without a starched collar; in Bermuda shorts, a tennis shirt and knee socks he looked strangely naked and vulnerable, but he was drinking beer from a paper cup and grinning through his sunburn.

"Play ball," somebody yelled. I turned to face the pitcher and there, for God's sake, was Frederick Lacey, Esquire, all dressed in white and glaring at me through his bristling eyebrows.

"Are you ready, Ben?"

"Yes, sir. Ready when you are."

Somebody behind me said: "No outs, nobody on base, let's go, Butler."

Frederick Lacey pushed the visor of his tennis hat back a little, wound up with surprising agility, and threw the pitch.

"Where'd you learn to hit like that?" asked Moynihan when I arrived at second base. "I never saw you lift anything heavier than a brimming glass."

"Accident. Has Mr. Lacey been pitching all afternoon?"

"You must be kidding," mumbled Moynihan. "Dick Harris is our star. We just put in the old boy this inning so he'd have some fun. Now Pennington won't have the heart to pull him."

I saw now that the great Mr. Harris (late of the Princeton varsity) was languidly picking his teeth in the outfield, down where the weeping willows hung into the creek. The sun was just sliding behind the roof of the barn and a flight of swallows wheeled over our heads.

Leslie Patch was at bat now, swinging stiffly from the shoulder. His jaw stuck out in one direction and his ass in the other. The first pitch looked all right to me, but Angus MacDonald, after some hesitation, called it a ball. Cheers and applause from the C & D crowd.

"The ump is drunk!" screamed Moynihan between cupped hands. "We demand a fresh ump!"

"Tut tut," I said. "That's no way to talk to your own client."

The next pitch was low and slow. Leslie Patch swung awkwardly and connected. The ball bounced toward Lacey, who stooped, fumbled around with it, and then whirled, throwing it to Moynihan. I hadn't budged from the base, and Leslie Patch now stood panting on first.

"Jesus," said Moynihan between his teeth as he returned the ball to Lacey.

"Your boss doesn't trust me," said I.

"Here comes the guy *I* don't trust," said Moynihan as Ordway Smith stepped to the plate.

"All right, now watch it," called Pennington. "Let's wake up in the outfield!"

"Why not?" I asked.

Frederick Lacey threw a wild pitch.

"Ever hear of the Pemberton Estate?" asked Moynihan.

"Sure."

"Your pillar of the community there just shoehorned his way into it."

"As what?"

"Special counsel."

Lacey threw a beautiful flat inside curve. Ordway swung with all his might — and missed. The Openshaws cheered and whistled.

"Special counsel to *your* bank? Good for Ordway!"

"Up yours, Butler."

Lacey tried to burn the next one in, Ordway swung again, there was a satisfying fat rich thwack, and I dashed toward third.

"Well, things look a little better now," said Ellsworth Boyle, leaning back against the fence rail. He was right. With the bases loaded both Atwater and Patterson Fox had struck out, but then Kellerman put one all the way into the creek and before Harris could get it out, C & D was leading 13–12. I was finishing my second paper cup of straight bourbon, and the afternoon meadow began to glow pleasantly, like the French Impressionists I had seen with Monica.

A twinge? Yes, and it hurt. I wondered where she was and what she was doing.

Over on the blanket, Sally and Marion were smoking and chatting idly with other wives who had come to join them, while Sheila Forrester sat a little apart, gazing into the distance. I started to walk over, but Boyle's voice stopped me.

"Ben, somebody said you were mixed up in those riots last night."

"That's right, Mr. Boyle."

"Well, tell us how it was."

Leslie Patch had come over, paper cup in hand, and so had Patterson Fox. Kellerman sat on his haunches, carefully preparing another drink for Boyle. Behind me a couple of the others stopped to listen.

"Well, it was quite an experience," I began, but it was hard to continue. These things had happened a few hours ago, less than ten miles away, and yet I could not seem to find words that would transport Columbia Avenue to Gladwyne. I tried to tell them about the screaming crowds and the fire and the crashing of the windows and Mr. Gold's

207

shotgun and how we had worked through the night in magistrate's court. I tried, but I couldn't make them feel how I felt, standing in the Golds' doorway, facing all those eyes. It sounded flat: somebody else's war story.

"Incredible!" Boyle shook his head. "The police just stood around and let them loot the stores like that?"

"Listen, the Mayor wants to get reelected," said Leslie Patch. "And as a matter of fact, the jigaboos are just getting back what those little Hebrews have been stealing from them all these years —"

A shout rose from the crowd behind us and we all turned. Lansing Merrit had made our third out, and the Openshaw team was moving in for the last inning.

Boyle decided to make me catcher, so I spent the next twenty minutes crouched between the Openshaw batters and Angus MacDonald, who was consuming one cup of beer after another, with the result that his rulings were becoming increasingly confused and pugnacious. I had to work pretty hard, but all my interest in the game was dissipated by Leslie Patch's remark, and by the casual attitude of the others; they were interested in the riots, just as they were interested in the Vietnamese war and the state of the stock market — well, not as much as in the stock market, because the stock market has a direct effect on your life.

"STEE-rike . . . I mean BALL!" yelled Angus Mac-Donald.

"Well which is it?" demanded the batter, who happened to be Frederick Lacey.

"Ball three," said Angus. "Three and two. One out. No one on base. Top of the ninth. Conyers & Dean: thirteen; Openshaw, Prescott, Pennington & Lee: twelve. PLAY Ball!"

I wondered what Marvin Gold was doing while I was here participating in this foolish ritual — all this in-group good fellowship and boozy conviviality among men who were busily trying to steal each other's clients. The papers had mentioned Sunday court, to dispose of the rest of the rioters; Marvin was probably back at work right now, trying to bring order to a seething city while these guys, these leaders of the bar, were playing softball in funny hats.

"STEE-rike three and yer OUT!" shouted Angus Mac-Donald happily, and Lacey stalked to the sidelines. It occurred to me that poor Angus had few opportunities to put down Lacey and the rest of this bunch. Corporate Trust men are the poor boys in the banks; their work is boring routine unremunerative clerical stuff, but since it involves huge amounts of money, there is always the risk of an expensive mistake, so these cautious underpaid men spend their lives trying to avoid hidden reefs, piloted and protected by their overbearing counselors.

Tom Moynihan came to bat. Kellerman was still pitching for us, his suntanned hairless chest gleaming with sweat. The first one came in very low, but Moynihan swung hard and knocked a high fly over third base. Atwater turned around after it, but he was too slow and the ball plopped into the field a yard ahead of him. Moynihan made it to second. The next batter, a tax man I hadn't met before, hit one straight toward Kellerman, who caught it on the bounce and fired it to Merrit at third. Merrit dropped the ball, so Tom Moynihan came steaming home to tie up the score. Screams from all sides.

Pennington came to bat: blue chin, six-feet-three of rugged leadership qualities, dressed in a T-shirt, faded Marine Corps fatigue pants, and dirty tennis shoes.

Kellerman threw another very low one. Pennington looked at it. MacDonald called it a strike and Pennington turned to me, frowning.

"What'd that look like to the catcher?"

"I never argue with the judge, Mr. Pennington."

"STEE-rike two!"

No question about that one; a nice curve, and Pennington missed by a mile. I couldn't get over the idea that Ordway Smith had persuaded the Bank to bring him into the Pemberton case; to Pennington and his men the enemy was not just at the gates; he was inside now. I fervently hoped that Fred Lacey would never catch me off base.

Kellerman paused to rest for a moment. It was getting late and he looked tired. Then he wound up and threw the pitch. Pennington stood still. It looked high to me, and I had to rise from my crouch to catch it.

Pennington turned around. Everybody looked at Angus, who rubbed his mouth.

"Strike three," he said, but not enthusiastically.

"What?" shouted Pennington, his face darkening. An indignant howl rose from the field and the sidelines. Pennington turned to me.

"Now you know goddamn well that went past my ear! Are you going to stand there —"

I had already chucked the sweaty glove. Our people were streaming in. "Mr. Pennington, I don't think —"

"Come on now, Bill, this is all in fun, isn't it?" Ellsworth Boyle clapped him meatily on the shoulder. "Tell you the truth," he said under his breath, "I tend to agree that our distinguished ump has shall we say passed the peak of his efficiency this afternoon." He chuckled happily and raised his voice again. "Tell you what, this game's way behind schedule anyway, a lot of these girls want to take their kids home to supper, why don't we stop right here and call it even?"

"Oh no," boomed Pennington. "You've got one more turn at bat and we don't need that kind of —" but Boyle's suggestion was already going into effect. The game was breaking up. People clustered around the tailgate bars for a last drink, and cars began to bump slowly up the lane, raising clouds of dust. A group of indignant Openshaws surrounded poor Angus MacDonald, all talking at once.

Kellerman came by, putting on his sweatshirt.

"Hey sport, will you do me a favor?"

A long story: Patrick Forrester had told him to settle a school bond issue Monday morning, tomorrow, but Randy's future mother-in-law, Mrs. Hyde, had previously commanded his presence in Berwyn to look at a gatehouse she proposed to rent for him and Roseann. He knew it didn't make sense, but I didn't know Mrs. Hyde, and in all honesty he was in no position to argue with her about anything right now —

"What school bond issue is that?" I asked.

"Some little place upstate, Roscommon Township School District. It's a general obligation issue, a small one. About eight hundred thousand. Forrester did all the work but then he just dumped the closing on me Friday —"

"Randy, I've still got a week at the Defender. I'm not supposed to do any work at the office —"

"Listen, this thing won't take you an hour; it won't take you *half* an hour. You've done dozens of them."

"Yeah, but I can't take the whole day off to go upstate somewhere —"

"It isn't upstate, it's across the street at the William Penn. Angus MacDonald knows all about it. Some guy from the School Board, the treasurer or somebody, is coming down, he's got the bonds all signed, and all the papers. Scout's honor, Ben, there's absolutely nothing to it except to deliver the bonds to the underwriters, pass the check to the school man, and run back over to the Defender. You could do one of these things in your sleep."

I thought about it. "What about the legal opinions?"

"Forrester's already signed them. They're in the file. The file's on my desk. Come on, Ben, be a pal!"

"What time's the closing scheduled?"

"Nine o'clock tomorrow morning. You can be all through and back in City Hall before court begins."

"Well . . . okay. You've checked the file, have you?"

"Absolutely. Perfectly clean little issue, all the papers are there, four complete transcripts, everything approved by the state, settlement certificates all made up, I mean there's just nothing to it, Ben. You'll see."

Sally Rochester detached herself from the cluster of wives and walked toward me. She looked remarkably ripe and wholesome, and I could not help but notice how many of the girls she knew and with what comfortable style she handled herself. She was at home in this crowd.

"Sally, I promised to take —"

"I know, Ordway told me. Can you — would you like to come out for dinner tomorrow night?" She looked down at the grass and pushed a twig with her shoe. "Jessie can feed the boys early and we can have dinner on the terrace and then you could take me to the movies. Or something."

"Sounds very nice. Especially the 'or something' part."

She actually blushed. "Come out whenever you're finished with your work. 'Bye, I'm going to take the boys home now."

Sheila Forrester said hardly a word as I drove out of Boyle's lane and down along the State Road. I tried to make conversation about the game, about how good it was that Pat was finally taking a vacation . . .

"Oh cut it out, Ben," she broke in sharply. "I know what's on your mind. Why don't you come out and ask? That's why I came to this ridiculous picnic, to look people in the eye, but nobody comes out with it."

She had not been drinking Coca-Cola.

"Well, Sheila, at the dinner —"

"Lord God, don't start on *that!* I know all about what happened at the dinner. Ordway came on Saturday morning and Ellsworth Boyle in the afternoon — both after calling to make sure Pat wasn't there. Everybody's so solicitous now, so eager to help, but I've been living with this for *months!*" Then she began to cry softly, while I cursed Ordway for sticking me with this mission.

"Listen, Sheila, he's going to be all right, he just needs a rest —"

"Oh for God's sake, what do *you* know about it!" She began to sob, holding her head in her hands. "Can you imagine what it's like to live with a man who's lost all contact with reality, who hates his life, who pays no attention to his children, who can't listen to anything except what's going on inside his own head?"

"Sheila, we didn't know anything about this . . ."

"No, and I didn't tell Ordway or Mr. Boyle and I don't know why I'm telling you — yes I do. Because I'm drunk now, that's why. I know I am and I don't care." She fished a crumpled Kleenex from her blouse and blew her nose.

"Pat just told me that he was trying to write something, working on a book —"

"Yes, yes, the damn book. He's got it fixed in his mind that he's a creative artist, you see, he always should have been a writer instead of a lawyer, and now he's got to write, only we're stopping him."

"We are?"

"We, us, me and the children. He's got to slave away at Conyers & Dean to pay the mortgage and the children's school bills and the car loans and everything else — did you know that he's three thousand dollars overdrawn at the office?"

"No," I said. She had no business telling me that.

She began to laugh harshly. "Here he is, the big successful lawyer, partner in Conyers & Dean, only we're broke and we owe everybody."

"Sheila, don't you think a lot of people have these financial worries?"

"Well, money isn't even his main worry, though God

213

knows it should be. His main worry is that he can't hear his voices."

"His voices?" I asked, incredulous. "What voices?"

"What voices? Mr. Butler, you're obviously no creative artist! Don't you know that an artist creates characters and puts them on the stage of his imagination and then listens to their voices so that he can write down what they say? Don't you even know that? *Everybody* knows that!" She took off the sunglasses and dabbed at her red brimming eyes. "And if you've got a wife who talks to you because she's lonely and children who want to ask their father questions and clients who want you to work on their deals and partners who expect you to communicate with them — well, they drown out the voices, right? So how are you going to do any writing if nobody will let you listen to your voices?"

I didn't know what to say.

"And what about time? You get up in the morning and you go to the office and you work until seven o'clock at night — lots of times until midnight — but when you do manage to get home, you've got to have a drink to unwind, or two or three drinks, and then you have dinner, and then you sit down in the library and try to write, and what happens? Nothing happens, you're too tired. So you build up all this anger and resentment against everything, against this trap you're in, and guess who you take it out on. Just guess!" Sheila made an effort to stop crying and blew her nose again. "Oh Ben, what's going to happen to us? Now he can't even do his work at the office any more. Did you hear about the soap company settlement in New York?"

"Yes, I did. But that wasn't really Pat's fault —"

"And even before that — do you remember that last issue you did with Pat — which one was it, last month . . ."

"Schuylkill Steel?"

"That's right. He wouldn't get out of bed that morn-

214

ing you had the closing. Just wouldn't get out of bed. I didn't know what to do. Finally I called Mr. Boyle and told him Pat had to take me to the dentist."

My palms began to sweat. Could something like that ever happen to me? What does it feel like when you're lying in bed in the morning and you can't make yourself get up and go to work? Your wife is standing there in her bathrobe and the children are going off to school and you know that you must get up and shave and dress and eat breakfast and get on the train, only you can't do it. So you turn over and put a pillow over your head but you can hear your wife's voice as she telephones your partner at his home and tells him the excuse she has invented . . . What does it feel like?

We were in Wynnewood now: big trees, comfortable stone houses set close together, winding narrow streets. Huckleberry Lane is hard by the Main Line of the Pennsylvania Railroad. I parked in front of Forrester's house.

Sheila thanked me for driving her home and asked me to come in for a drink. I knew it would be hard to extricate myself so I told her I had to get back to town, but I still wanted to know more about Forrester.

"How long has Pat been having these troubles?"

"Oh, he's been on this writing kick for quite a while, a couple of years anyway, but mostly all he did was talk about it. The real trouble began in February, when he ran into that Austrian woman again. That's what really set him off."

Suddenly I was in too deep to get out. "What Austrian woman?" I thought that my voice was shaking, but apparently she didn't notice.

"Well!" She sighed and let her head fall back against the seat. "You knew we went on a skiing trip to Switzerland last winter, didn't you? What are we doing going to Europe for two weeks when we don't have any money? Good question. We borrowed the money: Go Now, Pay

215

Later. It was all my fault, Pat was really shot from all that business in the fall; you remember he was doing about five deals at once for a while, and then there was a break, and my mother offered to come stay with the children, and skiing is the one thing we've always done together, we both used to be pretty good at it — did you know Pat was in the ski troops?"

"Yes, he told me —"

"Well, there was this crowd in New York who charter a plane every year, Pat's roommate's brother, Charlie Tillinghast, organized it, it doesn't really cost much more than going to Canada, so anyway I talked Pat into it, and we went along."

"This was to Austria?"

"No, the plane went to Geneva and then you take a train to St. Moritz, but when we got there it was raining. So what do you do? You sit around the hotels and drink, of course. Well, right at this time they were having the Olympic Games, the Winter Olympics — you know what they are? at Innsbruck in Austria. Somebody said, Why not take a look while we're here? so Charlie Tillinghast got together four couples and hired this Volkswagen bus and off we went through the Engadine to Austria. It was a beautiful drive, but I must say I realized later that Pat hadn't wanted to go, and the rest of us sort of forced him to."

"Did you get to see the Olympics?"

"We saw one event, a bobsled race. Charlie Tillinghast knew a very nice Austrian lawyer there in Innsbruck, they'd called him up from St. Moritz and he'd wangled some tickets for us, but then it rained in Innsbruck too. Everybody came off the mountain and went crowding into the bars — not bars, really, but wine cellars, where you sit at these long tables and drink white wine and they have a band in costume. This place we were in was mobbed — people from all over the world and local people, all milling

216

around and talking and drinking wine and the band was playing away oomp-pah-pah — well, all of a sudden this Austrian lawyer who was showing us around stood up and said to Charlie Tillinghast, 'Oh, here comes old so-and-so (I forget the name) he's one of the biggest steel men in the Ruhr, I'd like you to meet him, his wife is from one of our old families here, and he brought over this old man, very tall sick-looking old man and the wife much younger, about our age and damned handsome, so we all stood up to be introduced and then I saw her do this double take when she saw Pat. She sort of swallowed and turned white and said 'Oh, Mr. Forrester and I have met before,' and shook hands all around. You know, they shake hands all the time over there, even the women."

"What happened then?" I asked.

"Well, it was so obvious, I mean the two of them were sort of staring at each other and trying not to, and everybody else was pretending that nothing had happened, and Charlie Tillinghast invited them to sit down with us, but he — the old man — bowed and said thank you no, they had to meet friends somewhere else, and so we all tried to make some conversation about the bobsled race and this girl then collected herself and told me very nicely that she'd known Pat 'very long ago when he was a little soldier here,' as she put it, but it was terribly crowded and we were blocking the aisle, so then they said good-bye and disappeared. Well, then of course the others tried to gloss over the whole thing by kidding Pat and me — you know, big joke — but it fell flat, and Charlie Tillinghast started talking about the trip back to St. Moritz. They were going to spend the night somewhere along the way. So that's when I made my big mistake."

"What did you do?"

"I asked the Austrian lawyer could he get Pat and me a hotel room. Of course the town was jammed, but he seemed to know everybody and he looked like the kind of man who can produce a hotel room in a situation like that. I said I was too tired to start back to St. Moritz that night and I wanted Pat to show me around Innsbruck." Suddenly Sheila giggled. "You should have seen the faces of those girls! They thought I was nuts, and I guess they were right. But I thought that if he didn't get to see her again, to talk to her, he'd *never* get her out of his system. I thought I'd fix it so that he could spend some time with her, I mean what would be the point of hustling him off, if they felt this strongly after all these years?"

"He'd never said anything about Monica to you?"

"How'd you know her name was Monica?"

"You just told me," I said, feeling my heart pounding again. "You were telling how the lawyer introduced you . . ."

"Oh yes . . . Sure, I knew he'd had a girl over there, I mean after all he was twenty-three when I met him, he'd been in the war, I didn't think I was the first girl he'd ever been in love with."

"Did you stay over that night?"

She nodded. "The lawyer's brother turned out to be the manager of the biggest hotel, so we got quite a nice room, the others drove off in their bus, and Pat really did show me around the town for a couple of hours. Then we had dinner and went up to our room and then I said, 'Look, go find her and talk to her or screw her or do whatever you want but get together with her or you and I are just finished!' Well, he went through the motions of making a fuss, said I was crazy, imagining things, all that, but I just rolled over on the bed and wouldn't talk to him, so finally he put on his coat and walked out."

"Did he find her?"

"Oh, he found her all right. He didn't come back till two o'clock in the morning. He didn't go to bed with her, I would have known. Apparently they sat around someplace drinking and telling each other their troubles. At least he told me this long story about her, how her father had died and she'd had to run this estate all by herself and then she fell in love with a German officer who had come back from a Russian prison camp with her brother but then this man got bored with farming and ran off to the French Foreign Legion and got himself killed and then she finally married this old millionaire because he was kind to her, only *his* children didn't like her — my dear, you've never heard such a tale of woe, and I had the temerity to say that she seemed to have survived it all in pretty good shape, whereupon he went into a sulk and wouldn't talk about her any more."

"Then what happened?"

"That's all, really. Next day we rented a car and drove back to St. Moritz, the weather cleared up and we got in a few days of good skiing, and then we came home. But after that he began to pile into this writing business in earnest, I mean every single night when he wasn't at the office he'd lock himself into the library, nobody was allowed to make a sound — I mean he wouldn't speak to me, wouldn't speak to the children . . . Henry is thirteen, that's when a boy needs a father, it's impossible . . . Oh hell . . ."

A middle-aged woman came marching along the sidewalk, leading a dachshund on a leash. She looked straight ahead as she passed.

"That's all I need," said Sheila, blowing her nose. "Mrs. Forrester sitting in a car with a young man, and crying." She looked at her watch and opened the door. "Ben, the other kids will be home soon and I've got to fix them something to eat. Won't you come in for a moment?"

I declined again, but followed her up the walk. I wanted to nail down one more point. "Sheila, has Pat been in touch with this — this lady, do you know?"

She shrugged. "I suppose so. I guess she writes him at the office, but I don't know."

"Do you know where Pat is right now?"

Just then the earth began to tremble, there was a puff of wind and the hollow roar of an electric locomotive, and then the long deafening clatter of a freight train passing directly behind the house. We could not speak until it passed.

In the silence she said: "Isn't that awful? It isn't so bad inside, and we don't really notice it any more."

I waited. Had she forgotten my question? She opened the front door and turned to me. "Ben, I didn't tell any of this to Ordway or to Mr. Boyle, and I shouldn't have told it to you, so you won't repeat it, will you?"

"No of course not, Sheila." Where was Forrester? Maybe she hadn't heard me.

"Good-bye, Ben, thanks again for taking me home and for being such a good listener." She closed the door.

chapter 19

At eight o'clock on Monday morning I let myself into the silent empty offices of Conyers & Dean. The place had been sealed all weekend; the air was musty and dead. I walked along the grand carpeted hallways on the thirtieth floor, down the little spiral staircase and then through the endless narrow passages on the floor below, past all the cubicles with their open doors revealing some little trace of the men who spent most of their lives inside them: photographs of wives and children, a forgotten raincoat, a mounted fish, the ubiquitous law school diplomas . . .

Randy Kellerman's office was one of the smallest, tucked away around the corner at the very end of the corridor. The little room was jammed; books and files were stacked on the windowsill and the floor, and the gray steel desk was covered with carbon copies of letters, and memoranda written in pencil on yellow legal pads. On top of the heap was a slim red file envelope labeled #226-3487.00 SCHOOL DISTRICT OF THE TOWNSHIP OF ROSCOMMON $800,000 GENERAL OBLIGATION BONDS Lawyer in Charge: PF.

I sat down in Randy's rickety swivel chair and went through the file. He was right: a routine school-bond issue. I picked up the correspondence folder. The first letter was from a lawyer named S. Mifflin Rosenquist in Riverside, a county seat far up in the mountains along the northern tier of the state. Mr. Rosenquist said he was the solicitor for Roscommon School District, which intended to borrow $800,000 to build a new school. Did Mr. Forrester wish to act as bond counsel for a proposed general obligation bond issue? Mr. Rosenquist knew that municipal bonds cannot be sold unless they are accompanied by an opinion from a well-known law firm stating that the bonds have been legally issued and are valid and binding obligations; he also knew that the law firm acting as bond counsel usually draws all the necessary papers.

Of course Patrick Forrester wrote back saying that we would be happy to help with this issue and explaining all the steps to be taken by the School District.

I flipped through the rest of the correspondence folder, finding exactly what I expected: Forrester had sent Mr. Rosenquist all of the necessary resolutions, notices and certificates; Mr. Rosenquist had the resolutions properly adopted by the School Board and published the notices in the local paper. Then he had sent Pat certified copies of the resolutions and notarized proofs of publication from the Riverside newspaper. The bond issue was within the borrowing capacity of the School District, and did not have to be submitted to the voters for approval. A notice of sale was duly advertised, and the School District received a couple of proposals from investment banking firms. The bid showing the lowest interest rate came from First Hudson Corporation, and was accepted by the School Board. Forrester had the bonds printed and submitted the proceedings to the Bureau of Internal Affairs, which sent them back approved and embossed with the gold seal of the Commonwealth.

Then there was a lot of correspondence about the closing. Mr. Rosenquist wondered if the bonds could be delivered in Philadelphia. There was a ticklish local situation: should the eight hundred thousand dollars be deposited in the First National Bank of Riverside or in the Riverside Trust Company, or should it be divided between them? The School Board, under pressure from both factions, wanted to deposit the money temporarily with the William Penn Trust Company in Philadelphia until the local banks could reach an agreement. Mr. Rosenquist knew that this must sound rather petty and provincial to Mr. Forrester, but in a small town such issues can generate a lot of feeling . . .

Forrester wrote back that of course he understood the local problem; First Hudson would much rather take delivery of the bonds in Philadelphia, because that would save the cost of sending a messenger up to Riverside, and would also speed delivery to their customers.

It was arranged to have the printed bonds sent to Mr. Rosenquist who would have them signed by the president and the secretary of the School Board. The secretary and Mr. Rosenquist would then bring the bonds to the William Penn Trust Company, where Forrester would inspect all the closing certificates and would issue the legal opinion. Then First Hudson would receive the bonds and would pay the purchase price, which would be deposited in a special account with the William Penn Trust Company, to be drawn out whenever the School Board saw fit.

There was one more letter: Mr. Rosenquist would have to be trying a case in Riverside on the closing date; if Mr. Forrester would have no objection, Mr. Altdorfer, the School Board secretary, would come to Philadelphia by himself. Mr. Altdorfer would have all the papers and the bonds; he was quite familiar with the whole matter; and Mr. Rosenquist was sure that he could handle everything under Mr. Forrester's supervision. Mr. Rosenquist was sorry that the unexpected listing of an important negligence case would make it impossible to meet Mr. Forrester personally, but he wanted to thank Mr. Forrester for his splendid cooperation, and in view of the School Board's large projected building program, he was confident that they would be working together soon again.

That was all. I looked through the bond transcripts. Everything was there. Twenty-five copies of the legal opinion, beautifully mimeographed on Conyers & Dean letterhead and signed by Patrick Forrester, were tucked into a separate folder. The file was shipshape.

It was nearly nine o'clock, and I could hear voices in the corridor. As I stood up and put the file together, something in Mr. Rosenquist's last letter rose to the surface of my consciousness: ". . . impossible to meet you personally . . ." Then Forrester had not attended any of the meetings up there? That was a little unusual. On the other hand, why should he have driven five hundred miles on this routine matter, when Rosenquist was following all of his instructions to the letter and nobody had asked him to attend meetings?

I put the file into my attaché case and let myself out into the elevator lobby on the twenty-ninth floor.

When I walked into Room G, the smallest of the William Penn's boardrooms, three men were already sitting around the polished table.

"Well, look who's here," said Angus MacDonald, standing up. His nose was peeling, but otherwise he seemed the same as ever. "I thought Pat had turned this one over to Randy Kellerman."

I explained that I was standing in for Randy, said hello to the man from First Hudson's "cage," who was counting through the stack of bonds, and then shook hands with Mr. Altdorfer from Roscommon Township, a thin gray-haired little man in a blue suit, with a lodge pin in his lapel.

"Mr. Forrester couldn't make it, Mr. MacDonald tells me," he said.

"Oh, you're in good hands," said Angus MacDonald.

"Ben may look like a boy, but he's an old hand at the bond business, aren't you?" He slapped my back.

Mr. Altdorfer looked familiar. "Have we met before, sir?" I asked.

"Certainly might have, Mr. Butler." His friendly eyes squinted through the rimless glasses. "I come down to Philly pretty regularly for regional sales meetings. I'm in the insurance business, and our district sales office is over in Penn Center — Do you know Charlie Livingood? He's the eastern district manager for the company, that's Householder's Mutual."

I didn't know Charlie Livingood. The man from First Hudson passed over Bond Number 1 so that I could compare the signatures with those on the Officer's Certificate Mr. Altdorfer had brought along. The signatures on the bond corresponded with those on the certificate, and the other papers were in order too. The man from First Hudson turned over a certified check, signed a receipt for the bonds, packed them carefully into his big leather suitcase along with the legal opinions I gave him, and carried the suitcase out of the room.

Angus MacDonald and I showed Mr. Altdorfer how to endorse the check in the name of Roscommon School District; then he made out a William Penn deposit slip and handed the check to Angus.

"My goodness," chuckled Mr. Altdorfer. "You fellows don't leave me have that check very long, do you? I guess that's the biggest check I've ever held in my hand."

"Did you bring along the signature cards?" asked Angus.

"I sure did," said Mr. Altdorfer. He produced a set of William Penn signature cards, each signed by the president and the treasurer of the Roscommon School District.

Angus MacDonald said: "You see, Ben, they want to draw checks right away, so Mr. Altdorfer stopped in last week and asked me if we could have the checkbook printed ahead of time, and I gave him the signature cards to have executed. Saves 'em a little time."

"To tell the truth, Mr. Butler, we've gotten a little ahead of ourselves up there." Mr. Altdorfer scratched the side of his nose. "As a matter of fact, I told Charlie — that's Charlie Hines, our president — I said 'Charlie, as a businessman, I think you're putting the cart before the horse, I mean after all, suppose something goes wrong with the bond issue, then where are we —' "

"Mr. Altdorfer, I'm afraid I don't even know where you are right now. What cart before what horse?"

"They've already spent some of the money," said Angus MacDonald.

"See, here's the thing, gentlemen." Mr. Altdorfer looked at us earnestly. "We've just got to have this building ready next February. We've got kids sitting in the Legion Hall, we've got kids sitting in the church, and we're running two shifts at the old school. This is all elementary kids, you understand; the older ones we send in to Riverside. So the state only approved this new building in March, and it takes almost a year to get it finished, and the lawyer said it would take maybe eight weeks to get the bond issue sold, so we went ahead and got bids and let the contracts as fast as we could."

"So by now you owe the contractors some money?" I volunteered.

"That's right, Mr. Butler."

"I can't see anything wrong with that, Mr. Altdorfer. Your board just took a chance to get the job done. Now here's your money, go ahead and pay your contractors."

"Oh sure, I just wanted to explain why all the hurry about making withdrawals. Well, gentlemen, will that be all you'll be needing me for?" He put the checkbook into his briefcase.

"This is your copy of the bond transcript, Mr. Altdorfer. You'll want to keep it with the other records of the School District."

"Thank you, sir." Mr. Altdorfer put on his hat. "Haven't you forgotten something, young man?"

"What's that, sir?"

His eyes twinkled. "Your bill." All three of us laughed.

"That's all right, Mr. Altdorfer," I said. "Pat Forrester will send that along when he comes back from vacation. No hurry at all."

"Wish they were all as easy as this, don't you, Ben?" asked Angus MacDonald as he accompanied us to the elevator. "Mr. Altdorfer, you ought to see this fellow waffle a softball . . ."

chapter 20

"Why, this is an outrage!" shouted Judge Stellwagon.
Willis Donahue and I agreed with him, in unison.

Hector Ramirez shifted his feet.

"Am I to understand that this man's been sitting in jail for three months and there aren't any charges against him?" The Judge glanced toward the press table, but the reporters had gone. It had been a long Monday morning. There were still a lot of cases from the Saturday night riots, a constant stream of policemen and Negro prisoners in handcuffs, jostling and pushing and confusion and the high cheesy smell of people who had been in jail all weekend, but now finally the crowd was thinning out and I only had this one bizarre thing left. "Who's responsible for this, Mr. Donahue? Maybe we'd better send for Superintendent Walsh and get an explanation. Maybe the Grand Jury —"

I decided to interrupt. "If your Honor please, we've already discovered what happened. May I —"

"Sure, sure, go ahead." Judge Stellwagon dropped the release order and peered down at me over his glasses.

"Sir, Mr. Ramirez is a dishwasher at a diner up in Kensington. He's only been in the United States about six months, he doesn't speak any English, and he has no family here at all. His family's in Puerto Rico. Apparently he was living with some other men in a rooming house up above Spring Garden Street, and one night back in March there was a drinking bout and a man was knifed and the police arrested everybody who was there. This man, Mr. Ramirez, was held as a material witness."

"He couldn't have been held this long as a material witness," said the Judge.

"Your Honor, they made a mistake at the prison. They make out IBM cards for all the prisoners now, so that they can keep track of them quickly. When they made out the card for Mr. Ramirez, they should have coded the card 098, that's 'Material Witness' and then the card would have turned up every day on their automatic inmate review. But somebody transposed the digits and the card was coded 089." I handed the perforated IBM card to the clerk, who passed it up to Judge Stellwagon. "Oh-eight-nine means 'Conviction: six to twenty-three months,' so the machine would only turn up the card in six months."

"Is that correct?" demanded the Judge, turning to Willis Donahue.

"Well, it seems to be right, your Honor, but of course the man could have said something —"

"If your Honor please," I broke in. "You and I and Mr. Donahue would have said something. Mr. Ramirez had no idea what was going on. All he knew was that there had been a fight and he'd been arrested and now he was in jail. What finally happened was that he told this story to another Puerto Rican, a man who spoke English and knew his way around, and this friend advised him to ask for the Defender."

The Judge shook his head. Then he asked, "What about the knifing incident? What's happened to that case?"

"I think Mr. Donahue —"

"That case was dismissed by Magistrate Jakubowski," said Willis in a flat voice.

"When?" asked the Judge.

"March twenty-ninth," replied Willis.

"A couple of days after the arrest," I added. "All the other men were released at that time."

"Had the right holes punched in their cards, eh?" The Judge sighed. "An inspiring comment on the administration of justice. All right, where'd that release order get to?"

A clerk stood up to help him look for the order, and I called over the Spanish interpreter who had been sitting in the courtroom. We told Mr. Ramirez that he was free to go, and he listened to the flow of whispered Spanish without changing his expression. I had already tried to explain what had happened, but nothing seemed to reach him. After all, what can you say? The interpreter led him toward the door, and I put my files together.

"Call the next case," said the Judge, who was still signing papers. The next case was to be handled by a private lawyer, who came forward now.

"Oh Mr. Butler," said the Judge, suddenly looking up. "I hear this is your last week with the Defender."

"Yes, sir."

"I won't be sitting in here any more, but I want to say that you've done a splendid job. I've told Ellsworth Boyle."

"Thank you very much, Judge Stellwagon."

"Like to see more of you around here, but I guess there isn't much chance of that."

"Thank you, sir, I've enjoyed it." I sort of bowed myself away from the bar, and the Judge began to sign things again.

"Stick around," muttered Willis Donahue, leaning back in his chair. "This next one's gonna be good."

I looked at my watch. Marvin Gold had sent a note saying that he would pick me up for lunch. I decided that I might as well wait for him there, and sat down on the leather-cushioned bench reserved for lawyers.

They brought out three mean-looking young men,

white, dressed in T-shirts and blue jeans. Acne and dirty long hair and sideburns.

Their lawyer asked for a continuance.

"Why?" demanded the Judge.

"If your Honor please, the presence of children in the courtroom would, in my opinion, prejudice the interests of the defendants in a case of this nature . . ."

I turned around. Sure enough, there were three rows of girls in blue blazers. I had not seen them in the confusion. They were not exactly children, though; they looked like seniors at one of the finishing schools on the Main Line. I don't know how I had missed their teacher, who was sitting directly behind me: an elegant little blonde, wearing a rather tight striped seersucker suit, a straw hat, and white gloves. She seemed younger than some of her hulking pupils. Her frosty blue look turned me right around again.

Stellwagon had denied the request. "This isn't a jury trial, Mr. Logan. I don't think it makes any difference to this court who's listening to the evidence."

"But the nature of the testimony, your Honor —"

"Well, if these young ladies want to hear what goes on in court, they'll have to take it as it comes, I guess. It's part of life, that's all. Can we get started? Have these men made their plea?"

The trial began. It was a rape case, and a bad one. The victim was a fat gum-chewing blonde in her middle thirties, a waitress in a taproom near the ball park. After the place had closed one night, she had gone for a ride with these boys.

Willis Donahue was anticipating a defense of consent. After all, what did she think was going to happen? The real point seemed to be that they were drunk and got too rough with her, and so Willis had to extract all the details. The woman wasn't shy; she was mad and she wanted these guys to get stiff sentences. Even by the standards of Room

231

453, the testimony was becoming gamy. I looked up at Stellwagon. Wasn't he going to send the girls out?

"Mrs. Johnson, I still don't get the picture," said Willis. "Were you in the front seat or the back?"

She chomped her gum angrily. "I just told ya: they had me bent down over the seat. My-uh-legs was in the back, and my head was in the front. This one there was holding the back of my neck —"

"This one here — indicating Magruder?"

"Yeah, and them two was in the back."

"And what was the state of your clothing?"

"How's that?"

"Where was your dress?"

"They pulled it up over my head."

The Judge's eyeglasses glittered. He was watching the girls behind me.

"And where were your — uh, your panties?" asked Willis.

"They threw 'em out the window."

There was an exclamation behind me. "Why this is *ghastly!*" I turned around. The little school teacher was on her feet. "All right girls, we're leaving." Her voice was strained. Every face in the room turned toward her. "Hurry *up* now!" She stamped her foot. Reluctantly the girls stood up and filed into the aisle.

"Go on with your examination, Mr. Donahue," said Judge Stellwagon drily.

"All right, what happened next, Mrs. Johnson?"

She shifted her gum. "They had sex with me."

"Which one?"

"All of them."

"Well how, exactly, Mrs. Johnson?"

I got up too. I'm not sure why; I guess I was mad at Stellwagon. The teacher was just pushing the last of her girls through the swinging door. There are actually two sets of doors: first the inner set from the courtroom proper, then a little vestibule with doors leading left and right to witness chambers, then the outer doors to the hallway.

The girl in the blazer hurried ahead to join the others outside, letting the door swing shut behind her. The teacher and I were alone in the vestibule. I moved forward to open the door for her. She turned to thank me, and I saw that her face was glistening. She opened her mouth, her eyes closed, and she began to fall. I let go of the door handle and grabbed her by the waist. She slumped against my chest, but I couldn't hold her up that way; I had to get my other arm under her knees. She was surprisingly heavy. Her head fell back and her hat dropped to the floor. The leather purse dangled from its shoulder strap. Through the round windows in the outer door, her girls were staring at us like goldfish from a bowl. There was some movement behind the glass, the door opened, and Marvin Gold hurried in.

He shook his head in disbelief. "Butler, you really are —"

"She fainted," I told him. "She got her girls out of the room and then she just passed out and I caught her."

"Well, bring her in here." Marvin picked up her hat and opened the door to the righthand witness chamber, which contained a long wooden table, some chairs, and a water cooler. I put my burden down on the table, trying unsuccessfully to keep her skirt down, and Marvin filled a paper cup with water.

One of the blue blazers peeked around the corner. "*Miss Abercrombie!*"

"She'll be all right in a minute," I said, my hand on the doorknob. All the others were trying to crowd back into the vestibule. "Look, girls, just wait out there in the corridor, will you? We'll bring her out as soon as she feels better. Just stay right there." I closed the door.

Miss Abercrombie was already sitting up, her legs dangling over the table's edge. She was holding her head.

"Oh my word," she said softly, and drank the water Marvin gave her.

"Here, you'd better lie down again," I said.

She shook her head firmly. "No thank you, I'm *quite* all right, really." She looked from Marvin to me. "I must apologize, I can't imagine why I did that . . . but the things they were making that woman say . . . Are you connected with the court here?"

I introduced us and explained who we were.

"How d'you do, I'm Barbara Abercrombie, and I'm a teacher at Miss Beardsley's, though I don't know how much longer I *shall* be one when those girls tell their parents what they heard today." She chirped like a little English bird.

"Was it your idea to bring them into court?" I asked. "Somebody should have told you —"

"Oh, I thought it would be so instructive, a different side of life, don't you know, and it was all arranged by the Bar Association, but I should have *realized* what was coming, though I must say I was positively *hypnotized* by the sheer horror of it . . . Oh blast, now I've a runner in my stocking!" She jumped from the table and for a moment all three of us solemnly studied the back of her leg, which was definitely worth studying.

"Are you sure you feel all right?" I asked.

"Oh yes, *quite* sure, thank you. Just one moment, and I'll take away my girls." She opened her purse, took out her compact, and turned away to examine herself in the mirror.

"I'll just make sure those kids don't go away," said Marvin, giving me one of his enigmatic looks. He opened the door and disappeared. When I turned around, I met Miss Abercrombie's eyes in her mirror. They flicked away; she finished applying her lipstick, put on her hat, checked herself once more, and dropped the compact into her purse.

"Are you English?" I asked.

"Scottish, actually," she said, smiling. "Though I went to school in England."

"Ah — Have you been here long?"

She shook her head. "This was my first year. I should be sorry to be fired in the last week of the term."

"You won't be fired."

"Well, perhaps not," she agreed. "But thank you for rescuing me. If I'd fallen in a heap amongst those girls, there would have been a scandal."

"Any time," I said. "Ready to go?"

She nodded. I opened the door and followed her out to the corridor, where the chattering girls surrounded Marvin. They turned toward us.

"Miss Abercrombie!" . . . "Are you okay?" . . .

"All right, girls, we've had our excitement for the morning," she announced briskly. "Now we're all going to march over to the station and have some lunch . . . Yes, yes, I'm perfectly all right . . . Thank you . . . No, nobody's taking a taxi, we're all going back on the train just as we'd planned" She shook hands with Marvin. "Good-bye, Mr. Gold. Thank you *ever* so much. Good-bye, Mr. Uh —"

"Butler. Benjamin Butler."

"Good-bye, Mr. Butler, thank you again." She looked at me. It was there. She turned and led them down the huge echoing hall toward the northwest elevators.

"Good-bye, Mr. Uh," said Marvin in a high little voice. "It's been simply *ravishing!*"

The waiter had poured our second coffees before Marvin got to the point. We were sitting in the last booth at McGintey's.

We'd had a couple of drinks to celebrate the end of my term with the Defender. I knew he had something on his mind but I didn't ask him what it was, so all through the meal he described his Sunday: sweeping up the broken

235

glass, trying to locate a glazier when everybody else needed one too, the afternoon in magistrate's court again, the evening meeting of the merchant's association where a committeeman had promised that the City would indemnify everybody . . . I mostly listened, and as Marvin's problem worked its way to the surface the pauses became longer. Finally he sat back and took a deep breath.

"Ben, there's something I want to discuss with you."

"All right, shoot."

"Have you heard about Walter Simon?"

"No — Heard what?"

"The Governor's appointed him to the vacancy on Number Four Court. It'll be announced this afternoon."

"Simon's going to be a judge? That's *great,* Marvin!" It really was an unusually good appointment. Marvin stirred his coffee carefully as the full implication hit me. "And you're going to succeed him as Chief Defender."

"If the Board approves me," said Marvin.

"Come on! You know damn well they'll approve you. Boy, this is good news, Marvin. It's really what you deserve and — well, I want to wish you all the luck in the world."

"Thanks, Ben." Marvin looked pleased and embarrassed at the same time. "Of course, this leaves the Deputy Defender slot open."

"It does? What about Charlie?"

Marvin shook his head. "Not the type. A good trial lawyer, but too temperamental. He fights with the judges and he can't handle other people."

"And Bill Merangelo?"

"He's going to the D.A.'s office next month. And the others are either too young or not suitable for some other reason." He paused for a moment. "Ben, I'm offering you the job. I've talked it over with Simon, and we both think you're the man for it."

"Me? My God, Marvin . . . I really don't know what to say. It's very flattering of you, but —"

236

"All right, I know it's a startling suggeston, but let me give you my analysis." Marvin finished his coffee and began to unwrap a long cigar. "Now in the first place, the job pays fourteen thousand, which I assume is a little more than you're making now."

"Quite a bit more."

"Well, but in a few years they'll make you a partner and then you'll be making twice what the Defender could pay you, and eventually three or four times as much. If you want money, C & D is the place for you. But is money really what you want?"

I didn't say anything.

"I don't think it is," Marvin continued. "You've been having a ball trying cases in court. Will C & D let you do that? Answer: No. They don't have any criminal cases; they don't even have much negligence work. They have antitrust cases lasting five years, using batteries of lawyers at a time; a different kind of thing entirely, and you know it. But that's not all. What are they really doing up in that oak-paneled eagle's nest? What's the basic function?"

I shrugged. "Giving advice to businessmen? Protecting money?"

Marvin nodded. "That's right. Business, money, commerce, the things that make the wheels go round. Very important, no question about it. But, Ben, do you think it's the *most* important thing? Do you really want to devote your whole life to it?" He leaned across the table, his eyes magnified by the heavy glasses, and the words began to come at me like machine gun bullets. "Over here we're not dealing with money, we're dealing with *lives;* with *people.* We're dealing with assault and burglary and robbery and narcotics and prostitution and rape. We're dealing with the basic human emotions, the basic things in a man's guts. Hatred and fear and hunger. We're dealing with questions of guilt and innocence. Of men! Those are the really important things. Those are the things people write books and poems and plays about. Have you ever seen a play about a bond issue or an SEC registration?" He stopped, out of breath, and looked with surprise at the unlighted cigar he had squashed in his hand. With an embarrassed laugh he scraped it into the ashtray. "I sound like I'm in a play myself."

"No," I said quietly. "You sound like you mean it."

"I do mean it," he said. "But those are emotional arguments, and you're a cold-hearted corporation lawyer, or pretend to be, so let's look at the practical side. What does the *Gideon* case mean to us?"

"*Gideon and Wainwright?* Everybody knows what it means. The Supreme Court said that you can't try a man unless he has a lawyer."

Marvin nodded. "But what does it mean in terms of the judicial system? In terms of the administration of justice? Look at the implications, Ben. In this country, maybe seventy-five per cent of the criminal defendants have been tried without a lawyer — because they couldn't afford to pay a lawyer. Or they were advised by some lawyer who happened to be standing around in the courtroom, and the judge would say 'Mr. Jones, will you talk to this man,' and there'd be a two-minute whispered conversation, and then the lawyer would 'defend' the man. Well, that kind of crap is over and done with now. What *Gideon* means is that every single man, no matter how poor and ignorant, is entitled to exactly the same kind of legal advice as the Commonwealth gets from the district attorney, or that some tax dodger gets for a ten thousand dollar fee!"

"But here the Defender has been doing that all along, Marvin. You've been representing these people, and doing a good job —"

"Oh sure, sure, we've been doing the best we can, but it's been a very limited operation: only in certain courts, only people who can't raise bail — it's been an act of charity, and we've been a charitable organization. From

238

now on, after *Gideon,* a lawyer is a matter of right. We're going to represent a man from the minute he's arrested. We're going to go into the magistrate's courts and the juvenile courts, and the probation hearings; we're going to handle writs of habeas corpus, we're going to take appeals whenever we think it's necessary — in other words we're going to do everything a private lawyer does, and that's the way it should be. Why should the poor man get a different brand of legal service, a different brand of justice? For instance, how do you think it feels to be a Negro walking along the streets, knowing that the cops can brace you up against the wall any time they feel like it? You ought to see what goes on every night in those magistrate's courts, how they treat the people who are brought in off the street. You know what all this has caused? It's caused the poor man, especially the Negro, to hate the whole system. To you and me the law is a friend, something that keeps the world in order, something that protects us, protects our property — or is supposed to, anyway. But to them, the law's an enemy. So they don't pay any attention to it. How can things go on this way? You saw what happened on Saturday night. That was only the beginning, that was just a *taste* of what's coming — riot and destruction and murder in the streets. I can feel it coming, Ben. How can a city live if it's swarming with people who don't give a damn?"

Marvin stopped, took off his glasses, and wiped his sweating face with his handkerchief. His naked eyes looked small and tired. "And that's just the Negroes," he went on, putting his glasses on again. "What about the whites? The Negroes are rising, and the whites are scared of them. Not your friends out in Bryn Mawr and Paoli, sitting around their swimming pools. I'm talking about the people in the row houses, with armies of blacks all around them. People who ride subways. They're scared, Ben, and people hate what they're scared of. You should hear the talk in the

239

machine shops and the bars and the neighborhood stores. It's terrible, I just don't know what's going to happen to this town."

I felt a little overwhelmed by his outburst. "Well, Marvin . . . Look, I certainly agree with you that we're in the midst of very serious social problems, but I'm not sure how much the Defender can do about them."

"Oh, I'm not saying the Defender is going to cure all these things, but we can do an awful lot to help. I think we ought to be a place where every man who is being kicked around can go for help. If the magistrates and the policemen understand that the poor man has a lawyer too — well, they'll think twice before they clobber somebody —"

"And then your poor man will develop a respect for law and order?"

"I know, it sounds too pat," said Marvin, unwrapping another cigar. "Maybe I'm wrong, but I don't think so. What I'm trying to tell you is that the Defender will be right in the middle of the real problems of the day, struggling with the important issues, making new law. And those guys up at Conyers & Dean won't be."

It made sense, and I said so.

"Sure it does," said Marvin. "And all of this means that we're going to get bigger. *Much* bigger. If every man is entitled to a lawyer, who's going to supply the demand? We are. Who else is there? So that means you'd be coming in just at the right time." He smiled. "We're a growth industry."

"Are you thinking of this as a permanent job, or do you plan to go on the Bench too?" I asked.

Marvin shrugged. "I don't know. Maybe I'd like to be a judge someday, but first I want to make the Defender a real force in this city. And anyway, there's no shortage of Jewish lawyers who'd like to be judges. You know what they're short of?" Marvin lighted his cigar and regarded me steadily through the blue smoke. "They're short of white

240

Episcopalians with Ivy League backgrounds who want to be judges. The Deputy Defender is in the papers at least once a week. You handle yourself right for the next five years or so, and you could be the youngest Common Pleas judge in history."

The waiter brought the check and Marvin grabbed it. "No, this is my party." He counted the bills out of his wallet and put them on the table. "Think it over, Ben. We'd make quite a team."

As I turned the car into Sally's driveway, the sun was just sinking behind the top of the tallest oak. The Irish setters and the boys came running across the lawn; Sally walked behind them, smiling, wearing a white linen dress. I stopped the car, and the boys began jumping up and down, shouting something about an airplane and pointing up to the house. The dogs dashed back and forth, barking, and Sally grabbed one of them as she approached the car.

"Quiet! For heaven's sake, what's the matter with all of you? Robbie! Will you give him a chance to get out of the car!"

"The airplane! The roof! It's on the roof! It's on the roof!" They were still jumping up and down.

I stepped out of the car, and Sally said: "I'm afraid they've been waiting for you with a special project . . . All right Robbie, Andy, *stop* that insane jumping! Ben's tired, first of all he's going to have a drink, and then you can show him the problem and see if he can help you."

"No, no," screamed little Andy. "You *promised*, Ma. You *said* . . ."

I took Sally's arm and we walked across the lawn, surrounded by boys and dogs. "What's this all about?"

She pointed. High up on the side of the steep slate roof, about halfway between two dormer windows, was a small white cross. "It's sort of a glider," she said. "You shoot it with a rubber catapult. Bobby sent it to them, and

241

they've been playing with it all day. It flies beautifully, but look where they finally put it! The gardener offered to go up and get it, but he's sixty-five and I wouldn't think of it. There's no handhold up there. Do you think maybe you could put a ladder across from the window, and tie a clothesline around your waist . . ."

"Oh, it doesn't look all that bad," I said. That was a lie. It looked dangerous, but I was conscious of the little boys pressing around.

"Well, have a drink and we'll make a plan," she said.

"Oh hell, why don't I just get it over with; it won't take a minute, and then we can relax." I took off my jacket. "How do I get up there?"

As soon as I stepped out of the window I realized that I should have taken my shoes and socks off. The roof was pitched at a sharp angle; my soles could grip the slates only if I put my full weight on them, but to do that I had to stand up straight and could not use my hands. I knew that I should begin again, barefoot and with a clothesline around my waist, but the glider was only ten feet away. I let go of the windowsill and took the first step.

Your inclination is to lean away from the abyss and toward the "safe" side; I had to force myself to stand up straight. I saw now that the glider was resting against a little pipe that came up through the roof. I took the second step.

The glider was the size of a clothes hanger, made of rubberized cloth stretched over a wire frame. I took the last step and reached. As I shifted my weight my left foot slipped; I fell heavily against the roof and lunged desperately for the pipe. From below came a shout. I held fast to the pipe but my hand had dislodged the glider, which slid ticka-ticka-ticka-tick past my outstretched body and stopped in the gutter under the edge of the roof, some eighteen inches below my feet.

242

"Let it go, Ben. We'll get a ladder."

I looked down for the first time. Sally and the boys were standing in the shadow of the copper beech. Behind them were Jessie, in a white apron over her blue uniform, and the old gardener, who was wearing bright red suspenders. They were all shading their eyes to look up at me. The dogs were running in circles.

I released the pipe and let myself slide slowly toward the edge. When my toe touched the gutter I stopped. The gutter bent beneath my weight, but it held. I twisted down and around, and then I held the glider in my hand.

"Throw it! Throw it!" shouted Robbie.

I knew that I would never get back to the window unless I regained my feet; if I remained in this position, only the fire department would be able to get me off the roof. Very cautiously I put a little more pressure on the gutter, turned myself around, and brought my other leg up. Now I was sort of crouching on the edge of the roof, the glider in my right hand.

"Throw the airplane, Ben!" called Robbie.

With one foot in the tin gutter and the other on the roof, I slowly stood up. I could see a mile of trees and houses, the hills by the river, the tower of Bryn Mawr Hospital, the tall office building in Ardmore; right below was the clipped green lawn, now entirely in the shade of the enormous trees. The figures on the grass stood still, watching me. Everything was suddenly silent in the summer evening. Well, why not? I asked myself. Would this be such a bad life? I threw the glider. It shot straight down, then caught the air and rose again, a white bird against the green foliage, and banked into a lazy circle. The heads below moved to follow its course. I started to step out of the gutter. There was a loud tearing sound. The whole length of the gutter was coming off. As I fell, I saw the faces turning and heard Sally's scream.

243

book two

Book Two

chapter 21

Her arms were clasped around my neck and her body pressed hard against mine. We were floating high in the water. I saw the wave towering behind us, a wall of green shimmering in the sun, the white foaming top curling over. She was holding me so tight that I couldn't see her face; I couldn't even see her hair although I twisted my neck around . . . The wave loomed straight above us now, a cliff moving, and ever so slowly it blotted out the sky and fell . . . I couldn't breathe but she held on, saying, "I'm too old for this sort of thing. Please let me go and don't be silly," and Patrick Forrester was leaning in the doorway, wearing an overseas cap and an unzipped tanker jacket, holding a glass of brandy and watching us lying naked on the bed.

"What?" I tried to sit up but something moved inside my head and it hurt. It was dark. I was lying between smooth fresh sheets. The yellow quarter-moon was shining into the window.

"Do you feel better?" whispered Sally. "The doctor said to wake you up a couple of times during the night, just in case you have a concussion . . ." There was a movement in the darkness and the swish of silk as she pulled her nightgown over her head, and then the mattress compressed as she slid in beside me. "Oh darling, I'm sorry you hurt yourself, but it's such a good excuse to have you here." She wrapped her arms around me and kissed me on the mouth and then she put her hand between my legs, but it wasn't any good. I tried to remember what had happened. There had been a doctor, a fat young man in tennis clothes, the children's pediatrician? And then I had puked in the downstairs toilet and everybody said I was lucky that nothing was broken. The doctor didn't want me to drive home, so they put me into a guest room. I knew that I had just been worrying about something, only I couldn't remember what it was. It had something to do with Forrester. I turned over, and felt Sally fitting herself against my back. What had I been worried about? Was it Monica? She took my arm and asked, "Why do you keep looking at that picture, Ben?" A big Gauguin, a brown girl in a sarong, combing her hair. It was Fernanda Runcible. She turned to me and said, "Man, you better find them that shotgun." But we were in the Barnes Foundation and it was jammed full of Negroes, silently pushing and crowding each other to look at the paintings. I came face to face with my mother and Mrs. Ellsworth Boyle, and my mother said: "Ben, don't they need you at the office this time of day?" I thought I should introduce Monica but when I turned she had disappeared. Then Forrester was leaning in the doorway wearing an overseas cap and an unzipped tanker jacket, holding a glass of brandy and watching us lying naked on the bed. She didn't see him and she was kissing me, moving down my body kissing me and Forrester was watching quietly. Ellsworth Boyle and Leslie Patch, in black dinner jackets, appeared behind him. "You see, I told you so," said Leslie Patch. "He's just getting into mischief." I said, "Look, I can explain all this. We thought they'd have bathing suits, but there was only this one towel," and I pulled the damp towel out from under us and showed it to them, knowing that it would prove my point. Then Marvin Gold was shaking me, holding my shoulders and shaking me and shouting, his face an inch from mine, his eyes frenzied. "Wake up Ben! You've got to wake up and tell me where you put my father's shotgun. We've got to have it, they're killing everybody!" and his father and mother were desperately pulling out all the shoe boxes and throwing them on the floor, but the shotgun wasn't where I'd put it. I showed them the exact place, but it wasn't there, and the banging on the door became so loud that I had to hold my hands over my ears, and when I opened the door, the Park Guard said: "Keep your hands away from your body. You're a rotten lawyer or you wouldn't have to play tricks in the courtroom," and then I saw that it was Judge Stellwagon. "Your Honor, you just told me I'd done a splendid job!" I protested, but he jumped down off the bench and began chasing me. He's just an old man, I thought, but I ran just the same. I ran out of Room 453 and along the echoing corridor and then down (no, *up*) the long winding Piranesi staircases of City Hall, and when I looked around again I saw that it wasn't Judge Stellwagon any more; it was Frederick Lacey, and he was carrying a baseball bat. I knew that I had something terribly important to tell Marvin Gold (or was it Forrester?) so I ran and ran, but now I was running up on an escalator that was carrying me down. My goal was the frosted-glass door at the top. With a desperate effort I outran the moving stairs, seized the door handle, turned it, and plunged into the room. Marvin was behind his desk, talking to another man who sat with his back to me. "Marvin," I shouted, "I've got to tell you something!" (What? What?) and the man rose, shook hands with Marvin and turned around.

I sat up. Pale watery light filled the room, and outside the birds were singing. Sally was lying on her back, breathing heavily through her mouth. Shivering, I climbed out of bed and walked to the window.

Mr. Altdorfer, the man from Roscommon School District, was Maxwell Moriarty, the bad-check artist I had seen in Marvin's office that day.

249

Behind the trees the sun began to rise. I put on my clothes and examined my sticky-eyed stubbly face in the mirror. My back was stiff and my head still ached; perhaps the fall had scrambled my brains. Quietly I went downstairs, opened the back door and walked across the courtyard to my car. The setters jumped all over me, but they knew me now and didn't bark. I took the Roscommon file from my dispatch case, and then I strolled across the dewsoaked lawn, inhaling the cool morning air and trying to untangle myself from the cobwebs of the night.

If I was right — and Moriarty's face would not leave me — it meant that a skillful forger with a book of checks had access to an $800,000 bank account.

Back in the house, I sat down on the living room couch and tried to decide what to do. Should I look for Forrester? What could he do? No, the first thing was to block the account at the William Penn Trust Company. That meant Angus MacDonald.

It was too early to call, so I read through the whole file for the second time. I spread out the papers on the red Persian carpet and examined them carefully. They still looked all right. Nervous and bewildered, I wandered about the sleeping house, looking at the heavy Spanish furniture and the unopened leather-bound sets of Shakespeare and Trollope and the gold-framed paintings of dark forest scenes. A grandfather clock ticked monotonously. In the big gloomy kitchen I turned on the hot water tap and made myself a cup of Nescafé. At seven my patience was exhausted and I dialed Information.

Angus MacDonald's wife had to call him out of the shower. I apologized for disturbing him, and told him as little as I could: something was wrong with the Roscommon issue, and until I had time to investigate I wanted the account blocked so that none of the bond proceeds could be withdrawn.

He was dubious. "I don't understand what you mean, Ben. How can I put a stop order against that account without any authorization from the School District? It's their money, after all."

"Angus, I can't explain it to you because I'm not sure what happened, but I'm going to find out. All I know is that something's wrong."

"Ben, do you feel all right? You sound funny."

"I'm all right, Angus. Now please, will you do whatever's necessary to block that account? I've got to have some time."

Angus hesitated. "Well, I guess I could put a temporary stop against it when I get in this morning, but the checks could be presented anywhere, you know."

"But they'd be large checks, so the cashiers would call bookkeeping, wouldn't they?"

"Ben, if we dishonor a check without proper authority, we'd be subject to liability, wouldn't we? I think I ought to call Fred Lacey about this."

The thought of Frederick Lacey and the Messrs. Openshaw, Prescott, Pennington & Lee made me feel sick again. For an instant I thought that all this was still part of my dream.

I said, "Angus, this bond issue is our deal. Won't you give me one day to get it straightened out before you bring anybody else into it? You know I won't do anything to get you in trouble."

There was another silence. Trust officers are not encouraged to take chances.

"Please, Angus. I've never let you down, have I?"

"No, you haven't, Ben. We've got a lot of respect for your ability . . ." He took a deep breath. "All right, I'll put a stop against the account, but tomorrow morning I'll have to call Fred Lacey."

"Thanks ever so much, Angus. I'll have it all straightened out by then." I hung up and considered the next step.

251

The money belonged to Roscommon School District, so we would have to get proper authorization to move it to another account, where Moriarty would not be able to draw checks against it.

As I dialed Long Distance I realized with a sinking heart that Pat Forrester was going to be blamed for yet another fiasco. In this kind of work you are not allowed to have messes; blocks of securities and large amounts of money change hands with the smooth clicking of expensive legal machinery. The machinery is expensive because it is supposed to be infallible. I could already hear the voices in the officers' dining rooms: "What's the matter with C & D? All their deals seem to be falling apart. Well, it's an old firm . . ."

It took a long time to find the right man in Riverside. Although I gave her the name from the file, the operator could not locate the president of the Roscommon School Board. Finally I was talking to the Principal of the Riverside-Roscommon–Snow Mountain Joint High School, who was at home eating breakfast. I explained who I was and asked if he could give me some information about the Roscommon School District.

Yes, sir, he'd be glad to help me any way he could; Roscommon was just across the river, part of the same school system.

I said I wanted to talk to the president of the Roscommon Board about their bond issue —

"What bond issue?" asked the Principal.

"Why, their eight-hundred-thousand-dollar general-obligation issue — we had the closing yesterday —"

"Oh, you must have the wrong place, sir. Roscommon hasn't issued any bonds since — Oh before the war, and they're all paid off. They lease their elementary school from the joint school authority, matter of fact it's only two years old — Say, there's a Roscommon Borough down in Allegheny County, over near Pittsburgh, you know . . ."

252

I knew I didn't have the wrong place. "Well, perhaps I'd better call Mr. Rosenquist. He's the solicitor for the School District —"

"Attorney Rosenquist? You mean Mifflin Rosenquist?"

"Yes sir, he's the one who retained our firm —"

"Say, would you spell your name for me, please?" The Principal's voice had changed. I gave him my name and the name of the firm. Then I heard the line humming. "Well — ah, Mr. Butler . . . I don't know what's going on here, but I think you ought to know that Mifflin Rosenquist died over a year ago."

Again I thought: I'm still asleep; this isn't happening.

I don't remember exactly how we ended the conversation. As I hung up the telephone, Sally came into the living room. She was wearing a navy blue bathrobe and slippers.

"My God, are you working already? Ben, you're white as a sheet. Is anything wrong?"

Nothing much, I thought. Apparently Conyers & Dean has approved a bond issue that doesn't exist, and First Hudson Corporation has shelled out $800,000 for it.

"Ben, you really don't look well. I'll call Dr. Boyce —"

I assured her that I was feeling much better, but that I would have to do a lot of telephoning to straighten out something at the office. She frowned, but then she went back upstairs to dress the boys.

For the first time in my life I just didn't know what to do. Should I sound the alarm? Call somebody? Who?

And the story didn't make sense. How could a man fresh out of prison concoct a fraud of this complexity? How many people — how many lawyers, for that matter — would know enough about the bond business to write all those letters to Forrester?

I looked at the documents spread out on the carpet. It didn't seem possible . . . For example, you have to advertise everything in the local newspaper: the resolutions authorizing the bonds, and the request for bond bids. Wouldn't people in Riverside have seen these notices? I studied the proofs of publication: sworn statements from the editor that the attached notice was published in the *Riverside Gazette* on certain dates. Could you fake something like that? Suppose you wanted to; how would you do it? All right, suppose you sent the *Riverside Gazette* some innocuous legal notice — perhaps a notice of intent to organize a corporation — and asked for a proof of publication. Suppose you had your fake notice printed on newsprint by some obscure printer in New York or Philadelphia. Then you would just detach the real notice from the *Gazette*'s proof of publication and substitute your fake notice . . .

On Sally's writing desk I found a silver letter opener. Using just the tip, I peeled the notice headed "Request for Bond Proposals" from the proof of publication. It tore a little, but I could see immediately that there was no print on the other side. This notice had not been clipped from the *Gazette* or any other newspaper.

I sat on the desk and held my head in my hands and tried to fight down the panic. After all, I'd had a concussion, and then nightmares, and now I was drawing crazy conclusions from very few facts . . .

"Ben, what *is* the matter with you?" Sally was carrying a tray with orange juice, fried eggs, toast and coffee, which she put on the desk in front of me.

"Listen, I'm not an invalid," I said irritably. "I can come in there and have breakfast with you and the boys."

"I'm afraid you have to be an invalid for the sake of my reputation, dear heart. Andy just asked whether you're living here now." She went back into the dining room and I drank my orange juice. Then I called Marvin Gold at his parents' place and told him not to expect me for a day or two. I said I just couldn't give him any explanation except that it was a real emergency. Would he take my word for it?

"Of course, Ben. Is there anything I can do to help you?"

"You haven't seen Maxwell Moriarty again, have you?"

"Max Moriarty? No, I haven't, but I'll make some inquiries. You want me to ask at the Roundhouse?"

"No, don't talk to the police yet. This may all be a false alarm. But if Moriarty's still in town, I'd like to know about it."

"Okay, I understand. You think you'll be back later in the week?"

"I hope so, Marvin. Thanks a million for not asking questions."

The next call was harder.

"Sheila, I've just got to find Pat immediately. Have you any idea where he might be?"

"Oh Ben, he never tells me anything! All I know is that he went to New York, but I haven't the slightest idea where he's staying." She hesitated. "Ben, I just don't know what to say to you about that scene I made on Sunday night. I must have been out of my *mind* to tell you all those things, and I'd just *die* if I thought you'd tell anybody . . ."

By the time I finished reassuring her, it was nine o'clock. The switchboard operators at Conyers & Dean didn't know where Mr. Forrester was, and his secretary was on vacation too, but Mr. Rieger was handling Mr. Forrester's work; did I want them to ring Mr. Rieger? No thank you, I said, and hung up.

The Information operator had a number for M. Wesselhof in the Rittenhouse Connaught, but when I dialed that number I got another operator. The telephone had been disconnected at the customer's request.

I was really frightened now. If Monica was gone, did

255

that mean Forrester was gone too? If I didn't raise the alarm this minute, it might be too late.

I went upstairs and shaved and thought about it. When I came down again I made a few calls and located the rental agent for the Connaught. I had a client who was moving to Philadelphia and wanted two rooms and a kitchen on Rittenhouse Square, a quiet apartment with a good view . . .

"Gosh, Mr. Butler, I just had a two-roomer on the eighteenth floor, but I rented it yesterday. I can show you several others, but they're below the tenth floor. Of course they do look right into the Square —"

"You rented the one on the eighteenth floor yesterday?"

"That's right, the previous tenant had to move out in a hurry, some family emergency, but luckily it only took us a week to rent the place, so we let her out of the lease —"

"It took you a week — When did the previous tenant move out?"

"Lemme check with my girl . . . Helen, when did that lady move out of eighteen-oh-one?"

He was talking about Dotty Todd, the call girl. I heard some unintelligible conversation, and then the agent said: "Mr. Butler, this is our lucky day. My secretary just tells me that another tenant on the eighteenth floor is moving out this week, so we've got just what you wanted. When would you like to look at it?"

I had to find Monica; maybe this was the best way. "How about this morning, or is the tenant still in there?"

Again there was a pause while he talked to his secretary. "Mr. Butler, we're not sure if she's in there today, but if you want to walk over I'll be glad to meet you there and show you the apartment. It'll be a break for her if we can rent the place immediately . . ."

We agreed to meet at ten-thirty.

chapter 22

An hour later I was sitting on a bench in Rittenhouse Square, my eyes fixed on the entrance to the Connaught. The visit to Monica's apartment had been brief: she wasn't there. I had arrived promptly at ten-thirty. The agent, a fat little man in a silk suit, called me Ben a dozen times as he took me up in the elevator and chattered hard about the many advantages of the Connaught: marvelous location, fine construction with practically soundproof walls, fully air-conditioned, one of the most exclusive buildings on the Square. The first thing I saw when he opened the door was a wooden packing crate in the middle of the floor. It was open, and inside was the block of teak on which Monica had been working, only it wasn't just a block of teak any more; it was a bust of Patrick Forrester.

"The lady's some kind of an artist, I understand," said the agent. "Going back to Germany or someplace. I see she's packed up already." She was indeed; the tables and shelves were bare, and a neat stack of trunks and packing cases lined the wall.

"This is the bedroom in here, Ben. Notice the view. Isn't it terrific?" The bed was still made up and Monica's clothes were hanging in the closet.

"When do you think the place will be vacant?" I asked.

"When do you want it? The lady's leaving tonight, she

says. How about next Monday? The place is in perfect condition, as you can see."

I had to backtrack quickly. As far as I was concerned, the apartment looked fine, but I'd have to describe it to my client. Could I call on, say Thursday?

Five minutes later the agent had driven away in a taxi and I had found a bench in the Square from which I could see Monica when she returned. There was nothing to do but sit, so I sat.

Hours passed. The sun was high in the sky, gradually turning the city into a furnace. Everyone who could find an air-conditioned room was in it; the Square was empty. I mopped my sweating face with my handkerchief and tried to persuade myself that there was no reason to panic: this wasn't my affair. If Monica didn't show by five o'clock, I would find Ordway Smith and dump the whole mess in his lap. ("You mean to say you gave these people twenty-four hours' headstart?") But he'd told me to look out for Pat Forrester. And in a little corner of my mind I still wasn't sure that I was awake. My head was aching again. What if there was some perfectly good explanation for all this, and I raised a hue and cry . . .

"Feeding the pigeons, Ben?"

I looked up and jumped to my feet.

"Good morning, Mr. Patch. I'm . . . ah, I'm working on a case. As a matter of fact, I'm sort of watching for somebody . . ."

"Sort of watching for somebody, eh?" Leslie Patch's jaw muscles moved spasmodically. He put his briefcase down on my bench. "They use lawyers to watch people at the Public Defender, do they? I would have thought they'd have investigators . . ."

A taxi was stopping in front of the Connaught. The doorman leaned down and then Monica's head appeared. She was wearing sunglasses. "Will you excuse me, Mr. Patch?" I left him standing there and dashed across

258

the street. Tires squealed. "Ya stupid son of a bitch!" somebody screamed. The taxi driver and the doorman and Monica all turned to look at me.

"Monica, I've got to see you!"

"Why hello, Ben. Aren't you in court today?"

"I've got to see you," I repeated. "Can I come up with you now?"

"No . . . Ben, I don't think so. You see, I'm in a terrible hurry —"

"Monica, this is about Pat Forrester. I've got to find him. Something's happened at the office."

The sunglasses masked her expression. "Who is this? Who are you talking about?"

The doorman, who had moved back a few steps, was listening intently, but I didn't care.

"Jesus Christ, Monica, I know all about you and Pat! I've just got to find him. Please let me come up to explain. I've already been in your room, I know you're all packed to go, but you've got to listen to me!"

She bit her lips, hesitating. "All right, come along then."

I followed her through the soft luxurious coolness of the lobby and into the elevator. We rode up in silence, and then I watched her unlock the door, remembering how I was planning my assault the last time I had seen her do this.

As we went in she asked, "Who let you into my apartment?"

"Oh never mind that," I said. "It's not important. Monica, you know where Pat is and you've got to tell me."

She put her gloves and her handbag on the table, took off her sunglasses, and sat down on the couch. "Why?" she asked. I saw now that she looked drawn and exhausted.

I hardly knew how to start. Thinking something is

259

one thing; saying it somehow makes it more real. When you've issued the words and another person has received them, your thought has acquired a life of its own.

"Monica, you and Pat are going to run away together, aren't you?"

She examined her fingernails. "I don't know why I should discuss this with you."

"All right, don't discuss it. Listen to me and see if I'm wrong. You and Pat had a big thing in Austria after the war. Then he left, and both of you married other people, and then last winter you ran into each other again."

"Well, you have been talking to his wife," said Monica.

"You got the idea that he was unhappy. With his work and with his family and I don't know what else. Then your husband died, and you made up your mind to come over here and get Pat for yourself. Am I very far off?"

She sighed. "You make it all sound very simple. Very organized and very simple."

"Monica, if he runs away with you, how is he going to support his family? He's got a wife and three children."

"It's not a problem."

"What do you mean, it's not a problem?"

"I . . . We will make arrangements for them. My husband was — Oh Ben, it does not concern you, but there is plenty of money. It is not a problem."

She stood up. "I really must finish my packing now. I will find us something to drink, and then you must leave." She walked into the kitchen and opened the refrigerator. "There is not much left — oh, a bottle of wine. We will have our last drink together, Ben." She handed me the cold bottle of Orvieto and put a corkscrew on the counter.

"Monica, where are you going to take him?"

"I'm going to take him home with me, of course."

"To Austria? To your castle?"

"Yes, of course. Will you open that bottle, please?"

260

I peeled off the foil and inserted the corkscrew. "What's he going to do there, Monica?"

"He is going to finish a book he is working on." She reached past my head and put two glasses on the counter. I could smell her perfume. "Did you know that he is a writer? He is going to have his own workroom, with a view across the mountains and no sound except the cow bells, and he will work there every day, and no one will talk to him —"

"Except you," I said, pouring the wine.

"I have my own work. I will do my carving and run the farm and he will write, and in the evenings we will see each other." She raised her glass. "Well, *prosit,* Mr. Butler. You have been very nice to me."

I drank the cold wine and looked at her. The fairy princess, come to take Forrester to her castle in the clouds.

"Do you believe it's going to work out that way, Monica?"

"Of course," she said. "Why not?" But she took a dishcloth and began to wipe the counter, which wasn't dirty, and she continued to wipe the cloth back and forth as she looked into the spotless white sink.

"How *is* Pat?"

She didn't answer, but went on rubbing the cloth across the counter. Then she picked up her glass and drained it. "Give me some more wine," she said.

"Monica, you know he isn't well."

She whirled around. "No, he isn't well, he's sick!" she exclaimed. "But *I* am not the one who has made him sick! It was that stupid law firm of yours and that stupid wife with all those children, and that train he has to ride every day — What is it called, that train?"

"You mean the Paoli Local?"

"Yes, he says he can tell by the people's faces at which station they will get off, back and forth on the same train every day — Why should he have to live like that?

261

That is what made him sick, and I am going to take him away and make him do what he *must* do, and that will make him well."

"Oh, Monica, that doesn't make sense. He's got an important job, we need him and his family needs him —"

"You don't know anything about it!" Her eyes flashed angrily. "He could be an important writer, he could write books that people everywhere would read instead of wasting his life in this dirty town — you didn't know him when he was young, he wasn't yet twenty when he came to Innsbruck — much younger than you are now. He had been fighting in Italy and he was exhausted and depressed, but he wanted to tell about it, to tell what happened to him and his friends, to tell what was inside of him, you know, and I said 'Why don't you write down these stories?' and he began to do it. They were so *good*, Ben. Everybody liked them and he sent them to America and they were printed in a magazine. You should have seen the letters he received. And writing freed him from his depressions; he was a happy boy and I loved him." She smiled to herself. "Sometimes he was lazy and did not want to work, so I told him he had to bring me five pages every day before I would go out with him. A lot of girls sold themselves for five packs of cigarettes in those days, but all he had to give was five typed pages."

I filled our glasses again, and Monica began to tell me how she and Forrester had met. He had arrived at her father's castle early one morning in the summer of 1945 — a nineteen-year-old lieutenant with a truck full of soldiers. Some German stragglers were supposed to be hiding in the mountain pastures belonging to this estate, and Forrester had been sent to clean them out. While his men combed through the steep meadows and pine forests, he sat on a fence rail with the daughter of Count Ranzberg talking and smoking and looking far across the mountains to Switzerland. The next day he returned alone. "You are quite right," she said. "We had a 'big thing,' almost at once. My father did not like it, but there was nothing he could do. Patrick found a little room in the town, and I would come to meet him there. He brought over a typewriter from the CIC office and he would sit there and work on his stories. Oh, I think it was the happiest time —" She stopped, biting her lip.

"What happened?"

She shrugged. "What could happen? In the spring of nineteen forty-six they sent him home."

"He didn't . . . you weren't engaged or anything?"

"No, it was out of the question. In the first place, remember we were an enemy country. We were not even allowed to get married. But the main thing was, he was a boy, he had no money, no education, no training to do anything. He had to go back to begin college . . . Well, it just was out of the question."

"But you kept in contact? You wrote each other?"

Monica shook her head. "One day I called up his quarters and he was gone. Just gone. There was an English major there, a tall man with a moustache. He answered the telephone. You know what he said to me? He said 'Hard cheese, Countess, your Yank has flown the coop.' That is what he said to me!" Monica bit her lip again and drank more wine. "I will never forget that. *Never*. Then I received one letter. He said we both knew it was over because it had to be over, and he didn't want to have it dribble away with sad sentimental good-byes and more and more infrequent letters, he just wanted to end it with a sharp break, so that I would be able to begin with other people. At the time I thought he was terribly cruel, but later I realized he was right."

She never heard from him again until they were introduced in that crowded wine cellar last winter. Of course her husband sensed what had happened, and reacting very much like Sheila Forrester, he invented an excuse for driv-

263

ing up to Munich. Monica and Forrester had no trouble finding each other that evening."

"We went to a little bar and sat in a dark corner. I noticed that he drank quite a lot. Too much. Well, we just sat together and drank Scotch and told each other about our lives. It was so nice — it was — well, I can't explain it to you. Have you ever been listening to a noise, a motor running or something, and you didn't know it was bothering you until it stopped? That feeling of wonderful silence? That is how I felt with him, being with him."

"And that's when he told you that he was starting to write again?"

She nodded. "It was so terrible; he was trying to write, but he was discouraged, he never had time to write or to think . . . He had to work so hard at his job, and he didn't think the things he wrote were good enough. I told him he *must* make the effort, he must not be discouraged or let anything make him stop. We sat there for hours — And after that he wrote to me, and I wrote back. He told me that he was making some progress, but he still had the same problems — too much work, no time for himself. I did not like the way his letters sounded, though; they were terribly depressed and discouraged." She sighed. "Well, you know the rest. My husband died, very suddenly — he'd had a heart attack before — and I was all alone again, so I decided to come here and see Patrick."

"It's not the whole story, Monica." I was beginning to feel the wine now.

"No, you are right. When we saw each other again, we knew that we would have to stay together. There was just no other answer."

"And what about his family?"

She shrugged her shoulders again. "I am sorry for them, but this happens; people who should not have been married have to separate. It was a mistake. Should they spend their lives chained to each other?"

"So now you're going to fly away together?"

"No, not together. I am flying to Paris tonight, from Philadelphia, and he is coming on Friday from New York."

"Monica, I've got to see him before he leaves. You must tell me where I can find him."

"Why?" she asked.

"Because something has gone wrong at the office, at Conyers & Dean." She watched me, frowning, and I went on, choosing my words carefully. "This is something he set up, and if it isn't straightened out immediately, then there's going to be all sorts of trouble, because it involves a lot of money, you see. I'm sure that Pat can take care of it, can tell me what to do, but if he goes off to Europe and leaves this situation up in the air, well — they might decide to send somebody after him, and you don't want that, do you?"

She looked out across the shimmering city for a long moment. "I don't know . . . He has made his plans carefully and I don't want to —" She turned back to me. "Perhaps I can do this: perhaps I can reach him by telephone. If you will write down a message and a number where he can reach you —"

"Monica, I really ought to see him, to talk to him —"

"*No.*" Her voice came through clenched teeth.

I tore a page from my pocket diary and wrote the note. "I'll be in my room all afternoon and all night, Monica. It's terribly important."

"I will try," she said. "And now I really must finish packing, Ben." She held out her hand. "Good-bye again, I'm sorry that we have had such a short time to know each other. Perhaps you can visit us in Austria."

"That would be nice." We shook hands. She smiled and closed the door.

chapter 23

The window of Angus MacDonald's sterile green office faced the brick wall of another building. The electric clock on his desk said 9:35, and I had almost exhausted my supply of cheerful conversation. Through the open door I could look into the bustle of the William Penn's corporate trust department: men in shirtsleeves and girls busied themselves with piles of bond coupons and stock certificates, dealt with messengers from brokerage offices, and carried about stacks of IBM cards.

"It's really remarkable what those machines can do now isn't it, Angus? You remember you promised to show me how your computer can turn out a stockholder list in twenty minutes —"

"Sure, Ben, be delighted to show you, anytime, except I've got a closing at ten-thirty, the Electric Company Mortgage Bonds —" He arranged the pencils and the yellow pad into a different pattern, and checked his wristwatch to make sure it corresponded to the clock on his desk. "When do you think Pat will get here, Ben? I mean, we said nine o'clock . . . Do you want to call your office? After all, you know this whole thing is a little unusual, and I've got to get ready for this other closing . . ." He took off his rimless glasses and began to polish them with his handkerchief.

I stood up and walked to the door and took one more look along the corridor to the elevator lobby.

My eyes burned. I had just spent the longest night of my life sitting in my room, drinking Nescafé and praying that Forrester would call. He didn't. At some point I fell asleep in a chair and woke at eight o'clock when my cup crashed to the floor. My mind was befuddled with images of Forrester and Leslie Franklin and my father, something about my father and Forrester rowing in a boat while I was trying to swim after them. I went into the bathroom and shaved and brushed my teeth, and then I called the Pan American desk at the airport. After a lot of back-and-forth, they confirmed that Mrs. M. Wesselhof had flown out to Paris last night. I changed my shirt, stopped for a cup of coffee at the drugstore on the corner and then, feeling like a condemned man on his way to the gallows, I made my way through the muggy automobile-clogged city morning to Angus MacDonald's office at the bank.

The elevator lobby was empty. I turned around and walked back into Angus's room. When I was sitting beside his desk again I had finally faced that the fact that Forrester wasn't coming. Somehow I would have to handle this myself.

"Look, Angus, you've got this other settlement and I don't want to hold you up any more. I wanted Pat to explain this but he was in New York last night and I guess he missed his train or something."

I took a deep breath.

"Angus, the fact of the matter is we've been defrauded. The Roscommon issue doesn't exist. We've checked with the people up in Riverside. They never authorized a bond issue and they didn't issue any bonds and the man who showed up here on Monday was a crook who's probably in Brazil or someplace now."

Angus had stopped polishing his glasses and was regarding me with an indescribable expression. "You must be kidding, Ben."

"I wish I were."

"But, but . . ."

267

I leaned forward and slapped my hand on his desk. "No buts about it, Angus. It's Conyers & Dean's fault, we fell for it hook, line and sinker, and it's our job to clean up the mess, but since all the money is still in the account, nobody's hurt much. We'll have to explain it all to First Hudson, of course."

"Boy oh-boy oh-boy!" Angus dabbed his brow with the handkerchief. I saw that his hand was shaking a little. "Gee I don't know, Ben . . . I've never heard of anything like this . . . I mean, eight hundred thousand dollars . . ."

"You're right, it could have been a real disaster, but you remember I thought the man looked familiar, and when it came to me who he was I called the School District —"

"I don't think you should have put me into this position, Ben," said Angus, replacing his glasses. "Frankly, I'm a little disappointed in you." He swallowed, his adam's apple moving under the starched white collar. He began to draw little triangles on his pad.

"I didn't put you into any position, Angus. It seems to me I helped you to save the day."

"Well, how do I know that?" his voice rose querulously. "I mean, I'm not a lawyer, I think I ought to have some advice here. This is a serious matter, you realize that? I'm going to call Fred Lacey, he'll have to come down and take this off my hands." He reached for the telephone; it was all I could do to keep from grabbing his arm.

"Angus, don't you think we should discuss this with Mitchell Morris first? I mean, you know as well as I do that Lacey will blow this up out of all proportion, it'll be all over town this afternoon, do you think Morris will like that? I mean, it won't make his department look too good, and it's so *unnecessary*, Angus. If *he* wants to holler for your lawyers, then it's his responsibility."

Angus swallowed again, his hand on the telephone.

268

He looked out of the window, then at the ceiling, and then at the triangles he had drawn on his pad. "Maybe you're right," he said. My heart pounded in my ears. He dialed a number, spoke to a secretary, and then to Mitchell Morris. "Could I bring Ben Butler down for a minute, Mitchell? We seem to have a little policy matter I'd like your advice about . . . Fine, be right down . . . No, not more than five or ten minutes. Yes, Butler, from Conyers & Dean. That's right . . . Okay, be right down."

Angus hurried along the corridors and into the automatic elevator and I tried to stay in step. His face was paler than usual and his lips were compressed into a single line. Whatever happened today, he would never quite trust me again.

We got off the elevator on the second floor and marched across the expanse of the main trust department. The room was two stories high and a block long. On the thick brown nylon carpet stood rows and rows of square modernistic steel-and-oak desks, and behind each desk sat a carefully dressed vice-president. Some of them were dictating to secretaries, others were telephoning or reading their mail, and a few were already talking to customers. Everything was quiet efficiency; none of the desks were cluttered, the typewriters were muted, and the telephones didn't ring; they buzzed. In the front of the room, near the elevators, the desks were close together; as we walked down the aisle, the offices became more important and their desks stood farther apart. Mitchell Morris was in a separate office at the Broad Street end of the room, and his door was guarded by a handsome old lady with blue hair and a blue electric typewriter. "You can go right in, Mr. MacDonald," she said.

The office was not large, but the windows extended from the ceiling to the floor and looked out over Broad Street. As we came in, Mitchell Morris rose from behind his desk and Angus MacDonald started to introduce me.

"I met you at Ordway Smith's, Mr. Morris," I said, shaking hands across the desk. His face was still the color of rare roast beef. He wore a navy pinstripe suit, a blue-and-white striped tie and a white shirt with a buttondown collar.

"Yes, sure, remember you very well. Nice to see you. Sit down, fellows. Want some coffee?"

We declined the coffee, and Morris tipped back in his leather swivel chair. "What's the trouble, Angus?" He placed the palms of his hands together and held them under his nose, regarding us judiciously.

Angus began: Mitchell, he didn't know exactly how to explain this . . . it was the goddamndest outrage he'd ever heard of in thirty years of corporate trust work . . . eight hundred thousand dollars' worth of faked municipal bonds . . .

Mitchell Morris began to frown.

"Excuse me, Angus," I interrupted. "Maybe I can lay it out for Mr. Morris. Sir, the fact of the matter is, we've all been taken in by an extraordinary con man, a bad-check artist who just got out of prison a little while ago and somehow tricked our firm into approving a bond issue that doesn't exist."

Morris came forward in his chair and leaned on his desk. The air of calm deliberation was gone.

I told him the story while Angus MacDonald sat biting his fingernails.

"So you see, Mr. Morris, it makes us look very foolish. but there isn't any harm done, because the money's still right here in the bank, isn't that right, Angus?"

"Yes, that's right —"

Morris cut him off: "What do you mean no harm's done? The underwriters think they've sold this bond issue; in fact they've probably delivered the bonds. What are they going to tell their customers?" His color was changing from red to purple and the immaculate white collar seemed too tight for his neck now. "And you know they expect to make a profit on a deal like this," he went on. "They've got to borrow the money to carry the bonds until their customers pay for them, and they've got to pay interest on that —"

"Well, maybe I was overstating it a little, Mr. Morris, but the point is that we — that is, Conyers & Dean, will have to straighten things out with First Hudson, of course I realize that, but this bank —"

"And what about this crook, this guy who pulled the job? Don't we have to call the police?"

"That's just what I was wondering, Mitchell," said Angus MacDonald.

"Do you think that's such a good idea, Mr. Morris?" I asked, trying to sound calm and reasonable. "If this gets in the papers, somebody else might decide to try the same thing —"

"But aren't we concealing a crime here? My God, man, this bank has a position in the community, I mean I think we need some legal advice here, Angus!"

"Exactly my thought, Mitchell."

I could feel the situation slipping away. "Mr. Morris, this was really Patrick Forrester's issue, and I think you should give him an opportunity —"

Morris picked up the telephone. "Miss Perkins, will you get me Fred Lacey — Who? Oh, all right —"

The door opened behind me and I turned to see Ellsworth Boyle charging into the room like a bull, his jaw out and his brow beetling down over his eyes. Behind him towered Ordway Smith, also looking grim.

"Morning, Mitchell," shouted Boyle. "Understand we got a mess on our hands here."

"Yes, we do, Ellsworth," said Morris, as the three of us stood up. "It seems that —"

"Yeah, yeah, I know," said Boyle. "Got an appoint-

271

ment to see Jack Dawson right now. Will you come on up with me?" John Fitzherbert Dawson is the president and chairman of the board of the William Penn Trust Company.

"Why . . . sure, Ellsworth," said Mitchell Morris. There was nothing else he could say.

Wasn't Boyle going to take me along? I didn't understand what was going on. "Mr. Boyle —" I began, and they all turned. Boyle stared at me for an instant, started to say something, and then thought better of it. He turned to Ordway Smith, who had been standing quietly beside the door.

"Ordway, I think you want to have a talk with Ben, don't you? Maybe Mitchell would let you borrow his office for a few minutes."

"Why, sure thing, Ordway. Make yourself at home." Morris seemed dazed. "Ellsworth, do you mind if I bring Angus along upstairs? He's a little more familiar with this whole story, and —"

"Sure, sure, got to have Angus," boomed Ellsworth Boyle, adroitly moving both bank officers out of the room. "We'll see you a little later, Ordway," he said over his shoulder, and then the door closed behind them and I was alone with Ordway Smith.

I had never seen him looking so fierce. "Sit down a minute, Ben."

I was frightened now. "What's going on, Ordway?" I sat down.

He stood behind one of the beautiful Swedish chairs and grasped the back of it with his hands. "Ben, Pat Forrester is dead."

I heard the words and knew what they meant, but at the first moment they didn't seem to get inside me. I couldn't feel any emotion at all; it was as if Ordway were speaking to me through a glass wall.

"He died early this morning, in a crash on the Jersey

272

Turnpike. I'm sorry, Ben . . . I know how you felt about him . . . We all did, of course —"

"Ordway, what's going on here? Why did you and Mr. Boyle come bursting in — I mean, how did you know —"

"I think you know more about it than we do, don't you, Ben?" said Ordway, looking at me intently. "Last night about ten or eleven I had a phone call from Pat. I don't know if he was drunk or full of sleeping pills or what, but he was almost incoherent. He said he'd approved a bond issue that didn't exist and that you were going to try to straighten it out with MacDonald and that you wouldn't be able to do it alone and that I'd better get hold of Boyle and have him deal directly with the top level at the bank and at First Hudson, otherwise the firm would take a terrible hosing. Well, of course I didn't know whether to believe him or not, it was such a crazy tale, and he sounded as if he were mumbling in his sleep, so I tried to ask some questions but all I got was something about a moon and sixpence. Do you know what he could have meant by that?"

"Where was he calling from?" I asked, ignoring the question.

"I don't know. I asked him, but he didn't tell me. He kept saying 'Ben is out there on a limb and you'll have to get him off.' He said that at least three times, and then I asked where was he, why didn't he come back to straighten it out himself, I mean after all, then he became very vague and said 'Yeah, he ought to do that but he wasn't sure he could.' I mean it was weird. Frightening. I kept trying to pin him down about how it had happened and then he suddenly said 'Well, hotshot, take care of yourself and don't do anything I wouldn't do,' and then he hung up. Of course I called Boyle and he called Jack Dawson, and Dawson said to come over first thing in the morning. Then this morning at six o'clock Sheila Forrester called, in

273

hysterics. She'd just had a call from the Jersey State Police, who told her that Pat had driven headon into the wall of an overpass, somewhere near Hightstown."

"He was coming back from New York in a car?"

"I don't know where he was coming from, but he was in a rented car, though who would rent a car to a man in his condition is something I'd like to find out. This afternoon, as soon as we get this bond issue business straightened out, I'm going over to Hightstown to claim the body and to investigate this whole mess. Now what's the story, Ben? What the hell is going on here?"

I got up and walked over to the tall windows and watched the cars moving up and down Broad Street. Here was the cavalry. Forrester was dead and I could dump the whole mess on Boyle and Ordway Smith and go back to the Defender and forget about it. I knew that it was the only safe thing to do, and I also knew that I wasn't going to do it. I turned from the window and told Ordway Smith about the same story I'd told Angus MacDonald and Mitchell Morris: I had closed the Roscommon issue as a favor to Randy Kellerman who had been assigned to the job by Pat, and later I remembered that the man who picked up the bonds was Maxwell Moriarty, a con man I had seen at the Defender office, and this impelled me to call a school official at Riverside . . .

"But Ben, why didn't you blow the whistle right then and there?" asked Ordway. "When was that, yesterday? Why didn't you call me or call somebody?"

"Ordway, it was Pat's deal. He'd had so much trouble already, I thought I could find him and get him to come back to straighten it out —"

"Well, did you find him? Come on, Ben, out with it! Ellsworth Boyle is upstairs trying to pull the chestnuts out, but he doesn't even know what happened —"

"I got a message to him. I explained what had happened and that MacDonald had blocked the account and I

274

asked him to call me, but he didn't! *Nobody* called me! I sat there all night waiting —" To my horror, a disgusting noise came out of my throat, so I shut my mouth and swallowed quickly. "That's all I know about it, Ordway."

"For Christ's sake, this Moriarty or whatever his name is will be in Timbuktu by now."

"I guess so."

"Well, I suppose you thought you were doing the right thing. Now I'd better go up and help Boyle." He shook his head. "I don't understand any of this. If he was driving back to handle it himself, why'd he call me? Did he change his mind?"

"I don't know."

"Do you feel all right, Ben?"

"Ordway, I feel sick as a dog."

"Well, sure, I can understand that, old fella." His tone had changed again. He came over a little awkwardly and put his hand on my shoulder. "He was a great guy, a splendid lawyer and a good friend, and we're all going to miss him terribly. But you're still pretty young, Ben, and when you get older you'll discover that death is part of life. People die all the time. You talk to a guy one day and the next day you read the paper and he's dead. It's just the way things are, Ben."

I stood there and looked at my dispatch case, which contained the Roscommon file.

"Tell you what," said Ordway. "You let Boyle and me untangle this. You go back over to the Public Defender and put your mind on something else, and tonight have a good stiff drink and take a girl to the movies and tomorrow you'll feel better. All right?"

"All right, Ordway." Wasn't he going to ask me for the file?

He opened the door of Mitchell Morris's office, and we shook hands very formally. "I'll let you know about the funeral, Ben," he said. "Now you go do what I said; get

275

your mind on something else." He hurried toward the elevator and I walked down the marble steps to the main banking floor.

Out on the sidewalk it was blindingly hot. The sun looked like a blazing hole punched in the milky sky. The air was damp and still and stank of diesel fumes from the buses. I began to walk. I had to do something and I didn't know what else to do or where to go, so I walked and walked along the streets, seeing nothing and nobody. Perhaps subconsciously I did know where I was going, because an hour later I found myself in the middle of the Market Street Bridge, right by Thirtieth Street Station. I opened my dispatch case and took out the Roscommon file and threw it into the Schuylkill, watching it slide away on the thick muddy tide, sinking as it went.

Why? Why not? I turned around and walked back into the city center, walking and walking until my legs ached and my shirt was soaked, finally ending up in my room, shakily opening a bottle of Scotch and dialing Sally Rochester's number.

"Listen, I can't just drop everything and come in there in the middle of the day —"

"Please," I said.

"What's the matter, Ben? Are you still sick from that fall?"

"Please come stay with me," I said.

"Right now?"

"Right now."

chapter 24

*Remember O Lord thy servant Patrick, according
to the favor which thou bearest unto thy people, and
grant that, increasing in knowledge and love of thee,
he may go from strength to strength, in the life of perfect service, in thy heavenly kingdom; through Jesus
Christ our Lord, who liveth and reigneth with thee
and the Holy Ghost ever, one God, world without end.*
AMEN.

Silence, and then a great bustling as the congregation
rose. Again the organ vibrated the flagstones beneath our
feet with "O God our help in ages past, our hope for years
to come," and the expressionless men from Oliver Bair's
wheeled the draped coffin up the aisle. Sheila followed, heels
clacking, her face white and hard under the floppy black
hat. She was leading the little girl, who stared back at the
people in the pews. The two boys, wearing their blue
school blazers, walked behind with a man who might have
been Sheila's brother. The younger boy was crying.

When they had gone, there was some hesitation until
Mr. and Mrs. Boyle and old Alfred Dennison stepped into
the aisle, followed by Marion and Ordway Smith. Then
everyone began to move toward the doors. The church was
nearly full. Most of the office had turned out, with a sur-

277

prising number of wives; there were people from Schuylkill Steel and Baxter Instruments; and in one corner I saw a crowd of well-dressed young matrons who were apparently neighbors from Huckleberry Lane.

We moved from the cool darkness of the church into the afternoon sunshine; there was a flurry of talk as people greeted each other and formed chattering groups. The hearse and the two black Cadillacs with the family were just moving down the drive, on their way to West Laurel Hill Cemetery. I was glad that I wouldn't have to speak to Sheila. I should have gone to Hightstown with Ordway, I should have helped with the arrangements, and I should have driven out to call, but I was too much of a coward, used my court schedule as an excuse, and wrote Sheila a note. I thought about Monica, alone in some Paris hotel. How long would she wait for him? My letter had gone to her place near Innsbruck, the only address I had, so it might be days until she learned that he was never coming.

For a moment I stood alone at the edge of the crowd, and then I was surrounded by Kellerman, Atwater, Patterson Fox and a couple of others. They all wanted to know the same thing: What happened? Apparently they had not been told about the Roscommon issue, although Randy Kellerman demanded to know why the file hadn't been returned to his office.

"I don't know a thing about it," I said, and there was a groan of disbelief.

"Listen, I've been at the Defender, I don't know what goes on —"

"Why was he driving back from New York in the middle of the night in a rented car?" asked Patterson Fox. "Why didn't he take the train?"

"There aren't any trains that time of night," I replied, and then the group opened to admit Ordway Smith and Marion.

278

"What's this, a town meeting?" he asked. "Ben, have you got your car here?"

"Yes, sir."

"All right. Darling, Ben can drop me off at the Mitchells'. We've got some things to talk about." He took my arm and moved us away from the others.

"Okay," said Marion Smith, "but I think I'll go home and change first. Ben, you're taking Sally out to dinner tonight, aren't you? Ordway, I *do* think we ought to —"

"No," said Ordway sharply. "M'dear I've *told* you this is not the occasion! Ben and I have something else to discuss. One thing at a time, if you don't mind."

Marion pursed her lips, but she turned and walked quickly toward the parking lot, joined by Mrs. Boyle and one of the Huckleberry Lane ladies.

"Let's take a walk in the churchyard," said Ordway.

We moved through the crowd, greeting the people we knew, and stepped between the cars now lining the driveway. On the other side, in the shadow of enormous ancient copper beeches, was the old graveyard, nearly full now, used only by families whose ancestors are buried there. I followed Ordway's steps across the soft carefully manicured grass and past the rows of gravestones, until he suddenly stopped and sat down on one of them.

"Well, Mr. Butler," he said, "I think we'd better have a little talk — What's the matter?"

"Ah . . . Ordway, you're sitting on a gravestone . . ."

"Take a look at the name on it," he said.

I moved to the other side and read the inscription:

Thomas Edward Ordway
1820–1902

"I don't think my great-grandfather will mind," said Ordway. "You can sit on my Aunt Christine over there, or in the gras₃, if you'd rather."

279

I propped myself against the gnarled trunk of a beech tree and looked back at the church, where the cluster of mourners was melting off toward the parking lot.

"Want a cigarette?" asked Ordway. I shook my head. He extracted a Lucky Strike and lighted it with a thin gold Ronson. He inhaled slowly, blew out a cloud of smoke, and then fixed his eyes on me. "You're quite a cool cookie, aren't you, Ben?"

"Sir?"

"I've just been in Hightstown and New York, looking into Pat's death. Aren't you interested in what I've discovered?"

"Yes." I had to clear my throat. "Sure I am, Ordway."

"Yes, sure you are." He put his hands into his pockets and leaned forward to regard the glistening black shoes stretched out in front of him. His long yellow hair was neatly parted at the side and plastered down to the skull. "Well, I'd say at first I was most interested in what I *didn't* find. I didn't find the Roscommon file; in fact, nobody can find it. Kellerman says he told you to take it. Have you got it?"

"No."

"Curious, isn't it?"

I nodded. "Tell me about the accident. What happened?"

"That's also rather strange," he said. "Pat was alone in the car, a rented car, heading south on the Jersey Turnpike at four o'clock in the morning, and he drove headon into the side of one of those bridges — you know, those overpasses that carry other roads across the highway." Ordway studied the grass between his legs and then he went on. "The State Police think he must have been doing over eighty, and he drove right into a cement wall. It took them an hour to cut the wreck apart enough to get his body out."

280

"But how did it happen, Ordway? Was it an accident?"

Instantly the blond head turned and the gray eyes were on mine. "You have some reason to think it might not have been?"

"I —"

"Before you answer that question, I'd better tell you some additional facts. The only asset in Pat's estate, for practical purposes, is a life insurance policy."

"How much?" I whispered.

"Fifty thousand." He looked at me steadily. "With triple indemnity for accidental death."

"He must have fallen asleep at the wheel."

"That's what he must have done," said Ordway, looking down again.

Neither of us spoke for a few minutes. The doors of the church were closed, and the last car had rolled down the driveway. We were alone. The air was perfectly still, and the smoke from Ordway's cigarette flowed up into the beech leaves in a thin wavering plume.

"Where's the file, Ben?" He continued to examine the grass between his long, outstretched legs. In the shrubbery along the road a bird began to sing.

I closed my eyes and held my breath and jumped. "At the bottom of the river."

Ordway sighed. "You don't want me to ask the next question, do you?"

"No." If he asked, I would have to expose my deepest suspicion to another person, and thus breathe life to something that might otherwise just die in darkness.

Ordway looked at me for what seemed a very long time. The carillon in the church steeple began to clang, wafting the soft melody of an old hymn through the foliage. I couldn't remember its name. Finally he spoke. "All right, I'll take the opportunity you're offering, Ben . . . I

281

won't ask. But did it ever occur to you that if this comes out, people will think you covered up because you had something to do with it, and then you'd take the whole blame?"

"No," I said in all honesty. "That never occurred to me, Ordway."

"Well," he said. "Apparently it isn't going to come out. We had one hell of a time with First Hudson, but Ellsworth carried the day, as usual. They didn't even ring-in the Openshaw firm."

"What did he say to them?"

"Oh, you can imagine: terrible tragedy, Forrester killed rushing back to rectify a mistake, fantastically sophisticated confidence man —"

"Didn't they want to call in the police?"

"Sure, but Ellsworth convinced them that it wouldn't make sense. The guy hadn't actually gotten away with a cent, and the publicity would not only make us all look like damned fools but it might bring on a rash of these things. He was very persuasive, and in the end they bought it."

"Can they keep it quiet?"

Ordway shrugged. "They have so far. The salesmen at First Hudson were told that the issue was withdrawn because of legal difficulties, and that's what they've told their customers." He stood up and brushed off his trousers. "So that seems to be the end of the affair. One more question though: Do *you* understand exactly what happened?"

"No I don't, Ordway. I really don't."

"Well but how did they — I mean, whoever set this up must have realized he'd get caught, there wasn't a chance —"

"Not for six months, most likely," I said.

"Why not?"

"That's when the first coupons would be turned in

for payment. Until then, who would ever question the matter?"

Ordway nodded. "You're right. The money would just have been siphoned out of that checking account, and six months from now we would have had some job trying to pick up the trail. Wow!" He passed his hands over his eyes. "Well, Ben, there's nothing else I can or want to say right now, and nobody will ever know that we had this conversation, but you've kept your wits about you in a very difficult situation and may have saved the firm from a disaster, and those who know it aren't going to forget it." He looked at his wristwatch. "Can you take me over to Haverford now?"

The churchyard was still. As we came out from beneath the copper beeches and walked through the warm summer evening toward the parking lot, the carillons in the steeple began to play "Oh God Our Help in Ages Past."

chapter 25

As I drove up the long hill, the setters came bounding across the lawn. I turned into the cobbled courtyard behind the house, and almost ran into a brand new maroon Mercedes Coupe, with sliding roof and whitewall tires, which stood there gleaming fatly in the sunshine. I parked my battered Chevy, got out, and began to walk around the Mercedes. Behind me, the screen door of the kitchen slapped. I turned to see Sally striding across the court. She wore a white summer dress and carried a straw handbag.

"Hi," she said. "The boys are over at Bobby's mother's. Was the funeral as bad as you feared?" Her voice sounded strained.

"No, not too bad," I said. "Whose car is this?"

Her face flushed. "Do you like it?"

"Do I like it? It's the most beautiful car I've ever seen. Is it yours?"

She hesitated for a moment. Then she put her purse on the low stone wall beside us, put her hands on my shoulders, and kissed me quickly on the mouth.

"It's yours, Ben," she said, sounding frightened, "Happy Birthday, darling."

My birthday? My God, I thought, I'm supposed to be having dinner with my mother. Then I looked at her and looked at the car again and sat down on the wall. "Hey,"

I said and took her hand. She turned her face away. "Hey Sal? This car cost . . . this car must have cost nearly ten thousand dollars!" Her face was still averted. I couldn't quite believe she'd done this, but then I remembered Marion's argument with Ordway after the funeral. "Sally, you know this is impossible. What are you . . . I mean, what are you trying to prove? You know what people would say —"

"They'd say I'm trying to buy myself a man. And they'd be right." With a jerk she opened the straw purse, found a Kleenex and blew her nose. Then she began to toy with the three-pointed star on the shining radiator of the Mercedes. Children used to break the star off, so now it is mounted on a spring. You can rock it back and forth . . .

"Ben —" She took a deep breath and began again. "Look, we can't go on like this."

"Like what?"

"I can't just be somebody who comes running whenever you feel like getting laid."

"Oh, come on now!"

"No, that's exactly what's happening," she said, her hands nervously twisting the star. "On Wednesday you were tired and upset so you just picked up the phone and I was supposed to drop everything and fix you up."

"Well, you could have said no."

She turned to look at me. "But, Ben, I don't want to say no. Can't you understand that? I want to — Look, you asked me what I'm trying to prove. Well I got you this car to shock you, to knock you off balance, to make an impression on you." She sat down beside me on the wall. "Are you going to make me come right out and say it? I'm not some bimbo you can keep on tap for occasional use. If you want me, you've got to marry me. We're terrific together in bed, and the boys like you so much, and there's got to be a man around here, and I'm rich, Ben. You know that, don't you? We could have a good life together, and

285

it certainly wouldn't hurt you at Conyers & Dean —" She stopped abruptly and put her hands in front of her face.

I had to say something. "Did Marion see the car? I mean did you tell her . . ."

Sally nodded. Her eyes were closed. "You want to know what she said? She said 'You're out of your mind. He'll run like a rabbit.'" She opened her eyes again. "I suppose she's right, and I'm behaving like a lunatic. I'm supposed to play up to you and flirt with you and make you think marrying me is all your idea, but Ben, I just haven't got those talents. I can't do it. And I'm not an old maid, I've got to have a man, and the boys have got to have a father, and you know there are other people interested in me." She began to cry again. "The only thing is, I can't stand them!"

"Oh Sally . . ." I put my arm around her shoulder.

She twisted me off. "But I'm not going to hang around and be your mistress and hope that someday you'll make an honest woman out of me. I'm just not going to do it! So make up your mind." She expelled her breath, wiped her nose with the Kleenex, and regarded me with liquid eyes.

"You mean right now?"

"Right now."

"Sal, this is just crazy! Suppose I said 'Yes, great, let's go.' What would happen to us? How long would it last? You'd always know that you pushed — I mean, that you forced the issue, and you wouldn't even trust me, and all this business about your money, I mean —"

"You're squirming," she said.

"Of course I'm squirming. You're putting me in an impossible position, and I don't know what to say."

"Dear heart, there are only two things for you to say. One is yes, and the other is no."

"You're not really serious, are you?"

"Yes or no?"

286

"*Please,* Sally!"

"Yes or no?"

"Well then, *no,* God damn it!"

"Okay, I guess that clears the air," she said quietly, standing up. "Good-bye, Ben. I'm sorry I made such a scene, but at least we know where we stand."

"You don't want to see me any more?"

She bit her lip again and shook her head. Then she turned and ran into the house.

chapter 26

I think the sun woke me up. The window was open and the cool breeze smelled of early morning. A train clattered past, not far away, and I tried to burrow deeper under the covers. I touched her then; instinctively she turned and wrapped herself scalding around me, still asleep. Her face was red and swollen and partly buried in the tangle of straw-colored hair that now tickled my face.

I closed my eyes, feeling her breathing softly against my chest, but I couldn't fall asleep again. I felt no urge to make love. I felt lousy.

Why?

Very very gently I extricated myself from her embrace, turned over and looked around the little bedroom: a chintz-covered dressing table, shelves filled with paperback books, silver-framed photographs of her handsome parents and her brother in his RAF uniform, my clothes tossed in a heap . . .

Why did I feel so lousy? This is supposed to be fun.

After the fight with Sally I had gone to my mother's after all, but it was not a successful birthday dinner. I didn't want to discuss the various garbled versions of Forrester's death nor my prospects at Conyers & Dean nor the details of Randy Kellerman's wedding; finally my mother gave up and finished her grapefruit in hurt silence. I tried to explain that I couldn't explain what was wrong with me, but sometimes even your mother can get on your nerves so I thanked her for the gold pen-and-pencil set, gave her a kiss, and drove away.

But it was only eight o'clock. I had already studied my files for Friday's cases. I drove along Montgomery Avenue and thought about my empty room and then I remembered the Scottish girl, the teacher who had fainted into my arms in Room 453. By the time I found a pay telephone I remembered that her name was Barbara Abercrombie. She was in the telephone book, she lived in one of those apartment houses by Bryn Mawr station, she was home, and she would be delighted to join me for the nine o'clock movie. It was all very gay and informal. The film was Italian and obtuse. When it was over she took a long careful look at me and then announced that she had a bottle of good whiskey in her apartment.

It *was* good; we drank all of it.

A school teacher who faints at the description of a rape? Things are often not as they seem; it wasn't the testimony so much as the surprise of it and the fear of what her headmistress and the parents would say.

Well, counting Sally this would make — I tried to stop myself from thinking through the adolescent tabulation again. Childishness. Doubts. As to what? As I lay there watching the chilly wind flapping the window shade and listening to the Paoli Local grinding townward with its load of early commuters I suddenly understood that I'd had enough. This is supposed to be fun, but is it? When she wakes up there will be tears and protestations and God-What-You-Must-Think-of-Me, and then all the business of getting dressed together . . . I tried to remember how it had been, whether I had felt any special joy or closeness to another person or promise of happiness or *anything* more than the quick relieving bang and the cold satisfaction of another score, but there was nothing: a very nice girl, lonely, with hot pants and courage. She had chattered a lot about the differences between English and American men, and when she was drunk and turned-on she had used words that sounded funny emerging from her well-bred little face. The whole thing had been too easy: a ritual in which both participants moved automatically through their prescribed positions. In a few minutes the morning-after part of the program would begin, and I wanted badly to avoid it.

Reaching out with my right hand I touched the carpet and braced myself. Then, moving only an inch at a time and with the greatest of care, I was able to slide from between the sheets to the floor. While dressing I kept my eyes on her; once she moaned softly and turned over again.

I'm twenty-seven years old, I thought. Is this sort of thing going to look or feel amusing when I'm thirty-seven? Or forty-seven? Will I be paying for it by then?

I knew that I should leave a note, but I couldn't think of an appropriate message. It was not yet seven o'clock, so there was plenty of time for me to drive back to town, shave and change my clothes and then show up for the General Arraignment List in Room 653 — my last day in court. I could call her from my room. I set the alarm so that she would not miss her first class, and then tiptoed out of the apartment.

chapter 27

Thwak!

The little black ball careened off the front wall and chunked into my court, only a couple of inches from the side. My racket clicked against wood as I swung, but somehow I got it under the ball, which arced high up toward the blazing lights and then fell forward, striking the wall just below the red line. As it dropped toward the floor, Ordway Smith came pounding past me, swinging hard, while I dashed to the rear. He wasn't fast enough; the ball was too low, and he slammed it into the tin below the second line.

"Getting old," he gasped as he tossed me the ball. "What's that, thirteen to twelve?" His white T-shirt was transparent with sweat. I nodded and got ready to serve.

I hadn't played squash for six weeks. It's a funny thing: I'm the world's worst athlete, lazy and badly coordinated, but squash is something I'm good at. Since I didn't go to prep school I didn't have a racquet in my hand until my freshman year, but then I learned fast. I loved the game from the first moment: the enormous brightly lighted courts, the gleaming white walls flecked with black smears of rubber, the echoing shouts and thumping feet, even the sour jockstrappy smell — and most of all the hypnotic *thwak! thwak!* of the hard rubber ball being slammed against the walls.

291

It's almost like a dance. You have to watch the other guy hit the ball, and before it reaches the wall you have to sort of *feel* how it's going to bounce and then — instinctively, because there's no time to think — you have to figure how to return it via the front wall so that he can't get it. As the ball is fired back and forth, you forget everything else and lose yourself in the effort to outguess it. At least I do.

We had two pretty good rallies, but I took both points, which gave me the game and also the match, three-two.

"All right," said Ordway. "That's plenty for me." He wiped his dripping scarlet face with his towel. "You ought to go out for the Cup."

"Oh, I'm not in that league at all," I said, following him out the little door. We walked around the corner and down the stairs to the members' dressing room. Ordway stopped beside the house telephone. "Listen, Ben, I thought I'd have a sandwich sent up here with our drinks, because I'm due at a Museum meeting in half an hour. Would you like to join me, or do you have a date?"

I said that I was due at Kellerman's wedding dinner but would be glad to have a drink, so he called down for a martini, a Scotch-on-the-rocks, a roast beef sandwich, and a pot of coffee.

Under the stinging hot shower I wondered again what could be on Ordway's mind. He usually plays with his own friends: Harry Rex, or Stevens from the Openshaw firm, or Morris Patterson, a broker at First Hudson. When he asks me, it means that one of the regulars has canceled out at the last minute. I don't mind, and he is always very flattering about my game, which is better than his but nowhere near tournament level. This afternoon, however, he was crowding me into his schedule. Now he wanted to eat up here in the huge deserted dressing room.

When I emerged from my wooden cubicle, the boy was there with the tray. Ordway, freshly shaved and glowing pink, in shirtsleeves, collar unbuttoned and tie untied, was bending over the table, signing the tab.

As I looked at the pimply expressionless boy in the gray jacket, I asked myself for the hundredth time whether I would ever feel quite at home in the Racquet Club. There must have been other members who were kitchen helpers once; it's just that I've never heard of any.

When I was fifteen we were having money trouble. My mother was sick; she had earned nothing for six months, there were medical expenses, and we knew that I would be going to college soon. I went to see a man at the William Penn Trust Company, a man who had worked with my father, and asked if he could find me a good job I could do after school. A week later he called and said that they needed a kitchen boy at the Racquet Club. My mother made a fuss about it, but I took the job anyway, and that winter I spent every evening among the cigarette butts and empty whiskey bottles and piles of oyster shells in the kitchen basement. They paid me well and I have no complaints, but I suppose a place will always look a little different if you came in first through the servants' entrance.

The boy left. Ordway raised his frosty martini, said "Cheers," drained half the glass, and sank back into the soft leather couch with a contented sigh.

"Boy! A good workout and a good drink — Nothing like it. It's been the most godawful week: four estates on the audit list, plus a brief due in the Millington endless divorce matter, plus everybody running around in circles about Pat Forrester's death . . . Sit down, Ben." He popped the olive into his mouth. "Want to talk to you about something."

Drink in hand, I settled into the club chair beside him and waited.

"You're coming back on Monday, aren't you? I thought it would be more appropriate if I talked to you before that. Well . . . goddamn it, Ben, I really don't know how to put this, it's all Marion's idea." He swallowed more of his martini. "This business about Sally and the Mercedes . . . Marion and I want you to know that we're very much embarrassed about it, we think it was a — a loony thing for her to do, we think you handled it the only possible way . . ." He took a deep breath. "And we hope that you won't let it affect your friendship with us — or, for that matter with Sally."

I made some appropriate noise. "Oh sure, Ordway, you don't have to —"

He took another gulp. "You see, she's really a marvelous kid, but terribly eccentric. This thing with Bobby — there wasn't any reason for it. Bobby never claimed to be the brightest guy in the world, but he's a good boy and he loved her —"

"I thought he married his secretary," I said.

"Yes, he did, but after a couple of years of being treated like the village idiot by Sally. Oh well, that's water over the dam. Look Ben, I want to say — No goddamn it, I am *instructed* to say, that you shouldn't take Sally's statements, her — um, ultimatums, too literally. She makes these you know, *gestures,* that doesn't necessarily mean . . . Jesus, this is hard for me to say, but we think . . . Marion and I think that you'd be just the right person to handle her, and in spite of your . . . Well, after all, your father was killed in the war . . ."

"You mean you wouldn't consider me a fortune hunter?"

He looked grateful. "No, we certainly would not, Ben. We'd be extremely pleased, in fact the whole family would be —" He was going to say "relieved" but he bit it off. "She's a girl who needs a man with some brains, and some of the other aspirants who've been hanging around — Well, I guess I've delivered my message, haven't I?" He smiled and finished his drink.

"Yes, you have, Ordway. And thank you very much." That seemed noncommital enough.

"Not atall," said Ordway, sitting up to the table. He began to munch his sandwich. "Mmm, when you see the shape we're in on Monday, you're going to wish you were back in some nice peaceful rape case. Why, Phil Rieger was just saying —"

"Ordway, I wonder if I could take this opportunity to discuss something else with you."

"Um. Sure thing." He resisted the urge to look at his watch.

I told him about Marvin Gold's offer. Ordway nodded and bit into his sandwich again. "Um. Very good, Ben. We heard that you were doing a swell job over there, and this certainly proves it. Must make you feel very satisfied."

I still had Scotch in my glass, and I finished it. "Ordway, the thing is, I think maybe I should take the job."

Ordway's sandy eyebrows went up, and he stopped chewing. "You're joking!"

"No, I'm not," I replied, and while he silently ate his sandwich, I recited all the reasons Marvin had declaimed across the table at McGintey's. I wasn't as eloquent or as excited as Marvin, but I tried to restate the case he had made. Ordway's expression didn't change; he finished his sandwich, poured himself a cup of coffee, drank the coffee, and then lighted a cigarette.

When I ended my speech, Ordway was slouched against the back of the sofa, carefully blowing smoke rings toward the distant ceiling.

"What do you think?" I asked.

"What do *I* think? A wretch who's spent his life helping plutocrats hang on to their money?" He continued to look at the ceiling. "What difference does it make what I think? This is the age of public service, of service to the common man, and I'm a relic from the days of the robber barons. You've received the call, and you're going to heed it, aren't you? Isn't your mind made up?"

"No it's not, Ordway. That's why I'm asking your opinion."

He stretched out his long legs and turned his face toward me. "You really want my opinion? All right, I'll give it to you. In my opinion, this argument, which I assume is really Mr. Gold's argument, is a lot of horseshit. I mean, so far as you personally are concerned. Oh, I think he's perfectly right about the *Gideon* case; I think the Defender will be expanded, it may even become just as important as the District Attorney's office, for all I know. And no doubt the cops will have to become more careful about how they handle their prisoners. He's right about all that. But this talk about what's more 'important' — human emotions, rape and robbery, are more 'important' than business and money — Ben, that's just oratory, that sounds good when you say it fast, but does it mean anything? The fact of the matter is that the Public Defender does social work, meaning it takes care of people who are too poor or ignorant to take care of themselves. That's fine, that's great, we all support the Defender one hundred per cent. Everybody's supposed to help the poor, but does that mean the poor are more important than everybody else? Those prisoners you defended over there are really the dregs, the bottom of the barrel, the wreckage of society. I know that's a terrible thing to say, but isn't it true? They're the ones who couldn't make it, because they're discriminated against, or because they're uneducated or poor or stupid or maybe just plain lazy — whatever the reason, it's always the same ones who can't make a go of it and have to be helped. That's what we call social work. Is that what you worked your way through law school for, to do social work?"

With a grunt Ordway stood up and poured himself another cup of coffee.

"Now what do we do at C & D? What do they do in any big law office? To some extent we help rich people hang

296

on to their money, but mostly we give advice to corporations, to businessmen. That's how all these firms became so big — because they had to supply all the different specialists: the tax men, the SEC men, the antitrust experts — all the lawyers a modern company has to call on. Well, I don't need to tell you all this . . . The point is, we work for businessmen, successful businessmen, instead of people who've been arrested by the police."

"I know that, Ordway —"

"All right, what's more 'important,' social work or business?" He drank his coffee. "What I'm trying to explain is that business isn't just making money, grubbing for money. Business is life for most people. Business is their jobs and their children's future and security is their old age. If you'd ever been out of a job you'd understand that. That's what the world is all about, Ben. Most people don't go around robbing and stealing and knocking other people over the head; most people just try to do their work and get along and play by the rules — if they can find out what the rules are. And it's our job to tell 'em." He put his cup and saucer back on the tray. "What the hell, it's your life. You've got to do what you want, what you think is the most fun. Right now you think that trying criminal cases in court is more exciting than figuring out the best way for one corporation to acquire another. But will you still think so a year from now? Two years from now? How exciting are you going to find your hundredth rape, your six-hundredth drunken assault, your thousandth prison interview? You turned out to be good at criminal trial work, okay. But you're also very good at the kind of thing we do, and over the long pull what we do is more interesting. It really is, Ben. This idea that criminal law is more exciting, more dramatic — Well, if you want to know what I think — I think it's sort of an immature concept, and you'll grow out of it. Most of those characters who practice in

297

the criminal courts would switch places with you in a minute. Just try them!"

He looked at his gold wristwatch. "Well, I've got to get going." He walked over to the row of washbasins and, facing the mirror, began to tie his yellow foulard necktie. "Now let me tell you something else. In confidence. We really need you more than Marvin Gold does. Pat Forrester's death has left a big hole in the firm. He built up that securities group of yours, and none of the other partners have enough background or enough time to run it properly."

"I thought that Philip Rieger —"

"Oh sure, Phil is going to be in charge for the time being." Ordway leaned forward and grimaced into the mirror as he carefully adjusted his knot. "The trouble is that he has to spend most of his time on Eastern Oil matters. He's been doing almost nothing else for ten years, he knows that company up and down and inside out, and just between us, Ben —" he turned his face to me, "Phil is going to be president of Eastern Oil someday."

"Oh, I didn't know that."

"Yup. That's the story." Ordway squared his shoulders in front of the mirror, fixed the necktie to his shirt with a tiny gold clip, and disappeared into the first dressing cubicle. He came right out again, shrugging himself into his jacket. "This business of replacing Pat is just a stopgap. In the long run, we'll have to bring in someone from the outside, or —" He examined his reflection once more. "Or promote one of the associates way ahead of schedule. Do you read me?"

"I think so, Ordway."

He stood still, hands in his pockets, and looked at me. "Here's the point, Ben: I'm not promising you a partnership this year, or next year. You're too young, you haven't had enough experience. But the year after that — Well, Rieger will have to go to the oil company about then, and

298

who else is there? Keep working as hard as you have, and keep your nose clean, and you might be a partner in C & D by the time you're thirty." He smiled and put his hand on my shoulder. "Be quite a coup. First time in history."

"No," I said. "Pat made partner at thirty."

Ordway snapped his fingers. "Right, by God, so he did. Well, in any case it's not a bad accomplishment for a young lawyer — Ben, I've really got to run now. Want to walk down with me?"

We trotted down two flights of stairs, across the cavernous empty lobby and out the doors to Sixteenth Street. On the sidewalk Ordway began to crane his neck to see if a taxi was coming.

"It didn't do Pat much good, did it?" I looked up into the violet summer evening.

"What's that?" Ordway glanced at his watch again.

"I'm not sure I want to follow in Pat's footsteps," I said. "I'm only a technician, just as he was, and I heard him tell you that you could buy all the technicians you want."

Ordway frowned with annoyance as he understood what I was saying. "Oh for God's sake, Ben! TAXI!" A Yellow Cab turned north from Locust Street and came toward us. "You don't think Pat's work had anything to do with what happened to him, do you?" The taxi stopped at the curb and Ordway ripped the door open. "All that about buying technicians is so much nonsense. Oh, once in a while we may have to go out and find a specially trained man, sure; but almost always we train our own people, bring them up by working on our clients' problems, letting them grow right along with their opposite numbers in the companies we represent. As a matter of fact it's the hardest thing in the world to find a really first-class lawyer who is on the loose, and that's why we're going to have so much trouble replacing Pat. No, it wasn't the work that killed him. I suspect you know more about his troubles than I do, but my guess is that he developed some mental illness or psychosis from something that was wrong *inside* — you know, an illness. Hell, I could turn up with cancer tomorrow, or you could get run over by a car. I'm as sorry as you about what happened, but if you think the firm's at fault — Well, you're just wrong that's all. Whatever it was that killed Pat grew inside him. I really mean that, Ben." He gave my arm a friendly whack. "Thanks for the game. We'll have another talk next week." He climbed in and slammed the door, the taxi rattled away, and I walked slowly toward Rittenhouse Square.

book three

chapter 28

I woke with a neck-snapping jerk, and when my head
came up from the bench slab the first thing I noticed was
that the little colored boy was gone from the lip of the
fish pond. The evening was darker now; the sun had
fallen behind the tall buildings, the cloudless sky was the
color of saffron, and the Square was filling up again. Somewhere behind me a transistor radio issued the tinny throb-
bing wail of electric guitars. I looked at my watch. It was
almost seven-thirty: I would be late for Kellerman's wedding dinner. Stiffly I stood up and winced because my foot
had gone to sleep, and then I walked the three blocks to
my room. I climbed the stairs and slammed the door and
tore off my clothes and shaved as quickly as I could, and
when the telephone rang I was dressed in my dinner jacket,
standing in front of the bathroom mirror, operating on
a razor nick with a styptic pencil.

— Hello?

— Ben, I'm sorry I was out when you brought those
files back this afternoon. Looks like you did pretty well on
your last day.

— Marvin, I was going to call you on Monday —

— Listen, I've got a couple of things I want to tell you,
and my mother and father would like to meet you again
under — well, you know — under nicer circumstances, and
so I was wondering if by any chance you might be free

to come for dinner tomorrow night. It won't be anything fancy —

— Gee, Marvin, that's awfully nice of your mother and I'd love to come some other time, but tomorrow I've got to go all the way out to Chester Springs because a friend of mine is getting married and I'm in the wedding, and I don't know how long the whole thing may last, so I wonder if I could have a raincheck on that.

— Sure, we'll make it some other time, it's pretty late notice anyway...Well then let me tell you about these other things now. Weren't you asking about old Max Moriarty, the check man, the other day?

. . . .

— Ben? Wasn't that you that asked me? I think you saw him in my office once, when he was asking about extradition treaties —

— Yes . . . That's right. I did ask you about him . . . The reason was —

— Well, I don't care what the reason was, I just wondered if you'd heard that he's dead?

— Moriarty is dead?

— I heard about it from Captain Wheelock of the Frauds Division. Seems he tried to pass a big check in New York the other day, a check on one of our banks as a matter of fact, and the New York bank called up and of course the check was no good and the poor old bastard dropped dead of a heart attack right at the teller's window. It was in the New York papers, I understand. And then there's something else you might be interested in. Remember that girl with the jewelry in Rittenhouse Square, the colored girl . . . I've got her name here somewhere —

— Fernanda Runcible?

— Fernanda Runcible. She's in again.

— What for?

— Same old thing. Burglary, Larceny, Receiving Stolen Goods. She was working as a maid for a family out in

Cynwyd and now the lady is missing a fur coat and some diamond things and I forget what else.

— Have they got any evidence? They can't just pick her up because she has a record —

— Ben, I haven't got the slightest idea, I haven't even seen the file, I'm just telling you because it brings up what I wanted to talk about tonight: What about that offer I made the other day? Walter Simon will be sworn in next week and we're shorthanded as it is and I've got to fill the slots. What about it, Professor? Want to give it a whirl?

— Marvin . . . Let me say this: I've given it an awful lot of thought.

— Aha —

— And I don't need to tell you how flattered I am that you want me for your deputy, it's a terribly important public position and as you say it will get more important all the time —

— Mmm —

— And you know how much I liked the work and how much I admire what you're doing over there, and how you feel about the Defender as something that will show the Negroes that the law is on their side too . . . Marvin, I think it's just great and I wish you all the luck in the world and I'll do whatever I can to help you . . . But I don't see how I can leave the firm now. This may seem hard to believe but they really need me more than you do. My boss has just been killed in an accident —

— What do they have up there, sixty or seventy lawyers?

— But they're all experts or specialists of some kind, Marvin. They can't just be switched around into other fields.

— Yeah . . . I guess that's a problem I didn't know about. You see . . . I was thinking more in terms of the city as a whole — what's going to happen to the people who live here . . .

305

— Yes, I understand that, Marvin, I agree with you —

— People all crammed together and hating each other so much and sometimes you wonder how it's all going to end . . . Listen, can't you take a leave of absence for a year or so, to see how you like it on the outside?

— Well, maybe I could, but these places operate like escalators, you know. If you step off you lose your place and — Marvin, I've worked my ass off all these years to get in this particular position.

— Mmm . . . Yeah, I can see that you wouldn't want to lose your place.

— You do see that, don't you? They've trained me for a certain kind of work, and I'm good at it, and now they really need me. Maybe more than you do. You won't have any trouble finding good men for your staff, men with much more trial experience than I have.

— Oh, sure. Don't worry about it, Ben.

— Marvin, it was an unforgettable experience for me, I guess I don't have to tell you that, and I meant what I said about helping you. I'd like to serve on the Board of Directors and with the money raising and all those things —

— Sure, Ben. I know you'll be a big help to us. I'll speak to Simon about getting you on the Board . . . Well . . .

— Well . . . Look, Marvin, I'm a little late for something now, why don't we have lunch next week sometime?

— Fine. That would be fine, Ben.

— I can't make a date now because I'm not sure what'll be on my desk when I get back, but I'll call you early in the week. Okay?

— Right. Just give me a buzz. Any time.

— And be sure to thank your mother for me and tell her I'm awfully sorry about tomorrow.

— I'll do that. And have a good time at your wedding. I'll see you, Ben.

— So long, Marvin.

chapter 29

The enormous striped tent seemed full already, but I could see that the reception line on the terrace was still in action: Mrs. Hyde, Mrs. Kellerman, the bride and groom (both red-faced and beaming), the bridesmaids in their identical yellow dresses and huge floppy hats, and the queue of guests extending back through the French doors into the house.

The sides of the tent were rolled up so that the whole panorama was visible: "Hyde-A-Way," absurdly misnamed, massive, bristling with turrets and chimneys, the exact copy of Château de Montmort in the Ile-de-France, erected in these rolling Chester County hills by Roseann's great-grandfather, the railroad king; the long tree-lined driveway winding up through the hayfields from the township road; the lower meadow, where the parking boys were arranging the cars in numerical order so that they could be rushed back to the front door at the loudspeaker's command; the square brown caterer's vans, parked discreetly behind some pine trees near the kitchen courtyard; the white-jacketed waiters sliding skillfully among the guests bearing silver trays jammed tinkling with glasses of champagne and iced whiskey; and the guests themselves, masses of them, handsome, well dressed, self-assured, cool despite the stifling heat, all drinking, all smiling, all happily conscious that "everybody" was here, all performing their parts in this expensive folk rite.

The wedding itself had gone off without a hitch, as it should have; there had been a rehearsal — which I had missed — and most of the party had been through the drill before: three of the ushers, two of the bridesmaids and the best man were married (not to each other) and all of them had participated in weddings of this kind. The Episcopal service is mercifully short; only a few minutes elapsed between Roseann's majestic progress down the aisle on the arm of her stony-faced father and the release of the guests, which Randy's prep school roommate and I accomplished by rolling up the blue ribbons that blocked the pews.

Outside on the steps photographs were taken and then back on the lawn at Hyde-A-Way more photographs: the wedding party, the bridal pair alone, with his parents, then with her parents, then with both sets of parents, then the men were excused and the ladies rushed upstairs to prepare for their hour on the line.

Now that hour was almost over. I had consumed three glasses of champagne and was sweating profusely under my morning coat and ascot tie. The starched collar was too tight and pinched my neck, but there was nothing I could do about it.

"Hello, handsome." Sam Atwater squeezed between a waiter and two straw-hatted matrons. "Why aren't you over there with your girl friend?"

"Who's that?"

"Oh come now! The statuesque Mrs. Rochester, your great and good friend, I thought. She's over on the other side, surrounded by hungry-looking middle-aged steeple-chasers. Why'n't you go and extricate her? Oh by the way, have you seen Ordway? He was looking for you . . . Will you be in the office on Monday?"

"Yeah, I guess so . . .

Automatically we drifted apart, looking for other faces. Of course I had already seen her. She was at one of the round linen-covered tables, wearing a green dress and a big black hat, sitting between two lanky windburned older men who seemed to be competing for her attention. She was carefully not seeing me.

I plucked another glass of champagne from a passing tray and stepped out of the tent. The air was cooler, but not much. I tugged at my collar. You're afraid, I said to myself. You've been over and over it and you've made up your mind and now you're scared shitless. There is really something the matter with you.

"*Gawd!*" said a voice beside me. "They *finally* let us go, I thought I'd *die!*" The oldest and handsomest bridesmaid, a Long Island cousin of Roseann's, looked up at me. She was just out of Vassar and about to start a job at *Life,* and at the wedding dinner the night before she had delivered a pretty good toast, an obviously embroidered anecdote about her European trip with Roseann and their encounters with Italian sailors. She didn't like Philadelphia, though. "How can you *stand* this town," she had mumbled in my ear. "It's too simply square to *abide.*" Now she had done her duty on the reception line and she wanted a drink. As we stepped back into the tent the band began to play, and up on the platform Roseann and Randy did a few steps together, looking rather relieved. There was some cheerful applause, my friend most impressively knocked back a whole glass of champagne, Randy turned Roseann over to her old man, and then we were all dancing. The bridesmaid was light in my arms and chattered along in a touching effort to gain my full attention. "I Could Have Danced All Night" sang the saxophone and the violins; the platform was filling up and the musicians were already sweating. On the other side of the tent Sally Rochester laughed at something one of her companions said. A hand touched my elbow: one of Roseann's anthropoid brothers was cutting in. The girl gave me a dazzling smile and then turned just the correct anticipatory expression upon her new partner.

This was the time to do my duty dance with the bride, but I stepped off the platform and made my way among the tables. They were still laughing when I stood in front of them, and they all looked up at once.

"Sally, may I have this one?"

"Hello, Ben, don't you look nice. Do you know —" The men stood up, rather reluctantly, to be introduced, and one of them held her chair as she rose too. Then, without another word, she walked quickly toward the music.

When she was in my arms we still didn't speak to each other. There were so many dancers now that we could hardly move. The band was playing "It Was Just One of Those Things." My heart pounded in my eardrums now. My right hand covered the little roll of skin below her bra strap.

"Sal —"

She leaned back so that she could look at me, but she still didn't say anything. This isn't right, I thought. If you really wanted to, would it be this way? This hard? "Sal —" and then I jumped like an electrocuted frog because a hand had seized my elbow.

"Good grief, don't panic!" said Ordway Smith, grinning at me. "I just want one dance with my sister Sal. You can cut right back." Sweat was running into my eyes. Sally watched us expressionlessly. "Listen, Ben," said Ordway as he took her in his arms. "Go see Phil Rieger for a minute, will you? He's over there at the buffet and he's got a job to talk to you about. We've been trying to catch up to you all afternoon." The crowd closed around them.

Rieger was standing by himself, leaning forward a little as he carefully ate from a plate of lobster salad. He wore an immaculate blue summer suit, striped shirt, yellow tie —

310

every inch the future president of Eastern Oil Corporation. "Um . . . Ben . . . Glad to see you . . . Um." He finished the salad, put the plate back on the table and wiped his mouth with a linen napkin. Then he propelled me to the edge of the tent. "Look, we're going to have to put you to work in a big hurry. Do you by any chance know what a 'B' reorganization is?"

"Sure," I told him. "That's a stock-for-stock acquisition. We did one for Baxter Instruments when we picked up that transistor outfit in Cambridge —"

"Right. Fine." He looked relieved. "Well, they've got another one cooking now, a pretty complicated deal." He lighted a cigarette and told me the story: Baxter wanted to buy a drug company in New Orleans, which in turn owned a subsidiary in Mexico. The New Orleans company had several hundred stockholders, which might or might not mean that Baxter would have to register its offering with the SEC. "There's a man out at Baxter called Crossland, Executive V. P. Apparently you know him?"

"Sure," I said. "Jack Crossland, he used to work with Pat —"

"Exactly so," said Rieger. "Well, he's flying down to New Orleans tonight, to work out the details, and somebody's got to go with him."

"Tonight? Tomorrow's Sunday."

"Yeah, but they've got to move fast because some New York drug firm is competing with them and they've got a meeting set up for tomorrow. So somebody's got to draw up the reorganization agreement as soon as the deal has jelled, and then of course the Mexican operation will have to be looked into." He paused. "Can you go, Ben? There's really nobody else with the experience to handle something like this. Eastern Oil has just gotten into another mess in the Persian Gulf so I'm off to Paris on Monday and then probably on to Cairo next week, and with Pat gone —

311

well look, Ellsworth Boyle will be around if you need him, but you'll be able to cope, won't you?"

I swallowed; this sounded far more complicated than anything I had done before. "Sure, I guess so, Phil."

"Good boy! You'll need a back-up team here, of course. I'll speak to Boyle on Monday about getting you a tax man, Sam Atwater will have to check out the antitrust angles for you, and who do you want for the general corporate work? Randy won't be back for two weeks —"

"That'll be soon enough. I'll take the bridegroom."

"Okay, I'll tell him right now. Maybe he'll have to come back sooner but that's just too bad. They've got your airplane ticket at the counter, it's a Delta flight at eight o'clock. Here's two hundred bucks, we'll wire you more on Monday. Okay?"

"Yes sir," I said, putting the bills into my wallet. "I guess I'd better go home and get ready."

"Best of luck, Ben. I don't have to tell you how important our relationship with Baxter is." He clapped me on the shoulder and went off in search of Kellerman.

The champagne was foaming in my skull now. I walked back into the tent, leaned against one of the cool metal tent poles, and watched the dancers revolving more or less in time to the heavy insistent beat of the music. Here's the solution, I thought, feeling my brain swimming around and around like a floating compass: Go dance with Roseann and say thank you to her mother and go home and take off this costume and fly away to New Orleans and Mexico and by the time you come back you'll be all over this.

Why not?

The crowd on the dance floor shifted, and I saw that Sally was dancing with one of the steeplechasers now, pressed quite comfortably in his arms and nodding as he talked, but then he pivoted so that looking over his shoulder she saw me leaning against the tent pole — saw me seeing her see me — and there was something in her eyes, I don't know . . . I don't know how to explain what it was but then, without being conscious of having made a decision, I discovered myself moving toward them.